THE MYSTERIOUS WAYS
OF WANG FOO

THE MYSTERIOUS WAYS OF WANG FOO

VOLUME 1

Sidney C. Partridge

COACHWHIP PUBLICATIONS

Greenville, Ohio

The Mysterious Ways of Wang Foo, by Sidney C. Partridge
Volume 1
© 2015 Coachwhip Publications

This volume includes Series 1, Series 2, and half of Series 3.
No claims made on public domain material.

ISBN 1-61646-300-7
ISBN-13 978-1-61646-300-7

Cover: Bamboo © Veronique Gauthier.

CoachwhipBooks.com

CONTENTS

INTRODUCTION

SIDNEY CATLIN PARTRIDGE (1857-1930) was born in New York and educated at Yale (graduating 1880), Yale Divinity School (1880-82) and Berkeley Divinity School (1882-84). His Yale highlights included several prizes in English composition, becoming an editor for the *Yale Record*, and membership in several societies (including the infamous Skull and Bones). By 1885 he was an Episcopal priest in China, acting as instructor in natural science for a missionary college in Shanghai. He continued to teach for several years, until elected as the first Episcopal missionary bishop to Kyoto, Japan, in 1900. Partridge served there until 1911, when he was elected bishop of a western Missouri diocese. He remained in that post until his death. Partridge married Charlotte Ritter in 1884, but was left a widower in 1886 with daughter Helen. He remarried in 1901, to Agnes Simpson, and they had a second daughter, Amalia.[1]

Partridge wrote five series of stories illustrating Chinese life that were published by the McClure Newspaper Syndicate from 1918-1926. (Some reprints appeared as late as 1933.) These stories feature a Chinese detective, though the mysteries involved cultural misunderstandings as much as they involve criminal activity. (Of course, the imaginative solutions are rarely "fair play.") Each story gives insight into Eastern culture, and it is clear that Partridge had a real fondness for the people of China. Certainly, in creating such a positive character as Wang Foo, Partridge was acting against the trend in portraying fictional Asian characters as

7

part of a "Yellow Peril." A popular speaker, Partridge argued in one talk against the concept of a "Yellow Peril" with China and Japan, noting the popular error that the Japanese didn't trust each other, but stating that "the average Japanese are just as honorable and trustworthy as the average Chinese."[2]

It is likely that the cultural features in the Wang Foo stories were inspired by Partridge's own experiences. One such incident in Canton was published in newspapers as a humorous anecdote:

> Invited to visit the palace of the viceroy, the church-man was shown into the reception hall and requested to wait patiently while an almond eyed attendant went to tell another attendant to instruct still another to inform the viceroy of his presence.
>
> "I looked around the hall and finally discovered a beautiful modern piano over in one corner. Now, I can't play, but I like to try when nobody is near. So I sat down on the stool and began picking out *Home, Sweet Home*, with one finger. While thus engaged I heard the rustle of silk behind me and turned in confusion to confront his excellency smiling in the doorway. The viceroy made a low bow and with grave politeness said:
>
> "'Oh, great American, that does with one hand what it takes a poor Chinese gentleman's both hands to do!'" (3)

Notes

[1] Obituary record of graduates of Yale University deceased during the year 1929-1930. *Bulletin of Yale University* (1 Dec. 1930). No. 89.

[2] "No yellow peril, Partridge says." *Springfield* (MO) *Leader* (18 Feb. 1922) p. 2.

[3] "A viceregal jester." *St. Helens* (OR) *Mist* (12 Nov. 1915) p. 5.

THE JADE-STONE PENDANT

"CAPTAIN," SAID THE INSPECTOR, as he rose from his office chair and, turning toward the long open window, gazed out over the blue waters of the harbor, "we might just as well give it up. It is the most puzzling case I have ever had since I came to the Far East, just 17 years ago this month."

And Inspector Wallace of the Hong Kong police, reaching up to a little Chinese ebony shelf upon the wall, took from it a long Manila cheroot and, slowly and thoughtfully lighting it, watched the Peninsular mail steamer maneuvering toward her anchorage amid the forest of shipping.

"Yes, it certainly is a deep one," answered Capt. Brownlow, second in command, and, like his chief, a veteran of the Indian army. "We certainly have made a very thorough search. Every dive of stolen goods and every pawnshop in the colony has been combed, but there isn't the faintest trace of it. And here," pointing to a file of letters upon the desk, "here are the confidential reports from the vice consuls at Canton and Macao. They say they have done their best, but they are just as much in the dark as we are. There's only one thing left, sir; we'll have to send for Wang Foo."

"You are right, Captain. It takes a Chinaman to catch a Chinaman, as the old saying goes. Look him up, and meet me here at 9 tonight sharp. I am dining on the flagship and will excuse myself early."

While the foregoing conversation was taking place in the police inspector's private office, Lady Evington, wife of the Governor

There was a loud cry
and commotion in
the outer passage way
"A Thief, a thief, into the
river with him!"

of the colony, was just bidding goodbye to the wife and the daughter of the Admiral at Government House.

"Yes, I have about made up my mind that I shall never see it again," she said. "The Inspector told the Governor this afternoon that he considered it practically a hopeless case."

"And you are quite positive that it wasn't stolen at the reception?" asked one of the ladies.

"Quite positive," answered Lady Evington. "I remember distinctly looking at it and admiring its rich green color just before I laid it away in the case on my dressing-table, after the last visitor had gone. And," she added, with a great deal of emphasis, "I know one or the servants could not possibly have taken it, for my door was securely locked and bolted."

The article in question, that had so mysteriously disappeared from Lady Evington's dressing-table two weeks before, was nothing less than the famous jade-stone pendant that the Viceroy of Canton had presented to the Governor of Hong Kong in recognition of His Excellency's services in conducting the campaign for the relief of the thousands of sufferers from the great Pearl River flood. It was a wonderful jewel, of almost priceless value, and had for no end of years been part of the official insignia of the Viceroys of Canton, hanging from the center of a necklace of coral, over the gold-embroidered phoenix on the ceremonial robes.

The gift had been elaborately described in the English papers of Hong Kong, and the notices had been translated into all the native papers of the colony and of Shanghai, and it was generally recognized that no more striking token of appreciation had ever been presented by a Chinese high official to a foreign ruler.

His Excellency, Sir Arthur Wayne Evington, the Governor, had kept it securely locked in his office safe until the evening of the reception to the officers of the Army and Navy, when Lady Evington wore it for the first time in public. She had laid it on her dressing table just before retiring, and in the morning it had mysteriously vanished. That was all she knew. And that was all that anyone knew, although the entire official staff of attendants and servants had been most rigorously examined and cross-questioned. And so "The

Theft of the Vice-Regal Jade-Stone," as the heading in the papers ran, became the subject of gossip and speculation all up and down the eastern coast, from Singapore to Peking.

Capt Brownlow returned to his home after the interview and, summoning his faithful servant, Ah Sing, said:

"You savee Wang Foo, go catchee four piece chair-coolie, my wantchee go his house very chop-chop."

"You wantchee him catchee tief-man?" asked the ever-inquisitive Ah Sing.

"Never you mind what my wantchee," replied the captain, passing from his pidgin English into the more regular tongue of his mother country. "Get the chair ready quick and mind you don't tell anyone where we are going."

The light open-work sedan was got ready in a very few minutes and swinging on the shoulders of four stalwart coolies. The captain, followed by the faithful Ah Sing with a lantern, passed rapidly down Queens Road until they reached the Avenue of Fragrant Waters, and turning to the left, began the steep ascent of the Alley of the Red Cloud, stopping at last in front of a little doorway that bore the thrice interwoven symbol of "5–5–5," the Chinese emblem of good luck.

The coolies quickly put down the chair and, pulling their bamboo pipes from their girdles, sat down to smoke around the lantern of Ah Sing, while the Captain knocked at the door and was immediately admitted.

"Good evening, grandma," he said, with a smile, to the venerable figure who drew back the double bars, for some missionary had told him that that was always a polite form of address to any Chinese dame who had reached the age of 50. "Is Wang Foo at home?"

"The lord of our humble mansion is waiting to receive you," was the answer, as she ushered him into the little reception room and hastened to get ready the water pipe and the inevitable bowl of scalding green tea. The officer took the proffered chair, and soon a footstep was heard descending the narrow stairs that led into the upper loft, where the humble citizens of Hong Kong spend the sweet hours of night. Wang Foo, the man of mystery, stood before him.

Tall and slender and light of weight, clad in a long blue gown of delicate blue silk with an upper jacket of the lightest yellow, neatly braided queue with a tassel of white (indicating mourning for a parent), the host had all the dress and manner of the perfect Chinese gentleman. His face was the traditional oval, nose rather sharper than usual among his countrymen, while the high cheekbones would have located him in the northern rather than in the southern provinces. His skin was as smooth as child's, except on the forehead, where it bore traces of an ugly wound received many years before in an accident. But the eyes—these were what attracted the captain's attention, as they did that of everyone who ever talked with him. Narrow and slightly almond-turned at the outer edge, they were as piercing as an eagle's, and seemed—almost chameleon-like—to change their color with every changing glance. No one could have told their exact color, even in the strongest sunlight.

And the hands (he put out one of them to grasp the Captain's) were as long and slender as those of the fairy princess in the Chinese tales of childhood, with tapering nails of the most delicate coral pink. He would have been an interesting character study at any time or in any place; he was doubly so now.

"Good evening, Captain," he said, with a most gracious smile of welcome, before the English officer had had time to say a word. "I am highly honored to have you under my very humble roof. Please take a seat and let me know how I may have the pleasure of serving you. You surely haven't come to consult me about the robbery at Government House, have you?"

"That's just it," replied the Captain. "We may as well confess it, we're in a fix, and you seem to be the only one that can help us out."

"Did the Inspector himself send you for me?" inquired Wang.

"He did, sir, and he is anxious to see you about it. Of course, you know about the case?"

"I have read about it in the English papers," was the brief characteristic answer.

At this point grandma suddenly appeared with the Chinese brass pipe, which she placed before them on the table, with two bowls of smoking Foo-chow tea and a little tray containing some cigarettes for the use of the foreigner not accustomed to the native pipe. The host politely passed them to his guest and after a few minutes conversation on the weather and the ordinary topics of the day the captain arose to leave.

"At what hour, Mr. Wang, may I tell the Inspector to await you?"

"Say to him with the very best compliments, that he may look for me at precisely 9 o'clock tomorrow morning."

"At his office, I suppose?"

"Yes, at his office."

"Good night."

"Good night, sir, and, as the Chinese say, may lucky stars guide you on your way!"

As the captain rode along Queen's Road on his way home he kept saying to himself: "Wonderful man, that Wang. No doubt, he knows all about his countrymen and their tricky ways, but where did he get that smooth and polished English? Not a syllable of 'pidgin' the whole time I was there. Why, he speaks as correctly as an English schoolmarm."

He did not know that Wand had learned his English from the Bishop's own daughter in the old mission on the Bund, and polished and refined it afterward by a two-year residence in Melbourne. Long and faithful study had made him a master of it, as he was of his own ancestral tongue and its complicated literature.

"Venerable Grand One," he said, addressing the old lady, who had bolted the door after the departure of the foreigner, "where is old Chang?"

"He is resting in the outer court."

"Call him at once, and tell him to go to the Temple of the Queen of Heaven and ask for the Abbot, and say that Wang Foo desires the honor of his presence without delay."

"It is done as the master says."

In scarcely 20 minutes' time the old Abbot arrived, and after the tea and pipes they ascended the rickety stairs to the upper loft.

"Welcome, venerable father, to the humble shrine of Choo-Foo-Tse," said Wang Foo as they entered and took seats in the little study.

"I am honored beyond words in being admitted to the shrine that bears the name of the greatest scholar of the classics," replied the guest.

For two long hours they were closeted together, and the result of their consultations amounted to this: It was not likely that any Chinese official, even of the rank of Viceroy, would knowingly give to a European a jewel of such value and such National pride as the famous jade-stone pendant of the dynasty of the Tsings. Therefore, on first thought, what the Governor received must have been a cheap duplicate or an imitation, trusting that the European eye would never detect the difference.

But no Chinese thief would ever be able to dispose of such treasure without being instantly apprehended. Therefore, on second thought, the only conclusion was that the Viceroy actually did present the genuine pendant to the Governor, and the privately arrange for it to be stolen and brought back to him.

The guilty party, whoever he might be, must be sought in the Viceregal Yamen at Canton. But it must be done with the utmost secrecy, for the exposure of an official of high rank would mean almost certain death to the informer. An immediate trip to Canton and an entree into the inner Yamen must be the very first step in tracing the criminal.

"You are quite sure, venerable father," he said to the old ecclesiastic on leaving, "that your description of the jewel is correct?"

"Quite positive," was the answer. "See! Here it is as I copied it today from one of our rarest volumes in the Temple Library, entitle 'Jewels of the Imperial Line and Sacred Possessions of the Sons of Heaven,' No. 28—The Jade-stone pendant, or seal of the Tsing Emperors.

"The most perfect stone ever brought from the imperial jade-stone mints of Shen Si. It measures two inches in length by an inch and three-quarters in width and depth. It is of the clearest green, pure as the waters of the sacred sea. On it are carved the words of the motto of the great Tsings, 'Pure as this stone must ever be the imperial heart'. But that which gives it its priceless value and marks it as the very gift of high heaven to the Celestial line is this: that when held up to the direct light of the sun the crystal markings in its center outline the character for 'Tsing' or 'Pure'. There is and can be no other like it in the world."

"It is enough," said Wang Foo. "We are pledged to eternal secrecy?"

"By the oath of the Elder Brotherhood that is never broken," responded the Abbot, as he passed out into the darkness.

At precisely 9 o'clock on the following morning Wang Foo was announced at the Inspector's office and was immediately ushered into the inner room, where, after a most cordial greeting and a friendly cheroot, the following terse conversation took place between him and the English officer:

"I have sent for you, Mr. Wang, because I believe you are the only person that can unravel this mystery for us, if there is really any unravelling to it. I remember the wonderful way in which you cleared up the matter of the Hong Kong bank robbery last year, and everyone has heard of your help in tracing the harbor pirates to their dens and in convicting the Kow Loon murderers. You certainly understand these people better than we do. So we want you to find the thief that took Lady Evington's pendant."

"I need hardly say that it will be a pleasure and a privilege to serve His Excellency the Governor in any way or at any time," replied Wang, "and I take a special interest in this case because it concerns him and Lady Evington personally. First, let me ask, have you made a thorough examination of the premises and questioned Her Ladyship directly? Tell me the whole story, slowly and with every detail."

The Inspector sat down and, beginning with the ceremonies of the presentation of the jewel, gave his Chinese visitor all the facts that the police force under him had been able to collect. Wang listened very attentively, making now and then a note or two in a red leather case which he drew out of a copious sleeve of his jacket. His only interruption was an occasional, "Yes, I know all that; please proceed quickly," spoken in a nervous and jerking way.

When the Inspector had finished he rose and said: "It will hardly be necessary for me to call at Government House and make a personal examination of Lady Evington's apartment. We Chinese do not usually trace crime in that way. But out of compliment to their Excellencies and because they might otherwise question my thoroughness, I think I had better go. Kindly send an officer ahead of us and ask if we can have the honor of an interview in half an hour."

The officer returned in a very few minutes, and, accompanied by the Inspector, our Chinese prince of detectives, for such he was, visited Government House and heard from the Governor and Lady Evington in person the story of the robbery, and visited under their guidance the apartment from which the pendant had so mysteriously disappeared. On bidding the farewell, he bowed respectfully and said:

"This is the first of the new month; I ask just 15 days to look into the matter thoroughly. Whatever happens, you will see me or hear from me on the morning of the 13th, the Feast Day of the Yellow Dragon."

Wang Foo reached his home, and after the morning rice said to his faithful housekeeper:

"Venerable Grand One, I go away for a few days. Keep everything quiet and in order until my return."

"And to the Honorable visitors what shall the answer be?"

"The master is gone to the Quiet Glade for study and reflection."

"It is done as the master says."

He ascended the steep little staircase to the upper room and, locking the door, made the following preparations: He took from under the bedstead the little white pigskin trunk—faithful companion of every Chinese traveler—and disrobing himself entirely laid all his garments carefully in it. From the bookshelf he took a few ancient volumes—*The Analects of Confucius*, the *Doctrine of the Mean*, the *Book of Rites and Ceremonies* and a little copy of *Seals and Carvings of the Ancient Empire*—and tucked them carefully away underneath the clothing. Then from a drawer in his desk he drew a bundle of long strips of red paper, visiting cards of assorted ranks, and laid them with the books. To these he added his water pipe of cloisonné, a package of native tobacco, and a few necessary articles for his daily toilet. Last of all he opened a little lacquer cabinet, and drawing from it three octagon tin boxes, examined them carefully (they were marked "light," "medium" and "strong"), and, wrapping them carefully in a sheet of yellow paper, put them in the top of the pigskin trunk and closed and securely locked it.

Wang Foo, as we know him, did not reappear. But a half hour later a Singapore rice merchant, clad in the dark-brown garments of the southern provinces and followed by a coolie with a pigskin trunk and a roll of bedding on either end of a bamboo, passed rapidly down the Avenue of Fragrant Waters and joined the long line of passengers ascending the gangway of the afternoon steamer for the city of Canton. He found a vacant spot on the upper deck, and was waiting patiently for the final whistle of departure when he saw the familiar form of old Chang passing hurriedly by and apparently looking anxiously for his master. He hailed him:

"How did you know I was here?"

"The bamboo carrier told me he had brought a gentleman from our alley and I wanted you to receive this letter, which came just after you had left."

"It is well. Here is the wine money. Return at once, and let your words be few."

As the great steamer (she was a Hudson River boat years ago, that had weathered the Cape) pushed her way out through the deep waters of the harbor, the rice merchant tore open the envelope and revealed a tiny slip of red paper with these words:

"At Canton look out carefully for the Viceroy's second secretary. His real name is Fong, but he is known everywhere as the 'Black Fox.' He is dangerous to others, but he may be valuable to you."

Underneath was the seal of the old Abbot. He read it over carefully again, and repeating the words "Black Fox," "Black Fox," he tore it into a hundred fragments and tossed them into the foaming wake of the steamer.

Arriving at the great teeming city, the rice merchant, traveling under the name of Woo, engaged an upper room at the "Inn of Heavenly Welcome," and proceeded to unroll the matting roll of bedding and to make himself at home. It was a very warm evening, and he enjoyed sitting by the open window and breathing the cool air from the great Pearl River. The partition between him and the adjoining room was very thin and the boards so cracked that any conversation could be overheard by him without any effort at eavesdropping.

As he sipped his bowl of fragrant tea and tasted the little slices of preserved ginger which the servant had placed upon his table, he became suddenly conscious of a heated argument which was going on in the adjoining apartment. This was what he heard:

"I tell you there isn't a greater villain in the entire amen, and he has His Excellency the Viceroy completely in his power. He even uses his seals and his private keys. I tell you, Black Fox is the curse of Canton, and the city will never prosper till it is rid of him."

"Yes," said another voice, "I have even heard that he is suspected of having stolen the jade-stone seal of the Tsings, and that the Viceroy wore a clever imitation in its place."

The entrance of a servant with the evening meal ended the conversation abruptly here, but Woo, the rice merchant, had overheard enough to set him in a train of careful reflection and he passed the night in thinking and planning.

Early the following morning he set out for the Street of the Seal Cutters, and, sauntering leisurely along, he entered a shop where an engraver was hard at work at his little bench.

"Pray tell me," he said to the workman, "who is it that carves the seals for the officials of the Yamens?"

"Old Chow Foo, at the sign of the Jade-Stone Temple," was the answer, "has had that monopoly for many years."

Woo thanked him and walked along the crowded street until his eye caught the sign of the official engraver. He entered and asked to see the master of the shop. An aged workman, with large crystal goggles inclosed in rims of horn, came forward to meet him.

"I wish to speak to you on a matter of important private business," he said.

The master took him into an inner chamber and carefully closed the door. They waited a moment until the servant that had brought the tea bowls retired, and then Woo began:

"What did the Black Fox pay you for carving the imitation seal of the Tsings?"

The master carver tuned pale and stammered, "Black Fox—seal of the Tsings? I do not understand you, sir."

Woo leaned toward him over the teapot, and seizing him by the wrist with a grasp of steel, held him like a vise while he said, piercing him through and through with eyes of fire:

"Do not attempt to deny it, or your head will roll on the ground when his Excellency hears of it. You know well the penalty for forging an Imperial seal."

The seal-cutter winced and, trembling for his life, confessed it all. The Black Fox had come to him in the dead secrecy of night and paid him 200 Mexicans for duplicating the seal of Tsing and threatened him with instant death if he ever divulged it.

Woo relaxed his hold and the old seal-cutter sank down into his seat.

"That is all I wish to know," said the visitor as he rose to depart. "Cease your trembling. You are safe, on the one condition that you let no mortal man ever knew that this interview has taken place between us."

With that he unbarred the door of the inner room and in a moment was lost to sight in the crowded street.

The following morning Woo sat in the gatekeeper's lodge of the Viceregal Yamen.

"Does the second secretary accompany His Excellency to the Imperial Customs today?" He asked of the old gatekeeper, as he slipped a Mexican into his palm. "I am a visitor to the city and am most anxious to see him."

"He passes out in an hour's time," was the reply. "Sit here and enjoy your pipe and you shall see him."

Wood sipped the proffered tea and waited patiently for the official procession to pass. Ere long he heard the shouts of the out runners and the lictors, and soon he saw the outlines of the Viceregal sedan chair. He took a position of special vantage, and in the second sedan chair he saw the object of his search. There was no mistaking the Black Fox; he would almost any disguise. His Excellency the Viceroy wore the coral necklace of his office, but without the usual pendant, for the original was concealed in the inner robes of the secretary, while the imitation had been, all unconscious of the deceit, presented by His Excellency to the Governor of Hong Kong.

"The secretary is leaving on the morrow to visit his parents in the province of Four Rivers," volunteered the gatekeeper, as Woo rose to leave. "As the family is in deep mourning he goes secretly, in a citizen's blue gown."

The down river steamer for Hong Kong was loading at the Customs wharf, getting ready to depart at sundown. All day long, from early dawn, a traveler with a pigskin trunk and a roll of bedding had sat at the side of the gangway. He was apparently lost in the pages of a historical novel; in reality he was scanning intently every passenger who bought a ticket. Hour after hour he sat there, when at last his efforts were rewarded. A plainly clad gentleman purchased a ticket and was assigned to cabin No. 32. Instantly the watcher followed him and secured the other berth in the cabin.

Woo waited until his companion was ready to retire, and then courteously offered him a pipeful of tobacco, which was readily accepted. It came out of the little tin box marked "strong." The effect began to show itself at once, and his companion fell into a deep and heavy slumber.

Quick as a flash Woo was upon him and the long hands were searching the folds of his capacious sleeves. In an inner pocket, carefully sewed up, he felt a hard, square lump. Sharply pointed scissors soon cut it loose, and out of a silken wrapper rolled the seal of the Tsings!

Almost at the same instant there was a loud cry and commotion in the outer passageway, and Woo heard the ominous shrieks "Chan Tao Tsai Sui, Tsai Sui!" ("A thief, a thief! Into the river with him!") He knew only too well the swift and stern justice which Chinese passengers administered to those who were caught robbing them. He opened his cabin door just as they were dragging their victim by.

"Not in to the river," he cried; "throw him in here, and we will lock him up until the morning."

The crowd yielded for a moment, and he dragged the swooning wretch into the cabin. He bolted the door, and it was but the work of a few rapid moments to pull off the thief's ragged garments and substitute the blue gown of the secretary, and then to drag the drugged officer to the floor of the floor and clothe him in the cotton trousers of the river pirate. The crowd outside grew restless.

"Bring him out!" they screamed. "Into the river with him!"

They started to break in the door. Woo opened it, and ere he could restrain them they had dragged the helpless form to the deck and with a loud cry of vengeance had thrown him into the swirling water of the river.

IT WAS THE 13TH DAY OF THE MOON and the feast day of the Yellow Dragon, and Wang Foo and Inspector Wallace were ushered into the private office of Government House. His Excellency and Lady Evington greeted them most cordially.

"Well, Mr. Wang," said the Governor, "we are waiting anxiously to hear the results of you labors. We hope you have good news for us."

"Your Excellency," said Wang Foo, as he rose and drew from his left sleeve a tiny packet, "I have the very great pleasure of now returning to you and to Her Ladyship the jade-stone pendant stolen from Government House."

"Wonderful!" cried lady Evington. "Wonderful beyond words! How can we express our gratitude to you?" and she took once more the jewel into her hands and admired it.

The Governor opened a secret drawer in his desk and drew out a roll of Bank of England notes. "What reward do you think suitable for you services, Mr. Wang?"

"I accept no rewards, as you know," the detective replied. "My expenses are privately provided for; but if you have a vacant position in your office for a young interpreter, I should like to recommend my nephew."

"He shall begin his duties in the morning. And now let me ask who was the thief and how are we to punish him?"

"You cannot punish him, for he is not amenable to punishment by any court of justice."

"What a strange personality!"

"Sir, he has no personality. He is not a human being at all. Lady Evington's jewel was stolen by a magpie that flew into her apartment at night, and seeing the shining object lying detached upon the dressing table, picked it up in his beak and carried it off to the corner of the garden, where my trusty servant found it a few nights ago. We know of a number of similar robberies here in former years."

"By Jove!" said the Inspector, "strange, we never thought of the birds. I recall now a pearl robbery in Calcutta, years ago, where the gems were found in the garden, and a magpie was the guilty party."

As Wang Foo reached the door at the close of this interesting denouement he paused for a moment and, turning to Lady Evington, said with the most gracious of bows:

"Before I leave there is still greater pleasure in store for me." And drawing from his other sleeve a similar packet, he exclaimed to the astonished listeners: "Permit me now to hand to Your Ladyship the priceless jewel of my country. Here is the real jade-stone seal of the Tsings. What you formerly had, and what his Excellency the Viceroy presented to you in good faith, was only an imitation. The original was stolen by an attaché in his Yamen and the duplicate substituted for it. It has now been recovered, and I ask you to accept it at my hands. But," and here he smiled, "please don't leave detached jewels lying around on your dressing-table at night, when the weather is warm and the windows are open. It might lead you to suspect a perfectly innocent servant. Men are not the only thieves in nature."

"VENERABLE GRAND ONE," said the Prince of Chinese Detectives, "the tea has grown a little cold. Fill up the bowl again and hand me the pipe of cloisonné."

And opening his little window he looked out upon the green terraces of old Hong Kong, the Island of Fragrant Waters, and taking from the shelf the fourth volume of the *Analects*, he read again the words of Confucius the Sage: "The superior man toils and then he rests!"

So, as the cooling breezes blew in from the bay, Wang Foo fell asleep in his long chair of carved bamboo.

THE SANDAL-WOOD FAN

THE MORNING EDITION of the *Shanghai Daily News* of July 19, 191–, contained the following striking paragraph:

"Mysterious Death of the Taotai's
Deputy at the Wellington Hotel.
"Our readers will be sorry to hear of the sudden death last evening of Mr. Lo Ting Choo, the popular deputy of His Excellency Chang, Tao-Tai of Shanghai. He was attending a dinner given by the directors of the new Mutual Spinning Company at the Wellington Hotel on the Bund and was taken suddenly ill at the close of the meal.

"He was carried to an adjoining apartment, and Dr Hall-Clayton, surgeon to the British Consulate, was immediately summoned, but all his efforts to resuscitate the unfortunate gentleman proved unavailing and he died shortly before midnight.

"Mr. Lo was one of the most promising of the younger generation of Chinese officialdom and had always shown himself most courteous and obliging in his relations with European residents. His decease is a great loss to this community and leaves a vacancy which his excellency will find hard to fill.

"The usual reticence displayed by the attending physicians in commenting upon the case, and the

24

Chung, the Head Boy, Led the Old Priest Into the Private Dining Room and Gave Him the Most Vivid Description of the Scene.

refusal of the health officer to give any details to the
press, have thrown an air of mystery about the
occurrence which we hope in time will be satisfactorily explained, but which we must all very much
regret."

A week had passed after the above notice and the reading public of Shanghai had begun to forget the incident, when a little group
of men sitting on the porch of the Municipal Club, were joined in
the evening by three others.

They were the Chevalier Brouchard, Consul-General for France;
Dr Hall-Clayton (formerly surgeon of the 9th Punjab Artillery), and
James Mactavish, Esq, Director General of the new Mutual Spinning Company, one of the most prominent commercial enterprises
in all the Far East. It was a hot and moist July night and every
breath of air blowing up the river-channel was welcome to make
life endurable.

"Well," said the consul, as he replaced his glass of aerated water
and lighted his Manila cheroot, "have they come to any final decision as to that case of the Tao-tai's deputy?" He turned an inquiring look toward the surgeon.

"Mysterious as ever," was the reply. "Inspector Sharpley and I
have been closeted two hours this afternoon with Detective
Morehead—awfully clever chap, by the way, that Morehead; could
have given Sherlock Holmes any number of points and beaten him
at the game—but we don't seem to get any nearer to it."

"Was he in good health at the time?"

"Perfect, as far as the doctors know."

"Something must have been wrong, then, with the food. Chinese cooks are awfully careless in this sickly season and one never
knows what they may serve up to you. A little piece of tainted fish
or some over-ripe fruit may cost the unwary European his very life,
you know."

"Yes, true; but this was not in Chinatown or in a private house; it
was in the Wellington and every particle of food served there is under

constant and most careful inspection. The proprietor and chef are both old Eastern hands and know these risks as well as we do."

"Then," said the Consul, after a moment's pause, "the only thing is poison. You never can tell what these chaps may do, if one has a deep-seated grudge against another. I tell you, they'll stop at nothing. Couldn't one of the assistant cooks have smuggled it into a special dish on the table, or the table boy have dropped it in the wine?"

"Not likely," replied the surgeon. "We have gone into all that most carefully and we are positive that he neither ate nor drank anything that was not shared by all alike, and not another soul felt any bad effects whatever. No, I do not place any credence in the poison theory—unless—" and here he slowly rose and walked to the railing overlooking the sluggish river just below that seemed to conceal Oriental mysteries from European minds,—"unless it be some deadly drug that no modern medical man has ever heard of, and, you know, we haven't been working and studying and practicing in these wretched lands for over 50 years for nothing."

He touched the bell and the waiting Celestial instantly responded. "Boy, go catchee my 'ma-foo' and speakee he my wantchee trap just now go homeside."

The vision departed and having duly summoned the waiting horse-boy from the gate-house and his pipe, announced: "Tlap all leady now, sir," and the busy doctor bade the little company goodnight.

"That only shows," said Mr. Mactavish, "how little you can know about them, no matter how many years you may live among them. They'll outwit you every time. I wonder what the next problem will be that we will have to deal with."

"Well," said the Consul, "your company needn't worry. You got the property for your mill all right that you have been haggling for this last half year. He affixed the Tao-tai's seal to the release, didn't he, before he was taken ill?"

"Yes, he sealed it just before he swooned away, and that is the other strange and mysterious performance: for the release, as we all supposed—and the good Lord knows we paid and bribed every living soul in that blessed Tao-tai's yamen to get it, anyhow—the release was for the down-river lots and not for those up-river lots beyond the French concession. We're let in, you see, for 60,000 taels instead of 50, and now it's too late to change it."

"That's what Bill Nye meant when he said that their ways were 'child-like and bland,' wasn't it?" chimed in Capt. Burrows of the American steamer in port.

"Gentlemen," remarked the Hon. Mr. McAllister of His Majesty's Consular Court, as the little company broke up, "here is the case in a nutshell, I give it to you as I would to a jury. It is yours, go home and sleep over it and let the chief of police and myself know when you reach your verdict. A company of European capitalists decide to build a spinning mill in Shanghai and start looking for a suitable piece of land on the river front.

"After a long delay two pieces are offered to them; a downtown piece at 50,000 taels and an upriver piece at 60,000. As both are on actual Chinese soil, the seal and release of the Tao-tai are necessary before the purchase can be consummated. After no end of interviews with middlemen and consuls and Yamen officials, the decision seems to be in favor of the lower priced property and a dinner is arranged at the Wellington Hotel at which the principals are to meet, and the Tao-tai sends his deputy to affix the seal. All goes merrily until the coffee and cigars, then the document is produced and the deputy seals it and the transaction is complete. Now for the denouement; no sooner is the deed properly sealed than the deputy swoons away.

"He is carried out and, in spite of all that the most skillful English physicians can do, he dies within a few hours without regaining consciousness. On opening the deed later in the evening, to the utter astonishment of all concerned, it is for another piece of property at a much higher price! Yet every one present at the dinner was an eye witness of all the transactions and heard the deed distinctly read. Here are the three nuts for you, to crack, viz: (1) How was the deed exchanged, if exchanged it was? (2) Who was responsible for the deputy's sickness and subsequent decease? (3) How and why did it occur at just that critical moment?"

While these three problems were being submitted to the gentlemen at the club, the following conversation, bearing most vitally on the self-same subject, took place in the inner office of the Shanghai inspectorate general of police, between Chief Detective Morehead and his superior officer.

"I tell you, chief, it's beyond me and f I rather think it's beyond us all. I saw the Tao-tai's second deputy today and he tells me that they have worked just as hard over it as we have and they can't get any nearer to it. They understand their own people, and, I tell you—for I know something of their wily ways of forcing and torturing a confession out of a suspect—if they can't figure it out, there is no more use of you and me and any of the European men wasting any more time on it. Let's give it up and leave it alone for a while, and then perhaps later on something or somebody may 'turn up,' as old Dickens said, and shed a little daylight on the darkness."

"I am almost tempted to agree with you," answered the Inspector, "and yet, don't you know, I hate to acknowledge a failure. It puts us all wrong with the natives. This thing occurred in the Foreign Settlement and in our largest and best hotel, at a dinner right under our very eyes, and we not only can't find any clew to the mystery, but our best physicians had to let the poor chap die without even being able to tell us what he died of.

"Where will our boasted Western civilization and skill stand with the Chinese after this? Even if they haven't got many newspapers to read, this thing so my boy tells me—has been spread and gossiped all up and down the coast and river and every time they repeat it it naturally grows worse. It can't stand all those yellow papers that they paste up on the corners of their native streets where the crowds gather, but I shouldn't be a bit surprised to be told by some missionary that they say, 'How Chinese Government officials are trapped and murdered in foreign hotels!' Indeed, I have some papers like that in my office safe now."

"There's only one human being that I've ever heard of that can really help us, if we can find him, chief."

"Well, who is it? Not that mysterious chap from Hong Kong? 'Wily Wang Foo,' as they call him down there. You don't mean him do you?"

"The same; you remember how he traced out that fellow that stole the Governor's jade-stone signet, don't you, when all Hong Kong gave it up?"

"Yes, Indeed, I remember that ease distinctly, I don't believe we should lose face, do you, by sending for him now?

"It surely couldn't do any harm, sir, especially if we made it clear that we only wanted some temporary assistance."

"You're right, Morehead, we will wire for him tonight. As the old saying is, 'there is no harm in trying.'"

This will explain why the faithful Ah Sing, devoted house boy of Mrs. Morehead and personal valet of Detective Morehead, carried an urgent telegram (apparently from the Morehead residence, for it wasn't always wise to send official messages from the police of one port to another in a matter involving secrecy) for a private residence in Hong Kong that selfsame evening and trudged slowly with it along the Bund. The wires flashed it out into the ocean and down the Formosa Channel and around into the beautiful harbor of "The Valley of Fragrant Waters" and, ere the hour of midnight struck, a trusty messenger had summoned Wang Foo the "Wily" to an important mission in the great central seaport of Shanghai. Four days later the Messageries Maritimes steamer dropped anchor off the Woo-sung Bar and after a restful night at the "Inn of the Travelers' Peace" our famous detective, clad in the modest robes of a Chinese scholar, sent in his card to the private office of Inspector Sharpley.

"I am very glad to meet you, Mr. Wang," said the Inspector, extending to him a most cordial welcome, "for though I have often heard of you and of your wonderful ways, I believe I have never had the pleasure of personally meeting you."

"The honor is mine, I assure you, Mr. Inspector," replied Wang, in the most fluent and correct of English, "I appreciate you sending for me and it will be a privilege to serve you and the department in any way I can."

"The truth is, Mr. Wang, that we are in quite a perplexity here over a case that seems to have baffled the Chinese authorities as much as it has ourselves. Believing from what I know of your record, that you can help us in this matter, I have taken the liberty of sending for you."

"You refer, I presume, to the Wellington Hotel Incident, do you not?"

"Ah! You know of it, then?"

"Not all that I should like to know. I have read what the native and the foreign papers have had to say about it and I have heard it discussed at some Chinese clubs and—" he hesitated for a moment and then said, slowly and significantly—"other places where men are wont to gather."

"Suppose we go into the matter thoroughly now. I will tell you all I know about it from beginning to end and then I shall be glad to have you ask me freely any and every question you wish."

The Inspector suited the action to the word and gave Wang a complete account of the case, stopping only from time to time to answer some brief but very leading questions which his Chinese visitor read from a notebook in his wallet, and to which he jotted down what appeared to be very careful answers. It was long past the tiffin hour when he arose to go.

"Let me see," he said; "this is Wednesday, is it not? Next Monday evening, if all goes well, I should like to meet you here again. Let the time and place of our meeting be kept entirely quiet, and—" he raised his finger and placed it on his lips— "you will not consider it necessary to let anyone, native or foreign, know that I have arrived. We understand each other? I think we do! Good morning, sir."

IN THE THIRD ALLEY to the right as one goes north up the White Stag Passage from the central Boulevard or "Ma-Loo" of China's great seaport is the modest shop of the basket-maker, whose sign bears the symbols of the "Three-fold Blessing." It is the centre of a little colony from Hong Kong who make the baskets and chairs and sedans of willow, now so popular in the Western world. Thither, early on Thursday morning, came Mr. Wang Foo, with his white pigskin trunk and his roll of bedding, borne on the pliant bamboo of an aged coolie. There was no need of knocking, for there were no doors to unlock. Everything was open to the street and pass-erby, as the various members of the family all plied their daily tasks in full view of the world. The old father recognized him at once—they had been neighbors in the Southern isle—and rose and greeted him and placed the seat beside the table and brought the water-pipe and smoking tea.

"Venerable Elder-born, we greet you. Welcome to our humble home! Deign to be seated and refresh yourself. Alas, 'tis but poor hospitality that we can offer, our rice is coarse and the tea, we fear, is cold."

"Excuse me for thus intruding without the proper rites or cer-emonies. I am quite unworthy of your welcome and your kindness. Ten thousand thanks I offer and greetings from all your friends in Fragrant Waters."

In the little upper room, which he had occupied on a former visit, Wang Foo made himself at home, and from the basket maker's shop he sauntered daily forth to solve the mystery for which he had come to the northern city. Sometimes they knew him, some-times they knew him not, for the capacious pigskin trunk contained many and marvelous disguises.

In the morning early, as was his wont, he opened his little vol-ume of the Confucian *Analects* and chose therefrom his motto for the day. "Chuin-tse-woo-pen: The superior man bends his atten-tion to what is radical," he read, and then he closed it and said to himself: "Yes, we will begin with the fundamental things today. I will first see the place and then the people and then listen to what they said and did. The great master speaketh well to his little pu-pil!" And then Wang Foo disappeared from sight and an aged priest from old Thibet, carrying in his right hand a little flageolet and bell of bronze and in his left a bundle of tiny scrolls with ancient symbols and pious prayers and charms, passed out into the bust-ling highway of the broad Ma-Loo.

He came ere long to the servants' gateway of the Wellington Hotel and entering the courtyard crossed it and seated himself by the kitchen door. He took out his little flageolet and, fingering it skillfully, began to play one of the plaintive airs of his faraway mountain home. Music hath charms in every land on earth and China is no exception, so he was very soon surrounded by an admiring throng of listeners, who bade him enter and share with them their morning rice and tea.

"Listen, my children," he said, and he stroked his beard of gray—and there is no land where more deference and respect are paid to age—"listen to a tale of Thibet." And they gathered all about him, the cooks, the tableboys, the ma-foos, and the coolies and listened with eager ears and raptured gaze, as he alternately told and sang of a famous vendetta of the ancient days in which a noble warrior invited his rival to a banquet and then hired an assassin to kill him while he sat at meat.

"A wonderful story, venerable Father," said the head table boy, as the story was finished, and he took out from his girdle a few brass cash to purchase a prayer charm, an example which all the others quickly followed; "but those deeds were not confined to the ancient days. We have them now—and right here in this very house, where the deputy was poisoned scarce two weeks ago!"

"Here? In this very house? It cannot be. Tell me, my children, tell the old priest how the ancient deeds survive unto the present."

"Yes, tell the old Father all about it, Chang; you saw it and heard it all. Show him the room and tell him who was there," they cried in chorus.

Chang, the head boy, led the old priest into the private dining-room and gave him the most vivid description of the scene. He told him the names of every person present, showed him just where they sat and recalled every dish upon the menu. The old priest listened with the deepest attention and pleased Chang more and more by asking close and leading questions. "Tell me slowly," he said, "for I am old in years and I cannot take it all in like one more young. See, I will make some notes of it in this little book, that, if I return in safety to Thibet, I may tell this wondrous story of the modern days to all within the White Cloud Temple—for they will find it hard to believe, I fear."

Then the old priest, returning once more into the kitchen, took up his little flute and bells and charms, and with a "Bless you all, my children," crossed the pavement of the courtyard and soon was lost to sight in the busy streets.

Late that evening when the beard and wig and gown of the Thibetan priest had been exchanged for the short and comfortable Kwa-tse or short jacket of the Chinese student, Wan Foo lighted his pipe and, seated at the table in his upper-room, opened his notebook and began to think.

All was quiet, for the basket-maker and his family, weary with the work of the long and heated day, had retired early. He thought and thought. He read notes and made other notes. He compared persons, place and events. Gradually, as the night wore on, an outline seemed to frame itself before horn, indistinct at first, but gradually getting clearer, though here and there a piece seemed to be yet wanting. And this was the conclusion of it all.

1. Lo, the deputy, had been clearly murdered—killed by some subtle poison unknown to Western medicine, but the fatal working time of which had been carefully thought out.

2. The deed which was handed to him and which was seen by all and read to them, was not the deed to which he affixed the Tao-tai's seal. By some very clever sleight-of-hand, one must have been substituted for the other at the very table and between the moments of the reading and the sealing.

3. The administering of the poison must have been done by some person present in the room, but who timed the length of the meal exactly and the same person or a trusted confederate must have exchanged the deeds.

All this Wang Foo counted on as a good day's work, but within the next four days he must supply these three missing links to make the chain of evidence complete, viz: What was the poison? Who administered it? Who exchanged the deeds? The hoarse whistles of the up-river steamers warned him that there remained but three hours before the sunrise, so closing his secret diary and his notebook, he turned in to his well-earned sleep.

The next morning he rose rather late and took his noon-day rice with the basket-maker's family. In the afternoon he sauntered down to the Woo-sung Gardens and, finding a cool seat by the river's bank, sat down to meditate and look over once more the notes of the night before.

The junks and sampans gliding smoothly by on the incoming current, seemed to him like human characters in the drama he was trying to disentangle. Two foreign yachts with their graceful hulls passed by and then his eye rested upon a new Mandarin gunboat with her flags and banners, but just as she got within his range of vision, a loathsome beggar boat slipped in between them and the ragged lepers with outstretched palms gave him a strange feeling of revulsion as for a moment their ugly craft hid the little gunboat from his sight. He looked again and two large cargo-junks laden with cotton were following in their wake. He glanced down at his notes and read: "Six people only were seated at the table: the deputy, his secretary, Mr. Lee, the owner of the property; Messrs Mactavish and Owens, directors of the company, and last, but by no means least, Long Wing, the assistant Interpreter from the Yamen, who acted as general utility man and go-between."

What made him pause and shudder as he recalled this name? What made him compare him with the leper boat that hid the Mandarin from him on the river? He looked at the little diagram of the seats at table on that fatal night, and he saw that Long Wing's seat was directly opposite the deputy's. Another link in the chain was being forged most rapidly.

He hurriedly left the gardens and, taking a jinrikisha, told the coolie to take him to the old city gates. Descending there, he exchanged the jinrikisha for a sedan and directed the bearers to Taotai's Yamen, where he dismissed them and passed into the gatekeeper's lodge.

"Am I too late to see an officer today?" he asked.

"Whom do you seek?"

"Long Wing, the interpreter."

"Alas, Sir, he left for home a half-hour ago."

He called another sedan and started in the direction the gatekeeper pointed

"You fellows know Long Wing?" he asked of the forward bearer.

"Yes, sir; we know him well."

"Do you ever carry his sedan?"

"The Elder-born speaketh true, we often carry him, because both his bearers are ill at home."

"Did you carry him anywhere, per chance, on the evening of the 18th of the moon?"

"Indeed we did and on the 19th also."

"Do yon remember where you took him?"

"On the 18th we went to the mansion of the widow Wang, the one who sold her property for the foreign mill, and on the 19th we went into the foreign quarter and to the great hotel."

Wang Foo's thoughts were working faster as he saw the outline closing in. He stopped the sedan at the City Temple and, paying the coolies a double fare, said: "The night is clear, I will walk the remaining few streets." He crossed the bridge into the French Concession and took the first jinrikisha for the basket-maker's home.

Once secure within the upper room, he unlocked the trunk and, turning over slowly the well-thumbed volume called "The Poisons of the Ancient Dynasties," he came to this: "The berries of the South Formosa lacquer tree distill a noxious odor, which is stupefying and deadly in its effect. Concocted into an ointment it is one of the most virulent poisons known. It is generally spread upon a fan and the victim becomes quickly unconscious. Perfume of some kind is always added to conceal it."

Before his interview with the Inspector on the following Monday Wang Foo had ascertained these further facts: first, the widow Wang had left for a long journey to Pekin the day following the dinner at the hotel; second, Long Wing was formerly a resident of South Formosa; third, his brother, a compradore in the Peninsular S. S. Co, had deposited 5000 taels in one lump in the Anglo-Asiatic Bank on July 18th. Monday afternoon he completed the chain and when the doors of the private office closed upon him, the chief and Morehead, that evening, there was unfolded to them the various stops of a crime almost unparalleled in their long experience.

They were shown how Long Wing had accepted a bribe of 5000 taels from the widow Wang to have her property substituted for that of the other parties and how, to avoid suspicion, he had secretly passed this money over to his brother to deposit in the bank.

He had gone to the hotel earlier in the evening and under the pretext of arranging some flowers on the table had secreted the duplicate deed beneath it.

Then, at the critical moment, he had pushed the first deed onto the floor and in pretending to pick it up, had dexterously substituted the second for it and it was this that the deputy sealed. He returned later in the evening, looking, he said, for a lost memorandum, and had secured the former deed from underneath the table.

"But how did he come to go to the deputy's side?" asked the Inspector. "Please explain that to us."

"'Your Excellency looks warm,' he said," answered Wang Foo; "'let me refresh you with some fragrance from the Southern Isles,' and drawing a beautiful sandal wood fan from a box within his sleeve, he stepped to his side and began to fan him vigorously. The upper portion of the fan was covered with the deadly lacquer, you see, but the odor of the sandal wood concealed it.

"It took but a few moments for the poison to do its work, but those moments were quite enough for the impressing of Tao-tai's seal. In the excitement that followed, he deftly replaced the fan within its air-tight case so that no others were affected by it."

"But did not the secretary and others have their fans?"

"Ah! That is just the important point. It was the 18th of the moon, you know, and the book of rites and ceremonies is very strict about the etiquette of fans. Feather fans alone are used after the 15th of the moon, and these, you see could not have held the poison or concealed the odor of it. That is why sandalwood alone would answer."

"Morehead," said the Inspector, "you and I have still a few things to learn about our Celestial friends. Let us call this 'The Case of the Sandalwood Fan.'"

"Not a bad idea," replied the detective.

"In the third book of the *Analects* it is written: 'The Superior Man Is Careful to Follow the Rites and Ceremonies,'" said Wang Foo.

"Or, in other words," added the Inspector, "whenever he wishes to refresh himself, he should use the proper fan for the season!"

THE LACQUER CABINET

"I DON'T CARE WHAT IT COSTS, I want it and I propose to have it. Why, it would be the greatest curio in all my collection. Just think of it— a real Chinese ghost shut up in his own little cabinet and ready to come and go whenever I open the door, like a squirrel in his cage. Isn't it great? It will make those Indian Buddhas and those Burmese idols look like nothing at all, and, Just think, Tony, what a spiritualistic séance we can give when we get back to Syracuse, eh?"

"Well, old man, I suppose if you set your heart of it, you'll eventually get it, somehow. I don't believe I ever knew you really to want a thing—that is, a thing that money could buy that you didn't sooner or later put your hand on it, but it looks as if you were going to have a mighty hard task before you this time."

"The captain says—and the old skipper has been out here a great many years, you know—that no European has ever gotten his hand on a real genuine one yet, and there have been lots of travelers hunting curios out here before us."

The above remarks were part of a conversation between Mr. Reginald Wells, a wealthy young American tourist, from Central New York, and his college chum at Cornell, Mr. Theodore Towbridge (known on the campus as "Tony") as they sat in the smoking-room of the steamer *Nan-Ching*, en route from Hong Kong to Amoy. They were real globe-trotters of the traditional American type. They had started out on a trip around the world, and, incidentally on a good time, and at this present moment they were having their share of both.

38

Appearing as if by magic out of the darkness a great Ning-po rice junk crashed directly into them - Spotty was swept away in the flood and was seen no more

They had "done" India, the Straits, Java and Borneo, and now they were on their way north from Hong Kong to Amoy to fill full their huntsman's cup of joy with a genuine old-fashioned tiger hunt. They had heard incidentally of this sport in the south, but Col. Johnson, the American Consul at Hong Kong, had whetted their appetite for it to the keenest edge by showing them in his office the skin of a magnificent man-eater. "More than 12 feet long, gentlemen, from tip to tail! Had killed three children the week before I shot him—grandest sport in the world, I can tell you."

That was enough. Nothing would do but a tiger shoot. The consul made every preparation for them, and the crack steamer of the Southern Navigation Company was now bearing them rapidly toward the lair of the beast, armed not only with guns and ammunition, but with something equally important, namely, letters of introduction to the leading English firm of the port. Messrs Waring & Co had been notified by wire of their coming, and they were instructed from their bankers not only to entertain the travelers handsomely, but to have boats and coolies ready for the hunt

Just at the moment that we are introduced to these gentlemen in the smoking room of the steamer, however, the interest in the tiger had suddenly waned and the all-absorbing topic was the rarity and value of the curios which they had collected in the Orient. After listening patiently to their descriptions of the "unique" and "only genuine" articles which they had induced reluctant natives to part with at fabulous prices, Capt. Jones chimed in at last with:

"Well, you may have Buddhas and idols and Josses galore, but there's one thing you haven't got—and it's one thing money can't buy, either—and that's a genuine ancestral cabinet with the original ghost inside. I've seen lots of tourists offer for them—and mighty high prices, too—but nary a one did they ever get, for the Chinaman would rather die than sell his ancestor's ghost; and that's what they believe is really in the little tablet in the lacquer box."

"Regy," said Tony, from the opposite side of the room, "we've got more of these miserable curios now than we know what to do with. Why, you could stack the whole museum at Cornell almost

full with what we've shipped home already, and even if you do induce some disloyal Confusionist to sell his ancestor's ghost, it
would cost you a small fortune to buy it—so what's the use?"

Six bells rang out from the wheel-house just at this moment
and the appearance of the saloon-boy with, "Velly solly, gentlemen; but catchee lebbon clock must putchee out lights," ended the
conversation for the evening.

The good ship *Nam-Ching* dropped anchor in Amoy Harbor on
schedule time in the morning and the steam launch flying Waring
& Co's house-flag, with the head of the firm himself on board, came
out to meet the travelers and give thorn a cordial welcome to the
port and to the hospitality of the "hong," as such business establishments are called in the China seas.

They found everything in readiness for the up-river trip and
the hunt. Mr. Waring having put his own commodious house-boat,
the *Marguerite*, completely at their disposal, and having engaged
extra servants and competent native guides, they could start in a
day or two just as soon as they had rested from the sea trip. The
tigers were waiting for them, messengers from the interior having
reported further depredations from the beasts in the valleys of Foo-
King, to the north of them.

Amoy and its sights were soon exhausted and a picnic to the
famous White Door Temple, followed by a dinner to the little foreign community at the hong, completed their program in that Chinese city, popularly known as the "dirtiest at the Empire." They
were to go aboard the *Marguerite* late in the evening and start at
daylight the following morning, when something occurred which
made their visit one long to be remembered by their hosts as well
as by themselves; and thereby hangs our tale.

Mr. Waring had invited three or four fellow merchants, together
with Sir Warren Chelmsford, the British Consul (the American
Consul being at home on furlough), to join them at dinner and
after the coffee the subject of conversation very naturally turned
to tigers and the various experiences of Europeans who had gone
in search of them. When this had been thoroughly thrashed out,
Mr. Wells turned to the consul and said:

"Sir Warren, I am very anxious indeed to secure for my collection of curios a genuine gold-lacquer cabinet with the ancestral tablet of some Chinese family. You are an old and experienced resident of the East; how would you advise me to go to work to get it?"

"Ah, Mr. Wells," replied the consul, "you are not by any means the first one that has asked me that question, and I can only say to you what I have said to all the others; that they are absolutely unobtainable. The Chinese are the most reverential and particular people In regard to the spirits of the departed, and any disrespect shown to them calls down upon the culprits the dire vengeance of the gods. In their 'superstition,' as we ignorantly call it, they firmly believe that one of the ghosts or spirits of the dead—and every individual possesses three—enters into the ancestral tablet of the lacquer tablet.

"It remains there while the doors are closed, and passes in and out when the doors are opened. It must be most respectfully treated; offerings of rice and tea and wine must be regularly supplied to it and 'spirit money,' as they call those strips of gold and silver paper that you see scattered around the cemeteries, must be provided for all its contingent expenses. When any of these are neglected, misfortune of some kind will surely fall upon the family. To injure one of these tablets while it is 'vivified,' as they say, is an insult to one's ancestors, and to destroy it or to sell it to a European—which is the worst insult of all—is a crime which not only surpasses murder, but outrages the entire community where it occurs. So, you see, now, why none are ever offered for sale."

"Not for any amount of money? Money is very powerful, you know, in overriding superstition. We found that over and over again in India, didn't we, Tony?"

Addressing himself to his chum, he went on. "You remember that old abbot who sold us his father's pet idol that had protected the family for 50 years, don't you? He was terribly shocked when we offered to buy it for £20 and almost drove us out of the temple; but the morning we left Benares he came around early to the back door of the hotel, and sold it to us for £15. Don't you think, Sir Warren, that if it was generally known here that 200 or 300

Mexicans would be paid—on the quiet, of course—for a cabinet and tablet and ghost complete, some noble scion of a Chinese family would be willing to risk it?"

"Perfectly hopeless, sir; it has been tried again and again."

The inevitable result of this conversation was to make Mr. Wells hunger more than ever for the forbidden fruit, and he there and then resolved that he would not leave China without it—even the supreme attraction of slaying a "man-eater" began to pale before his determination to secure the ghost and the cabinet, if it took the very last pound on his letter of credit.

When the *Marguerite* lifted her anchor at daylight in the morning, the coveted cabinet was aboard, securely locked in a sole leather suitcase and hidden away under the lower berth of the cabin.

How did it ever get there? Let us see.

When Ah-Woo, the faithful house boy of the Warings (and son of Sam-Tok the compradore), come into Mr. Wells' room late in the evening to assist him in packing his baggage, he looked carefully around, closed both the windows and then mysteriously proceeded to lock and bolt the door. Having taken these precautions, he produced from the inner recesses of a commodious gown a carefully wrapped package of yellow silk and. placing it on the dressing table, remarked to the rather astonished traveler:

"You can savee, my blongee Ah-Woo, my master callee 'Spotty' 'cause my catchee smalpox (pointing to the decorations left by that dreaded disease upon his face). My have hear you speakee last night wantchee buy cabinet with Chinaman's spilit inside. No can buy store side. Suppose culioman sell, mandalin kill he. Have catchee one piece this side can seclure my great-glandfather ghost inside he. Suppose you pay me five hundred dollar, my givee you, my no can sell."

Spotty here proceeded slowly to unwrap the covering of silk and from it he brought forth a beautiful little cabinet of the most exquisite gold lacquer and set it upon the table. It measured about 10 inches in height and about five inches in width. It had two little doors in front, clasped together with bars of delicately carved bronze, and when these were opened they revealed within a golden tablet with the posthumous titles of a man of noble rank. There could be no doubt about it, it certainly was the genuine article. Spotty explained it all in the most fluent "pidgin English."

He showed the opening in the top of the tablet through which the spirit of the departed entered and the seals that guaranteed his presence, and then, solemnly drawing forth from his sleeve an ancient dagger, turned to his astonished visitor and said:

"Suppose my no talkee tlue, you can killee me now."

"All right, Spotty, I'll take your word for it. Put away that dagger; I don't want to murder anybody for all the old curios in China. Here's your 500 Mexicans. Wrap it up carefully and put it away in my grip and stow it under my berth on the boat."

Spotty counted the money over slowly and carefully and rolled it up in his capacious girdle. He packed the cabinet according to directions and then, as he reopened the windows and unlocked the door, he added, significantly pointing to his throat, "You no tellee any man till you get Melica side. Suppose Mandolin savee my pay you cabilet, he choppee my head off so fashion."

The tide at Amoy is one of the worst on all the Asiatic coast, rising and falling over 14 feet, and making navigation for small craft exceedingly dangerous. Spotty did not return on the steam launch that took the travelers to the house boat, but called a sampan of his own and directed the boatman to take him to the lower city.

The outgoing current swept the fragile little sampan along and in a very few minutes they were opposite the customhouse wharf and they turned to pass in between the buoys, when, appearing as if by magic out of the darkness, a great Ningpo rice junk crashed directly into them and overturned the sampan in an instant. The boat man managed to seize a bamboo rope hanging over the side and clambered on board the junk, but Spotty was swept away in the flood and was seen no more.

THERE WAS AN UNUSUAL EXCITEMENT in the market street of the town the following morning and the news spread quickly from mouth to mouth that one of the servants in the foreign hong had been seen in the act of robbing his ancestral hall. An old egg peddler from the country had brought the news. He had been resting quietly by the roadside partly hidden by the bushes and had seen Spotty climb over the wall of the enclosure, enter the hall and depart a few minutes later with a bundle under his arm. On looking through the window, he saw to his horror that the ancestral cabinet was missing from the central shelf. He recognized Spotty at once from having seen him at the kitchen door of the hong where he stopped to sell his eggs to the cook.

Before night the news had reached the Tao-tai's yamen and the runners were sent to arrest the house boy, but returned with the statement that he had disappeared and had left no trace behind him. Under the old law of China by which a parent is held responsible for the sins of a child, the runners returned in the morning and, seizing the compradore, dragged him away to the yamen to be held there until his son should give himself up.

Mr. Watsford was sitting at his office desk when the second house boy rushed in to him with the news that Hoo-Sam-Lok, his compradore and right-hand man, was actually a prisoner in the hands of the native authorities. He could scarcely believe his senses, but when he realized it was true, he seized his hat, and, ordering his private launch to be ready immediately at the wharf, hastened at once to the British Consulate.

"Well, Chelmsford," he said, in a great state of excitement, "here's a pretty how-do-you-do. The Tao-tai has arrested my compradore because his son Scotty stole a miserable little tomb-stone out of the cemetery last night and they are probably bambooing him up at the yamen now. My whole hong is upset by this stupid nonsense and I want you to go or send over there at once and order him released."

"I am sorry for you, Watsford," answered the Consul, "but you see it's on Chinese soil and entirely outside my jurisdiction."

"Do you mean to tell me that the British Government can't send over there and get that chap free? Why, it's outrageous."

"The only thing that I can do for you is to go over there and ask the Tao-tai personally to see that he is kindly treated until the son turns up."

"Well, for goodness sake go quick, then; you know what those yamen runners are when they get a foreign employee into their hands—they'll have his very life blood if he doesn't pay up handsomely."

The Consul and the merchant returned in the launch to the yamen and after an interview with His Excellency received his assurance that no harm would be done to the prisoner, but that he was obliged to hold him in confinement until every effort had been made to secure the person of Scotty.

Two full weeks passed by, but not a trace of the criminal could be found. The Tao-tai then sent a dispatch to the Consul telling him that the town was in such a state of excitement that unless Scotty turned up within six days he would be obliged to apply the torture in order to secure a confession from the compradore and thus appease the people.

"Good gracious," said Watsford, "isn't there any human way of catching the villain and saving his poor, innocent father from those infernal demons? Why, if they once get at him they'll kill him, sure as fate."

"I have been thinking over it a good deal," answered the Consul, "and I have decided to wire to the Governor at Hong Kong for Wang Foo."

"And who is this Wang Foo?"

"The most remarkable man in the colony. They call him the 'Mysterious.' He is a Chinese gentleman of means who gives his whole time and attention to ferreting out criminals, and seems to succeed when all others fail. His record as a detective among his own people is certainly wonderful."

"Wire for him at once. Tell them to send him on the very first ship and look to me to foot the bills."

The man of mystery arrived on the appointed date and after his usual very careful and painstaking inquiries, together with private examinations of all the parties Interested, proceeded to his interview with His Excellency, the Tao-tai. He was most courteously received and after the tea-drinking, requested that all the attendants be retired and that the doors to the private apartment be securely closed and locked.

The Tao-tai reluctantly granted his request. They sat down facing each other upon the couch of honor and took up the tobacco pipes. Wang lighted the paper fuse and, looking his companion straight in the face, made with it certain passes in the air. The Tao-tai appeared confused. Wang continued the motions and with the smoke outlined two ancient Chinese hieroglyphics. "Phoong-Hwia," exclaimed the startled official as he rose, "The Brotherhood!"

"The same," answered Wang, as he calmly replaced the fuse in the holder. "You have not forgotten me, then? You remember the case of Long Chow and how I saved you from official disgrace? The time has come now for you to repay that favor."

"What favor do you ask?"

"The relief and justification of Hoo-Sam-Lok."

"But suppose I do not grant it? What then?"

Wang leaned forward and, gripping the official's hand, held it like a vise.

"If you do not, the official promotion to provincial judge which you are expecting in a fortnight's time will mysteriously fall through! Do you understand?"

"But how can I satisfy the people's demands? They know that a crime of the most heinous nature has been committed and the heads of all the clans and guilds in town are clamoring at my gates for torture and for trial. If I refuse to gratify them, I am a ruined man. How can I break the laws and traditions of the Empire?"

"Listen!" said Wang, still gripping the Tao-tai's hand. "Is it not written in the *Analects*, 'The superior man adjusteth the punishment to the time?' You know he is innocent—absolutely innocent—you also know as well as I that there are ways of going through these forms without injury to the victim? 'Fak Ching, fak-ching'— 'punish lightly,' you know how. See that it is done! I demand it in the name of the Brotherhood! Farewell!"

The following morning Wang Foo the detective met Mr. Arthur Watsford by special appointment in his private office, and, after pledging him to secrecy as absolutely essential to the release of the compradore, addressed him in these words:

"Mr. Watsford, what I am about to say to you will probably astonish you, but you have lived long enough in China to know that there are more astonishing things here than any European has ever dreamed of.

"I want you to leave this case absolutely in my hands, and I guarantee that the prisoner will return to you on the 30th of the month, without a trace of his unfortunate experiences, thoroughly well and sound and able to resume his duties. He will come back to you with the respect of the Chinese community, completely vindicated of any charge of complicity in the crime of his son, but in the meantime he must pass through the ordeal which the traditions and beliefs of my people insist on. Do you trust me?"

"Mr. Wang, I do so, perfectly."

"Then telegraph at once to the firm in Foo Chow to which Mr. Wells had letters from here and have them instruct him to take the steamer direct from there to Shanghai. He must on no account return to Amoy. His presence here would thwart all my plans and be almost certain to start up an incipient antiforeign riot. The sooner he is out of sight the sooner will this unfortunate purchase of his be forgotten.

"As for the rest, leave everything to me. No matter what rumors or reports come to you of the officials' treatment of the compradore, I will bring him back to you myself, safe and well, on the 30th of the month. If you attempt to interfere in any way— through the consulate or otherwise—I will not be responsible for his life."

There was something in his voice and manner that inspired confidence and trust and the merchant pledged himself to comply with his every request.

On the morning of the last day of the month, true to his promise, Wang Foo appeared at the office of Waring & Co, and by his side, smiling and well, walked the familiar form of Hoo-Sam-Lok, the compradore. Amid the rattling noise of packs of firecrackers they were welcomed into the hong and all sat down to the joyous feast of welcome which the staff of native employees and servants had provided.

"Well, Hoo," said Mr. Watsford, as he extended his hand, "the old firm is certainly glad to see you back! Here's to your health and happiness and may I express the hope that the whole generation of globe trotters and tiger hunters will hereafter leave Amoy alone; for they have certainly made us trouble enough."

"There's just one thing I would like to ask you, Mr. Wang," said the consul, as he bade the detective goodbye on the returning steamer, "and that is: How did that fellow ever pass through that ordeal and live? My chair coolies tell me that he was 'snaked' and 'cangued' and 'bomboood'—they saw some of it themselves in the Tao-tai's courtyard—and any one of those is enough, the Lord knows, to finish an ordinary mortal."

Wang smiled and answered, "Oh, that is simple enough when one knows the inner methods and secrets. You see the copper snakes around his arms which were supposed to be filled with boiling water were really cold."

"But my coolies saw the steam coming out of them?"

"They thought they did, but it was only tobacco smoking in the spouts."

"But the circular scars upon his arms?"

"A little red and blue paint made that look very natural."

"And the wooden cangue or collar of a hundred pounds?"

"The wood was all carefully hollowed out and the collar was really no more uncomfortable than some of the stiff linen ones you foreigners wear."

"Well, how about the 60 blows of the lictors' bamboo? They say that sometimes half that number will cripple a man for life?"

"That depends upon the weight of the bamboo. Some are natural wood; some are laden with lead—these are the deadly kind—and others are so carefully split open along their length that though they sound like heavy weights they are really no more painful than tappings with the lightest cane."

"The whole thing, then, was really a farce from beginning to end, wasn't it?"

"That depends upon the point of view. It was necessary for the populace to be convinced of the culprit's innocence and this could only be done by testing him in the way they understood. They would never have taken the Tao-tai's verdict, so he had to convince them, and he did it."

"One question more—the lacquer cabinet; what of that? Did Spotty really steal his ancestral cabinet and sell it to the tourist? You know, I have my doubts."

"No, he did not really steal it. He borrowed it, intending to return it in the morning, but the poor chap was drowned by the sinking of his sampan."

"And was that proved?"

"Yes, the boatman told the story at one of the tea stands on the river bank."

"What was it, then, that was packed with the baggage on the boat?"

"O, that was an imitation, skillfully substituted for the original in the cabin."

"Then if Spotty had lived, he would probably have never been found out?"

"Probably not, for he would have replaced the cabinet in the morning."

"And what would you say was the real value of the treasure which Mr. Wells took away for which he paid $500?"

"It would be hard to tell—I should say $5, possibly $10; who knows? He is happy with his curio. Let us be happy also and leave well enough alone."

THE IVORY CHESS-BOARD

IT WAS JUST THE CLOSE of the tiffin hour in the colony of Hong Kong and Sir William Rollins, head of the great English firm of Rollins & Co, chemists and druggists, was sipping his coffee in the little dining room of the Church Hospital for Chinese. He was the guest for the hour of his old friend Dr. Bradlaw, the surgeon, who had come out with him to the East just 20 years ago.

"Well, Doctor," he said, "how about the opium question? Are you still struggling with it as you were five years ago when I left the Colony and went home?"

"It is just about as bad as ever, Sir," replied the surgeon. "In spite of all the Government restrictions and regulations, they seem to smuggle the vile stuff in and we get it in the hospital all the time.

"The police and detectives do all they can to ferret the rascals out, but what can you do when your own countrymen are the chief offenders? It's the foreign druggists that are really to blame, Sir Rollins, and"—he looked toward his guest most significantly—"you'll pardon my saying it, but Rollins & Co is not above suspicion."

"What! Do you mean to tell me that after all my efforts of years to banish opium from this community my own firm is supposed to be actually selling it to the natives? Impossible!"

"Not impossible at all; the illegal traffic is going on right under your very eyes, but you are not sharp enough to catch them. Why only a few days ago I found a patient here taking some of your new

n England you say, "The very walls have ears," but in China ✣ ✣ ✣ The words were scarcely uttered when down with a crash came the Japanesse screen by the pantry door and out sprawled the house boy

cough lozenges for his throat, and when I examined the package carefully, it was filled with the choicest and most expensive Patna opium. What do you say to that, eh?"

"What do I say? I vow by all that I hold sacred that I will probe that thing to the very bottom, and the man that did it—be he Chinaman or Englishman—shall not only be instantly discharged, but I will hand him over to the police, without any mercy."

"I sincerely hope you will, Sir, and not only help us in the crusade, but also redeem the good name of your firm; for my Chinese nurses tell me that there is always some way of getting it at your establishment, if they only know the secret, or have a 'pull' as the American doctors say."

There was a grand shakeup in the leading drugstore of Hong Kong the following day and the police made one of the cleverest hauls of opium that the papers had ever recorded. Padro Madero, the trusted Portuguese clerk (in charge of the native department) somehow or other got wind of it and disappeared for parts unknown just before the officers reached his residence. Hundreds of dollars' worth of the "golden earth," as the Chinese euphoniously call the drug, were discovered under various disguises.

Boxes of cough lozenges, quinine, headache powders, tonic pills and a dozen other popular articles sold to Chinese customers, were found to have been carefully cut open, filled with opium and then resealed to avoid detection. The entire foreign and native staff were summoned before the firm and given a lecture, accompanied with threats of dismissal, which ought to have been effective in forever after preventing a dram of the poison from being sold over their counters. Sir Rollins received a flattering compliment for this in the papers and was personally congratulated, as a public benefactor, by His Excellency the Governor.

In less than three weeks from the above occurrence an anonymous letter, postmarked Canton, was laid upon Sir Rollins' plate at breakfast. He tore it hastily open and read as follows: "You have evidently, Sir, made most conscientious efforts to rid this community of the opium curse by trying to prevent the sale of it through your clerks, but the missionaries of this district have positive evidence through their native converts that you have been thoroughly hoodwinked and that the importation and sale of the drug is still going on, though in a way that you cannot detect. Consult the man of mystery and perhaps he will throw a little light upon the subject."

Sir William Rollins was furious. He rose and paced the floor. He crumpled the letter up and threw it into the waste-basket and then, after a few moments' thought, picked it out again, smoothed it and placed it carefully in his wallet.

"Boy," he cried, "catchee my chair chop-chop, my wantchee go city-hall side."

Arrived at the city offices, he sought a private interview with the chief inspector and, laying the letter on his desk, sat down and said: "Well, what do you police chaps say to that?"

The Inspector read it over slowly and carefully and, after a few moments' hemming and hawing, replied: "I rather imagine that the 'Wily One' is the only man in the colony that can really get at the bottom of it."

"And who is this 'Wily One,' as you call him?"

"Wang Foo, the Mysterious. Haven't you heard of him?"

"Do you mean the native detective that recovered the Governor's jewels?"

"The same, but he wouldn't care to be known as a native detective. He is a gentleman of means who takes a special pleasure in ferreting out criminals, in the interests of what he calls the Confucian standard of justice. He won't accept any pay—just does it for the sake of the cause, don't you know—and I must say that he is the cleverest one of his kind I ever came across."

"If you know where he lives, send for him and ask him to do me the honor of dining with me at the hong this very night."

The Inspector touched a bell and gave orders to his deputy to seek out Wang Foo and invite him to dinner at Rollins & Co's at 8. Promptly at the appointed hour the chair-coolies put down their burden at the doorstep and a tall Chinese gentleman was ushered into the drawing room. It didn't take five minutes for every native servant and employee in the establishment to know who the distinguished visitor was.

The coolies told the gate-keepers; they in turn told the cook and the head boy, and it passed with lightning rapidity through the house; even the female servants and the amahs peered over the staircase to get a glimpse of their fellow countryman who—to their minds at least—was conferring an honor upon the foreign firm by condescending to accept its hospitality.

"Mr. Wang," said Sir William, greeting him most cordially at the door of the drawing-room, "I am certainly delighted to see you and to welcome you to the humble home of Rollins & Co."

"It is an honor, sir, which I appreciate most keenly. The name of 'Lo-Ling,' or 'Green Forest'—which you know is the humble attempt of my countrymen to pronounce your Scotch family name in the symbols of their Oriental tongue—is a household word up and down this entire street.

"No foreign hong stands higher in the native estimation. The large golden tablets of appreciation which your grateful customers have hung on your walls show this in far more flowery words than mine, though, perhaps"— and here he bowed and smiled— "you do not always read them."

"No, I regret to say, Mr. Wang, that though a resident of many years in the Island, I have never taken the time to learn to read the language. But my compradore has translated some of them for me and they certainly are flattering, especially the one where it says: 'He prepares his golden pill of immortality.'"

"Yes, that is about as high a compliment as one could pay to a manufacturer and dealer in medicines. It would especially appeal to the Taoists, to those who seek the fountain of youth, as you call it, and who claim to have the secret of the elixir of life.

"It must be a remarkably rejuvenating tonic, sir, that called forth such a testimonial. I should like to see this tablet myself and"—he nodded, looking carefully around the room to be sure that he was not overheard—"I must buy a bottle of the medicine."

"For yourself, sir? Allow me to send you a box of half a dozen with my compliments."

"Not so much for my own personal use as for my personal satisfaction. I have long had an especial interest, in tonics and life-givers of every kind and I love to"—here he looked directly at his host—"I love to analyze them, sir."

The dinner was soon announced and the house-boys took an especial pride in the native guest's perfect familiarity with the European menu and the ease and refined dignity with which he handled the "Iron chop-sticks of the outside kingdoms," as they felicitously termed the knife and fork.

Over and over again the host tried to introduce the subject of the evening, but every time that he did so, Wang Foo dexterously turned it aside and with upraised finger significantly said: "By and by, Sir, by and by." When the cigars had been lighted and the opportune moment seemed to have at last arrived, the host dismissed the attendants with: "Boys, you all can go kitchen-side now, my wantchee talkee Mr. Wang." As the last blue gown and cue disappeared behind the pantry screen, the detective smiled and, rising from the table, remarked: "Sir William, in England you say, 'The very walls have ears,' but in China, not only the walls, but the floor and ceiling and the very furniture seem to vie with each other in the fascinating occupation of eavesdropping. Let us seek some quiet spot—it is a pleasant evening: what do you say to a stroll in the public gardens or to a ride on the inclined railway to the Peak?"

"Whichever one you think most secluded."

"Well, let it be the Peak, then."

The words were scarcely uttered when down with a crash came the Japanese screen by the pantry door and out into the room sprawled the number two houseboy, with the fragments of a glass bowl in either hand. Could he have overheard?

"Didn't I tell you boys to keep out of here?" exclaimed their master, angrily.

"My velly solly, master, but my forgottee finger bowl. Please you 'sclusee me."

"Never mind the finger bowls—just pick yourself and that glassware up and get out, chop-chop, do you hear? And you tell number one boy that'll come out of his wages. Yes"—turning to Wang Foo—"It's just as you say, Mr. Wang, you never can really get rid of them;

they're all around you day and night. There's absolutely no privacy for a white man in this country at all."

A few minutes later found them seated in one of the little tramcars and being drawn up on the cable-road several thousand feet into the air. They alighted at the Peak station and walked out on the terrace of the great frowning rock that, Gibraltar-like, overlooks the Island and the Estuary of Fragrant Waters—England's Eastern stronghold of Hong Kong.

What a view spread out before them! What a fascinating panorama of twinkling lights! Far away to the east, the broad red beams of Ly-Ee-Moon Lighthouse; directly opposite, Kow-Loon and its forest of shipping; to the west White Gull Island the Pass to Canton, and directly below them the great city and colony of Victoria with its teeming population of Orient, and, out in the middle of the harbor, the French flagship radiant with its hundreds of colored lanterns in honor of the "Day of the Bastille."

They selected a quiet seat near the parapet and Wang Foo began: "Sir William, I know full well why you have sent for me and, ere we proceed to business and details, I want to tell you how much I and my Chinese fellow citizens of the better class appreciate your earnest efforts to rid my country of this cursed drug that is sapping its vitality.

"In the Book of the Great Learning the Master says: 'They who governed the people well learned first to control themselves.' How true this is! Without self-control how can we hope for genuine progress in any race? You and I are working together for the moral uplift of my people—we must look upon opium as our deadly foe."

"It is, alas, England's National disgrace that she forced it on you. Every Christian man in the Empire realizes that now and feels the humiliation of it."

"That is past history now, sir, and much as we regret it, we have to face the problem of the present. China is growing much of her own opium now and will grow much more if the Indian market is cut off. I take more than a usual interest in tracing out this case, because of the high moral issue that is involved."

So they talked and talked, far into the night. The merchant told all he knew and Wang, gently but pointedly plied him with questions, the answers to many of which went into the little leather notebook. The outcome of it all was simply this: a steady stream of the forbidden drug was flowing into the Chinese quarter and Rollins & Co were supposed to be the means of it. Yet the most careful scrutiny on the part of the firm and the closest watching on the part of the police and authorities failed to discover any clew to the guilty parties.

They rose and started back, for the last tram-car for the night was ascending the incline. Suddenly, without a sound of warning, a smooth, round stone fell directly out of the sky and struck Sir William on the shoulder. He started with a cry—more of surprise than actual pain.

"Some miscreant is attacking us. Who and what can it be at this hour of the night?" he said.

Wang stopped and his keen eyes searched the entire terrace. "There is no one here, sir. It probably is some playful lad who has tossed it up from below the parapet. I hope you are not hurt—"

"No, not at all. Just frightened for a moment, that is all."

The detective stooped to pick the missile up and, as he did so, noticed to his surprise that it had wrapped around it a bit of yellow paper. It had writing on it! Before his host could see what he was doing, he slipped the paper into the sieve of his silken jacket and tossed the stone unconcernedly away.

Safely down on Queen's Road once more, they bade each other good night and a friendly jinrikisha rattled away to the Alley of Fragrant Waters, where Wang alighted at the "Gateway of the Triple Five" and climbed the steep little stairway to his upper chamber. The Venerable Grand One had already retired, but old Chang poured the smoking tea and lighted the pipe of welcome.

"The master is returning very late tonight."

"Yes, but it has all been for the interest of 'Wu-Jen,' the 'Five Virtues,' Chang."

"Ah, then, the Master's time has been well spent."

Wang closed and barred the upper doors and lighting his little lamp, sat quietly down at his table and carefully unrolled the yellow paper from his sleeve. It contained just four lines of poetry—no heading, no name. It ran as follows:

> "He who thinks and thinks aright
> will read these lines between.
> Poppies bloom in the open light,
> Ivory in the forest green."

Who had thrown the stone with this mysterious warning and what was its inner meaning? He thought and thought, and came to this conclusion: someone at the hong had overheard the word "Peak" and had followed Sir William and himself to the summit by the little pathway that climbs up by the side of the tram.

He had tied the message to the stone and thrown it over the parapet. The words of the poem were intended to be a friendly clew to the object of his search, without divulging the slightest hint as to their author. Someone was trying—this was clear—to help him, but who and why? He fell asleep with the question only partly answered.

The following afternoon a venerable figure, clad in the old and faded blue gown of a scholar and leaning on a bamboo staff, was wending his way along the river street. He came to the old Canton wharf and, attempting to hobble across the thoroughfare, was nearly knocked down by an English pony-trap that rushed by in the most reckless way, while the occupant shouted: "Get out of the way there, you miserable old coolie." He reached the sidewalk and a Chinese police officer, with that respect for old age which puts the Westerner to shame, at once came to his assistance.

"Venerable Father," he said, "It is dangerous for you to be crossing the foreign street alone; let me offer to assist you."

"A thousand thanks, my son; I am all right now, only a little shaken with the excitement. Is there some friendly place near here where I can sit and rest a moment?"

"Most certainly; see, right across the way is the foreign medicine shop of the Green Forest. I will take you over to their Chinese tea-room, where you will be most welcome."

Suiting the action to the word, the policeman escorted the old teacher to the native room of Rollins & Co, where he was instantly made at home and a bowl of tea and a pipe were placed at his disposal.

As he rested and refreshed himself, he glanced around the room and his eyes surveyed the scrolls and tablets hanging on the walls. They described, in many and poetic ways, the virtues of the medicines for sale within.

One in particular seemed to interest him more than all the others. It hung right over the central archway and on it were inscribed the words; "He prepares the golden pill of immortality."

"That wondrous medicine," he asked of the native clerk, "the pill of immortality, do you sell it here? And what would it do for one as old and as feeble as myself?"

"It is the greatest tonic of the age, Venerable Elder-born," he answered; "it will restore your spirits and make you feel quite young again."

"The price—for the smallest box?"

"Two silver coins of the smallest size." But, seeing the books the old teacher carried with him, he at once added; "For the students of the great Master's words, one coin will be quite enough."

The old man slowly unwound his girdle, and, producing the money, took the box of pills and, rising from his seat, bade them all "good day."

"May you heap up the mountains of riches," he said as he passed out.

"May a little of your light ever beam upon us! May the lucky stars guide you on your way!" they all replied.

Two days after the above occurrence Wang Foo had his second interview with the head of Rollins & Co, and among other questions he asked was this:

"Sir William, has your firm any branch establishment whatever in the Colony?"

"None whatever."

"No other drug or medicine shop, then, has the permission or the right to use the sign of 'Lo Ling' or 'Green Forest'?"

"No, sir, a thousand times no—that sign is registered at Government House and you know how the Chinese regard the stealing of a business sign."

"Yes, it is a most serious offence and in the native courts severely punished. They sometimes take away a man's business for all the rest of his life. You are quite positive you have no 'other store'?"

"Absolutely positive, sir."

"The police know of none, then?"

"How could they? They have the strictest orders to arrest anyone, foreign or native, using the sign of 'Lo Ling.'"

"Sir William, I am going to say something that will surprise you—but I say it on the pledge of your strictest secrecy until this case is all complete—I was in your 'other store' last night!"

Was Wang Foo telling the truth? Was he really in the branch store of Rollins & Co the night before? Was there such a place? That Wang Foo, the famous exposer of crime, had really made such a visit no mortal knew except himself—but that the old scholar who trudged slowly homeward from the hong had taken a roundabout way through "Ivory Alley;" that he had carefully scrutinized the sign of every ivory-carver in that narrow passage; that he had finally found one where, under the bright golden characters, it said, in a fainter color invisible to the careless passer by, "Branch of the Green Forest for the special distribution of the Golden Pills"; that he had entered the shop and departed with a tiny packet of pills in his sleeve—and that on his return to his home that evening he had carefully compared the contents with that of his afternoon purchase and smiled a smile of intense satisfaction at the result—all this was most certainly true! And so, as he took out of his secret drawer the yellow paper with its poetic message, he said to himself: "I think I will just change this into prose."

And this is how it read: "Poppies bloom in the open light," became, "Opium is being openly sold in the Colony"; and "Ivory in the Forest Green" became "Rollins & Co are dealers in ivory." What possible connection could there be between these two articles? What had the tusk of an elephant to do with the juice of the poppy? This, you see, was just the missing link that needed to be found, and the sound of the mysterious symbols of the language supplied it, for the words for "elephant" and "tusk" when pronounced with a slightly different accent became the words for "fragrant" and for "opium" and the chain of evidence was complete!

The good ship *Mandalay* of the British India Steam Navigation Company was plowing her way patiently homeward against the northeast monsoon and was due in Hong Kong very early the following morning. After the captain's dinner in the evening the passengers enjoyed a farewell concert in the saloon, gave their customary contribution to the Sailors' Orphans' Fund, and then went below to their cabins to finish their packing—all except the little group of "genial souls" who adjourned to the smoking room for a final rubber.

Chief Engineer McIntosh and Mr. Alexander Hartwell of Boston took comfortable seats in the corner to enjoy just one more game of chess and the latter pressed the button and called the boy: "Please bring the chessboard," he said.

"Velly solly," was the Celestial's answer, "ship chess-board go makee bleak, s'pose you wantchee, my can bollow Compladore. He gottee velly nice piece, all ivoly."

"All right, bring it along."

The boy reappeared in a few moments with a large and handsome board of inlaid ivory and a box containing an exquisitely carved set of chess-men of the same material. The Chief and the passenger played until eight bells announced the midnight hour and then rang for the boy to return the compradore's board.

"Compladore go sleepee just now," was the announcement; "he talkee you can puttee that board your tlunk side, he boy come hotel catchee to-mollow, can do."

Mr. Hartwell was quite agreeable to the suggestion. Packing the chess-men carefully away he took them to the hotel in the morning and, sure enough, the smoking-room boy called for them at noon.

Now all this would have been quite natural and beyond a possibility of ulterior motive if the Chief, who was tiffining with Mr. Hartwell, hadn't happened to remark: "That's 20 trips I've made with that boy and every blessed time he lends that ivory board to some passenger and comes to the hotel to get it the next day—I suppose they give him a handsome sumshaw (or tip) for the use of it."

Nobody in particular noticed the Chinese gentleman, who had followed the engineer ashore and who now sat at the next table to him and noted everything he said—why should anybody? He was apparently just an ordinary visitor, and there didn't seem to be anything out of the way in his strolling along Queen's Road—even if the smoking-room boy was just a few paces ahead of him—or in his turning up into Ivory Alley, or, in fact, of his pausing for a moment in front of a certain Ivory-shop and noting very carefully the sign, after the boy had entered and closed the shop door behind him. Why should not any Chinese gentleman have done this?

The *Hong Kong Daily News* of the following Sunday had an interesting article headed, "Important Arrest of Opium Smugglers." Among other things it said:

"Our local police, cooperating with Chinese detectives, unearthed a new nest of opium smugglers and dealers yesterday in Ivory Alley. It seems that the compradore of the steamship 'Mandalay' has been in the habit of lending a handsome ivory chessboard to some foreign passenger and then getting the passenger to bring it ashore in his own baggage in order to avoid suspicion and searching. The entire board was filled in between with the choicest Patna opium and every one of the chess-men was hollowed out and fitted with a cylinder of tin containing the drug. Ah Wang, the ivory carver, was a confederate of the steamer-boy and shared the profits with him. The rascals had stolen the good name of Rollins & Co and had secret signs on their shop indicating to the habitués that the drug could be had within. We

are very glad that our esteemed citizen, Sir William
Rollins, and his firm have been cleared of any complicity in the matter, and we trust the native papers
will make this perfectly clear."

"At the same time, Sir William," remarked Wang Foo, as he
accepted the merchant's proffered gift of a box of Havanas, "I think
it would be just as well to take down that tablet now, don't you?"

"Which tablet?"

"Why, the one where you say you 'prepare the golden pill of
immortality,' because, you see, 'golden pill of immortality' is a well-
known synonym for the choicest brand of opium."

"What! Do you mean to tell me that I have actually been advertising the drug for sale in my own store, and right under my very
nose, Sir, every day of my life?"

"Not necessarily so, sir, because, you see, there was always the
ambiguity in the term, and good people gave you the benefit of the
doubt."

"And was it so in that ivory shop also?"

"Ah, no; there it was quite different, and this illustrates one of
the niceties of our written language. You see, some of the Chinese
characters are written from right to left and some from left to right.
The initiated scholar can instantly recognize the character or line
that has been reversed.

"The ivory-carver had the word for pills so written that the users of the drug knew at once what it meant, while the ordinary
passer-by, and"—he smiled as he spoke—"and the police supposed
it was the innocent tonic of immortality. Besides this, you see, the
play on words and sounds between 'tusks' and 'opium' rendered
the game doubly fascinating to the native mind, that always takes
a special delight in that sort of resemblance, of which the European knows nothing."

"Well, well," said Sir William, "after all, Mr. Wang, human nature is very much the same all the world over. Those of us who
know the 'open sesame' get into the game, and those who don't,
stay out. Isn't it so?"

"That, I believe, is one of the things the Master meant when he said: 'The West has its wise men as well as we,'" replied the man of mystery.

THE BAMBOO IDOL

"WELL, MOREHEAD," said Inspector Gubbins of the Shanghai Police to his chief assistant, "that batch is settled, anyhow. We won't have any more barber rows on the Harris wharf for a little while now.

"The Mixed Court magistrate gave them 60 blows apiece and two weeks' wooden cangue on the spot where the fight took place. You know, it isn't such a bad idea, this punishing a man on the place where he commits the crime; it gives them all a good chance to see justice administered."

"That's so, chief," answered the assistant, "I've sometimes thought it wouldn't be so far out of the way to have a little of it in the old country. That's what they used to do in the old days of the stocks and whipping-post, you know, and, after all, the wooden cangue is only another form of stocks. But doesn't it remind you of the Arabian Nights, this silly nonsense about barbers?

"Just think of a fight in London and a lot of barber chaps nearly killing each other just because they didn't go to the same church! They're worse than Mahometans, they really are."

"Is that what started it? I didn't hear the first of the evidence."

"Why, yes; you see two old barbers of the barbers' guild have had the monopoly of shaving the coolies on the Harris Wharf for years, and yesterday along came a couple of new chaps who don't belong to the guild and don't worship the same barbers' idol and set up their shop, and up starts the fight with those Chinese razors. They're sharp, too; the second mate of the *Shoo Pow*, who rushed in to separate them, came near being badly cut."

S uddenly a wild demon shriek was heard and ※ ※ ※ ※ a missile was hurled through the air directly at the goddess ※ ※ ※

"Just another case of 'Him no chin-chin same joss,' as Detective Chang says when I ask him what starts the ordinary street wheelbarrow fight, oh?"

"They certainly are mighty clannish, Sir."

The foregoing conversation between the Inspector and his assistant in the inner police office was hardly over when a knock was heard at the door and the native officer on duty brought in the chit-book from the British Consulate and handed a message marked "urgent" to his chief.

"Well, here we are again; I wonder what's up now? Perhaps the barbers are at it once more."

"Perhaps it's a lot of their friends come down to the wharf to get even with the other fellows. They often do that, you know."

The Inspector tore open the envelope, saying as he did so to the officer:

"You tellee coolie waitchee answer."

The message read as follows:

> To Inspector Arthur Gubbins, Shanghai Police:
> Sir—In the absence up-river of Sir Thomas Bradley, K. C. M. G., the Consul General.
>   I beg to request your presence, without delay, at the Consulate, to consult about a disturbance of a very serious nature that took place in the Settlement last evening. I am, Sir,
>   Very truly yours,
>   William Walpole,
>   H. B. M. Vice Consul, in Charge.

Handing a reply to the waiting messenger, the Inspector turned to Mr. Morehead and asked, as ho passed the paper over to him. "What's this? Any report from headquarters or from the branch station about a row last night?"

"Not a word, Sir; the docket is all clear."

"Well, perhaps there's some reason for the native officer's keeping it secret. I'll go right over and see what it's about."

He put on his long uniform coat, took his official cap from the hook, and, hurrying out to his waiting jinrikisha, ordered the coolie to take him to the Consulate. He was ushered at once into the private office and after the usual greetings was asked to take a seat at the Consul's desk, the doors having been closed and the curtains closely drawn.

"Gubbins," began His Majesty's representative, "I'm in a quandary and I've sent for you to help me out. I've been a good many years in the service and I flatter myself that I know these people pretty well, but every now and then something new turns up and I find myself as puzzled as an ordinary globetrotter on his first arrival. You have had a good deal of experience in dealing with them, too, but I imagine that sometimes you get into a fix as well as myself and then you have to—"

"Have to send for some old missionary who speaks the local lingo to worm it out of them," said the Inspector, helping to finish the sentence.

"Yes, after all, we study and study, but the people who live among them day and night are the only ones who ever really 'get under their padded vests,' as my chief says."

"That's so, and yet, do you know, old Dr. Johnson of the Mission Hospital told me only last week that sometimes he's just as badly off as we are, and he's been out here 40 years and speaks the lingo like a native."

"He's right, he's right—well, here's the case: This morning, when I came down to breakfast I notice my No. 1 boy had his head all plastered up. I asked him what was the matter and all I could get was, 'My makee fallee down stairs last night.' Now that would have gone all right if the No. 2 boy hadn't come in a few minutes later with a bandage around his eye, and when I asked him if he had fallen down stairs, too, he stammered and said, 'My comee in velly late, no can see that gate, have hittee eyeside.'

"I began to be a little suspicious when I saw two of them crippled up, but I could have passed their Chinese yarns even then, if I hadn't met Anderson and Broadmoor at the club this noon and heard them say that there must have been a fine old house-boy

fight last night, for both their boys had black eyes and other to-
kens of a scrimmage, on last night out on the Bubbling Well road,
for both his boys are laid up and, for all I know, perhaps a dozen
others, and yet none of us can find out a blessed thing about it.
There evidently was a big row somewhere, but where or how, or
why nobody knows."

"That's very strange, sir, for no report has come in to us, I'll go
right back and have every officer on night duty examined. But first
would you mind my calling in the boy and asking him a question
or two?"

"Certainly not; I'll ring for him."

The No. 1 boy came promptly. "Where was that fight last night?"
asked the Inspector, very pointedly.

"My no savee," was the only reply.

"Call no. 2 boy," said the consul.

"Where was that fight last night, and who gave you that eye?"

"My no savee," was the only satisfaction he received, though
the question was repeated several times.

After other ineffectual attempts to get any information out of
the stoical servants, the Inspector rose and said: "You see, sir, how
absolutely impossible it is to get anything out of them; you might
just as well address your questions to a stone wall. I'll go back to
the office and get the native detectives on this thing at once."

Every Chinese and every Seik policeman on night duty in the
settlement appeared before the chief during the next 24 hours and
was closely questioned as to the scrimmage in which, up to the
latest report from outside, over 30 servants in foreign employ had
been badly injured. The only answer was that not a sign of any
disturbance had come to their notice!

The Inspector was nonplused and sent for Morehead.

"Call Detective Chang and have him go into this thing thoroughly," said the Inspector. "Tell him to use all his native tricks
and ferret this thing out. There's been a big fight here, right under
our very nose—for these chaps couldn't get far away—and the whole
department is responsible for it. Now don't leave a stone unturned."

The wily and skillful Chang and his assistants had the case committed to their charge, but after a week's careful investigation, they were obliged to report, in the brief but significant phrase of the house-boys, "My no savee." The mystery simply deepened day by day.

"Do you mean to tell me that your entire force isn't able to locate this affair?" asked the consul of the Inspector, after the latter had reported to him their somewhat ignominious failure.

"We've done the best we could, sir, but their lips are sealed like the tombs of Egypt. They'd die before they'll let out a word. You see, if it had been in the native city, we might get at something by torture, but that's agin the law in the British settlement. Time is the only thing, Sir; if we wait long enough, some one of them will be sure to leak it out, but—" here he paused for a moment—"it may be months, perhaps years."

"Well, Gubbins, we may as well confess it, we're pretty helpless, aren't we?"

"I am sorry to say it looks that way, Mr. Walpole."

"Have you thought of getting that clever chap up from Hong Kong? He might get at it as an outsider, you know."

"You mean Wang Foo, the Mysterious?"

"Yes, I think that's his name. The one who recovered Lady Evington's jewels in the famous robbery case. Why not send for him—on the quiet, of course—and let him got to work at it, without any suspicion?"

"There's no harm in trying, sir."

And this is why, a week later, Wang Foo bade adieu to the Venerable Grand One at his humble home in the Red Cloud Alley, and directed his faithful coolie to carry his pigskin trunk aboard the English mailboat, lying at anchor in the harbor of Hong Kong, the Fragrant Waters.

Not far from the side gate to the European Cemetery, on the outer edge of the foreign settlement at Shanghai, is a pathway that winds through a grove of clustered bamboos and brings one to the Temple of the Foo Chow Guild. It is a favorite resort of the Fukinese residents of the port, but a white man rarely visits it, for the path is rough and winds by the side of a slimy creek whose waters give forth most offensive odors.

Passing through a series of brick white-washed archways, one comes at last to the shrine, which seems old and dilapidated and has nothing of architectural beauty to attract a visitor. On either side of the courtyard are rooms containing the coffins of those who have died in Shanghai and who are awaiting eventual transportation back to the "Foo" or "Happy" Province, where their bones will rest in peace by the side of those of their ancestors. Two old priests and a handful of lazy coolies comprise the living outfit. Twice a year, however, the place is a scene of lively ceremonies; in August on the Feast of the Returning Souls and in March, on the birthday of the Queen of Hades, when the venerable idol of bamboo which stands in the center is exhibited to the admiring and adoring crowds.

It is a curious old relic, this idol, scarce a foot and a half high and delicately carved out of the most popular wood of the country. No one knows how old it is, nor who was the man who made it— the tradition indeed being that it floated down one day from the clouds on the back of the hairy turtle of the ancient tales. It is, however, the protecting and guardian divinity of all those who come from the Happy Province. To it they are bound to pay their devotions and they violate its wishes at their peril. One of its hands holds a slender wand and the other is raised as if in the act of blessing.

One August night, on the eve of the Feast of Returning Souls, a motley crowd were assembled at the shrine. The air was filled with the odor of burning incense, gongs to call back the waiting souls from earth to Hades were being beaten and offerings of rice and tea and wine and imitation money were being presented to the Queen. Suddenly a wild demon shriek was heard and as a voice in the crowd called out. "Back to Hades with your people, miserable deceiver of humanity!" a missile was hurled through the air directly at the goddess and, striking the uplifted hand, broke off two of the bamboo fingers which fell at the feet of the awe-struck devotees.

Pandemonium reigned in an instant. Yells and execrations filled the air, and every man seized his neighbor in an attempt to apprehend the desecrator. In the midst of the confusion a tall, wild figure, his face flushed with native wine and his eyes starting from their sockets, broke through the crowd and, screaming, "Away with your worthless bamboo idol!" he dashed toward the gateway and was lost in the darkness before any one could stop him.

"A Ning Po man, a traitor from another Province," they cried. "Seize him! Kill him!" It was all too late, he was gone.

After various attempts to rescue order and quiet, the form of an old white-bearded man arose and, standing on the upper steps, motioned them to silence. The inherent Chinese respect for age secured him a hearing.

"Listen to the old one! Listen to our father!" they cried.

"My children from the Happy Province," he said. "We will avenge this insult to our goddess." And raising his long and bony arm toward Heaven he cried: "The curse of the Bamboo Queen and the Hairy Turtle be upon the villains from Ning Po."

Shouts of approval greeted this announcement and there and then the pledge was sealed.

AFTER A QUIET NIGHT at the home of his old friends, the Hong Kong basket-maker and his family, Wang Foo, attired in the modest gown of the Chinese scholar, presented his card at the office of the Inspector of police and was at once admitted to the inner sanctum.

"I am very glad to have the pleasure of meeting you, Mr. Wang. My esteemed predecessor. Inspector Sharpley, has told me of you and of your wondrous ways."

"The pleasure is mine, sir, and it is always a privilege to serve you and the department in the interests of law and justice. You have done me the honor of sending for me and now my time and my talents—such as they are—are entirely at your disposal. As Yuen Yuan the great disciple of Confucius said, 'To make no boast of talent, nor show of merit were my wish.'"

"There certainly are great things in those ancient books of yours, sir, I often wish that I could read them."

"I would that all Europeans were more familiar with the masters words," replied the visitor; "It would help them better to understand my people."

"Well, sir, now to the case before us. The morning is yours, let us go into it thoroughly. If you have no objection, Chief Detective Morehead will share the conference with us. He is a splendid fellow and knows all the circumstances as well as I do. May I offer you a mild cheroot, sir?"—opening a fresh box of Manlius—"Capt Wemyss of the flagship just brought them up from the Philippines. They ought to be good ones, for the old sailor is quite a judge."

Wang Foo with the politest of bows accepted the proffered cigar and the Inspector began his tale, while his guest listened most attentively and took the usual copious notes.

"We are face to face, sir, with a most mysterious and, at the same time, a most annoying occurrence, which if left unsolved, will reflect most seriously upon myself and all the members of the force. The circumstances are briefly these: On a certain morning some 25 or 30 house-boys and servants in European employ are discovered to be suffering from cuts and bruises, more or less serious, which were evidently the result of a midnight scrimmage somewhere in the settlement.

"We have made the most thorough investigation, but up to the present time we cannot find a trace of the place where it occurred or of any of the circumstances. Everything is reported, officially, as having been perfectly quiet that night throughout the entire district, yet every one of these boys bears the marks of a most serious row."

After answering several detailed questions of Wang Foo, he continued: "The strangest thing about it all is that these are not coolies or rowdies at all, but the quietest and most law-abiding class of native servants, and not one of them has ever been up before the police for a disturbance. Now, what in the name of goodness, could be the motive for such an attack upon them—for attack it evidently was—and, furthermore, why are they so everlastingly mum about it?

"They have done all in their power to conceal the effects of it and every mother's son of them has declared it was an accident or his own fault—of course a perfect pack of lies from beginning to end."

The Chinese detective thought long and carefully and, after referring again to the little leather-covered note-book which he had drawn from his sleeve, propounded to the foreign officers these three inquires:

"You are quite positive that all the boys who were injured belonged to the house and not to the office staff?"

"Yes, sir, I believe every one of them was a domestic servant. But what possible difference could that make?"

Wang Foo's only answer, as he lighted another cheroot out of the box, was a quiet but significant smile.

"There were no coolies or horseboys injured in any way?"

"No, sir; as far as we know, every one seems to have been either a number one or a number two table-boy."

"Just one thing more, Mr. Gubbins; did you notice at all carefully the nature or form or shape of the wounds or bruises? Have you any theory as to the kind of instrument or weapon they were inflicted with? Anything foreign or native? And were they apparently all inflicted with the same club or knife—or whatever it was?"

Assistant Morehead answered for his chief:

"Yes, there was one queer thing about it, I noticed it when we had them up here for examination and I made them unroll the bandages. Many of the scars looked like a three-pointed star."

"What kind of star, sir, did you say? A three-pointed star?"

"Yes, a sort of three-pointed star with one point longer than the other two. Don't you remember my saying, chief, that they all must have seen stars—that was my little joke, don't you know?"

Wang Foo arose and prepared to leave.

"Gentlemen, this requires careful study and, above all, secrecy. I will call upon you again in exactly 10 days and let you know the results. In the meantime, you will consider, if you please, that I am still—as far as the public is concerned—living quietly in Hong Kong. Good morning!"

"Ten days," said the Inspector, after the visitor had departed. "Ten days. Morehead, make a careful note of the date, and don't let anything interfere with your being here all day, mind that."

"I'll be right on deck, sir; you can rely on me for that. And in the meantime, I suppose"—placing his forefinger on his lips—"mum's the word, sir?"

"Mum's the word," replied the chief, as he rang the office bell for his jinrikisha.

In the quiet and retirement of the upper room in the basket-maker's house, the man of mystery was at work nightly upon the problem. A week had already passed by since his interview with the officers and slowly, one by one, he was forging the links in the chain of evidence.

Two things were already perfectly clear: first, it was an inter-provincial row and, second, it must have been in some way associated with the provincial honor, or they would not have leagued themselves together to keep it secret. Fear of some kind had sealed their lips.

Fear of what? Evidently of the anger of some local god. As regards the former, every victim was in the house-boy class, and a careful list of the homes where they were employed showed that, without exception, they were Ning Po men. This was clinched by the fact that the office staff and the horse-boys were from Canton and the coolies natives of Shanghai, and not one of them had been touched. It was an attack upon the Ning Po clan alone.

As regards the second point, something must have occurred to cause a rival clan to make the assault; but how, or when, or why? This was the puzzle. Wang Foo recalled the words in the great classic: "The princely man stands by his kinsmen," and he knew that it must have been a carefully planned and a concerted action. They were all in it—and they were in it together.

But the star, the wounds in the shape of the star that Morehead had described, the star with one point longer than the others, what of that? He lighted his little cloisonné pipe and leaned back in his wicker chair, repeating these words over to himself:

"A star with three points; one point longer than the others—longer than the others." His eyes rested upon the ceiling, where hung the tablet with the household motto:

"The Perfect Rest of the Bamboo Heavens."

Why did he start up so suddenly? Why did he jump to his feet with a sudden inspiration? Why? Because, right above him shone the golden outline of the three-pointed star of his search, the ancient Chinese symbol for bamboo. Yes! There it was, with one point oblique, one horizontal, and one vertical, longer than the others! The mystery so far was solved; every one of these victims had been struck with a weapon cut in the shape of the character for bamboo! Truly had the Venerable Grand One blessed him on his departure with, "A happy star guide thee on thy way!"

The following afternoon a native traveler, with beard and cue of gray, haled a wheelbarrow coolie plying for hire on the road of the Bubbling Well and asked him:

"Knowest thou the way to the Temple of the Bamboo Idol?"

"Aye, Father, I know it well. Take thy seat upon my barrow and for 30 coins of brass I take thee safely there."

"Fellow, I give thee 20."

"'Tis well, my daily rice-bowl is not yet filled; take thy seat upon the barrow and begrudge me not the wine-money at the close."

The traveler descended at the gateway of the Temple and for a few coppers induced the unsuspecting priest to unlock the shrine. He bowed reverently before the idol and, noticing the missing fingers, asked how it came about.

The old priest hesitated, but finally, as a tribute to his age and simple manner, told him the story of the riot and the curse of the Queen of Hades and the Hairy Turtle pronounced upon the villain from Ning Po. They sat down together and drank their tea and smoked the pipe of hospitality. The guest finally inquired, as he rose to leave: "And did they find the Ning Po man and wreak the curse upon him?"

"No, they never found the man, but some of the guild of Foo Chow men, I hear in private, redeemed the honor of the Bamboo Goddess, and gave the Ning Po guild the sign of the sacred tree, by beating them with the temple staffs."

Inspector Gubbins looked at his watch.

"Morehead," he said to the waiting Assistant, "it's past 10 now and Wang Foo was due this morning." Scarcely had he uttered the

words when the office coolie brought in the card of the expected
visitor. He was most cordially greeted, welcomed to a seat, and
after the door was carefully locked, the interview began.

"Well, Mr. Wang, we hope you have brought us cheering news."

"I bring you news, Sir, most certainly, but whether it is exactly
cheering or not will remain for you to say."

The Chinese detective then proceeded to unfold his tale. It was
simply the old story, somewhat complicated, of an inter-provincial fight, in which superstition and religious fear had played a
prominent part. The man from Ning Po who had hurled the stone
at the bamboo idol was in a state of intoxication, and had been
taken by his barrow to the Foo Chow Temple instead of to his own.

Not realizing at all what he did, or what the consequences would
be, he had, in his drunken rage, assaulted the idol of the rival clan.
He had escaped and had probably, on returning to his sense, fled
to parts unknown. Some members of Foo Chow guild, having
pledged themselves to avenge the insult to their protectress—and
fearing if they did not do so, that she would wreak her vengeance
upon them and their families—had hired three low fellows of the
yamen-runner order to disguise themselves as Ning Po visitors and
obtain admittance to the meeting of the Ning Po guild, which the
house-boys were innocently attending. They armed themselves
with the temple-clubs, carved with the symbol for bamboo, and
suddenly turning down the lights, struck at every member of the
guild within their reach, shrieking as they did so: "The curse of
the Bamboo Idol and the Hairy Turtle." And then they escaped into
the darkness.

"But why didn't they seize them there and then? Do you mean
to tell me that 25 or 30 men would allow themselves to be thus
held up by three?"

"Not ordinarily, of course, but you see in this case, the suddenness of it and the religious fear completely paralyzed them."

"Well, why didn't they report it to their masters and to the
police? Why all this air of mystery about it and this lying out of
it? Were they ashamed of it?"

"Partly so; but, you see, this was a matter of the guild and one of the first principles of a Chinese guild is 'Keep out of the clutches of the law,' and no one wants to be the one to involve the others in trouble.

"The moment they heard the words, 'Curse of the Hairy Turtle,' which always strikes terror to the native heart, they knew that some Ning Po man had desecrated an idol somewhere, and the words, 'Curse of the Queen of Hades,' identified it at once with the Temple of the Foo Chow guild. So they at once agreed to keep it absolutely secret."

"But how will it be settled up between them?"

"O, that will be all adjusted in a few days by a mutual feast at some tea-house, and, justice having been done, and 'face' saved, as they say, they will smoke the pipe of peace and drink the wine of harmony, and all will go on merrily again. 'To restore mutual harmony,' in the words of the Master, is the great virtue of human life."

"Just one question more, Mr. Wang, that puzzles me; how did those chaps in the Temple know that the assailant of the goddess was a Ning Po man? Was it his clothes?"

"O, no, not necessarily; they knew it at once from his accent—you see the dialect is quite different there from here or from Foo Chow."

"What are we in the department to do about it, then?"

"There is absolutely nothing that you can do about it, gentlemen, and, in the words of your own Western wisdom, I advise you to let well enough alone. The guilds and clans prefer to settle their own affairs under their own roofs—"

"Or," interrupted Morehead, "as we say at home, don't interfere in a family squabble."

"Yes, that's it," replied the man of mystery.

THE PEACOCK SCREEN

"YOU MAY REST ASSURED, Mr. Consul, that this department will do everything in its power to unravel the mystery and to discover the thief. This is the third time that the store has been broken into, for, you see, they carry a very attractive line of goods, but in the other cases we traced the men and caught them before they left the colony."

The foregoing remarks were addressed by Inspector Wallace of the Hong Kong police force, to the Hon. Mr. Masuda, consul for Japan, as the latter was about to leave the Inspector's private office. He had been to interview him on the subject of a burglary, a few nights before, in the establishment of one of his countrymen.

This was the well-known firm of Takimoto & Co, dealers in curios and Japanese works of art, whose show windows were almost opposite the main entrance to the Honk Kong Hotel, and whose store was a rendezvous for tourists and treasure hunters of every kind.

"Thank you," replied the official from Tokio, "I'm sure you will. You know that Mr. Takimoto is one of our most respected residents in the colony, and he and his friends feel this loss very keenly. What especially worries him is that there was not only the theft of a very valuable work of art, but it was accompanied with wanton destruction of property, as if someone was trying to do him a personal injury."

"If there is anything of that kind in it, we will be sure to find it out, sir, but I am quite sure it could not have been an agent of any

Mr Takimoto rushed forward screaming in his native tongue... the two clerks were paralyzed with fear it was gone - evidently slashed out with a knife

of the other curio dealers in Queen's Road, for they are our finest Chinese citizens. It would only be some cheap shop-keeper down on the water front that would descend to that."

"These international jealousies are pretty strong, sometimes, Mr. Inspector."

"Yes, I know they are, but I am sure the standing of your firm is too high for that, sir. Messrs Takimoto & Co are very popular with their Chinese neighbors and subscribe liberally to all their charities. It must be just a case of simple villainy—the thief may have injured himself in the dark, or he may have been frightened away or something else may have occurred to anger him and he just took his spite out on the first thing he came across; I've often had them do it."

"I hope it is nothing more. Good morning, sir."

"Good morning, Mr. Consul, and tell Mr. Takimoto that we are just as much interested in this as he is and that I have put my very best men to work on the case. We are sure to hear something in a day or two."

The Japanese visitor stepped into his waiting jinrikisha and was whirled away in the direction of his consulate.

"Brownlow," said the chief to his assistant, as they resumed their seats in the office, "our friend from Tokio seems quite worked up about this case."

"Yes, sir; they feel very sensitive about anything happening to one of their countrymen, especially in a port like this. But, as I said to Mr. Takimoto's head clerk, 'there's nothing personal in this at all—it's just plain out-and-out robbery, that's all, and it might have happened to any English firm just the same as to yours.'"

"Have you put the native officers to work on the pawnshops?"

"Yes, sir; we're having a thorough cleanup of the whole lot."

"Then have all the European hotels warned to look out for curio dealers and peddlers trying to sell to tourists, and have an officer at the gangway of every steamer to catch them if they try to get on board. It's almost sure to go to one of those two places, you know."

"As you say, sir," replied the faithful Brownlow.

MRS. WALTER WEATHERSTONE, wife of the head of the firm of Weatherstone & Co, Australian merchants, was very proud of her drawing-room and of her wonderful collection of art and curios which adorned it.

She had been gathering them here and there for a number of years and now she felt quite sure that there was really nothing finer in the colony—or even in Shanghai. Indeed, this was the tribute which admiring friends and visitors paid, who were her guests at teas and receptions at which she presided with the grace of a veritable Oriental queen. Needless to say, she was one of Messrs Takimoto & Co's best customers and they had a standing order to notify her when any new and very attractive article was to be offered for sale.

Just at this time they had put on exhibition a superb piece of Japanese embroidery, and Mrs. Weatherstone had already cast envious eyes upon it as a centerpiece for the drawing room. It was a screen, set in a richly carved frame of lacquer and measuring some five feet in height and four in width. The figure was a peacock with outspread tall and the handiwork was by Nishimura's finest artists. Four men had worked continuously upon it for over three years and so delicate and so perfect was the needlework that the creature seemed to stand right out from the screen and every individual feather to be quivering with motion.

Nothing approaching it in beauty had ever been seen in Hong Kong—but the price! Ah, that was what made even the richest resident and the most lavish tourist pause, for the figures in Mexican dollars ran up into the thousands!

"My dear Mrs. Atherton," said our hostess to her old friend who had just arrived on the mail steamer from Sydney, "you must come down with me to Takimoto's tomorrow and see that perfectly exquisite peacock screen. I am just hesitating about it for my drawing room and I should love to have you tell me what you think of it. Now do come—and bring both the daughters with you. I have an appointment with them to show it to us at noon. You see, I am making it early, because the American mail arrives in the afternoon and I should feel dreadful to have some rich traveler from the States take it away from me."

As the town clock was striking the noon hour on the following day, the four ladies were ushered into the reception room of Messrs Takimoto & Co, where the head of the firm was waiting to receive them. The screen was placed on a raised platform between two windows, where the best light for viewing it could be obtained, and when the ladies were duly seated, the manager motioned to his two Japanese assistants to uncover it.

It had been carefully concealed beneath a heavy curtain of yellow silk, which served not only to exclude the dust, but also to protect the delicate handiwork from the strong rays of the sun. The clerks stepped forward and standing, one on the right side and one on the left, proceeded to lift the curtain with all the solemn impressiveness of a pair of Cathedral vergers unveiling a masterpiece of Raphael's. They had hardly raised it a foot when the ladies simultaneously, cried out: "Why! Something has happened to it!" and almost in the same breath: "It is gone—it is gone!" Mr. Takimoto rushed forward screaming in his native tongue: "Osoroshii koto! Osoroshii koto!" (A terrible thing, a terrible thing!) The two clerks were simply paralyzed with astonishment and fear.

Yes, It was most certainly gone—not unscrewed from the frame or carefully removed, but evidently slashed out with a thin sharp knife as a European thief often cuts a valuable canvas from the wall. It had been done during the night and evidently done hastily and with poor light, as evidenced by the ragged edges of the silk and the scratches made by the knife on the lacquered frame.

Yet the thief had stopped long enough—wishing to postpone the hour of detection—to replace the curtain of yellow silk and even to tie together again the knotted cords and tassels that held it in place.

"Who could have done such an awful thing, Mr. Takimoto?" inquired the ladies, as soon as their composure was recovered enough for them to speak.

"Some robber, I suppose, who hopes to sell it to a tourist," he answered, "No native would steal it for himself."

"And is there no chance of recovering it?"

"Well, we have an excellent police service here, and I am sure they will do all they can to find it before it is smuggled out of the colony."

"You must be sure and let us know if they got it, won't you? We admired it so much that we almost feel the loss is ours as well as yours."

"Ladies, I thank you! I thank you a thousand times!" replied, the manager, bowing his customers to the door with all the grace of a Samurai of Old Japan.

The case was at once reported to the authorities and Capt. Brownlow had responded in person and gone into the matter most thoroughly, before the interview at the beginning of our chapter between the Japanese consul and the chief inspector.

More than a week passed by, but no trace of the missing peacock. The police at all the ports from Singapore to Tientsin had been wired to and the Japanese themselves had notified their own officers, but it had vanished completely from sight. The firm of Takimoto & Co had received no end of personal visits and letters from sympathetic friends in the colony, all of whom seemed to feel it as a direct reflection upon them that such a valuable work of art should have been stolen from their midst.

Among the callers, none were more outspoken in their regrets, than the Chinese merchants of Queen's road, many of whom were prominent in the same line of business. One of these, Mr. Loong Foy, of the establishment of Wan Cheng & Co ("Myriad Perfections"), importers and exporters of curios, finally took it upon himself to present his plea to the Police Department in person. He waited upon the Inspector the following day.

"Mr. Wal-la-cee, we all too muchee shame-face this side," he began, "cause tieffee man come my store steallie five tousand dollar, how fashion?"

"Well, Mr. Loong," replied the chief as he ordered the office boy at once to bring the tea and pipe for his visitor, "while this is a serious loss for Mr. Takimoto, it must be exceedingly gratifying to him and his friends to know how high he stands in the community and how much you feel for him."

"How you tinkee, Mr. Wal-la-cee, can catchee tat tieffee man? My friend, Chinee Mandalin, talkee my no can savee 'cause b'longee fashion stealee, no all same Chinese fashion."

"It is hard to say who took it. It may have been a foreign sailor— they sometimes steal curios and valuable native stuff and carry it on board the mail steamers to sell to the passengers when they get out to sea—but I think it is much more likely to have been a native thief in league with some of those hotel runners."

"S'pose one week more you no can catchee he, I tinkee velly good talkee Mr. Wang Foo come this side look see."

"He certainly is a very able man in ferreting out crime among the natives and has helped us several times."

"S'pose he come more chop-chop, more bettor. S'pose waitchee long time, tief can walkee Canton side—no can catchee."

"If the native detectives don't get any clue within a couple of days more, I shall be glad to have the assistance of Mr. Wang in the case, sir."

"My chin-chin you talkee he—he all same China joss, can see night-side, can savee what side tieffee man go, verry good."

With this complimentary comparison of the Chinese detective to a native divinity, Mr. Loong bowed his way out from the Inspector's office and returned to the house of "Myriad Perfections" in time for the afternoon rice. Four days later Wang Foo, Capt. Brownlow and Mr. Takimoto met by appointment in the latter's private reception room, from which the precious piece of Japanese embroidery had been so ruthlessly stolen.

A fair little maid in silken kimono and brocade sash stepped softly into the room and placing upon the center table of cherry wood the little tray with its teapot and tiny bowls, the sauces with the crisp sembei or rice cakes and the box of barley sugar paste, disappeared as silently as she had entered. After the guests had refreshed themselves and accepted the delicate cigarettes which the host produced from his cloisonné case, the investigation be-gan. Mr. Takimoto described the discovery of the theft and all the attendant circumstances. The assistant inspector told all that he knew and what had come to him from the native officers and added a few suspicions of his own. Mr. Wang listened very attentively, stopping them now and then to make a few notes in a little book which he drew from his sleeve.

"I should like, first of all," he began, "to be shown over this apartment where the robbery took place."

"With pleasure," replied his host, and, rising from their seats, they followed him about the room while every door and window and screen was carefully examined.

"Has there been any change whatever in the furniture of the room since that night?" he asked.

"None at all—everything stands now exactly where it did then."

He took his stand in the center of the room and carefully surveyed its contents.

"Every door and window has European locks and hinges, has it not? There are no Japanese screens or sliding panels?"

"Yes, sir, everything is absolutely secure, and the room is locked and bolted every night. No one but myself holds the keys."

"That lacquer cabinet is almost large enough for a man to conceal himself behind it, is it not?"

"Well, a small sized person might possibly squeeze in between it and the wall."

"Who cleans and dusts the room?"

"Old Deaf Lee the coolie is the only servant allowed to enter here, and I go over it after him every time."

"Is this old servant really deaf?"

"Quite deaf, sir: that's the reason they gave him the name."

"Please send for him."

The coolie was promptly summoned and put through a rigid examination in his native tongue while the two guests stood and tried to gather what they could from his gestures, for the language was entirely beyond them.

"That is all, gentlemen, and now I must ask the privilege of a few days' leisure to give this matter the thought and attention that it deserves."

This closed the interview and, bidding them goodbye, Wang Foo sauntered out into the highway and walked leisurely in the direction of the avenue of Fragrant Waters. Reaching his home, he said to the venerable grand one: "I want a quiet afternoon and evening—bid any guests return upon the morrow."

"It is done as the master says," replied the aged attendant, as she carefully bolted the outer gate and went to prepare the tea. He ascended the steep steps into the upper room, and when the boiling tea and fragrant pipe appeared, he removed his silken jacket and sat down to ponder over what he had seen and heard. He recalled the words of the Confucius:

"Wade the deep places,

Lift thy robe through the shallows,"

and suiting his actions to the sentiment, gathered up the folds of his flowing garments and laid him down to meditate.

Far out in the blue waters of the harbor, the China merchants steamer *Hai Loong*, or *Sea Dragon*, was lying at her anchorage surrounded by a swarm of boats and sampans. Her flag was at half-mast, for she carried under a canopy on her deck the great wooden coffin of the Victory of the Double Liangs, whose funeral cortege was proceeding to his Ancestral home in Pak Hoi.

A huge passenger junk was just approaching her sides and noise and confusion reigned supreme as the soldiers on board attempted to force a passage for her to the steamer. When she finally was made fast, a long line of servants and retainers clambered on the gangway, clearing the way for two high officers of state who had come to pay their respect to the great departed one. They were Chang the Fan-Tai (or Treasury General) and Woo the Tao-Tai (or Intendent of the Circuit). They were of equal noble rank, so, in addition to the embroidered ceremonial robes and disks, each wore the three-eyed peacock feather in his hat, one with the knob of blue crystal and the other with the knob of red coral.

More than two hours were taken up with the elaborate ritual prescribed in the Book of Rites and Ceremonies and they were escorted back to their junk with profound bows and expressions of gratitude on the part of the Viceregal mourners. Once safely back in their little cabin, they both breathed long sighs of relief and proceed to exchange the uncomfortable uniforms for the easy garments of every day life.

"Well, we got safely through it," exclaimed Chang.

"The luckiest escape of our lives!" answered Woo.

Just why it was called a lucky escape will appear from the following incident, and thereby hangs a tale.

Two nights before, while they were bringing some baggage aboard the junk, a careless boatman had slipped and dropped a circular oilskin case into the water and in spite of frantic efforts to save it, it sank before his eyes. It contained the official hats and decorations—the most important part of their regalia.

When it became known, the officials were furious. They ordered the soldiers to seize the boatman and beat him then and there. He fell upon his knees and shrieked for mercy, but all his cries were useless. This left them in the most serious predicament, for it was impossible to obtain official decorations short of Canton, many miles away, and to fail to appear at the proper hour at the viceregal ceremony would be a most serious and damaging reflection upon them—even endangering their official rank, should it reach the ears of the court censors at Peking.

The boatman's family, almost paralyzed with fear, started to scull the sampan back to the wharf, but not before the deputies had taken the number of their English license "42" and screamed at them: "Bring back that parcel before tomorrow, or your father dies the death!"

They tied the sampan to the wharf and hurried to their home; Wen Sang, the eldest son, addressed the weeping mother:

"Give me every dollar you have concealed beneath the floor."

She hurriedly took a knife and, prying up a brick beneath the couch, took out a roll of yellow paper and handed it over to him. He counted it—"Twenty-seven dollars! It is not enough; give me that silver anklet" (pointing to the heavy band of precious metal which the Chinese boatwomen wear instead of putting their savings in the bank). She worked it off her ankle with difficulty and pain and handed to him all her worldly wealth.

"Where are you going now?" she asked.

"To consult Old Lang the fortuneteller at the Temple of the Queen of Heaven."

"Go! And may the lucky stars guide thee on thy way!"

Old Lang sat at his little table in the temple court when Wan Seng arrived. It had been a busy day with him and more than 20 customers had learned from him the decrees of fate and received advice on matters of personal importance. They waited till a quiet moment and then the boatman's son told the story of the accident, of the seizure of his father and of the frantic efforts they were making to save his life.

The seer turned over the pages of a musty volume that lay before him, made some mystic symbols on a tablet and, raising up an urn containing slips of carved bamboo, shook them solemnly in the air as he bowed thrice toward the shrine of the Queen. One slip fell out and lay upon the table. He picked it up and deciphered the characters upon it. "Imperial effort," he said. He repeated the words over slowly. "Imperial effort"—and, playing upon the similarity of sounds, added, "Substitute work."

He turned to his anxious customer and wrote upon a slip of yellow paper, "The fates decree that every effort must be made to find a substitute." He accepted the proffered fee and said, "Go to Tak Foy, the hatmaker of the Dragon alley, and toll him to have the two hats ready by the morrow."

The little shop of Tak Foy carried only a very limited stock, so after a thorough search along his dusty shelves and in the various boxes and trunks which stood about, he could only find two official hats of the rank in question, and these he agreed to sell to his customer for five and twenty Mexicans.

"But the feathers, the peacock feathers with three eyes," exclaimed the lad, "these are the most important thing of all; where can I get them?"

"Nothing but the decree of heaven could bring them in this island," was the saddening answer. "The Bird of Confucius wears them only for those of noble rank. But buy the hats and try the fortune teller's words, 'to find a substitute.'"

Scarcely knowing what he did, he laid the price upon the counter and departed with the carefully wrapped bundle in his arms. He passed down the Dragon alley and walked rapidly along Queen's Road till he came to the narrow passageway that separated the house of Takimoto & Co from the adjoining establishment.

He paused and hesitated for a moment, then said to himself: "I will go and see my Uncle Lee, who lives a few doors above, and beg him to advise me."

He found the door, opened it and climbed the rickety stairs to the humble abode of him who was known as "Deaf Lee, the coolie."

What they said and did, and what the uncle planned to save his brother's life had better be told by Wang Foo himself, the unraveler of the mystery.

"A VERY CLEVER CAPTURE, Mr. Wang," said Inspector Wallace to the Hong Kong man of mystery, when a few days later, they met by appointment at the scene of the now famous robbery. "But," he added with pardonable pride, "I think it only just to the Department to say that we have suspected Deaf Lee from the very beginning.

"He was questioned and questioned and his room has been thoroughly searched, but not a word of confession could we get out of him, nor could a trace of the missing embroidery be found. The detectives have shadowed him every moment since, but he has not gone to any place where he could dispose of it. And, then, Mr. Takimoto had such confidence in him and trusted the old deaf creature so implicitly that it rather threw us off the trail. Would you mind telling us what led you to fix it so quickly upon him?"

"Well, after a careful study of the apartment, I felt very sure that it had not been broken into from without and so my conclusion was, very naturally, that it had been stolen from within. The next question was the time. Mr. Takimoto saw the screen covered himself late in the afternoon, and when it was opened at noon the next day, it was gone; the theft must clearly have taken place during the night or early in the morning. Now," he said, very slowly, as he sipped his cup of Japanese tea, "we come to the important question of the man.

"No one was in that room between these hours—for the proprietor had it securely locked—except Deaf Lee, and he was only there for some 15 minutes or so, dusting it out at the close of the day. He must have watched his master closely and, taking advantage of a temporary absence, have slashed out the peacock with a very sharp knife, tucked it away under his gown and rapidly replaced the covering and tied the heavy cords—in fact, gentlemen, that is exactly what he did—he confessed every word of it to me yesterday."

"Under torture, Mr. Wang?"

"Oh, no, not under torture, but under the pressure of a Chinese fear that very few Europeans would understand."

"And pray what was that? It must be something entirely new to us."

The detective rose and walking over to the frame from which the ragged edges of the silk were still hanging, he turned it completely around and calling their attention to a fragment of white paper which the knife had cut in half, he pointed his tapering index finger at it and said:

"Gentlemen, this paper, which was merely a small label pasted on the back of the screen, contains the Chinese symbols for 'Peacock.' They are 'Con Chok,' the 'Bird of Confucius.' That first symbol is the family name of the great Sage, sacred beyond words to every son of the Celestial Empire. To tear that word, to step on it, to desecrate it in any way, is an insult to the gods of literature—but to plunge a knife through it, as the thief in his hurry did, is to bring down upon him and all his family the vengeance of high Heaven.

"When I charged him with it yesterday he fell fainting on the stone floor of his cell! But to continue my story, gentlemen, when I made my first examination of the frame from which the embroidery had been cut, I discovered that the thief in his hurry had cut into the head and neck of the bird, thus ruining the symmetry of the figure and making it practically impossible for him to dispose of it without very careful repairs, and"—here he turned to Mr. Takimoto—"our friend the manager will testify that the skilled workmen who could do that are only in Japan, and the number of them is very limited.

"This led me to conclude at once that it was not the figure of the entire bird that he wanted, but only the outspreading tail with its beautiful feathers. Some one, somewhere, was willing to pay a very high price for peacock feathers—who could it be? The Chinese answer suggested itself at once: It must be some high-ranked official. On investigating further I found that the only ones who had been in or near the colony at that time were the two dignitaries who attended the Viceroy's funeral."

"And how did you connect them with the robbery?"

"Oh, a little Chinese interrogation of the head of the boatmen's guild brought that all to the light. I found that the soldiers on the official junk had seized the boatman for his carelessness in dropping the hats and feathers overboard and had threatened him with death, unless his family provided others to take their place. None could be procured here in Hong Kong in time for the ceremonies, so Deaf Lee was induced to save the day and also his brother's life by cutting the embroidered ones out of the frame."

"His brother's life?"

"Yes, you see he was the boatman's own brother—our Chinese families are very much interlaced."

"But how did you find that out?"

"Ah, gentlemen, you must really excuse me—it would be difficult to explain that to a European audience."

"But surely silk feathers would not be stiff enough to decorate a hat?"

"Oh, a little rice-glue fixed that, and then, a long goose-feather inserted in the middle gave them the necessary rigidity and made them look quite natural."

"Deaf Lee, then, will be tried at the next Criminal Court?"

"No, gentlemen," interrupted Capt Brownlow, who had entered the room unobserved, "he will not be tried by any court, for he swallowed opium in his cell two hours ago!"

"Tien Ming! The Decree of Heaven!" cried Wang Foo, as he rose and pointed to the ceiling. "The Decree of Heaven—let not mortal man presume to question it."

THE CLOISONNÉ VASE

MIDNIGHT HAD JUST STRUCK from the great clock on the tower of the Shanghai Customhouse, when flames were discovered bursting out from the huts of the opposite side of the river. They were so dangerously near the foreign signal station that the U.S.S. *Shenandoah*—fortunately close at hand at the customs buoy—sent a boat crew ashore to assist in putting them out.

They were just in time, for the railing around the signal staff was already on fire and the signal man was climbing down his ladder with his few worldly belongings in his arms. The sailors quickly organized a bucket brigade and succeeded in extinguishing the conflagration before any further damage was done to the customs property, but not before a half a dozen native huts had been destroyed.

Lieut. Gleason, in charge of the party, did what he could to quiet down the excited villagers, who were rushing hither and thither, shouting and screaming at the top of their voices, but it was not until a police boat appeared on the scene that anything like order was restored. The native sergeants, armed with clubs and long bamboo staffs, drove the crowd back from the signal station and threatened them in their own dialect with every kind of punishment if they did not instantly retire.

The women seemed more difficult to manage than the men. They wore frantically dragging their children about by the arms, and while trying to save their few household goods were screaming out the names of those who were lost in the smoke.

94

In the midst of the confusion an old man suddenly arose - no one seemed to see or know where he came from-holding a glass aloft, cried out: * * " the water of heaven quenches the fire of the earth!"

In the midst of the confusion an old man suddenly arose—no one seemed to see or know where he came from—and holding an old glass bottle aloft, cried out, as he poured the contents of it on the last burning shack, "Tien ping ching sui! Tien sui hsie di hwo!" (The crystal stream from the Heavenly vase! the water of Heaven quenches the fires of earth!)

His words were like magic in their effect. The villagers quieted down and even the native soldiers and policemen regarded him with awe and allowed him to empty the bottle in peace. To be sure, there wasn't very much "fire of earth" left for his "water from Heaven" to quench, but what there was did its duty most effectively, as far as the native mind was concerned, and that was the all-important thing for the moment. It was far more satisfactory to them than the yellow water of the Wang Poo—or even the puffing efforts of the English fire-engines from the Settlement, which had once crossed the river—and, as their flowery language expressed it, "The charm of the Heavenly liquid had dampened the ardor of the fire-god," and all was well.

A few evenings later, Lieut. Gleason and some of his brother officers from the *Shenandoah* were dining at the American Consulate, when the conversation turned upon the incident of the burning village, and he related the appearance of the old man and the magic bottle.

"I've heard a great deal about their curious native ideas and superstitions," he said to Mrs. Cortelyou, the consul's wife, "but this is the very first time I have seen them practically illustrated. I don't know who the old chap was—though my cabin boy tells me he was the head of the village, or something of that kind—but he certainly had them in his power, all right. Why, they had more faith in that quart of holy water than in all our ship's fire buckets."

"They must have the same charm over them that the medicine men have over our Indians in South Dakota," replied Mrs. Cortelyou. "My husband was attached to one of the Army posts there as surgeon, years ago, and he says many of my houseboys' stories remind him exactly of his experience among the red men."

"I wonder if you would mind calling the boy in for a moment; I am curious to ask him a question or two. The truth is, this thing grows more interesting and mysterious every day, and I am anxious to find out more about it."

"Why, most certainly," as she laid her hand upon the table bell.

"Boy, you can savvee that Hwang Poo fire last week?"

"My can savvee."

"Who b'longee that one piecee old man pour bottle water that fire side?"

"B'longee villages number one head man, catchee long whitee beard."

"All same joss man?"

"No all samee—he have buy dat water joss house side, velly good putchee out fire."

"You can savvee what side that joss house makee sell?"

"My no can savvee. S'pose you talkee cook, he can savvee; my b'longee Ning Poo man, no can savvee Shanghai joss."

"They evidently do not worship the same divinity in these two places," interrupted the consul, "and their local jealousies are such that no one of them will give any information about the other."

"I suppose it would mean a row in my kitchen during the dish-washing," said his wife, "if the Ning Poo house-boy cast any reflections upon—or revealed any of the secrets of—the temples of the Shanghai idols."

"Perhaps so; religious rivalries have certainly caused us a good deal of trouble in the world before this. Why, when we were on the Indian station we used to hear of them almost every day at the Bombay Club. Don't you remember what they told us there, Watkins?"—turning to his brother officer.

"The British Government certainly has a merry time keeping them from jumping at each others' throats," replied the genial Watkins.

"Well, I suppose we shall have to drop the subject there, for it would never do for the Navy to sow the seeds of disorder in the consular staff, but I am on the track now of that joss house and I won't be happy till I get it."

When the party broke up and Lieut. Gleason was being sculled back in a sampan to the ship, he had definitely made up his mind to solve three problems, viz: (1) Where was the mysterious temple that sold the firewater? (2) What was the heavenly vase from which flowed the crystal stream? (3) How could he get his hands on some of the precious liquid? He only hoped that the *Shenandoah* would stay at the buoy long enough for him to solve them. His little cabin already contained a number of very rare and interesting curios collected on the cruise.

Buddhas and idols innumerable were there, but they had all been bought on hearsay evidence as to their merits—here was something that he had actually seen the working of—the more he thought of it the more he longed for a glimpse of the "heavenly vase of the crystal stream" and the more positively he made up his mind that he must have it, even if it took the last Mexican dollar on his pay check.

In the meantime, the burned-out villagers were preparing to rebuild in their very humble way, but before anything whatever could be touched, they had to give the usual theatrical exhibition in honor of Kwa Sheng, the fire god. It was his anger that had been aroused and in consequence of this he had thrown his burning torch in their midst and now it was necessary to put him in good humor again by inviting him to a play.

After no end of haggling over the cost of it in brass cash, a company of strolling actors had been engaged and a rough stage and scenery of matting had been erected on the site of the fire and a comfortable seat provided for the dreaded divinity.

Gongs were beaten, firecrackers were exploded and the special tea and rice-cakes for his "Majesty of the flames" were duly provided. The ceremonies lasted three days and were as heartily enjoyed by the visible crowds as by the invisible personage who they all implicitly believed occupied the principal seat.

The poor homeless wretches who had not been permitted to seek shelter—(for to take in a fire-victim is to incur the anger of Kwa Sheng and to interfere with his discipline)—crawled into the remaining cabins and soon the work of reconstruction was under way in the village of Lo Ka Doo.

"It's a mighty strange thing, Morehead," remarked Inspector Gubbins of the Shanghai police to his chief assistant, "that it's always that village on the south of the signal-station that gets on fire, and never the one on the north of it. Now that's the third time within a year, and there must surely be some reason for it.

"You can make up your mind that someone's got a grudge against them and just starts the blaze—it's far too regular to be accidental. Let's put two of our best natives on the case and see if we can't get at the bottom of it—if we don't, the next thing you know that village on the south will catch fire and that's right next to the tea go-down with thousands of chests of the new crop stored in it."

In accordance with his chief's instructions, Morehead summoned the two cleverest local detectives in his office and instructed them to go across the river and stay until they found out exactly what the cause of the fire was.

After a week's wandering around from village to village and indirect inquiries addressed to boatmen and coolies at the little tea-stands, where they appeared in the guise of poor students seeking recreation, they returned with a very interesting story. This was the gist of it: the two villages of Hai Ka Doo and Lo Ka Doo, situated on either side of the foreign signal station, had been for many years rivals in ferrying farmers and other country folks across the river in their sampans.

The recent wreck of a junk, however, had turned a current of the stream so that the little wharf of the south side was no longer available and the line of passengers on foot now all passed to the north. This started the trouble and it wasn't very long before one night an attacking party, led on by four old grandmas, each over 60 years of age (which secures immunity from Chinese law) proceeded with baskets of decayed vegetables from the southern village to the northern and began to hurl them right and left at the heads of their rivals, shrieking as they did so, "Tao liao wo tik fan wan! Tao liao wo tik fan wan!" (You have overturned our rice-bowl! You have overturned our rice-bowl).

The northern village waited a week or more before deciding upon the best and most effective way of returning this celestial compliment and finally took the advice of a famous fortune teller on the Shanghai side. He bade them proceed at night to the twin graves of the southern village's fathers and "stop up the spirit holes."

This would prevent their spirits from getting out of the graves at night and going wandering about, and they would wreak their vengeance on their own people by sending the children smallpox or contracting with the god of thunder to hurl his bolts at them.

When the residents of Hai Ka Doo found out that this awful insult had been actually offered to the spirits of their dead, their anger knew no bounds, and, proceeding to the Temple of the God of Fire, they purchased several bundles of joss-sticks, which they soaked in kerosene oil and then from time to time hurled them into the thatched roofs of the northern village—hence the three-fold conflagrations of which the Inspector spoke.

"Well," said the English officer to his two Chinese assistants, after they had finished their explanation, "what can be done to stop a repetition of it? How long are they going to keep on setting each others' houses on fire? That's the point that interests me."

"S'pose you seclure 20 piecee joss-man, pay he twentee dollar, givee number one Chinese feastee, pay twentee dollar more—allee gedder forty dollar, Chinaman talkee Pei Lee, hab savee face, all ploper, no more fightee, can do."

"So you mean to tell me that the small sum of 40 Mexicans, expended on a native feast and on hiring a lot of those dirty, ragged priests to burn joss-sticks will make the proper apology and adjustment and prevent any more fires on that side of the river?"

"Me thinkee can do."

"By Jove! It would be worth the customs' while to pay it just to protect their property," replied Mr. Morehead, as he closed the interview.

THE LITTLE TEMPLE OF THE SACRED WHITE STAG was situated south of the extreme end of the English settlement and just outside the international boundary line. This made it very convenient for its devotees to visit it and sip their native wine in its courts and settle their little native disputes without any interference from the foreign police, whose views on the drinking and gambling and fighting question were known to be somewhat severe.

It consisted of the usual three courts with the surrounding sheds and in front of the inner shrine was the figure of the white stag bearing aloft on its interlocked horns a handsome vase of old Pekin cloisonné. Over him were large tablets with these words upon them: "His flesh is food! His horns are medicine! His tears are pearls!"

It was commonly reported that business was not as thriving at the temple as it used to be, and that the income of the priests was steadily falling off. To be sure, two years ago there had been a sudden miracle and the Sacred Stag had been discovered shedding his tears of pearls and these had been retailed at a high price to the worshipers as panaceas for all bodily ills, but this had lasted only a few short weeks and now it was becoming necessary again to appeal to the miraculous to replenish the temple coffers.

This state of things accounted for the secret meeting of the five old priests one evening, with "Old Nine Spot" the Abbot presiding. A shrewd business-like figure he was, bending over the tea-stand and smoking his little pipe, his shining bald head revealing most clearly the three rows of the nine burnings of the moxa at the time of his taking his vows.

"Brethren of the Order," he said, "the time has come for serious action. The cash boxes are lower than they ever were before— a miracle alone can save us. What shall it be?"

"Well," replied Brother Two, "it must be something new and striking. Our people are not as easily attracted now as they were before the foreigners came. Let us take time and do it well."

"Our Sacred White Stag has wept his pearls and shed his horns and cast his teeth," said Brother Three, "let him now do something different from them all. I have thought over it long and carefully and I have outlined the great miracle in my mind—will you hear it?"

"Our listening ears bend toward thee in the pledge of secrecy," they all answered as in one voice.

"The precious relic of the Dukes of Loo which Our Sacred Stag bears aloft upon his horns is supposed to contain the very dew of Heaven, is it not? As the Book of Poetry says, 'Heaven's crystal waters glisten on his branches.' Well, let the vase of cloisonné overflow in a perpetual stream and as the waters fall into the bronze basin at his feet, let us catch them in little bottles of glass and sell them for the cure of all diseases. Believe me, this will be the grandest investment we have ever made."

"It sounds most attractive," Bald Old Nine Spot, "but how will your plan be carried out? How will you keep the vase always full and overflowing so that the people do not suspect the truth?"

"It can be done in a new and very wonderful way, but—" and here he hesitated—"we—we shall need help from someone that is without."

"From without?" they all cried in unison.

"Yes, without that it is quite impossible."

"But can he be pledged to eternal secrecy?"

"He divulges one word on the penalty of his life!"

"Shall we accept the plan of Brother Three?" inquired the Abbot. All rose, and, slowly and reverently bowing, gave the mystic signal of assent by raising the right hand and moving it through the air in three interlocking circles. The meeting over, they dispersed to the several duties of the night

Brother Three was very busy for the next few weeks, coming and going from the temple at all hours of the day and night. Old Bon Lee, the egg-peddler, who lived in the mat shed opposite the temple gate, thought he saw him always choose the nights that were particularly dark and stormy for his trips to town—and sometimes he thought he saw him bring a mysterious looking stranger with him—but he knew the priests well enough to realize that they were not like ordinary beings, and as his position at the gate depended upon their favor, he did not question their doings or talk of them to strangers—except just once to a stranger who kindly bought all his eggs for the day and asked him many questions about the coming and going of the priests and who came there to visit them.

He had seemed like a visitor from another province, for he spoke the local tongue with difficulty, and his dress was different from the dress of those who daily passed by the temple gates. But old Bon Lee's memory was getting feeble now, and he forgot all about the stranger in a few passing days.

JUST ACROSS THE LINE from the Temple of the Sacred White Stag, and inside the border of the English settlement, was the modest little home of Johnson the Eurasian. He was an interesting member of that large class in every Eastern port which occupies the middle position between the two races represented in their parentage, but who, at the same time, seem to be socially ostracized by both.

He had been formerly attached to the staff of one of the Shanghai newspapers, where his knowledge of both peoples and of both tongues made him valuable, but he had been driven off by the jealousy of some of the Chinese employees, and since then he had been glad to earn a few odd dollars by almost anything that offered itself.

On the particular evening in question he was entertaining two native visitors in his little parlor, where all the doors and windows were securely sealed and the air was filled with the odor of smoking tea and incense. One was Mr. Hop Tuk, the magistrate of the Chinese District immediately opposite, and the other was none other than our friend, Brother Three.

They were engaged in a most absorbing conversation and evidently were discussing a plan of deep interest to every one of them. The words "dollars," "cash," "price of a bottle," etc, could be easily detected. Finally the magistrate arose to leave.

"Gentlemen," he said, "500 taels must be positively guaranteed me as my reward for the official protection of the miracle—not a cash less will I accept. Pledge it to me now and I will be as silent as the Buddhas of stone and permit no one to trouble you. If you refuse to agree to this, my soldiers will allow the mob to wreck the temple, just as soon as they think they are being deceived, and the reputation of the great White Stag will be forever ruined."

"'Tis a very high price to demand of the poor priests," answered Brother Three; "make it 400 and we will sign the paper now."

"No! Not a cash less, though the evil angel smite me. You call yourselves 'poor priests'; why, you will be rolling in riches before the moon is full, and eating and feasting like Princes. Come! Five hundred now—or nothing. What do you say?"

The other two participants withdrew into the corner of the room, where the magistrate could not hear them, and spent some moments in a heated discussion, which finally ended in their bringing forth a roll of yellow paper and a little box of seals, which they placed upon the table.

"And how much down?" asked the priest.

"One hundred down is the very lowest," replied the officer.

Out of an old and greasy girdle came forth a roll of bank notes and 100 taels were counted over and a receipt therefor signed and sealed—the remainder to be paid on the first of each succeeding month. Hop Tuk passed out into the darkness and the Eurasian and the native continued their preparations for the miracle.

"You are quite sure about the pipes? Two weeks will complete the line?"

"That is ample time if the nights are good and dark. We must work very carefully and slowly while the foreign police are on the Settlement patrol. If they should catch us, all would be lost."

"You can trust me absolutely—every foot will be laid with my own hands, and I know just the hour the patrolman passes the corner. Beyond the line, you know, he dare not go."

"Two weeks—two weeks to lay the pipes," repeated Brother Throe to himself, as he sipped his tea. Suddenly he started, for the old servant who had quietly entered the room was bending over him with the boiling tea kettle in his hand and ready to fill the bowls.

He looked as blank and innocent as the wooden idol that stood upon the mantle, but he might have overheard, he might have overheard. No, impossible; the suspicion vanished as soon as it came and the old priest returned to his roll of bedding in the temple bunk, assuring himself that all was well.

By the 15th day of the coming moon all would be ready for "The progidy of Heaven"; the Sacred White Stag and the Cloisonné Vase would bring untold blessings to all subscribers and the temple funds would run up into the thousands! So thinking and planning he fell asleep and dreamed of the golden palace of Kwai Shen, the God of Riches.

WANG FOO THE MAN OF MYSTERY from Hong Kong was simply making a social call upon Inspector Gubbins of the Shanghai police. He was on his way home from Pekin, where he had been summoned by some Chinese officials of high rank to assist them in unraveling a Government plot and had not, at least this time, been sent for to assist the officers of the English Settlement.

It occurred to the Inspector, however, that before he left for the South he might be able to help the department in a very practical way by giving them—from a purely Chinese standpoint—the "true inwardness" of some of the progidies and miracles with the aid of which the various temples wore relieving the populace of their hard-earned cash.

"Mr. Wang," he began, "If your steamer passage is not already engaged, we should like very much to have you explain to us something that is taking the attention and the money of hundreds of the natives and is attracting the curiosity of the foreigners who have heard of it through their house boys and coolies."

"Fortunately, sir, I am in no great hurry and I shall be glad of the few extra days of rest in the settlement. Let me know how I can have the pleasure of serving you."

"Well, sir, it is a supposed miracle that has taken place in the Temple of the Sacred White Stag, as they call it, and it's just outside the Concession line so that I can't control it or send my men there to investigate."

"What is the nature of the miracle?"

"I haven't seen it myself, but Morehead looked in there the other day and it seems there is a white stone stag there holding up a cloisonné vase on his horns and there is a perpetual stream of water flowing from it into a bronze basin, where the priests are bottling it up and selling it to the natives for all kinds of superstitious purposes.

"The mystery, of course, is where the water comes from. There doesn't appear to be any connection whatever between the vase and the rest of the outfit, and yet it keeps flowing and overflowing all the time."

"This is very interesting," replied the Chinese detective. "Of course, I have heard and seen many so-called miracles in the temples and shrines of the country—and, incidentally, have been obliged, for the protection of my people, to expose not a few of them—but this one is quite new to me. May I ask your secretary to kindly write down the exact location of the Stag Temple? I shall take pleasure in looking it up."

The same evening, Wang Foo, disguised as an unsophisticated countryman, alighted from a wheelbarrow at the south end of the Settlement and followed the line of foot passengers proceeding to the miraculous water, He found everything as the Inspector had described it. There was the figure of the Sacred White Stag; there was the old vase of cloisonné perched high upon his horns, and. sure enough, there was the overflowing water dropping into the bronze basin below!

He waited patiently until the long line of devotees moved on and he was able to get close to the wonder. He reached the surrounding railing, about four feet away from the image itself, and here his further progress was barred by the ever-watchful priests who guarded their source of wealth most zealously. He bought a circular describing all the various virtues of the sacred liquid and paid a handsome price for a medium-sized bottle, guaranteed to extinguish with its magic properties any conflagration, however serious.

The closer he looked, the more marvelous it all became to him and the deeper was his desire to fathom the mystery. All that he had seen hitherto in other places seemed coarse and commonplace compared with this. Whatever it was, it was certainly very well and skillfully done.

The vase was poised on the very tips of the creature's horns, with no apparent connection with anything around it, and yet the stream of water was evidently flowing steadily through it. All thought of returning to Hong Kong was banished from his mind and he resolved to stay in Shanghai until he had unearthed the secret.

A few days after the above visit Inspector Gubbins received a very cordial invitation from Mr. Wang to join him on a trip to the Temple of the Stag, and, he added: "If you have any European friends who are interested in Eastern miracles please bring them along."

The party was duly formed and included in its number Lieut. Gleason (who, now he had discovered the original source of the magic waters, was more set than ever on purchasing the vase), the British Vice Consul and a half dozen others. They stood in a group in the inner court and anxiously awaited developments.

The critical moment finally came—Old Nine Spot had just harangued the crowd with a vivid description of the miracle and a rehearsal of the virtues of the waters, when Wang Foo arose and motioning the assembly to silence cried out: "I have a special message from the source of the heavenly waters. The Spirit of the White Stag bids them cease. It is now"—holding up his watch —"five minutes to nine by the customs time. When the great bell tolls at 8 the waters will flow no more!"

Consternation fell on all the assembly. The priests were white with rage. "Heed not the scoffer," they cried. "Who is the child of earth that dares to cross the will of Heaven? Ten thousand curses rest upon him!"

"Wait and see! Wait and see!" cried the crowd.

The moments ticked away and the great hands on the customs clock drew nearer and nearer to the fatal hour of nine—suddenly the first stroke of the heavy bell rang out, all eyes turned to the sacred vase, the stream of crystal liquid grew less, and less and when the bell had ceased its tolling, the waters of Heaven had ceased to flow. It took but an instant to transform the temple crowd from a gathering of superstitious worshipers to a perfect mob of infuriated dupes.

They broke through the rails, knocked the cloisonné vase from its perch—just in time for Wang Foo to seize it and hide it under his robe—dashed the rows of glass bottles to the ground, and picking up the first thing that they could find, beat the priests unmercifully and compelled them to flee for their lives from the temple precincts. The miracle was over and another was added to the long list of frauds with which the simple-hearted people had been deceived.

"BUT WHAT LED YOU to suspect the connection with the city water works?" asked Lieut. Gleason, as he listened to Mr. Wang's most interesting story.

"O, that was very simple," was the modest reply, "I had a bottle of the miracle water analyzed by the city chemist, and I knew from his report that it could only come from the city pipes. I naturally turned to the nearest point from which they could tap the supply and I found it in the first house in the settlement, which happened to be that of the Eurasian.

"The old servant responded to my bribe and told me of the midnight meeting and the bargain with the magistrate. It was an interesting line of evidence to follow up from there the various steps by which Johnson made the connection with the city water and buried the long and slender pipes of lead under the roadway and the temple courts, digging the trench with his own hands.

"The Sacred White Stag was already hollowed out for some previous occasion, so that did not have to be repeated, but, of course, the boring of the horns and of the vase and the fitting of them together took a number of days and some very careful work. The old servant, whom I paid handsomely to turn off the water at exactly 9, played his part so effectively that the multitude were properly impressed and the exposure was fittingly dramatic."

"So I suppose this will forever end the miracle business at the Temple of the Sacred White Stag?"

"O, no, not at all; business will simply be suspended along those lines for a year or two and then the people will forget it and a now miracle of a different nature will take place and all will go on merrily as before."

"In the meantime, what of the vase of cloisonné?"

"I pray you accept it as a little memento of the occasion and say, if you wish, that it was the gift of an humble disciple of Confucius, who believed in the teaching of the Master that it was his duty always to undeceive the people."

THE SCROLL OF WOVEN SILVER

IN THE RECEPTION ROOM of Dr. Roger Campbell, surgeon to the English Hospital at Ningpo, there hang many scrolls and tablets which have been presented to him by grateful patients whom he has relieved of sickness and disease. The most highly prized of them all is the one which hangs directly over the mantel and bears the inscription in golden characters:

> "He gives his skill and wisdom
> To save the lives of men."

It is a painting on silk, by one of the famous old artists of the early days and consists of a Chinese landscape, with a venerable white-boarded figure in the foreground and a waterfall and cloudy mountains in the back.

Just how it came to be presented to the doctor and just how his skill once saved a human life is one of the most curious and interesting of the many experiences he has had in his Eastern life.

The Hong Kong *Daily Press* of a date not so many years ago contained the following item:

REGRETTABLE INCIDENT IN THE COLONY

"We are sorry to have to record the killing of a British seaman by some of the mourners in a funeral party yesterday. All the particulars are not yet at hand, but as far as can be ascertained at

Hung Chee, the "Lunatic" as they called him, had deliberately killed McLean by filling his mouth with sand and clay thus choking him to death. The coolies had no interest in the matter beyond standing by and seeing the white man worsted

present, it seems that Hugh McLean, an able-bodied seaman of H. M. collier *Ben Lomond*, attempted to cross the funeral procession of our esteemed citizen, Mr. Tak Hoy (late compradore of the Ningpo Rice Company) and, stumbling against the carriers of one of the banners, was knocked down and beaten or choked to death before he could be rescued.

"The jinriksha coolie who was pulling him escaped and gave the alarm and all the parties concerned were apprehended by the police, who are giving the case their careful investigation.

"Such unfortunate occurrences were not unknown in the early days of the white man's residence here, but it has been many years since anything so serious has happened to disturb our usual friendly relations with our Chinese citizens. We trust that on investigation it will be found that there was some misapprehension on the part of the funeral party and that there was really no intention on their part of inflicting fatal injuries."

"WELL, BROWNLOW," said Inspector Wallace to his assistant, the following evening, as they were going over the case at headquarters, "what have we got so far? You see, it's a little different from a merchant vessel; this was a Naval collier and so the officers and sailors on the station are all stirred up about it and swear they'll have justice done and all that sort of thing."

"Yes, old Collins, the skipper, stopped me on Queens Road this morning and said it was one of the most brutal murders he had ever heard of, and, in his opinion, they ought to hang the whole 'funeral gang,' as he called them."

"What did you get out of the riksha man? I suppose, as usual, he was so scared he wouldn't say a word?"

"No, sir, he calmed down all right after we assured him they weren't going to harm him and gave us the story all straight. It was just this way: you see, they were marching along with gongs and firecrackers and all that sort of thing, and about 20 coolies were carrying the big 'long life box' with old Tak Hoy in it, when they reached the crossroad down beyond the Happy Valley.

"McLean had hired the coolie to pull him all over the Island on a kind of spree and he turned up there just as the chaps carrying the silk banner in front of the coffin got there, and, as he cried 'Get across quick, John!' the coolie tried to pass in front of the box, and of course they bumped into each other and then the trouble began.

"The riksha upset and the banner fell down and then the procession all stopped, and they piled on top of the sailor and beat him and yelled all sorts of curses at him—you know how superstitious they are about crossing a funeral—and then, not content with that, they rammed sand down his throat and choked him to death.

"Now, that's the plain truth of it, sir. I don't suppose they really intended to kill him, but when they get wild and excited like that, they're as bad as the Malays running amuck, and they don't stop to think of the consequences."

"Can you find out exactly who did the choking?"

"You see, Sir, we've questioned closely the box-bearers and they all agree—and this is the strangest part of it all, sir—that it was old Tak Hoy's own son. It seems he's a kind of half-witted chap, that's only been down here from the Ning Po country a short time."

"I suppose he felt it his duty to avenge the insult to his dead father, didn't he? That seems to be the Chinese idea."

"That's what they all think. Sir."

"Have the natives been able to get him yet?"

"They're out after him now, Sir. It seems the old women of the family will have him surely before morning."

"See that he's closely locked up when they bring him in, and don't let any of his family or friends see him on any account."

"Right you are, Sir," answered the faithful Brownlow.

The Scroll of Woven Silver which had been carried at the funeral of Tak Hoy, the Compradore, was, from a Chinese standpoint, a curio of surpassing value. It was not only an original hand painting on silk by the brush of the Immortal Liang Lu, the court painter of the Tsing Emperors, but it contained something that the native mind and taste especially admired.

The waterfall in the background, which appeared at first sight to be a part of the painting, was a piece of exquisitely delicate silver embroidery, and the same was true of the long gray beard of the patriarch in the foreground. The curious fact was that they were exactly the same shape and size, so that the waterfall could have been exchanged for the beard without making the slightest difference in the perspective of the picture!

Thus it was a literal illustration of the ancient saying: "His silver beard is as the falling of the mountain waters." It had been presented to the Compradore's family many years before and hung immediately over the central mantel, between the bronze clock and the vase, making the "ornaments three" of a perfectly fitted native reception room.

After the passing way of the aged merchant it had hung in the place of honor over his "long wooden home" (as the receptacle for his mortal remains was euphoniously called) and was admired by the many mourners and sympathizers who came to pay their visits of condolence.

It was fitting and proper that it should be carried in the funeral procession when the day fixed by the lucky soothsayer had finally arrived. Suspended from the middle of a handsome teakwood frame, and covered with little streamers of colored silk, it was proudly borne before him by four bearers clad in the regulation garb of sack-cloth while the hired mourners and weepers walked behind.

Everything passed off satisfactorily, as far as the admiring crowds on the streets were concerned—and an elaborate funeral is one of the treats of their lives—and the procession had already left the streets of the Settlement far behind, when the very unfortunate accident occurred which turned the occasion into another tragedy, and caused an evening of very unpleasant tension in the usual peaceful Island of Fragrant Waters.

Every house-boy and chair-coolie on the street was discussing it and the teahouses were buzzing with excitement, while long processions of curious ones walked out in single file to the scene of the trouble. The naval authorities, fearing resentment on the part of the Marines and sailors, very promptly suspended all shore leave. Some of the European residents were apprehensive of a race riot, but the stern British sense of law and wider prevailed and nothing whatever occurred in the nature of an outbreak.

In his little upper room in the Alley of the Red Cloud, Wang Foo, the thoughtful scholar and man of mystery, was thinking it all over and sharing with his better fellow-residents a feeling of the deepest regret that anything so unfortunate should have occurred to stir up the embers of that race antipathy which he was trying to quench.

He was not perfectly satisfied with the case as Brownlow had presented it and felt very sure that the evidence was far from satisfactory or complete. To his mind the attempted crossing of the funeral procession was, of course, only the ignorant and innocent act of a sailor, while he quite appreciated the irritation it would cause to the native bearers and mourners. That they should have attacked the white man in their anger he could understand, but the choking him to death with mud and sand was a punishment far more terrible than he had ever heard of in recent years.

There must have been some reason for it in the native mind. The more he thought of it, the more mysterious it seemed. He pondered over it till late at night, repeating to himself the words of Confucius, "To find the root, to find the root," and resolved to call on Inspector Wallace in the morning.

He was just starting out for the office when three bearers deposited a sedan chair in front of his door and the card-bearer announced to him that Mr. Tak Hoy's daughter-in-law was awaiting an interview. Old Chang, the gate-keeper, quickly threw back the bolts when he saw a visitor had arrived, and summoned the Venerable Old One to receive the lady.

He ushered her to the principal seat in the lower room, bowing most respectfully and repeating the ancient greeting: "Graciously deign to take the higher throne."

The tea and pipes were quickly brought, and after the usual formalities, the object of her visit was introduced. Amid sobs and tears she rehearsed to the famous detective the story of the funeral and of all the unfortunate consequences that followed the encounter with the sailor at the country cross-road.

"I have come to you, sir," she said, "because the foreign policeman tells me that you are very wise and skillful in explaining to them these troubles with our people. They have taken my husband away and put him in the prison, and they will kill him when the month is over. How can I save him? O, sir, how can I save him? I know he is innocent. Ho gets angry sometimes, I know, but he would never strike a man—never in his life. The others killed the foreigner—the others killed him."

"Were you an eye-witness yourself of what happened?"

"Yes, sir, I saw it all. I was in the first sedan chair behind the mourners."

Wang Foo begged the visitor to calm herself and after a little interval began to examine her as to some of the minor details, the answers to which he carefully dotted down in the little leather-covered notebook. He inquired especially about her husband and found that he was, as had been reported, only a poor half-witted creature and a sufferer from epilepsy.

She had been betrothed to him in early infancy and her sad married life had been the consequence of the rigid Chinese code which forbade the breaking of the betrothal contract. He had always been the butt of the family jokes and a general scapegoat for the sins of others. She was positive that in this case he was the innocent victim of another's crime, "Pei tik jin ta yang jin sze liao!" she cried. ("Some other man killed the foreigner.")

A ray of hope began to dawn upon Wang. If Tak Hoy's son was really an imbecile, he knew that the English law in its justice could not hold him responsible. But, more than this, he felt it possible that he was being charged with another man's crime and might be entirely innocent, as his wife believed. He resolved to ferret it out at all costs and dismissed his visitor with this assurance.

Arrived at the Inspector's office about noon, he found him in earnest discussion with Sir William Beaumont, the Crown Advocate, regarding the murder and its participants. Both gentlemen were his personal friends and, knowing his deep interest in the case, they readily admitted him to their circle.

They went over the evidence together and it certainly looked very damaging. The four bearers who carried the silver scroll had confessed—probably to relieve themselves of the charge of the direct murder—to striking the sailor, but insisted that they had done so lightly, and Dr. Bradlaw of the Mission Hospital, who examined the body, did not find any serious bruises upon it. They all agreed that "Fung Chee," the "Lunatic," as they called him, had deliberately killed McLean by filling his mouth with sand and clay and thus choking him to death. These five were the only ones implicated, as the box bearers, being wharf-coolies and not friends of the family, had no especial interest in the matter beyond standing by and seeing the white man worsted.

It had been absolutely impossible to get anything satisfactory out of Fung Chee himself, and so the law would have to take its course.

Murder had been committed, and even if the death penalty could not be inflicted, imprisonment for life would probably be the sentence. "And who will act as counsel for the defense?" asked Wang Foo, as the advocate rose to go.

"John Crowder of the firm of Illingworth & Crowder will have charge of the case for the defendant, at the Governor's request."

"It couldn't be in better hands."

"Ah, you know him, then?"

"I not only know him, but I have the highest respect for him as one of the ablest and fairest young barristers in the Colony," replied Wang. The Crown advocate looked a little disturbed at this remark of the detective, but said nothing, and bidding them a rather formal adieu hurried out to his waiting jinriksha.

Mr. John Crowder was certainly to be the lawyer for the defense, but Mr. Wang Foo was, without any question, to be his guide and adviser. They had many and long conferences together during the next few days, but the door were tightly sealed and neither the crown advocate nor the Inspector—much less the public—knew

what was being said and done. In view of the fact that it was a international murder, his excellency, Sir Arthur Wayne-Evington, had
ordered a preliminary hearing at Government House, at which the
naval and military commanders and the Chinese Consul General
were to be present, and the date set was exactly fifteen days from
the morning of Wang's last interview with the English lawyer.

Three entries in the detective's little notebook were underlined
with red as being of special importance: First, the very strange
remark of Fung Chee to Brownlow: 'Him chow chow glass! Him
chow chow glass!" which the latter at once interpreted to mean
that the criminal's real intention was to have killed his victim with
broken glass if could have gotten it—the most devilish way of destroying life; second, the comment innocently dropped by Surgeon Bradlaw at the inquest that McLean was evidently thrown into an epileptic fit by the overturning of his jinriksha; and, third, the shrieking out of the word, "Yang! Yang!" ("Ocean! Ocean!"), by the murderer as he forced the clay down his victim's throat—which the coffin
bearers at once interpreted to mean, "Throw him into the sea!"

What was the strange and mysterious connection between epilepsy, broken glass and the ocean? This was the problem that presented itself to the mind of Wang as he lay, thinking, on his bamboo couch, and, to help solve it, he sent Old Chang for the Abbot.

"Venerable Father," he said, as the old priest from the Temple
of the Queen of Heaven entered, "my humble cottage is much honored by your presence. I pray you take the seat of dignity."

"For a long time I have not had the pleasure of your gracious
smile: may all the blessings of the Buddhas Three be yours! I am
here to serve you—let me know how an humble disciple can assist
the learned pupil of the Sages."

After the usual ceremonial greetings were over, they proceeded
to the quiet precincts of the upper chamber and the interview began. They talked long and earnestly and, as even in China two heads
are better than one, new light began to dawn upon the problem.

They cleared up the mystery of the cry of "Ocean," that that
was merely a synonym for "Foreigner" or "Ocean man" and the
Abbot remembered that in Ningpo it was the word for "Sheep" with

a slightly different tone. "Him chow chow glass" was (with the exchange of the letter "l" for "r") an attempt to say, "The sheep eats grass." So far, so good—the connection between the sheep and grass was clear, but the mystery of the choking with the sand or clay was still unsolved, so, acting on the Venerable Father's advice, Wang Foo decided to engage passage on the first steamer for Ningpo.

Four days up the China coast and the vessel glided slowly to her wharf amid the rows and rows of junks and cargo boats. The latter—as well as the foreign steamer—wore all adorned with large goggle-eyes upon their bows, enabling them, according to the native notion, more clearly to see their way in the darkness.

"What for that junk boat have got eyes fore-side?" was the usual foreign inquiry, and the native pidgin answer was always the same:

"No have got eye, how fashion can see? S'pose no can see, how can savvee what side walkee?"

Our detective selected a room at the "Inn of Tranquil Waters," and after a good night's rest, sent in his card in the morning to Dr. Campbell of the English Hospital. He was most graciously received and ere long had deeply interested the surgeon in the mysterious Hong Kong murder.

What he ascertained from him and what they planned together to save the life of Fung Chee belongs to a later day in the story. Suffice it to say that Dr. Campbell promised to give up his practice for a week and to be on hand in the Colony at the time set for the preliminary hearing, while Wang Foo returned on the steamer a few days ahead.

THE COMPANY HAD ASSEMBLED at Government House. Sir Arthur was in the judge's chair; on his right sat Rear Admiral O'Connor of His Majesty's Navy and on his left Col. the Hon. Lloyd Chatham, in command of the Lancashire Regiment, now garrisoning the Colony. The lawyers occupied seats at the green baize table in front of them and places of honor were reserved for the Chinese consul and his suite.

Sir William Beaumont, the Crown Advocate, opened the case and described all that took place on the fatal day. He read the testimony of the various witnesses taken under oath, and concluded with an appeal for the full penalty of the law, "which, unless duly administered, would endanger the life of every European in His Majesty's colony."

Mr. John Crowder arose to open for the defense. There was an impressive silence as all eyes turned toward him.

"Your Excellency and Gentlemen," he began, "I am proud beyond words to stand here today and plead for the release of an entirely innocent person—"

"That remains yet to be proven—" interrupted the Governor.

"It shall be proven; Sir, beyond the shadow of a doubt," he continued. "I am not dealing today with the assault upon sailor McLean by the bearers of the banner. That was a small matter, comparatively, and was only an outburst of passion against a supposed insult to the departed.

"I claim that the same thing would have taken place in England, if a Chinese sailor had attempted to break up a funeral procession. People's feelings are the same in this matter alt the world over.

"I propose to show, gentlemen, not only that my client is entirely innocent of the charge of murder, but that he was actually trying to save human life at the very moment that he is accused of having tried to destroy it.

"Dr. Bradlaw of the Hong Kong Mission Hospital will be my first witness and will testify that McLean was suffering from an epileptic fit at the time of the accident." (Dr. Bradlaw being unable to be present at the moment, Mr. Crowder read his testimony to the above effect.) "We have with us today Dr. Campbell of the Ningpo Hospital, who has come all this way out of interest in the case and who will now explain the circumstances to you."

Dr. Campbell arose and addressed the Governor:

"Your Excellency and gentlemen," he said. "I have often been called upon to explain to my European friends the curious and, to our minds, superstitious ways of this people, which often involve them in serious difficulties with the white man.

"We have a very interesting instance of this before us today. It is the firm belief of the country people in our province that when a man falls in an epileptic fit his soul has temporarily departed from

his body and the soul of the sheep has come in for the while to take
its place. In order to preserve the patient's life it is absolutely necessary that the sheep be fed on grass or hay until the soul returns.
This explains why they instantly pluck up the first bunch of grass
they can find and force it into the victim's mouth!

"Fortunately, I happen to remember the prisoner. My hospital
books show that he was treated by me for this very same disease
some years ago."

"You are quite positive about the record?" inquired the Admiral.

"Perfectly positive, sir."

"Having been a victim of it himself, and having had the 'sheep
and grass' treatment applied to himself, he naturally vividly remembered it. Poor, half-witted creature that he is, he saw the sailor
fall in the fit and the excitement brought back to him his own experience. He naturally rushed for the first grass or hay he could
find and pushed a handful of it into the patient's mouth.

"Now comes the sad and unfortunate sequel: being Winter time,
the grass was withered and in his anxiety to sustain the quivering
life, he unconsciously pulled up a quantity of gravel and clay with the
roots, and it was this that choked the patient to death! Of course, if a
European medical man had been close at hand we could have prevented this in time, but you see, it was a long distance outside the
Settlement and he expired before any help could reach him."

The effect of the doctor's testimony, given slowly and consis-
tently, was like magic. The Governor conferred for a moment with
his colleagues and then arose and addressed the assembly:

"This is a glorious day of triumph, not only for British Justice,
but equally for British skill and mercy. The life of a native subject
has been hanging in the balance and we have come dangerously
near to convicting of a capital crime an apparently perfectly innocent person.

"Dr. Campbell, this entire community, both foreign and native,
owes you a debt which it is hard to estimate, and which only goes
to show how careful we must be in procedures of this kind and how
dependant we are upon the intimate knowledge of the Chinese ways
which your learned profession and your devoted work have brought

you. Inspector Wallace, you will at once release the prisoner and restore him to his family."

"I thank Your Excellency for these gracious words," replied the doctor, "but the credit for the saving of this man's life belongs not to me, but entirely to your honored fellow-citizen, Wang Foo, whose untiring devotion to the cause of right and truth, and whose trip to Ning Po, were the means of bringing this release about. Give honor to whom honor is due!"

"Mr. Wang," added His Excellency, "it is not the first time that this colony has profited by your skillful and unselfish labors in the cause of justice. We are all deeply grateful to you and I express the feelings of all my colleagues present when I say that we are justly proud of numbering you among our fellow-citizens.

"You have helped us in this and many ways to bring about peace and harmony between foreigner and native and your work today will insure even a better relationship between us than was have ever known before."

The Chinese detective, who had been modestly occupying a seat in the rear of the room, arose and bowed his acknowledgments.

"I have merely tried, Your Excellency, humbly to carry out the teachings of our Master, who taught the people in days of old to 'Search out the root and find the way to harmony.'"

The family of Tak Hoy, the Compradore, insisted on presenting the famous Scroll of Woven Silver to the detective.

"No, not to me, but to the foreign doctor," he replied, as with gongs and firecrackers the procession of grateful Chinese bore it to his residence. "You owe this life to him!"

And this is why the scroll now hangs above the doctor's mantel.

THE MANDARIN COAT

"YES, MY DEAR, it is perfectly genuine. The captain took it to the consulate yesterday and had the vice consul examine it thoroughly—you know he is a great authority on all this sort of thing—and he looked the matter all up in his books with his Chinese secretary and he says there is no doubt whatever that it is the genuine official robe of the Prime Minister and must have been worn at the Imperial audiences.

"How they ever came to get hold of it is a mystery to me. I suppose it must have been overlooked in the hurried departure from Pekin and, of course, the very first soldiers that came along just helped themselves to it with all the other loot. They had no idea of the value of it and naturally sold it to the first Chinaman that made them an offer."

"What a superb opera cloak it will make, won't it?"

"Yes, that's really what I wanted it for. The last thing Louise said to me when we started on the cruise was: 'Now, mother, remember! The one thing above all that I want you to bring me is a real Mandarin coat. I don't want any cheap embroidered thing that can be bought in the London shops; I want something especially nice, with this richest old gold embroidery and all that, and'—she was most emphatic about this something with a history, you know, 'the robe of the Prime Minister or some Oriental grandee with a magnificent title that will dazzle the other boxes at the opera when I walk in with it.'"

"And what did you say to that?"

123

A Blinding Flash and It Was Gone

"I said: 'My child, if money can buy it!' But, to tell you the truth. I never dreamed of such good luck. Why, we've only been in Shanghai three weeks and here this prize falls right into my hands with hardly an effort."

"You certainly are a fortunate woman, and I know that when Louise appears in it—and she will wear it more gracefully than any other girl in the world—she will be the very centre of attraction and even the glasses in the royal box will be leveled at her."

The foregoing conversation took place in one of the rooms of the Astor House and the parties concerned were Mrs. Wadleigh, wife of Captain Thomas Wadleigh, of H. M. S. *Albatross*, of the China station, and her friend, Mrs. Cornelia Seymour, a wealthy widow from Adelaide.

The garment which was the subject of their admiration was a long and exceedingly handsome official robe, with all the curious insignia of the highest rank and evidently intended to be worn at the court ceremonials. Others of a similar pattern and style were on view and sale at the handsome Cantonese stores in the Nanking road, but even a cursory examination would show that they were of far inferior quality. It certainly was a treasure and the good lady was justly proud of it.

She obtained it in a rather curious way—almost accidentally, we might say. It happened that one day Jim, the tailor (proprietor of one of the best-known outfitting establishments in the Hongkew road), was measuring the captain for a smoking jacket, and Mrs. Wadleigh asked him if he ever had a chance to secure a genuine Mandarin coat.

"You wantchee buy Mandalin coatee?" he inquired. "S'pose you wantchee, my can tly catchee one piecee. But"—he added, with a curious expression of mingled doubt and suspicion—"you savvee b'longee velly dear just now. Two thlee hundled taelee must pay. Bye'm bye I come look see."

"Well, whenever you get a really fine one, bring it in and show it to me, and we will talk about the price. But mind! No trash of the kind they sell to tourists in the shops."

"All light, can do," was the Celestial's laconic reply, as he finished his measuring and his cue disappeared through the doorway.

Scarcely three days after this a gentle knock at Mrs. Wadleigh's door announced the presence of Jim, who entered and bowed as he deposited a bundle and a mysterious little pigskin trunk upon the floor.

The bundle contained the smoking jacket for her husband and the pigskin trunk, after its brass locks had been carefully opened, revealed another bundle within, wrapped in long folds of faded yellow silk. Jim the tailor's eyes fairly danced in their sockets as he proceeded to lift the contents out on the table and to unroll the mummy-like bandages.

"See, Missie!" he exclaimed, "this b'longee No. 1 Mandalin coatee. My have see plenty pieces fore-tim—this b'longe more beauty, more beauty. No have got Shanghai side."

He unfolded the garment and held up for her admiring gaze the very thing that her daughter longed for, and that she had almost given up hope of finding in the settlement.

"And you guarantee this to be a genuine coat of a noble of rank?" she inquired, as she adjusted her glasses and begun to examine the embroidery and ornamentation more critically.

"Yes, Missee, me can seclure this b'longee velly high Mandalin. Foleign man talkee, 'Pline Minister.' He wear China Emperor house. My speakee tlue. My pay you look see two thlee day, can take Consul man side, he can savvee."

She was so fascinated with the coat, and Jim seemed so thoroughly in earnest about it, that she accepted his offer to keep it for a day or two and get the consul and others to pronounce upon its genuineness and appraise its value.

"But, Jim," she said, "this isn't part of the palace loot, is it? Where did you get it? Now tell me truly."

"My China fliend have catchee—he talkee my can sellee for he," was all that she was able to draw out of him.

"And the price?"

Jim assumed a very serious and thoughtful air—"For you, Misses, five hundled dollar, my talkee velly cheap."

THE NIGHT WAS DARK and the sky overcast. Drops of rain were falling through the freshening gusts of wind as a sampan man sculled his little craft against the outrushing current of the river and headed for the customs jetty. He had only one passenger on the seat beneath the matting awning and he was coming ashore from the Tientsin steamer lying near the opposite bank.

He was a rough seafaring type of man, but one of the kind whom the boatmen are glad to have for fares, because Jack pays more liberally than his friends ashore. He jumped up the jetty steps and tossing the coolie a 20-cent piece exclaimed; "There! Take your double fare, old chap, and hurry home before the storm drowns you out." The boatman seized the coin, and crying: "Tankee you, Masseter," sculled away again into the darkness, while his generous donor hailed a jinrikisha, and pointing to the Hongkew bridge, cried: "Chop-chop go that side."

The tiny two-wheeled vehicle rattled across the bridge and down the Hongkew Road until a pull at the coolie's cue stopped him rather suddenly in front of the shop that bore the sign of Jim, the tailor. Trotsky, the Russian, alighted and passed within.

"Is your Master Jim at home?" he asked of the assistant who was showing a fellow sailor a roll of cloth.

"Yes, Sir, inside have got."

A pair of rickety Chinese doors at the end of the long counter opened apparently of their own accord and the well-known face appeared.

"Come this side," said Jim, as he beckoned to his visitor, and Trotsky followed into the inner room.

What went on inside was only partly audible in the outer shop, but it was evidently a heated discussion, growing more so every moment. Suddenly Jim appeared, and motioning to the assistant, said; "B'longee velly late now, can shuttee up shoppee, go home side." In less than five minutes from the time the command was given, the shop was closed and locked and the two were left alone.

"Well, where's the money for that Mandarin coat that you promised me over a week ago?" asked Trotsky.

"My no catchee," was the answer.

"You're a liar and a thief. You've got it here, somewhere. Now hand it out, quick, too, or I'll break every glass in your shop and"—he added with a threatening gesture—"every bone in your body, too, do you hear?"

"My no havee; how fashion can pay?"

"Come, quick, out with 200 Mexicans or I'll smash that old safe (pointing to an iron box in the corner) into junk."

"Foleign man no have pay me, my no can pay you. 'S'pose you come back tomollow?"

"Tomorrow? Never! I want that cash here and now. Now, out with it—where do you keep it?"

Ho reached for the table and, pulling open the drawers, throw the contents to the floor, the scissors and tapes and spools rolled out, but not a sign of coin. Angered at his disappointment, he raised his arm as if to strike the tailor when Jim, dashing across the room, pulled back the bar of a window and, with one leap, landed on the sidewalk outside.

"My callee policee-man! My callee policee-man!" he shrieked, and rushed off down the street. On the second corner he ran right into an English constable, and the two hurried back to the shop.

"What's the row now?" asked the officer.

"He wantchee klllee me."

"He wants to kill you? Who? There isn't anybody here!"—as they burst open the doors of the shop and found not a trace loft of Trotsky.

"Sailorman, he wantchee klllee me. My speakee tlue."

"Nonsense, your shop is empty. You've been drinking, Jim, that's what's the matter with you. Or smoking too much opium, eh? Nobody wants to hurt you—now shut up shop and go to bed. Sleep off your bad dream." And the constable, laughing good-naturedly, returned to his beat.

When Trotsky came to his senses, after his rather exciting flight through the window, he concluded that the wisest thing was to evade the clutches of the law for the present, even at the risk of losing the two hundred Mexicans, which Jim had promised for the coat.

He hurried away in the direction of the wharves and, turning a corner, took another jinrikisha and rode for a mile along the banks of the river. He came at last to a row of one-story semiforeign houses and alighting at one of them, took a key from his pocket and unlocked the brass padlock on the door. He entered, and striking a match, lighted a little glass kerosene lamp and set it on the table in the middle of a poorly furnished room.

Two dilapidated chairs, a cupboard or two and a row of foreign trunks completed the outfit of the front apartment; the room in the rear—there were only two—boasted a stove, a few kitchen utensils and an iron bedstead with a couple of native quilts.

He lighted his pipe, and taking out of one of the trunks a well-worn notebook, begun to turn over the leaves as he muttered to himself: "Three hundred Mexicans! Three hundred Mexicans! Well, that's not such a bad week's work for loot that didn't cost me fifty.

"Hang that Chinese liar, Jim; I suppose he's getting four times as much for them as he gives me. But he can sell them to his customers and I can't. According to my reckoning there must be five hundred dollars' worth left in those trunks yet—I must try and work them off on some of those other tailors before the police get on to it and crib the whole establishment. Those two last glasses of vodka on the steamer nearly finished the Jim and me part of it tonight, though. I wonder if he will croak now? Never! He's in it just as bad as I am, the old thief." And locking up the trunks, he turned in to sleep on the Chinese cotton quilts.

INSPECTOR GUBBINS of the Shanghai Municipal Police was trying on an overcoat in the identical inner room where Trotsky and Jim had had their encounter, when his eye happened to rest upon a handsome piece of Pekin embroidery lying upon the table. It attracted his curiosity and he said:

"Jim, where did you get that, and who is it for? I didn't know that you dealt in that sort of article."

"B'longee Navy man's wifee makee buy," was the answer. "My no makee this cide. S'pose sometime wifee come my shop 'longside husseband, talkee me can catchee."

"That looks to me mighty like some of that Pekin loot that's been going around the Settlement and that we've been trying to get our hands on. Come, now, tell me where you got it. All that is stolen property, you know, and the Chinese authorities are asking us to help catch the thieves."

At the sound of the word "thieves" Jim started and looked a little frightened.

"You know, Jim, according to English law, the receiver of stolen goods is just as bad as the thief, don't you?"

"My no savvee man have stealee; sometime sailor man come this side wantchee my buy things. He talkee my can sellee foleign lady hotel house, he no can. So my makee buy."

"Now, look here, Jim, you're too good a chap to get into that kind of business, and I warn you now to keep out of it. You can't afford to got in jail and ruin your custom. Just hand that stuff back to the chap you got it from and if any more of them come in here you send them straight to me and I'll fix them, see?"

"My can savvee," was the only answer from the now thoroughly frightened tailor, who there and then mentally resolved to have no more dealings with Trotsky and his gang, even at the enormous profits that had come from this underhand dealing.

Just how he was going to get out of the Mandarin coat transaction was the principal thing that worried him. He had already offered it for sale to Mrs. Wadleigh and Trotsky would be sure to come back again for his money.

If he came back in a state of intoxication, so much the worse for the shop and for Jim's personal reputation and safety. He made up his mind to get out of it at any cost. He would go to the hotel, take back the coat under some excuse, and return it to the sailor. As a consistent beginning of this resolve, he seized the embroidery from the table and hurriedly rolling it up, hid it away in one of the recesses of the iron box in the corner and started off for the hotel.

Mrs. Wadleigh was fortunately at home when he arrived and told Charlie, the hall-boy, to show him to her apartment.

"Good morning, Jim," she said, as he entered, "have you decided to come down on the price of that coat yet?"

To her utter surprise he replied: "My velly soly, Misses, but my no can sell you that coatee."

"You can't sell it to me—why, what do you mean? Has someone else offered you a higher price for it? I suppose you want $600 for it now, eh?"

"No wantchee any more dollar, Missee, my fliend talkee he wantchee that coatee his side. My must pay he back."

His customer now grew indignant, and, seeing the possibility of her precious treasure slipping away, decided to stand upon what she considered her European rights.

"No, Jim, you can't have it back. I don't care who your mysterious friend is or how badly she—for it must be a 'she'—wants it, she positively cannot have it. That coat is mine and I propose to keep it. Possession is nine points of the law. You can have your $500 as soon as my husband comes ashore, but you cannot have the coat."

The Celestial argued and pleaded, but to no avail.

"S'pose my no pay he back, Missee, my fliend wantchee killee me."

"Nonsense, that is just your old Chinese way of trying to frighten me. Tell me who your friend is and we will have the police take care of the 'killing' part of it. Here comes the captain now"— as the naval officer entered the room.

"Tom," she said, "what do you think? Here is Jim saying I can't have my Mandarin coat. He actually refuses to sell it to me."

"At the $500 figure?"

"Yes, at the original price he put on it when you were here."

"All rubbish! Someone else has probably heard of it or seen it and offered him an extra $50, that's all."

"That's exactly what I told him, but it didn't do any good. He still wants it back."

"Well, he can't have it. A bargain's a bargain. I'll go right down to the hotel desk now and cash this check for the money and he'll have to take it whether he likes it or not."

The captain suited the action to the word and, placing the bills in the tailor's hands, gently but firmly pushed him out into the hall and locked the door.

"Louise came pretty near to losing her opera cloak, didn't she, dear?" he said to his wife as he lighted a cigar and sat down to enjoy the evening paper with the account of the Hong Kong races.

"I never had such a fright in my life," replied Mrs. Wadleigh, bringing out the coat from the glass case, whore she had hung it, and again proceeding to admire the exquisite workmanship.

Jim started back for the shop and was just turning the corner of the Hongkew road, when whom should he run into but the identical Trotsky. Fortunately for both of them, he was sober and in a fairly agreeable mood. Jim decided to get out of it as quickly and as pleasantly as possible, so, putting on his sweetest smile, he addressed the sailor:

"Good-morning, Masseter, suppose you wantchee that money now, my can pay."

The effect on Trotsky was electrical. He unbent at once and the two proceeded back to the tailor shop and into the inner room. There the 200 Mexicans were duly counted out and, rolling the bills and stowing them away in his pocket, the Russian remarked: "I've got more of the same kind in the trunk, Jim, if you want them, eh? What time shall I come back tonight?"

"My no wantchee any more. You no come back this side. S'pose you wantchee sell more lootee, more better you go some odder shop. Too muchee robbery."

The astonished Trotsky pleaded, but all in vain, Jim was obdurate and insisted that this be their last transaction. There seemed to be no other way out of it, so the receiver of stolen goods bade him adieu—remarking as he did so: "Well, goodbye, then, you and I have made a pretty good thing out of it, anyhow. I'll find some other chap that knows a Chinese bargain when he sees it."

"MRS. WADLEIGH," SAID THE VICE CONSUL, as they were sipping afternoon tea in the Japanese room, "I wonder if you wouldn't like to meet one of the most interesting men in China before you leave Shanghai?"

"Why, I should be most delighted. Pray tell me, who is he? You know one really doesn't have a chance to see anything of the real higher class here. We seem to be confined to compradores and shop-keepers and all that sort of person—except an occasional official, and they are so dreadfully stiff and formal."

"Well," continued the consul, "this gentleman's name is Wang Foo and he is one of the best-known residents in Hong Kong. He is a cultured Confucian scholar, of private means, who has made a special study of all sorts of Chinese crimes and has been remarkably successful in unraveling many mysterious cases in both the Settlements.

"He seems to have a sort of natural instinct for seeing into the ways of his countrymen, which few, if any, Europeans ever possess. It was he who discovered the whereabouts of Lady Evington's jewels, in the famous robbery case, you remember."

"Why, certainly, that's the very same person that Capt. Aldridge told us about when we were coming up the coast. He told us not to fail to meet him and talk with him if we ever had the chance. But just one question: does he speak English or only this awful jargon they call 'pidgin'? You know it is so unsatisfactory to try to carry on a conversation in that house-boy lingo."

"O, put your mind perfectly at ease about that. He speaks English as fluently as either you or I do."

"How delightful! Where can we find him?"

"Well, he is in the outer office now, and if you don't mind, I'll just bring him in and introduce him."

"Please do."

The consul disappeared for a moment and then returned with the Man of Mystery, who greeted the ladies most courteously and, joining in the company's conversation, appeared perfectly at his ease. Mrs. Wadleigh was charmed with him and nothing must do but that he must consent to be one of her guests at a little birthday gathering which she was planning in her husband's honor.

"Now, Mr. Wang," she added, "you surely must come and do, please, bring something very mysterious with you!"

Wang smiled a gracious acceptance of the invitation, saying, as he did so: "Mrs. Wadleigh, your request reminds me of the English lady's invitation to Mark Twain, the American humorist, you remember, when she said to him: 'Mr. Twain, please come to my house and be funny.' One cannot always do these things to order, you know."

The problem of being very mysterious off hand rather perplexed the detective as he took his departure, but his ride home through the streets of the settlement suggested to him an idea which he proceeded to develop as the evening wore on.

It happened to be the evening before the ascension heavenward of Tsao Chuin, the god of the kitchen, and all the native population were preparing their paper sedan chairs and coolies and garments to accompany him on the Celestial Journey. He was writing his record of the year and would report on arrival the behavior of all the different members of the household. This explains the avidity with which they purchased packages of molasses taffy (of which the divinity was exceedingly fond) and placed it in his mouth before his departure, so that when he reached the heavenly shores he would be so busily engaged in chewing that he would be unable to talk!

As the jinriksha passed a very large establishment, where paper garments to be burned in Tsao Chuin's honor were being sold, Wang stopped and, entering, requested an interview with the proprietor. What they said and planned over the tea-bowls and pipes leads up to a very interesting event, which we mustn't anticipate.

"YES, IT IS QUITE TRUE," remarked the Consul, as the company passed into the drawing room after the elaborate birthday dinner, "that aged cloth and even silk becomes very inflammable. I remember when I was stationed in Egypt that often valuable mummies were destroyed in this way just through the carelessness of some Arab dropping a spark on the wrappings. I am told that the same thing has happened in India and I have no doubt, Mr. Wang"—turning as he spoke these words to the detective—"that the same is true in China, is it not?"

"Quite so," answered the Chinese visitor, who up to the present time had been disappointingly natural and not a bit mysterious,

"now, that beautiful Mandarin coat of Mrs. Wadleigh's, for instance"—he rose and approaching the glass case in which his hostess had hung it, to the utter surprise and dismay of the company,
took the garment out, and, without removing the gauze cover which
dimly concealed its beauty, before anyone could protest or stop
him, struck a match and touched its lower border!

There was a blinding flash, a burst of flames and in an instant
the priceless Mandarin coat was nothing but a bundle of crum-
bling ashes! He threw open the glass door and, rushing out with it,
deposited it on the veranda—as he did so, every electric light in
the room suddenly went out. It was only a moment before they
burst out again, but Wang Foo was missing! Yes, Wang Foo was
gone, but look! Who is this elegant Chinese official coming in
through the other door?

"Ladies and gentlemen," said the Consul, "allow me to present
to you His Excellency Chang, formerly Prime Minister of China!
He wears, as you all see, the identical robe of state which the daughter of our charming hostess is to wear as an opera cloak at Covent
Garden next Winter."

"Safely passed through the flames," added Wang, as with a most
gracious bow he approached the astonished Mrs. Wadleigh and sat
down beside her with the Mandarin coat adorning his handsome
figure.

"You see," he said, "I have brought 'something mysterious' with
me."

"Explain it! Explain it at once!" they all cried in unison.

"A perfectly simple matter, when one knows the secret," calmly
replied the wonder-working Wang. "I happened to find a Mandarin coat of paper in a native shop that was such a clever imitation
of the genuine article that it occurred to me to show it to you as an
example of real Chinese skill.

"The house boy kindly exchanged it for me before dinner, and
the covering of gauze prevented your detecting it. Our good friend
the Consul entered into the secret with me and kindly introduced
the subject of inflammable garments at the opportune moment.

You all recognize the fact that every good magician requires a confederate."

"And do you mean to tell me that it was the paper coat and not the real one that hung in that cabinet all through the evening?" inquired Mrs. Wadleigh.

"Words were never more truly spoken—you see the real one was waiting for me outside on the veranda when the proper time came to put it on."

JIM, THE TAILOR, still continues business at the old stand in Shanghai and makes uniforms for His Majesty's Navy; and every variety of garment for European civilians, but, heeding the timely advice of the inspector of police, he no longer deals in Mandarin coats— even at their fabulous values.

THE GOLDEN CARP

No European student of China and its ways has ever successfully completed the list of the many and various uses to which its wonderful plant, the bamboo, has been put. There certainly is no more remarkable illustration in nature of the adaptation of a plant to man's needs than is furnished by this graceful and pliant grass—for, strictly speaking, it is really that, and not a tree.

It grows anywhere and everywhere, and with such rapidity that its progress can be easily marked from day to day with the naked eye. Indeed, one of the awful punishments of the early code was to tie a culprit securely down over a pointed sprout and allow it gradually to force its way through his prostrate form, thus killing him by inches.

From the cradle to the grave it is the Celestial's faithful friend and servant. He is rocked in it in his infancy, fed with it in his childhood, supplied with every variety of utensil from it in his manhood, and finally carried on it to his last "happy home." His house, his furniture, his tools, his books, his chopsticks, his nets, his pipes—the staff that sustains him and the rod that smites him—an all part and parcel of the same heavenly plant.

No wonder that they gratefully speak of it as one of the gods' best gifts to man. Over 60 varieties, no two of them alike, are mentioned in the native books, and the literature on the subject is inexhaustible.

"Bamboo encouragement" is a familiar term to every Chinese schoolboy. He knows that when a little gentle stimulus is needed

When the stoker struck him he cried out "Swim up the dragon pool, you golden carp! Swim up the pool!" -:- -:- -:-

to make him "back" his books more thoroughly, the ever-ready "graceful grass" in the teacher's hands will furnish it on the moment. In this he is at a little disadvantage as compared with the American boy, who can see the rod and sometimes dodge it, for he recites with his back to the instructor and—unless there be a convenient mirror at the back of the school room, which there never is—the chastening and stimulating bamboo does its fatal work before he can avoid it.

The Chinese professor of the native lore takes no chances with his game, and he generally aims pretty straight. And this is how it comes to pass that a few judiciously administered blows—even in later life—to bring out the truth, are popularly known as "Bamboo encouragement."

"The prisoner seems to be a little modest or diffident about answering my questions," a magistrate will say in a native court: "he needs a little encouragement." And the lictors proceed forthwith to "encourage" him with some 15 or 20 well-directed blows, which generally has the effect of loosening the strings of the tongue and enabling him to incriminate his neighbors.

These introductory remarks explain the peculiar phraseology of the suggestion which Tak-Loy, assistant compradore at Royce & Co.'s warehouse made to Mr. Royce himself when the latter accused the head wharf coolie of stealing.

"There surely is a lot of thieving going on right here under our very noses, and you can't tell me that he doesn't know about it. Of course, he knows all about it and is getting a big squeeze out of it himself. But I can't get any satisfaction out of it. He swears the tallies are all right when they leave the gangplank, and all right again when they get to the go-down with the rice-bags, and yet we are nearly a thousand pounds short on the *Chip Sing's* cargo alone, and she is a small boat, don't you know."

"Mr. Loycee," replied the compradore, "I think more better we encoulage he how fashion you tinkee?"

"Encourage him! Why, good heavens, what do you mean? Make him steal more?"

"Please you s'cluse me. No stealee more. My talkee China school encoulage, all same bamboo."

"O, you mean to beat him, do you? Is that what you call your bamboo encouragement? Well, how are you going to do it without all of us getting into the Mixed Court and paying more than the whole thing is worth?"

"P'laps more better you talkee policeman first. S'pose he can savvee, all light, s'pose he no savvee, more better bamboo that number one coolie."

"All right, we'll put the police on this the first thing tomorrow morning."

CHIEF DETECTIVE MOREHEAD of the Shanghai office was engaged in a private conversation with Wang Foo, the famous detector of crime, when Mr. Royce's card was sent in from the outer room.

Mr. Wang had been requested to come up from Hong Kong (at the earnest solicitation of Dr. Cortelyou, the U. S. Consul) and co-operate with the local police in their attempts to solve the mystery of the murder of an American subject, and they were discussing the details of the crime just at this moment.

"We will have to suspend the conversation for a while, Mr. Wang, for this gentleman has come to consult me about a complicated robbery case and I know he is anxious for an immediate interview."

"Certainly," replied the gracious Chinese guest, "would you like me to call again a little later in the day?"

"Not at all, I want you to remain right here, if you kindly will, for I am sure you will be interested in this case, and I have no doubt you may be of some very practical help to us. Won't you stay?"

"Always at your service and that of the department, Mr. Morehead."

Mr. Royce entered, and, after having been introduced to Wang Foo, expressed himself as especially pleased that he could be present at the interview. The three gentlemen took seats and the officer motioned to Mr. Royce to begin.

He gave a full and detailed account of what had taken place on the wharf and in the go-down and ended up by saying that he had no doubt whatever that some very skillful thieving was going on all the time—and that the head wharf coolie was in league with the gang—but in spite of the most careful watching, not a trace of anything could be found.

As an illustration, he cited the case of the *Chip Sing* with 500 bags of rice. Every bag was examined on leaving the ship and a bamboo tally given for it to the coolie, who carried it across the wharf to the go-down, and who then handed his tally to the compradore and received his few coppers cash in his hand. There was absolutely no chance for any tampering with the bags, for they were watched from the time they left the ship until they were deposited on the go-down floor.

Now for the mystery: the bags were weighed at Swatow on leaving and then the iron hatch was securely locked; they were weighed again on being taken out of the go-down at Shanghai, and they were several hundred pounds short! Not a human being had had access to them on board the ship—the mate swore to that, for he held the keys—and they had been constantly and securely locked on shore.

The only possible suggestion was rats, but rats unfortunately cannot gnaw through the steel plates of a steamer or the galvanized sides and floors of a warehouse; and, then, rats always leave traces of their work in the holes in the bags and the scattered grains of rice lying about.

"You are quite sure the bags were all intact?" inquired the chief.

"Absolutely so—every one of them is examined to see that no strings have been cut when it is brought ashore."

"It certainly looks like ghosts, Mr. Wang, doesn't it?" turning to the quiet but very interested listener.

"Yes; you know the Chinese believe that hungry ghosts are particularly fond of rice, especially of this fine Swatow variety," smiled the man of mystery in reply. "But—they like it cooked, not raw, and they never cook it themselves, so you see they are dependent upon their human friends to secure it and cook it for them.

"Ghosts are made the scapegoats for a good deal in China, as they are in England, but they are never guilty of purloining uncooked food; that, I am obliged to say in their defense, is a purely mortal pastime. So, gentlemen, I am afraid we shall have to rule out the ghosts as well as the rats."

"What theory or explanation have you to offer, then, sir?" inquired Mr. Boyce.

"It would be impossible for me to offer any explanation offhand, sir—whatever conception I may already have formed mentally—without a careful survey of the scene of the supposed robbery and. the privilege of an interview or two with the parties most nearly concerned. Perhaps Mr. Morehead would do me the honor to show me over the scene tomorrow."

"Delighted to do so, Mr. Wang, at any hour that may suit Mr. Royce."

When the same party of three met a few evenings afterward, Wang Foo took from his sleeve the leather-covered notebook, in which he had entered the data of the robbery and, accepting the Manila cheroot which his host tendered him, leaned back in his chair and, looking at Mr. Royce in a strange, quizzical way, asked slowly but distinctly:

"You say that every bag of rice was weighed carefully at Swatow and again at Shanghai?"

"Yes, sir."

"And you found a difference of several hundred pounds?"

"Yes, sir; in fact, nearly a thousand on the consignment."

"And you have taken every precaution and made every effort to find the loss, but without success?"

"Indeed we have, sir, but the leak goes on as merrily as ever."

"I dislike to seem discourteous in differing with you, Mr. Royce, but there is one precaution you didn't take."

"And pray, what is that?"

"You weighed the rice-bags—but you omitted to weigh the coolies!"

"Weigh the coolies? What do you mean, sir?"

"Why, simply this; the excess weight of the gang of coolies at the close of the day would be about equal to the weight of the stolen rice. It's like the law of specific gravity, you know; the weight of the article is equal to the weight of the water which it displaces."

"Do you mean they stole it and hid it in their clothes, then?"

"I most certainly do, sir."

"Well, when and how did they steal it? Solve the mystery for me and I will acknowledge you are indeed a wonder."

Wang Foo put his long hand up his right-hand sleeve and drew out therefrom a slender piece of bamboo about eight inches long. It was hollowed out and the end was sharply pointed like a pen. Attached to it was a long bag resembling a stocking with a very small leg and a very large foot.

"Here, gentlemen, is your solution. You see this is neither 'rat' nor 'ghost'; on the contrary, it is something very simple and human. The coolie who carries the rice-bag has this apparatus concealed beneath his clothing. The bag is fastened around his waist and the bamboo is concealed in his collar. When he is given the bag on the ship he places it on his right shoulder and steadies it with his right hand, his left hand grasping the tally-stick which the compradore collects.

"Now for the trick—with his right hand under the bag he pushes the bamboo pipe up through the meshes until he reaches the grains of rice and then they begin to flow slowly but surely down through the tube into the stocking. The rocking motion of his body as he walks assists the flow—like good exercise for the dyspeptic—and before he reaches the go-down he has several pounds inside his garments. He then draws the bamboo down into his collar and no one is ever the wiser."

"Did you ever see anything cleverer than that, Mr. Morehead?" asked the merchant.

"It certainly beats me," was the chief's brief but emphatic answer.

"And, pray, what do they call this diabolical invention, Mr. Wang?"

"I am told," replied the detective, with a rather significant smile, "I am told that they call it 'The little bamboo assistant or encourager.' Your compradore suggested a little 'encouragement,' did he not?"

"Yes, but not exactly that kind."

"True, not exactly that kind, but still of the same bamboo, was it not?"

"Yes, I believe it was—a wonderful plant, when all is said and done, Mr. Wang, is it not?"

"One of heaven's best gifts to man," replied the Chinese scholar, "as the ancient saying goes:

How restful by the waters cool,
To watch its graceful waving!"

"As far as the case itself is concerned, Mr. Wang," remarked Dr. Cortelyou, the consul, to his visitor from Hong Kong, "it seems clear enough to the American eye, but you know I haven't been here four years without realizing that in every one of these international rows 'there's always a little nigger in the woodpile,' as we say in the United States. You are familiar with that phase, are you not?"

"O, yes, indeed, sir, though I am told that in Boston they express the same sentiments a little differently."

"Ah, how is that?"

"I believe they say that 'there's a lurking suspicion of a diminutive son of Africa's having concealed himself in the accumulated kindling,' or something to that effect."

"Diminutive son of Africa is very good," laughed the consul.

"Yes, you know the difference between Boston and Chicago, for instance, in the mode of expression reminds me of the difference between the classic language of the literati of China and the vernacular of the provinces, sometimes. I suppose you find it so in every country, do you not?"

"As far as my limited travels permit me to judge, I believe you do—but to go back to our case: the evidence all shows that there had been bad feeling between the second mate and the stoker for some time, owing to some row on shipboard, and it finally culminated in this Hongkew scrimmage when Jackson attempted to throw the fellow into the creek and he had to hit him back, as he says, in self-defense.

"Of course, Jackson was drunk at the time, for he and some of his cronies had been imbibing at that 'Happy Anchorage' place near the bridge, and I suppose when he came out and saw the stoker he thought it would be a good chance to get even with him on shore. Now, when men are under the influence of liquor they generally come through all right, as you know, when a really sober man would succumb, but in this case he must have fallen very heavily on the pavement, for the doctor said his skull was fractured when they picked him up."

"Well, where is your nigger in the woodpile?"

"Why, just here, Mr. Wang, and this is really the reason why I have sent for you; the jinriksha coolie and the others all testify that when the stoker struck him he cried out, 'Swim up the dragon pool, you golden carp! Swim up the pool!' And in spite of all my efforts, I cannot find anybody who can explain these words.

"Now, what had Jackson to do with a dragon pool and why did the stoker tell him to 'swim up'? There seems to be some mysterious hidden meaning in these expressions and the more I think of them the more I am convinced that there's some connection between them and the murder."

Wang Foo looked very thoughtful for a moment. "Have you inquired of the missionaries?" he asked.

"Yes, I have had a number of them in here with their Chinese teachers and all that I can find is that 'The carp swims up the dragon pool' is a phrase which is used to signify literary ambition. They tell me that it hongs on the walls of Chinese schools and is engraved on the slabs of ink and painted on the covers of the books and all that sort of thing.

"The idea seems to be that as the carp struggles up against the current of the stream, so the scholar ought to struggle onward and upward against all obstacles."

"They are quite correct, Mr. Consul; it is one of the most treasured phrases in our literary life, and would be instantly recognized by any Chinese scholar."

"True, but what in the world has a literary phrase to do with a couple of sailors and a street fight? That's what puzzles me. They are about the last words in the world you would expect to hear from the lips of a second mate—to say nothing of an ordinary stoker."

"Yes, sir, they are hardly part of the language of the sea, though a good many native sailors would remember them from their early schooling, as they learn these sayings very early in life."

"Still," persisted the consul, "I am perfectly convinced that there was some special reason for the use of the words and that when we find that reason we shall have some additional light thrown on the case. Now. Mr. Wang, I appeal to you. You are the only man in China who can help me out, and I shall never rest content with the evidence until I do."

"Be assured, sir, that I shall do everything in my power to assist you, but, as you well know, these things take time. I hope to see you again in—shall we say a week?"

"A week from tonight, Mr. Wang, and my good wishes go with you."

When Wang Foo reached the home of the basket-maker, where he always stayed while in the settlement of Shanghai, he enjoyed with them the humble evening repast of rice and eggs and pork and cabbage, with some choice Hong Kong pickles which they had saved in his honor, and after the tea and pipes he mounted the little stairs to the upper room and gave himself to thought—and work.

A gentle knock was heard at the door and. opening it, he saw before him little Toy Ching, the basket-maker's son.

"Is the honorable guest very busy just now?" he timidly asked.

"Not at all, little prince; pray enter and be seated."

The lad entered, but reverently remained standing—he would not dare to sit in the presence of the scholar.

"Would the venerable elder-born hear him 'back' his morning's lesson?"

"With pleasure. Give me the little book."

It was the eighth chapter of the *Analects*, and the subject was "The Three Duties of a Gentleman." Carefully they went over the words together: "To banish from his hearing all violence and levity; to set his face ever to the truth; to purge his speech of all that is low and base."

"I fear I have greatly worried the teacher," Toy Ching said, as he bowed his thanks and bade his guest good night.

"To teach without being weary—is not that true joy?" replied the gentle scholar as he bade his pupil depart in peace. "Stay a moment; what have you painted on the cover of the book?"

The boy held up the volume to his gaze, and Wang Foo read these golden words:

"The carp swims up the pool."

The sailor, the stoker, the carp and the pool—what was the mystic spell that had linked these four together? That was the problem, and he would begin to try to solve it on the morrow.

THE PARTITIONS BETWEEN the upper stories of the ordinary Chinese houses in the settlement are not always of brick or even of plaster, but of thin boards so full of cracks and knotholes that they have to be pasted over with paper to secure even a semblance of privacy. This, which would be most objectionable to European tenants, does not seem to disturb the native mind in the least.

They seem to accept the condition of things very philosophically, and the fact that domestic squabbles occasionally occur does not in the least affect their serenity of mind, even though several families enjoy the proceedings together.

Once in a while, however, things are said and done that if overheard are apt to cause trouble, and such was the case on the evening when the Chang family, at a certain number in the Lucky Star alley, discussed its private plans in the full hearing of the Choo family, who rented the adjoining apartment.

Now it happened that the eldest son of the Changs was a close literary rival of the eldest son of the Choos, and they were both soon to take their departure for the great examinations at the capital.

To whom would the coveted honor go? To a Chang or to a Choo? Perhaps to one—possibly to neither.

Every encouragement had been given them by their relatives and friends and all sorts of good wishes had been tendered them. They had both burned large quantities of midnight oil in perfecting their studies and, as far as the public mind was concerned, both were equally well fitted for the contest.

There remained just one all-important thing, viz; the consulting of the soothsayer at the temple and the selecting of the lucky day and hour for the departure. This detail was duly attended to and the young men set off for the capital.

It was the last day of the third session, the most critical time of all in the Chinese mind, and the one when they needed the utmost concentration of thought on the literary tasks before them, when Chang, the father, announced to his family in the upper room that he was going to "seek the omen of the golden carp" upon the morrow.

"If the carp swims up the dragon pool, our son will win," he cried; "It is the unfailing omen of the gods of literature. If he swims down—he fails. At exactly noon the carp will give the answer."

Through the cracks of the partition the Choos had overheard it all! A hurried secret consultation followed and it was resolved to thwart the plan of the Changs at any cost. Early in the morning Choo, the father, hastened to the Temple of the Golden Carp outside the Eastern Gate. He sought the head priest and thus addressed him in the privacy of the inner court:

"Venerable father, which way swims the Golden Carp tomorrow?" pointing to the rock-work pool before them.

The old priest eyed him carefully—"One cannot tell beforehand the ways and whims of the Sacred Fish," he answered. "He may swim up; he may swim down; 'tis not for mortals to control him."

"Listen!" said old Choo, as he opened out before him a palm filled with silver coin, "tomorrow at exactly noon, he swims down the pool, not up—you understand?"

The priest's eyes glistened as he saw the coin. He hesitated for a moment, than seized the proffered bribe. "Silver may sometimes change the course of gold," he said; "Is it not so written in the Book of Changes?"

Punctuality was not of paramount importance at the Temple of the Golden Carp and so it came to pass that it was exactly noon by the ancient time-piece of the temple when the city time was only 11, and this was also the reason why the aged priest mistook the sailors for the Changs when they presented themselves at the Dragon Pool.

"That fortune teller in the other temple is a villain and a cheat," exclaimed the stoker. "I follow my aged father's guidance and seek the omen of the Golden Carp. If he swims up, then I slay Jackson— if he swims down, then the second mate slays me! Watch him closely, for my life depends upon it!"

They stood in silence before the pool while the great golden fish lay quietly at the bottom of the water. The old priest seized a gong and struck it twice, then blow a shrill note or two upon a little pipe. The fish suddenly started and rising almost to the surface shot down like an arrow to the further end of the enclosure.

"He swims down! He swims down!" cried the sailors, and rushing out into the roadway, jumped into their jinrikishas and started for the river.

Just an hour later, old Chang appeared at the Dragoon Pool and watched the priest go through the same performance. The Golden Carp swam up!

"The Omen! The Omen! He wins, he wins!" he cried with joy. "My son shall wear the Golden Button of the Second Degree; honor at last has come to the family of Chang."

WANG FOO, THE CONSUL and Inspector Gubbins were closeted together in the inner office when the time came to unravel the tale. The man of mystery explained it all. He showed how the stoker's family, after listening to his tale of the mate's cruelty, had made him swear on the altar of his gods to avenge the insult to the family name; how he had decided to meet Jackson somewhere while on shore and fight it out with him, if need be, to the death; how he had been driven at last to consult the great Omen of the Golden

Carp and how, when the mate attacked him, he had shrieked out the words, "Swim up the Dragoon Pool!" fearing the man would drown him in the river. He told the story of the Changs and Choos and how the mistake in time had led the priest to mistake one party for the other, and had saved the day for both.

"Mr. Wang," the consul said, as he rose and took his hands, "you have done a splendid work for truth and justice in clearing up this mystery. We know more about the Chinese people and their ways and thoughts to than we ever did before. I thank you."

"But just how did you got hold of this gold-fish-temple connection with it?" asked the Inspector with some interest.

"O, that came about quite naturally. Some teachers in the school my little friend attends told me of it and the sacred fish, and I thought I would look it up. I happened to notice the old clock was an hour off, so that led the old priest, for a few coins, to tell me the story—you see, I was disguised as a brother priest myself and that threw him off his guard."

"And how do they work the gold-fish trick? I mean, how do they make him swim up or down?"

"O, I learned that in the old temple at Foochow, where they train them. It takes five years or more to train a carp like that. You see, one blow on the song means 'Up' and two blows means 'Down.' The wooden post that supports the gong goes deep into the earth and connects underneath with the pool; this enables the sound to be carried through the water—the fish couldn't hear it through the air—that's what mystifies the people."

"Just one question more, Mr. Wang, if you please, before we part; what earthly connection has all this with the case of the rice-stealing on the wharf, that you showed up so cleverly?"

"Why, you see, that involves some Chinese family connections that you European gentlemen do not often take note of—but which we always particularly inquire into. The wharf-coolie's wife lives next door to the basket-maker's where I stay, and we heard the whole story from her.

"In her anxiety to exonerate her husband she let out the words, 'Those rice-coolies have longer socks on their shoulders than they have on their feet,' and this led me to suspect the little bamboo trick, of which I had once heard in Hong Kong."

"But why didn't he expose them himself?"

"Gentlemen, his life wouldn't have been worth a Mexican dollar if he had. They were 30 men against one. Times were hard and they were desperate for food—that is all."

"I think, after this, we will weigh the coolies as well as the rice," remarked the Inspector. "Eh, Mr. Wang?"

"Yes, and bring your own scales so that they can't tamper with them beforehand!"

THE PEARL OF HOY HOW

IT WAS CERTAINLY a glorious New Year's Day in Hong Kong, the beautiful island of "Fragrant Waters." Not January the first—no, no, not that at all, for that is, to the happy Celestial, merely the ignorant European's distortion of the sacred calendar of antiquity—but February the 14th, the glorious day fixed by the silver moon, the radiant Queen of the starry heavens, and not by the glaring sun of the noonday.

And how wonderfully she accommodates herself to the Oriental's inherent dislike of a hard and fixed regularity! She never dates it alike on any two following years, but like the unveiling of her smiling face—her waxing and her waning with the changing months—she draws the curtain forward and backward as the seasons come and go and so gives to all her children the fascinating charm of variety.

Indeed, the cold, calm, businesslike way in which the Western man celebrates the dawning of the year has led them, in the various ports of China, to imagine that Dec. 25, and not Jan. 1, is the real changing of the calendar.

"Yang Jen go nien" (the Ocean Man is passing the year) is heard on every side at Christmas and the little rice-paper cards which are sold everywhere with the words, "My chin-chin you Melly Klismas," are universally supposed to be the New Year's greetings.

Queen's Road and all the other business streets were a blaze of golden glory. Red banners and streamers floated in the air, beautiful lanterns of all fantastic shapes hung out from every available

H produced from the inner folds of his capacious robe a number of jewel-cases and laid them out ※ ※ ※ In spite of the fact our travelers had been warned ※ ※ ※ they went into perfect raptures over one.

point, while the constant din of firecrackers without vied with the music of the three-stringed fiddles within.

Every business house, from the great hongs along the water to the humblest shops in twisting alleys, was closed and its doors hermetically sealed with the long strips of red paper, bearing their good wishes and their blessings. "Kai men ta chik" and "Sing nien wan foo" ("Great luck on opening the door" and "Myriad blessings of the New Year") greeted one on every side.

Everyone was happy and every man that had a new coat or a new hat or a pair of new shoes had them on. The last neighborhood row, the last family squabble, the last dunning for debts has ceased promptly at the stroke of midnight and now all was bowing and scraping and good cheer, as the "pipes of harmony" and the "wines of peace" passed around.

Of course, every jinriksha and sampan fare was either doubled or trebled. It was hard enough for even these poor coolies to be working on the great day of the feast, and mean beyond words must be he who would begrudge them the extra wine-money.

Every old resident in the Colony knew this and cheerfully paid accordingly, but the tourists in the hotel could hardly be expected to grasp the situation.

This explains why Col. and Mrs. Witherspoon, wealthy globe-trotters from St. Louis, U. S. A., were calling for the police at the hotel entrance, when the men who had pulled them from the steamer wharf insisted, in somewhat violent tones, on an addition to the fare.

"I gave them a dime apiece, and that's more than enough for hauling us less than three blocks," exclaimed the irate colonel. "They're regular sharks—worse than the cabbies in Naples."

"Twenty centee! Twenty centee! B'longee New Year, China New Year ussee pay more money," cried the coolies in unison.

"Not a cent more, if I die for it. Now get out of this, quick, every one of you, or I'll have the whole lot of you in jail." The foremost runner started to take hold of the tourist's sleeve and hold him back, just in time to dodge a blow from his heavy walking-stick, when a handsomely dressed Chinese gentleman who had been an eyewitness of the occurrence stepped in between them and, in the most perfect of English, attempted to explain.

"I hope you will excuse these men, sir. They really do not mean to be exorbitant or to do you any harm, but you see it is the great feast of the year with them and they are accustomed to an extra consideration, that is all. Just step into the hotel, sir, with the lady and I will settle with the jinrikisha."

"You don't mean to say that you are going to pay it yourself, do you?"

"O, never mind about that, Sir; that is a very trifling consideration. You see, the respectable Chinese especially dislike to have any unpleasantness on the holiday. It doesn't look well, and"—he added with a smile—"they believe it betokens bad luck for the rest of the year. Please pass right in, sir, and forget it."

"Well," answered the Colonel, quite taken aback by this unusual courtesy, "I am sure I am greatly obliged to you, sir. Here is my card, and I hope we may meet again before we leave the Island."

Wang Foo, the "man of mystery"—for it was none other than he—accepted the card with a gracious bow, and was on the point of opening his case to return his own, when Mrs. Witherspoon called to her husband from within and he was lost to sight in the corridor.

"Here are two extra cups of wine for you," he said to the coolies, as he proceeded to explain and to calm them down. "Do not blame the ocean man; he means well, but he does not understand our native customs. His New Year is over, a month and a half ago. Here, take this extra silver for good luck and may the god of riches beam upon you."

The coolies eagerly accepted the proffered tips, bowing low as they did so, and saying: "Venerable Father, a very Happy New Year to you. You have indeed exhorted men to be harmonious."

Just what interesting part Col. and Mrs. Witherspoon played in the events of the following weeks belongs to a later portion of our story.

THE PENINSULAR AND ORIENTAL STEAMER *Bombay* was making her regular 24-hour stop at Ceylon on her schedule eastward and all her passengers had gone ashore to spend the night at the Colombo Hotel. This not only made a very pleasant break in the monotony of the long sea journey, but also enabled them, to escape the noise, confusion and dust of the steamer's coaling.

The afternoon had been spent in driving about in native garries, visiting the fascinating jewelry shops and watching the jugglers and fakirs on the hotel verandas. Borabjee Sam, who kept one of the finest arrays of sapphires, rubies and pearls on the island, was of course on hand with his wares, as he always was on the arrival of every mail steamer, and did the usual thriving business with the travelers. He was particularly attentive, on this evening, to a lady and gentleman from the U.S.A., who had paid him the compliment of looking over his showcases and purchasing a few moderate priced stones.

He was very anxious that they should grant him a private interview in their apartment, where he might show them some of especial treasures, without exposing them to the vulgar gaze of the other guests. His request being finally granted, he produced from the inner folds of his capacious robe a number of leather and velvet jewel-cases, and opening them, laid them out in order on the table for the admiring gaze of his customers.

"And you guarantee every one of these stones to be perfectly genuine and flawless?" asked the lady.

"Absolutely so," was the unhesitating answer; "if you have any doubt about it, you may take them to London or Paris or New York and have your own jeweler examine them, without paying me a dollar. If what I say is true, you can send me the money by mail."

"That is remarkable confidence to show in perfect strangers," she added. "You never saw us before in your life. Suppose we should take this beautiful ruby away with us and never write a word to you about it; how would you stand the loss?"

"Madam," said the Cingalese merchant, bowing profoundly as he did so, "I have trusted many Europeans with my jewels to take away and I have never lost a dollar! I have been in the jewelry business many years and, I think, I know ladies and gentlemen when I see them."

In spite of this very generous offer, the lady decided not to avail herself of it and merely selected a few little stones at their cash value and insisted on paying for them on the spot. Borabjee Sam seemed to be hesitating for a moment and then drew forth from his sleeve the last of the little cases. He smiled significantly as he opened it—

"I wish to have the pleasure of showing you this, though it is not for sale." He held it gently up to the light—the most perfect and beautiful pearl on which they had ever laid their eyes!

"Not for sale—what do you mean?"

"I mean it is not for sale at any price that you would be willing to pay. This is the famous 'Pearl of Hoy How,' brought to Ceylon three years ago by a Chinese merchant from that little island. He finally disposed of it to a cousin of ours and from his hands it came into mine. Nothing more absolutely perfect has ever been exhibited in Colombo."

In spite of the fact that our travelers had been warned against the danger of being too enthusiastic over native jewels—for this inevitably raises the price proportionately—they went into perfect raptures over the one now before them and the end of it all was that when the *Bombay* blew her whistle the following morning, the precious pearl from Hoy How was securely locked in the bottom tray of the lady's trunk in her cabin, and the bank account of Borabjee Sam was some four thousand Mexicans to the good.

The good ship continued on her long voyage, touching at Penang and Singapore, and some two weeks later came to anchor under the frowning Peak of Hong Kong, all unconscious of the treasure that still lay hid in the trunk. Yes, there it lay, as Mrs. Witherspoon, its proud owner, believed—for it was none other than she that had purchased it from its owner, Borabjee Sam—and would have continued to lay concealed there for the rest of the voyage to Japan had not the temptation just to look at it once more been too strong to resist.

So, on a quiet afternoon off the coast of Formosa, she locked herself in her cabin and gave herself the exquisite sensation of—

discovering that the famous Pearl of Hoy How had vanished into the thinnest of air! Gone! Absolutely gone! Not a shadow of a trace of it remained!

IN THE LITTLE UPPER ROOM at 5-5-5 in the Alley of the Red Cloud, Wang Foo was closeted with his old friend the Abbot of the Temple of the Queen of Heaven. They had finished the first bowl of fragrant tea, had chipped the dried watermelon seeds—which were always believed to give aid to reflection—and now were slowly and methodically smoking the pipes of peaceful thought.

On the table before them lay two pieces of paper: two most significant messages from two most different sources. Like the tides and currents in the beautiful harbor beneath the windows, one had flowed in from the Eastern world and one from the Western, and they had met and encircled themselves together by the shores of "Fragrant Waters."

One was white, the other was yellow. One represented Europe, the other Asia. One bore the heading of the police department of Hong Kong and was written in round, school-boy English, the other which had been made of the roughest rice-straw, was covered with the ancient symbols of far-away Cathy.

The first had come through the regular agency of His Britannic Majesty's Post Office, the other had come through the very irregular agency of being torn from a poster on the wall at the end of the alley. And yet, in spite of this worldwide difference in form and style, the messages of their contents were identical.

The former read as follows:

"Office of the Chief Inspector, Department of Police, Victoria, Hong Kong.
"To Wang Foo, Esq, Alley of the Red Cloud:
"My Dear Mr. Wang—We are in receipt of a wire from the Department at Yokohama, stating that a lady traveler on the last P. and O. Mail was robbed while in the Hong Kong Hotel of a pearl of the value of several thousand dollars. The jewel was purchased

by her at Colombo and, she claims, was quite a famous one, being, known as 'The Pearl of Hoy How.'
Our department is working on the case here, but I
feel that we need your cooperation in case the jewel
has fallen into Chinese hands.

"I shall be glad to have you call at my office at
any hour after tiffin tomorrow, and, in the meantime,
shall be glad to know from you whether this reported
famous gem is known at all among our Chinese fellow-citizens in the Colony. I am, sir, yours very truly,
"Archibald A. Wallace,
"Chief Inspector of Police."

Wang Foo read it over very slowly and carefully to the Abbot,
translating each separate word as he did so. He had no need to
translate or interpret its yellow companion, for the symbols were
clear and distinct. What they said was:

"Those interested will take notice.
The Pearl of Hoy How arrives this week. And will
leave the next. Act according to the agreement! The
reward is sure!"

The postman had delivered the Inspector's letter to Old Chang,
the gatekeeper, the same forenoon and Wang Foo was thinking over
the words "Pearl of Hoy How" and repeating them to himself as he
was returning from a series of New Year's calls.

He stopped at the corner of the Avenue of Fragrant Waters to
invoke a blessing upon an aged cripple whom he had often be-
friended, and, as he stood there, his eye happened to glance upward at the yellow notices on the opposite wall. He started back a
step in utter astonishment—right before him were the very words
he had been repeating to himself, the identical "Pearl of Hoy How!"

He stepped up to the paper, tore off carefully the portion containing the notice and folding it up in his hands, inserted it
between the pages of the little leather notebook; not, however,

before he had very carefully, with the aid of his crystal spectacles, inspected the entire wall and found that there was not another line or word bearing upon the subject!

The Abbot spoke: "There is no heading and there is no signature. Did you notice that?"

"Quite so, Venerable Father," replied the Detective. "It is anonymous and of course intended to catch the eye of someone who is passing and who wishes to avoid suspicion."

"But why did they not send it through the mails?"

"Ah, a guilty conscience dreads the post office, I have often noticed that."

"Are there not some words from the Sacred Classic of the Christians carved above the entrance in the foreign tongue? I have so been told."

"O, yes, a famous line: 'As Cool Waters to a Thirsty Soul So Is Good News From a Far Country.'"

"Is not that conclusive proof that the hand of the foreigner is in this?"

"It does not actually prove it, but it makes it very likely."

So the two friends talked and talked, and thought it over in the clouds of their own mild native tobacco until the town clock struck the hour of 11. They had reached the following conclusion, viz: A robbery of a very valuable gem had undoubtedly taken place, and apparently while the owners of it were guests in the hotel.

Several parties must be implicated, for it was evident from the yellow notice that a confederate had wired the notice of the purchase from either Colombo or some intervening port, so that it was being looked for on the arrival of the *Bombay*. The Hong Kong agent in the crime must have familiarized himself with the plans of the travelers and possibly hastened their departure from the colony.

The confederate would probably follow on the very next steamer, receive the gem from the hands of the thief, pay him the agreed upon reward and then leave for some European or Australian port where he could dispose of his treasure with much less suspicion than he possibly could on the Island.

The very first step would be to get into confidential touch with the telegraph office and try to trace the message. With this agreement they gave the sacred sign of the Brotherhood—the solemn pledge to inviolate secrecy—and parted with the blessings of the night.

Early the following morning Wang Foo sought an interview with Mr. Robinson, the courteous head of the Great Eastern Telegraphs. The Englishman became deeply interested in the case, and promised to extend to his visitor every facility for tracing the message.

Two difficulties, however, stood in the way: first, all messages over the cables were considered strictly confidential and could only be delivered to the police on the request of the authorities; and, second, they were usually in private codes and their meaning known only to the recipients who held the key. The first was easily disposed of. Wang drew out from his wallet a little card and handed it to the manager. It read:

"To the Great Eastern Telegraphs:
Kindly extend to Mr. Wang Foo any courtesies
in the interests of the Department of Justice.
Arthur Wayne-Evington,
Governor of Hong Kong."

THE SECOND DIFFICULTY he felt could be solved by a package of code books in the drawer of his desk at home.

A copy of every message, other than those to the well-known firms in the colony, was laid before him and he spent a careful hour in looking into two piles, one of which he mentally labeled "probable" and the other "improbable." He requested the privilege of taking the latter with him for further examination and they were duly sealed up in the manager's presence and tucked away in the capacious sleeve of brocade.

In the afternoon he went by appointment to the office of the Chief Inspector and there heard from him all the details of the robbery, as far as the police had been able to trace it—and the very plain truth was that they had not been able to trace it at all.

"The trouble is, Mr. Wang, that we have nothing whatever definite to go upon. The wire from the Department in Yokohama is very brief and unsatisfactory. It merely states that on arrival at the Grand Hotel the tourists found that the jewelry concealed in some clothing in the bottom of a cabin trunk was missing and as it had only been opened once between Ceylon and Japan—and that right here—they at once jumped to the conclusion that the theft had taken place in the colony.

"We have, of course, interviewed the managers and carefully questioned the room-boys and servants, but their minds are as might have been expected—a perfect blank upon the subject.

"My only hope is that possibly the reputation of this jewel might be known to some of the native dealers here, and that through your influence we might get on to the track of it, that is, supposing any attempt has been made to dispose of it in the colony, which seems to me very doubtful."

The Man of Mystery hesitated. Should he or should he not reveal the story of the mysterious yellow paper that he had torn from the wall. How could it help the Inspector? Would the ends of justice allow him to break his pledge of privacy to the old Abbot without his permission? He quickly decided to keep the secret to himself for a while longer—that is, provided none of the native detectives had seen it and noted it.

"You have thoroughly questioned the Chinese officers as to any knowledge on their part of the 'Pearl of Hoy How?'" he asked.

"Yes, sir, Capt. Brownlow has gone all over it with them and sent them to the pawn shops and sailors' dens and they report that it has never been heard of."

Wang Foo's mind was relieved. He had feared that many copies of the notice had been posted up on the city's walls, but evidently there was only one, and that one was now safely in his own possession.

The afternoon was getting late and as he had still a number of ceremonial calls to make, he bade the Inspector good day and, with a promise to call again in the course of the week, he joined the

long line of well-dressed pedestrians on Queen's Road and banished the subject of the robbery from his mind.

A WEEK LATER Inspector Wallace, Capt. Brownlow and Wang Foo
met again by appointment at the department office.

"Well, Mr. Wang," began the chief, "what new light have you to
throw upon the 'Pearl of Hoy How?'"

"Only this," replied the visitor, with a smile of intense satisfaction, "the pearl has been found and is now in my possession safe
and sound. If you two gentlemen will do me the honor to be my
guests at a little informal gathering at my humble home this
evening, I shall be glad to hand it over to you."

"Found!" exclaimed the chief. "Well, Brownlow, that certainly
is a new and mysterious joke on us, and the department. I wonder
if there are two of them."

He handed Mr. Wang a piece of yellow paper—it was a cablegram from Yokohama—which the detective respectfully received
and, putting on his large tortoise-shell spectacles, proceeded to
read aloud:

> "Department of Police, Yokohama, Japan,
> "To the Chief Inspector, Victoria, Hong Kong—
> Pleased to report that valuable jewel known as 'Pearl
> of Hoy How' reported stolen in Hong Kong hotel has
> been discovered by detectives concealed in clothing
> in trunk.
> "Yamashiro Taburo,
> "Chief Inspector, Yokohama Police."

He folded the paper, handed it carefully back to Sir Wallace,
slowly removed his spectacles and remarked to their utter astonishment:

"Gentlemen, I cannot allow a little matter like the finding of
the pearl in Japan to interfere with my proposed plans for your
entertainment this evening. I shall expect you promptly at 8 and"—

he added with an especial emphasis—"I shall be true to my word and return to you, there and then, the beautiful 'Pearl of Hoy How!'"

"What do you make out of it, Brownlow?" inquired the chief, as they resumed their seats and cigars after Wang Foo's departure.

"It's surely too much for me," replied the captain, "but I can tell you one thing, you and I are certainly going to have the great surprise of our lives tonight when we get to his house in Red Cloud Alley, mark that!"

Promptly at 8 o'clock, old Chang drew back the outer bolts and admitted the two foreign officers to the dwelling of Wang Foo, where they were most graciously received and made to sit in the highest row of the red-cushioned New Year's chairs.

The smoking tea and the trays of sweetmeats were promptly introduced and placed before them, but, out of deference to their European lack of skill in handling the Chinese water-pipes, Manila cheroots, of a specialty fine grade were substituted for the latter token of hospitality. The hour passed pleasantly away and the hands of the clock upon the mantel pointed to 9 before they realized it. The great detective rose and spoke:

"My honored guests; it is the hour of 9, a symbolic hour of good luck, I believe, in all Eastern lands. Allow me to have one of the greatest pleasures of the Happy New Year's season and to present to you the matchless jewel, the original and only genuine 'Pearl of Hoy How.' Venerable Old One!" he called through the curtain that concealed the inner apartment, "bring in the 'Pearl!'"

At the word of command the ancient dame appeared, not bearing a jewel in a casket, but leading by the hand one of the sweetest little Chinese maidens that their eyes had ever looked upon! She was beautifully dressed in all the brightly colored silks of the festal season and looked for all the world as if she had just stepped off some daintily painted fan or screen.

She gave them the sweetest of courtesies and modestly blushing at the presence of the European guests, cast her bright little eyes downward to the floor.

The two astonished officers instinctively rose and returned the salutation, then sat down and awaited the coming explanation.

"What is the mystery, Mr. Wang?"

"It is simply this, gentlemen, the theft, or supposed theft, of the jewel at the hotel has been indirectly the means of unearthing a far more serious and dangerous crime; namely, the stealing and selling of a human life!

"This dear little girl was rescued by me three days ago from a gang of villains who stole her from Singapore and were preparing to sell her to a Portuguese theatrical troupe of Macao.

"She was brought up to the colony concealed in a lifeboat on board a steamer, and her coming and going corresponded almost exactly with the dates of the arrival and departure of our friends, the tourists."

"But what led you to connect the two and to suspect the stealing of the child?" asked the interested and puzzled Inspector.

"Well, that was brought about in a very interesting way that would be a little difficult for the European mind to unravel," replied Wang Foo, with a smile. "An anonymous notice, posted on a wall of the city, conveyed the intelligence to someone that the 'Pearl of Hoy How' would arrive on a certain ship and that she was to be met and taken charge of according to a previous agreement.

"This is hardly language that would be used for a mere jewel, and so I naturally suspected a kidnapping or something of that kind and here is the result of the suspicion."

"And was the notice wired up from the Straits?"

"No, we searched every telegram, but without a clew. The notice was brought up by some of the crew of the coaster that left two days ahead."

"And what are you going to do with the little 'Pearl,' now that you have rescued her? Send her back to Singapore? That would be an awful pity."

"Oh, no, gentlemen; that life for her is finished. She will pass into the care of some kind English ladies in the Colony."

"And how about the gang who stole her?"

The man of mystery looked carefully about him to see that every door was closed, and then, with his long uplifted finger motioning for silence and attention, he said: "If you have a half a dozen pairs of good, reliable handcuffs at headquarters, I think I can show you a few Chinese and Portuguese wrists that they would gracefully adorn for the remainder of the New Year's season!"

"Brownlow!" said the Chief, as he rose to bid them good night, "let us go home and polish them up!"

THE GREEN SEDAN

"CHIAO LAI! CHIAO LAI!" shrieked the two forward coolies as they pushed the people right and left in the crowded streets of Kowloon to make way for the burden on their shoulders. "Lai Liao! Lai Liao!" echoed back the two coolies at the rear as they struggled to keep pace with those in front.

"Sedan coming! Sedan coming!" was the cry that opened up the way for the chair between the long lines of pedestrians like a wedge, and "It has come! It has come!" was the signal to close up the ranks again as the bearers hurried along. The multitude—always patient and pliable—were a little more ready than usual to yield the right of why, when they saw that the bearers wore the blue jackets and red-tasseled hats of official servants and that the sedan chair was covered with the green cloth of the mandarin and not with the ordinary blue of the civilian.

They hurried along until they came to the canal that divided the Chinese city from the British Concession and turning sharply to the right reached the stone bridge of The Silver Cloud and passing over entered His Majesty's dominions of Kowloon opposite Hong Kong, better known in their own flowery tongue as "The Nine Dragons That Face the Fragrant Waters."

"Hia Chiao! Hia Chiao!" shrieked the forward crew. "Lower the Sedan! Lower the Sedan!" "Hia Liao! Hia Liao!" "It is lowered! It is lowered!" responded the rear guard, as the caravan came to a sudden halt and deposited their burden at the feet of Capt.

167

HE TRACED
THE CHINESE
CHARACTER FOR
"CASH"

Brownlow of the Colonial Police and two English and Chinese deputies, who were waiting there to receive them.

The officer who accompanied the chair, and who had been riding closely behind it on his shaggy Mongolian pony with his string of jangling sleigh bells, descended and, bowing low to the foreigners, drew forth from his voluminous sleeve a red leather wallet, and opening it, handed the captain a document covered with vermilion seals. The latter, unfolded it and, with the assistance of his secretary-interpreter, read as follows:

"Yamen of the Northern Hsien, District of Kowloon, Canton, 19th Day of the Fifth Moon.

"To His Excellency, The Governor of Hong Kong, Greeting—Sir, acting under instructions from His Excellency the Taotai of this circuit, we hereby hand over to your authority for the administration of justice, the person of one Ling Took, accused of murder within the limits of the European colony. The prisoner is being conveyed out of the Chinese boundaries in an official chair (instead of being chained, as usual, in an open basket) to avoid suspicion and to prevent any attempt at rescue on the part of his fellow villagers, who are reported to be lurking in the vicinity.

"With respect and compliments, I am, sir,

"Wang Ching Tang,

"Magistrate of the District."

"Well, Mackintosh," said the Captain to his deputy, "the prisoner certainly is traveling in style this time, eh? Squatting in a mandarin's chair is a lot more comfortable than being hung to a bamboo pole with a bunch of rusty chains, mark my words."

"It surely is, sir," replied the deputy, "and it's mighty clever of them to smuggle him through the town that way, isn't it? If they'd just brought him through like one of the regulars, he might never have reached us at all."

"Have those hand-cuffs ready when we take him out. I don't know whether they've got him safely ironed up inside there or not and, you know, they're as slippery as eels and we can't afford to lose him now."

"Right you are, sir."

"Here, Ching," turning to the interpreter, "just ask our friend the cavalry-rider if he's got him securely fastened inside the chair."

Ching turned to the officer and rattled off enough words—according to Brownlow's idea—to have said the thing over about 15 times in any other tongue and the officer, on his part, rattled back about the same quantity of expletives, accompanied by the most expressive and emphatic gestures.

"He's all right, sir," said Chung, "he's ironed hand and foot and locked to the back of the chair. He can't move an inch."

"Who's got the key?"

"The officer here has the key, sir, and we can take him right out now."

"All right, open the sedan up, then."

They started to unhook the heavy front curtains, which completely concealed the personage within, when they were interrupted by the clamoring of the chair-bearers for wine-money. "Yang Lao Yea! Yang Lao Yea! Ching Chiu Chien!" they cried, bowing and scraping and extending their palms into the very faces of the officers; "Ocean Mandarin! Ocean Mandarin! Please grant the wine-tip."

"What's the matter now? O, more cumshaw, is it? Well, I suppose they've a hard job to get him here, so give them two Mexicans for the four of them and tell them to keep quiet. I suppose it would be beneath the dignity of the official to accept anything, wouldn't it?"

"O, yes, sir, he couldn't take anything openly before the coolies, but I'll just slip a $5 note into his sleeve while they're looking the other way, sir, and that will make it all right with the dignity. He'll save his face and the money at the same time."

"Well, what are the beggars saying now? For goodness sake! They don't want more, do they?"

"O, no, sir, they are just expressing their thanks to you, that's all."

"What's this Yang something they're always saying?"

"Why, that's 'Ocean Mandarin,' sir, their politest title for you all."

"'Ocean Mandarin'! Do they take us for Admirals or navy men of any kind?"

"Not at all, sir; the word 'Ocean' simply means 'foreign' and applies to anyone who comes from across the seas to China; and, not knowing your exact rank, they simply say 'mandarin' and that covers it all."

The native officer drew from his belt a bunch of curious brass keys and lifting the double curtains called to two of his assistants to help him unlock the prisoner. he started back and throwing up both his hands wildly into the air, shrieked out, "He has escaped!" Sure enough, he was gone—chains, handcuffs, padlocks, and all. But he had left something very significant behind him; something grewsome and tale-telling that would add a ghastly interest to the mystery of his going.

"What's this!" cried Brownlow, as reaching inside he tried to draw forth from the back of the chair a bloody knife that had been plunged—evidently with great force—right through the cushion into the wood behind. He worked it loose and holding it up to the astonished gaze of his deputies saw that it was—not a dagger such as the old warriors carried—but a common sharp-pointed carving knife such as is used by the ordinary Chinese cook in the kitchen.

"Is this murder or is this a threat and a warning?"

"Both, I reckon," said Mackintosh, "but what's that piece of paper sticking to it?"

The captain drew from the blade a piece of yellow paper with Chinese symbols upon it. He was about to ask the interpreter to read it when he suddenly changed his mind and folding it carefully up placed it in his wallet and added significantly; "There's just one pair of Chinese eyes that's going to look at that for me, and Wang Foo's the man that owns them. Here! Wrap this knife carefully up in your handkerchief and take it back with you to headquarters," he said, as he handed the weapon to his deputy, "and mind you don't lose those cash that are tied around the handle, see?"

The captain entered the sedan and striking a match looked around very carefully for any further signs of the prisoner or of bloody legacies that he might have left behind, but there was nothing whatever to be seen; everything inside seemed to be in perfect order.

He stepped out again and ordered the deputies immediately to place the four chair-bearers and the officer under arrest, as they were on British soil and would be needed as witnesses if not as important accessories to the crime. Alas! He was just too late. They, also, had vanished like the mysterious occupant of the chair. The moment they realized what had happened, each one fled in a different direction. "Tung-Si-Nam-Pok" (East-West-South-North) they screamed, and to these various points of the celestial compass they scampered, throwing away their official hats and jackets as they did so, for they knew only too well that the sword of the executioner would be awaiting them if they were caught.

The tail of the Mongolian pony was the only thing left in sight as he disappeared over the bridge of the Silver Cloud with his rider, who likewise bade a very unceremonious farewell to His Britannic Majesty's dominions.

"Well," remarked the philosophical Mackintosh, "Mr. Ling Took has certainly been 'took,' and all that's left for us now is to find out who did the taking. I suppose, captain, we'd better lug this sedan with us back to headquarters."

"By all means, it will form an important link in the evidence—that is, if we ever get any evidence."

Four wharf coolies wore quickly hired and the green sedan was carried on board the Hong Kong ferryboat, followed by the police party who were returning rather crestfallen minus their expected prisoner, but guarding very carefully two rather important mementos of him, namely: the magistrate's official transfer and the bloodstained kitchen knife with its mysterious slip of yellow paper and the string of copper cash.

THE PRECEDING CHAPTERS of the story, up to the time of the discovery of the empty sedan-chair by Capt. Brownlow and his officers, were briefly as follows: Ah Sam, faithful servant and number one houseboy of Mr. and Mrs. Morton of Peak Road terrace, Hong Kong, had mysteriously disappeared about two months before and, in spite of every effort of the police to trace him, he had failed to reveal his whereabouts.

There seemed to be but two possible solutions, viz: Either he had left for parts unknown—possibly the Colonies or America—to secure a raise of salary, or he had fallen overboard from a sampan in the harbor, while crossing to visit his relatives on the Kowloon side. About a month after his disappearance, however, an entirely new aspect was given to the case by the finding of a yellow paper parcel on the front doorstep of the Morton residence with these words written upon the cover, "For the man who overturned my rice bowl!"

On opening it, it was found to contain the hat and gown of Ah Sam with a kitchen knife spotted with blood, and driven through a thick piece of red paper cut in the rough shape of a human heart!

Mr. Morton very promptly put the whole case into the hands of Inspector Wallace of the police, with the result that suspicion at once centered on Ling Took, his former cook, whom Ah Sam was reputed to have been the cause of discharging.

The native detectives explained that the phrase "overturning my rice-bowl" was merely the current expression among servants for "engaging another man in my place," and the paper heart with the knife blade driven through it was a delicate and significant way of saying "That is what I would like to do to you if I could get hold of you."

The enclosure of the hat and the gown—which were positively identified by Mrs. Morton's and the servants as being Ah Sam's—seemed to indicate that Ling Took had secured his heart's desire and wreaked his vengeance on the houseboy. Now as all Asiatics have a habit, after committing a crime, of returning, almost without exception, to the haunts of their native town or village—probably with the idea of securing the propitiation of their local divinities—the authorities naturally sought for the missing cook in the Kowloon district and it was not very long before they discovered him concealed in the garret of a bean-oil shop which was presided over by his mother's uncle. Two little street urchins had recognized him one day and volunteered, quite innocently, to lead the yamen-runners directly to the house.

He was promptly seized and dragged by the cue to the yamen, where, in spite of his shrieks for mercy and the loud protestations of his relatives and friends, he was given a preliminary bambooing—"just to quiet him down"—and thrown into a loathsome cell.

The Taotai, acting under instructions from His Excellency the Viceroy of Canton (who was quite anxious for political reasons to keep on good terms with the Governor of the colony), had ordered to have him handed over to the English police and arrangements had been made to meet them at the international boundary by the Bridge of the Silver Cloud on the very day that our story opens.

In the meantime, his relatives and acquaintances had left no stone unturned to secure his release. Every dollar in the native bank and every bit of cash that could be borrowed or "squeezed" out of the business of the family had been offered for bribes, but, strange to say, so far without success.

As a last resort they threatened mob violence, and papers attached to stones and tiles were thrown over the walls into the magistrate's courtyard announcing that neither he nor his jailers would ever reach "the foreign devils'" boundary alive.

Late on a Monday evening two runners were sent out from the yamen; one bore a message to all the teahouses and gathering places of the town that Ling Took would be delivered over to the foreigners on Wednesday morning, and the other bore a sealed message to the Governor that he would be handed over at The Bridge of the Silver Cloud at noon on Tuesday. The mob gathered early on Wednesday around the yamen gates, and, increased from 100 or 200 to nearly 1000—friends, loafers, vagabonds, curiosity-seekers and all the rabble of a Chinese town—demanded in forcible terms the release of the prisoners.

Suddenly a company of soldiers armed with spears and old-fashioned muskets appeared at the entrance and, with the beating of two large gongs, raised a banner with these words upon it: "Let all the people take notice! By order of His Excellency the Viceroy,

Ling Took the murderer was handed over to His Excellency the Governor of Hong Kong for punishment yesterday morning. Let all the people now quietly disperse, or most serious consequences will follow!"

Realizing then that they had been outwitted by their own officials, the crowd took the only satisfaction that was left them, and, heaping curses and execrations upon the heads of all in the yamen, they threw all the available stones over the walls into the courtyard, and bespattering the whole front of the Hall of Justice with mud, slowly and sullenly dispersed.

The prisoner, on the morning before, having been securely ironed on hands and feet, and having also been duly gagged to prevent an outcry, was in the magistrate's presence chained to the chair of his secretary's sedan, and, the curtains being closely drawn, was smuggled out of town without arousing even the slightest suspicion.

What became of him and how, without disturbing the sedan in any way and without attracting the notice of his bearers who were both before him and behind him, he escaped and left the bloody knife in his place, was a genuine mystery, destined to baffle the minds of Chinese and Europeans alike.

IN THE UPPER ROOM at No. 5-5-5 of the Red Cloud, Wang Foo, the Prince of Detectives, was resting in his bamboo chair after a day of rather strenuous labors. Old Chang, the gate-keeper, had been dispatched with a message to the Abbot at the Temple of the Queen of Heaven and the Venerable Grand One, matron of the establishment, was boiling water in the kettle to have it ready for the tea bowls when the visitor should arrive.

Of course he had been interested in the case, even long before Inspector Wallace called to consult with him about it, for there was nothing concerning the welfare of the community, especially in the matter of the administration of justice, that escaped his notice. Disguised as an itinerant seller of books, he had been on several trips to Kowloon across the harbor and had chatted with many a tea house proprietor and with underlings of the magistrate's yamen and had drawn out from them the general consensus of opinion regarding the green sedan and the mysterious disappearance of Ling Took. Referring to his little leather notebook, he had tabulated the various theories under three separate heads:

First—Those who believed that he had never been put into the chair at all, that the magistrate had been bribed to release him secretly, and that the knife and the bloody paper were all part of a well-thought-out plan to deceive the public.

Second—Those who insisted that the accompanying officer had released him and had bribed or drugged the coolies while on the way from the yamen to the international boundary.

Third—Those who attributed it all to "Tien Ming" or "Heaven's Decree" and believed that the demons of vengeance had spirited him away to the Court of Yo Wang, the Ruler of Hades. Revolving these all over in his blind, he decided to refer them to his venerable friend and counselor the Abbot, for no one of them was at all satisfactory to himself, although the Inspector and the police had practically settled their minds as to No. 2 and laid the guilt at the door of the officer and the chair-carriers, whose sudden departure and flight only served to confirm their decision.

There was a knock at the outer gate, and the voice of old Chang was heard calling: "Open from within!" The Abbot entered and the Venerable Grand One received him with due solemnity.

"Is the Master within the Palace Courts?" he asked.

"He awaits your Highness' presence under our cottage roof," was the reply.

Wang Foo at once descended the little stairs and after the ceremonial tea and pipes they mounted together to "The Hall of Quiet Meditation," which was one of the euphonious titles of the Confucian scholar's study.

"Well, what progress have we made?" began the ecclesiastic.

"Here are the three lines of public opinion," replied the host, as he handed over the notebook with his comments.

The visitor drew out from his sleeve an ancient spectacle case of shark skin and slowly opening a pair of crystal goggles adjusted them to his eyes.

He read slowly and carefully and then said, as he laid the book upon the table, "No one of these is correct. No one of them satisfies my mind. There is something underneath all this which neither the public nor the police know anything about. You noticed the red cord which was tied about the knife handle? How many brass cash did it have upon it?"

"Exactly five."

"You have here the upper curtain of the sedan, have you not?"

"Yes; I borrowed it from the police yesterday, as you requested."

"Good! Let me examine it carefully. You notice the small cash embroidered in the corners? They are also exactly five. Now look very carefully at the red seal in the center of the paper through which the knife was plunged; do you not see the dim outline of five separate cash?"

Wang Foo looked up and his eyes met the abbot's. He knew from his tone that they were on the eve of a great discovery. "Speak on, speak on, venerable father," he cried in his eagerness: "tell me, I pray you, what secret is in your mind."

The Abbot hesitated a moment and glanced around the room. "We are safe here?"

"Absolutely so."

"Close the window and draw the curtain, for we know not where human eyes and ears may lurk."

He took a brush and dipping it in the ink, traced upon the paper before them the Chinese character for "cash." He divided the two halves apart with another brush of red, and as he did so said: "It is KO, the same sound as brother, the meaning is clear. It is the secret order of the Five KO's or Brothers and the five cash constitute their mystic sign. The whole thing is the work of the Brotherhood and it only remains for us to find out exactly who are in it and why they released Ling Took."

"You believe, then, that the sedan is the special property of the Brotherhood and is used for their secret meetings?"

"Most certainly I do. It is used to carry the trusted ones to the place of meeting and there is some way by which they can enter and leave it without detection, and"—he nodded with especial

emphasis—"it was by that way that Ling Took escaped. Go to Headquarters tomorrow and examine the base of the chair and especially the floor-boards and report to me in the evening at the
Temple."

It was late in the evening of the following day when Wang Foo
entered the Abbot's private apartment and reported to him the
results of his investigation.

He had found that instead of being securely nailed on as usual,
the entire floor-boards were in a solid frame and that on releasing
two wooden pins, which could be easily pushed out with the hand,
the entire inner chair could be removed without touching the rest
of the sedan. He explained it all carefully to his host.

"Exactly what I supposed. So if the sedan were placed over a
trapdoor the chair and its occupant could slip through it without
disturbing even the curtains, could they not?"

"Venerable Father, it is as you say."

The Abbot went on: "Now, somewhere between the magistrate's
yamen and the Bridge of the Silver Cloud, that sedan was stopped,
and"—he added most significantly with a gesture of his uplifted
hand—"the chair and its contents went down through the trap. The
prisoner was then unbound, the knife and the paper plunged
through the cushion and the chair returned to its place again before the bearers moved on! Do you see it now?"

"Venerable Sagacious One, I do."

"We need only one link more in the chain. We must find the
exact house in front of which the bearers rested with their burden.
We must mark the spot carefully for it will not only give us the
clew to the Ah Sam murder case, but—which is of far greater importance to our country—it will enable us to reveal to the Viceroy
the much-looked-for secret meeting place of those dangerous
insurrectionists, the Brotherhood of the Five Brass Cash."

WITHIN LESS THAN 10 DAYS from the meeting of Wang Foo and the
abbot the Vice Regal authorities at Canton had accomplished the
unearthing of the headquarters of the rebels and the ringleaders

were safely lodged in the Provincial Prison. A careful investigation revealed the following facts:

First—The sedan had stopped for the usual 10-minute "tea and smoke" in front of the "Rest House of the Heavenly Genii" not 100 yards from the old city gate of Kowloon. When the bearers put it down the poles just touched the edge of the resthouse sign, the front coolie indicating the place very carefully.

This brought the base of it directly over the trap door in the sidewalk, which was made of a heavy piece of timber swinging on an oiled pair of hinges. This coolie was a member of the Brotherhood and had been carefully instructed by his superior officer in the band, who was none other than the magistrate's secretary; the other coolies were entirely innocent.

Second—Ling Took was taken down through the trap, released and sworn in as a member of the Brotherhood as a reward for his safety, and the bloody knife and paper plunged through the seat cushion in the chair, which was then pushed upward and fastened in its place. Being an official chair, it was very heavy and the difference in weight was not noticed by the bearers.

Third: The Magistrate acted in good faith and was entirely innocent. The Secretary, himself an important officer of the Secret Brotherhood, suggested the use of the official chair, having been bribed by the relatives of the prisoner to secure his release in some way. He was accustomed to attend the weekly meetings of the Order by being carried to this spot in the sedan, and after entering the trap to substitute another person in the chair, who was then carried by the unsuspecting coolies to the ferry-boat and continued on his way to Hong Kong for the night, returning the same way before daylight in the morning. The uniforms being identical, the Chinese official hat was pulled down over his eyes and a pair of large horn goggles prevented the coolies from recognizing any difference in the face. Of course he never spoke to them, so there was no danger of detection from the voice, all directions as to time, etc., having been given before leaving the yamen.

"BUT WHAT ACTUALLY BECAME of Ah Sam?" inquired Inspector Wallace of Wang Foo, when the latter had completed his final denouement in the Office at Headquarters. "Did Ling Took actually murder him or was he drowned in the harbor?"

"Neither," replied the detective, "the two knives and the paper hearts were merely threats to keep him away from the Colony. They frequently scare each other out of a town that way."

"Well, where is he now? Has he ever turned up?"

"Just now," replied the Man of Mystery, as he glanced at his watch—"just now it is a quarter to one, and I imagine he is engaged in the peaceful occupation of passing the soup in the dining room of the Shanghai Hotel, for," he added with a smile, "that is where he is now serving as the number-two boy."

"And what of Ling Took? Will he slip out of their hands as he did out of ours? They caught him when they raided the den, didn't they?"

"No, he happened to be away on the day that they seized the others, and none of the Brotherhood would divulge his whereabouts."

"Well, where do you yourself think he is? He surely wouldn't go back to the oil-shop again, would he? What do you think has become of him?"

"I might answer that question very appropriately in the words of the Classics, Mr. Wallace. Do you recall what Confucius said to the great Tze Loo when he asked him where the old cook had gone? It is written in one of the last chapters of *The Analects*."

"I am afraid, Mr. Wang," replied the Inspector, "that my recollection of those old philosophers is a trifle rusty. What was it the old sage said?"

"Why, simply this: the lord of the kitchen who had killed the fowls and dressed the millet and feasted the disciples, had mysteriously disappeared and Tze Loo asked the Master where he thought he had gone, and the Master merely replied in his terse and dignified way. 'Yin Chik,' 'he is hiding!'"

THE PHANTOM JUNK

ALL WAS BUSTLE AND CONFUSION at the wharf of the China Mutual Navigation Company in Shanghai on the July afternoon that the good ship *Tien Pao* was taking on her passengers and cargo for Ningpo. And when we say "confusion," we don't mean the orderly American kind that we are accustomed to, but the real Chinese variety, which is a very different thing.

To the ordinary visitor from Western lands it was simply pandemonium let loose. Coolies were rushing in every direction with bags of rice and beans and compradores (or "overseers") were shrieking to them at the top of their lungs. Native passengers were pushing and jostling and only the huge nets spread out on either side prevented their falling overboard into the river.

The only quiet spot seemed to be the little forward gangway, where a few European passengers were climbing up to the cabins especially reserved or them.

Ching, the first pilot, was on police duty here with a long bamboo to indicate forcibly to the Asiatics that "East Is East and West Is West" and that they belonged only on the after part of the steamer. Order soon came out of chaos as the whistle blew for the departure.

Capt. Clarke—ever popular with his European passengers—took his place on the deck just in front of the wheelhouse, Ching pulled in the little gangplank and shut the gate, and with the order "Let her go!" the chains rattled along the aides and the *Tien Pao* swung out into the stream.

181

"Great Heavens! It's the devil's own junk again a-sailing through the trees."

She had been an old P. and O. coaster in her better days and was certainly the worse for wear, but she was holding her own with the larger and finer liners because of the significance of her name—which with the Chinese meant everything. "Tien Pao," or "Heavenly Protection," was their great guarantee of safety and it was a lucky day for her owners when those great golden characters were painted on her sides.

Even the hundreds of little red paper slips which were tossed into the stream as she churned up the foam could add but little as offerings to the river ghosts when high heaven had her under its benign protection.

Down she steamed between the two long lines of shipping. Over the Hoo-sung Bar and out into the yellow waters of the great delta of the Yangtze, the father of Chinese waters, and took her course southward toward the Islands of Poo Too. All went well until just after the hour of dinner when she started to enter the Black Camel Channel and sighted straight ahead the warning beacon on the cliff near the dangerous reef known to navigators as the "Camel's Hump." What happened to her there—in spite of the protection of the heavenly name—was told in the "Extra" issued early the next morning by the Shanghai *Dally News*:

> "Extra—Serious Maritime Disaster—The Ningpo
> Liner *Tien Pao* a Total Loss on the Poo Toos."
> "The S. S. *Wing Pao* of the Coast Mutual Navigation
> Company arrived this morning early, bringing the
> officers and passengers of the S. S. *Tien Pao* of the
> same line, which went hard and fast onto the Camel's
> Hump Tuesday evening while trying to avoid a col-
> lision with a large Ningpo junk.
>
> "Although a strong ebb tide was running at the
> time, her passengers and mails were safely landed
> in the ship's boats near the Hai Toy beacon, where
> the native officials did everything in their power to
> make them comfortable until the returning steamer
> was signaled and took them off the following day.

"Capt. and Mrs. Gerald Duncan of Melbourne and the Misses Jones of the English Church Mission School at Hangchow were the only European passengers on board.

"They speak most highly of the conduct of Capt. Clarke and his officers, who did everything possible to allay excitement and to insure the rescue of the Chinese passengers and who never left the ship until the very last one had been safely landed."

Not very many days after the above "extra" things had settled down again to their usual routine in the maritime circles of the settlement at Shanghai and the morning issue of the *Daily News* announced to the world that a Court of Inquiry would assemble at His Britannic Majesty's Consulate on Aug. 1 to investigate the loss of the Coast Mutual Navigation Company's steamship *Tien Pao* on the "Camel's Hump," and that said court would be made up of the following officers, viz: Captain, Hon. George R. Wemyss of H. M. S. *Rainbow*; Capt. Lewis M. Pilsbury of the Blue Funnel Liner *Achilles* and pilot John A. Mosely, senior of the Lower Yangtze Pilots' Association.

Under ordinary circumstances the sessions of the court and the verdict they would render would not have attracted a very great amount of attention. Seafaring men up and down the coast would have talked it over and commented upon the fairness or unfairness of the Judgment and Capt. Clarke's personal friends would have given him their usual sympathy and then the circumstances of the wreck would one by one have dropped out of the public's mind—just as the timbers and planks of the old *Tien Pao* were dropping into the waters of oblivion with every rising tide that broke over the Camel's Hump.

But the circumstances, on the contrary, were of such an extraordinary nature that before the court had been in session a week the *Tien Pao* wreck and the very mysterious testimony and surroundings were the universal subject of conversation from one end of the town to the other! It was not only discussed at all the clubs

and afternoon teas, but it got into the native papers and compradores and coolies alike enjoyed whole columns of it over the pipes
and tea bowls. They called it "The Strange Story of the Devil Boat,"
but Mrs. Walpole, the wife of the British consul, had most felicitously named it "The Mystery of the Phantom Junk" and this happy
title helped to extend the circulation even farther than it might
otherwise have gone.

What was this "Mystery" and why was the junk called a "Phantom"? Listen! The testimony of Capt Clarke, under direct examination and under cross-examination, was perfectly clear and distinct—nothing could be more so. In a very condensed form, it was
simply this:

Just before eight bells on the evening of Tuesday, July 11, he
was standing on the forward deck of the steamer, right in front of
the wheelhouse, and was talking to Capt. and Mrs. Duncan, when
he noticed a bank of fog settling over the outer Loo Choo Islands
and working its way rather quickly toward the Blade Camel Channel, through which the ship would soon have to pass.

He excused himself to his passengers and, entering the wheelhouse, sent Jackson, the first mate, down to his supper and himself took charge of the course, with Ching and Chang, the Chinese
pilots (known on board as "Dead Eye" and "The Admiral") at the
wheel. They kept on their regular "so'west by west, half west," with
the Hai Toy beacon straight ahead, although the strong ebb was
drawing them a little nearer the cliff than usual, when the fog
seemed to settle right across the southern half of the channel, and
they changed the course half a point to give the "Camel's Hump" a
generous margin.

Suddenly, without a moment's warning of horn or gong or bell,
a great black junk appeared on the starboard bow, driving at full
speed with every sail of matting set and headed directly for the
Tien Pao.

There was only one chance to avoid the collision and Clarke
took it. "Hard-a-starboard!" he shrieked to Dead-Eye and The Admiral, and they threw the wheel over like old and experienced
helmsmen. "Away over with it!" as he pulled with all his strength

on the whistle handle and sent out the danger signal. "Away over with it—for your lives!"

"Belongee way ober, Sah," was the answer of the faithful two. The good old *Tien Pao* reeled over to her side as she swung around under the strain, then righted herself for a moment, gave a great forward plunge and with a crash like a thunder-bolt landed right in the center of the reef.

"Full speed astern—full speed astern!" The gongs rang out in the engine room and the propellers did their best, but it was too late. The steamer shook like a leaf but refused to budge—she was there to stay, and Capt. Clarke and his officers hastened to attend to the saving of the lives in their care.

"Where is the junk?" was the very first question. "Did she clear the reef?" The fog seemed to lift like a curtain and roll itself out into the ocean; the channel was clear from end to end and the junk has vanished into air. Not on the reef or rocks; not sailing the channel; not on the shore—no! Gone! Dissolved like the "baseless fabric of a vision." Not a sign or trace of her remained.

"You have seen that junk?" cried the captain to Ching and Chang. "What side he walkee?"

"Chinamen talkee him b'long all samee debbil boat—no can savee what side him walkee—s'pose him fly away, hab got debbil wings. Velly bad joss see dat debbil boat—all times makee ship reckee—velly bad joss."

Pale as ghosts and trembling all over, these poor victims of the wrath of some native divinity crouched along the deck, ready to throw themselves into the sea, when Jackson, the mate, recalled them to their senses with,

"Here, Dead-Eye, you and your mate get to work here quick and help lower this boat."

Capt. Clark was, as said, perfectly clear as to the junk. He knew it was a Ningpo coaster from the black lines and the high poop and he was very positive as to all its sails being set and as to the course which threatened his steamer.

He could hardly realize the suddenness with which it seemed to loom up out of the fog nor had he any explanation to offer of its almost miraculous disappearance. But he and old "Dead-Eye," the pilot, were the only human beings who saw it! Not another person on the steamer—officer, passenger or member of the crew—saw any sign of the junk before or after the wreck.

Nay, more, the testimony brought out that it was practically impossible for any vessel of that size to have been in the Channel without having been seen before or after the closing-in of the fog.

The testimony of Ching, the pilot, who was very closely questioned through the official interpreter, entirely corroborated that of the captain, but went a little more into details.

He was quite positive it was a Ningpo junk, of the large sea-going class, with three masts and high poop; all the sails were set and it was coming directly toward the steamer on a course that would certainly have struck her on the port bow if she had not at once put her helm hard down to avoid it. He saw the great goggle eyes on the junk and the tusk-like prows that made it look like some monster of the seas, but he had not been able to decipher the name.

One piece of incidental description—which, by the way, seemed especially to interest the sea-faring men present at the Court—was the fact that she had three flags flying, one on the foremast, one on the mainmast and one on the jigger.

Each flag had a white arrowhead in the center and they were flying from a bamboo framework that held them out taut and made them instantly visible and not to be mistaken for anything else.

All the large Chinese shipping firms at Shanghai and at Ningpo had been appealed to, but none of them knew of any junk company whose sign was the three white arrows; and so the mysterious black flags began to have the mingled fascination and horror of the skull-and-crossbones of the old-time Western pirates.

The Court of Enquiry decided to take a recess of a week to enable its members to visit the scene of the disaster in person and to make further private investigations regarding the characters and histories of the principal parties concerned.

No verdict had been reached, but the general opinion seemed to be that the captain would be acquitted, because he had chosen

the safer and wiser course when suddenly placed in a most difficult position that required prompt and decisive action.

And so the whole question was "thrown into the ring" and the
community was left to decide for itself just what it was the captain
saw—if, indeed, he really saw anything at all. In a word, what was
the phantom junk? Where did it come from and where did it go to?

That was enough to keep all the gossips and talkers at homes,
at the clubs and in the streets busy during the next 10 days and to
abstract from them every variety of opinion. Everyone that had ever
had any thrilling experience or a "spooky" or ghostly nature trotted it out and touched it up for the occasion—and made it doubly
horrible if it had been at sea and not on the land.

Old skippers drew out of the sea-chests of their memories tales
and stories of serpents and dragons, phantom ships and spectral
visions of the deep.

Some joked about it, some laughed and even ventured to ask
what Capt. Clarke had eaten for dinner that night, as if his vision
of the junk had been merely a torture of the demon of indigestion.

Some looked serious—some merely shook their heads and said
nothing. It went so far that even the Public Library had special
calls for volumes of the weird and grewsome, and "The Ancient
Mariner" was taken down from many a shelf and read over again
in the silent hours of the night.

"What of Clarke and the phantom junk?" became the test-word
that divided the coast ports from Hong Kong to Tientsin really into
three separate classes. We will call them "A," "B" and "C," as follows:

Class A believed him to be absolutely honest and to have been
the innocent victim of a temporary delusion or mental aberration.

Class B believed him to be honest, but weak and his vision of
the junk to have been the result of some stimulant or drug.

Class C believed him to be absolutely dishonest; to have concocted the junk story to deceive the public and to have wrecked
the steamer for the sake of her insurance.

Each one of these classes had its own arguments to bring forward and its own precedents and examples, but, on the other hand,

each of them seemed to have been thoroughly and satisfactorily answered by the testimony on the other side. Those who knew him intimately claimed that he had never been the victim of delusions of any kind whatever, but was an exceedingly even-tempered and well-balanced man.

All the stories as to the possibility of his having been intoxicated were at once ruled out by the fact that he was known to be a strict total abstainer. So, when old Tompkins, the tea broker, remarked at the club tiffin that it was nothing at all to see black junks after a spree—for he always saw red and green and painted ones with monkeys and parrots on them when he "went out to sea"—his joke recoiled upon himself.

The idea that the captain had actually put the steamer on the rocks intentionally—which idea was only held by a very few of the residents—was based on the fact that he was known to have bought a considerable share of the company's stock and that he had been overheard to say on one occasion that "he hoped the old girl would lay her bones on the rocks before she got much more cranky." That being a very common remark, however, among the skippers assigned to the old and worn-out coasters, it failed to have much effect upon the court.

Wide and divergent as were these opinions there was a most striking agreement upon one point, viz: that no real junk had ever appeared upon the scene and that what the captain saw was entirely subjective. The European mind seemed to be a unit on this, but it utterly failed to shake the testimony and the obstinacy of old "Dead-Eye," the pilot, who swore with a choice variety of Chinese oaths that what he had seen was decidedly objective.

"My talkee tlue, my no speakee lies, my no smokee opee, my no dlinkee wisky, my no go clazy makee fool pidgin. My can savee look see debbil junk come dat side. My b'longee pilotee more 10 years time; how fashion you tinkee my no can savee? Chinaman pilotee no b'longee fool."

So the public still awaited a permanent solution of the problem.

THE SEAGOING TUGBOAT *Hercules* of the Shanghai Lighter Company had been chartered to take the consul, the members of the court, Capt. Clarke, Mate Jackson, "Dead-Eye" Ching the pilot, and several European and Chinese witnesses down to the Poo Toos and the scene of the wreck, and was all ready early Monday morning for the trip, when word was received by the agents asking them to hold the trip over until Friday, as very important business detained the consul and it was absolutely impossible for him to leave. Just what this urgent call for postponement really meant nobody seemed to know, but rumor had it that important evidence in the case was being expected from another port and the consul thought it best to wait for it.

What really happened was simply this: he had come to the conclusion to send for the one man in all China who could help him to unravel the mystery, and had cabled to Hong Kong for Wang Foo, the prince of all native detectives.

Remembering his former successes in matters that had baffled the English police and his wonderful skill in getting at the real facts underlying the Chinese secretive ways, he felt that the case of Ching the pilot could be safely put in his hands, and this would undoubtedly throw valuable light on the case of the captain. Wang Foo replied immediately, stating that he would leave on the French mail Monday, and requesting a private, day's interview with the consul before his departure for the Poo Toos.

No detective appeared at the Consulate and the consul did not go to Police Headquarters to meet any such officer—as far as any one knew—but he did spend several hours Thursday afternoon and evening in the inner apartment of a large native drugstore where a supposed physician from Hong Kong wished to explain to him in detail the merits of a remarkable new cure for the opium habit, in which cures the consul was known to be deeply interested.

The *Hercules* steamed away promptly on Friday morning and on arriving at the scene of the wreck the whole matter was gone into most thoroughly. At the request of the court Capt. Clarke took her over the exact course that he had followed on that day, showing exactly where he sighted the fatal junk and how by the sudden turning to avoid the collision he was driven right on the Camels Hump.

The party expressed a wish to go on board the hull of the *Tien Pao*, the forward part of which was still intact, though the after half of the vessel was rapidly breaking up. The sea was moderate enough for small boats to approach with safety and the visitors climbed on board. The captain took them to the wheelhouse and showed them just where he and "Dead-Eye" stood when the junk loomed up in front of them and he gave the order to put the helm hard over.

Not the least interested among the spectators was the consul's new house-boy who was accompanying him as a personal valet and who listened to every word of the captain's with remarkable attention.

Nobody, however, noticed him, nor the fact that he occasionally made notes in a little Chinese book in his sleeve; nor that he lingered behind the others when they passed out of the wheelhouse onto the deck, nor that he took out a little pocket flashlight and eagerly examined every nook and corner of the room, nor that he got down on his knees and carefully searched the floor, and, finding there a few pieces of broken glass, wrapped them in his silk handkerchief and carefully tucked them away in his girdle—nobody noticed this; why should they? He was only a servant in attendance upon his master.

Nor did anybody pay special attention to the fact that he seemed to be on very good terms with "Dead-Eye," that he talked with him and smoked with him nearly all the way down and back and asked all kinds of interesting questions about a Chinese pilot's life and invited him to be his guest at the Tea-Garden-Theatre in the Nanking Road that evening—nobody, I say, paid any especial attention to these things, except the Consul himself, who after the theatre that evening had a long and secret interview with this self-same house-boy in the office and listened with eager attention to every word he had to say.

THE COURT OF INQUIRY at His Britannic Majesty's consulate was again in session, having been postponed a week owing to the "unfortunate indisposition"—so the papers stated—of a very important witness. The room was crowded with spectators, who awaited with no little eagerness the final settlement of the case and the solution—if solution there was to be—of the mystery of the phantom junk which had wrecked the good ship *Tien Pao*.

"Capt. Clarke," began Sir William Walpole, the vice consul, "there is one very important point which seems to have hitherto been overlooked in the examination, and that is the question of the glasses you used when you saw the junk through the wheelhouse window. The window, of course, was open, was it not?"

"Yes, sir, being a warm Summer night, all the windows were wide open."

"You had a perfectly clear field of vision, had you not? No person was standing by outside upon the deck? Nothing was in the way?"

"Nothing whatever, sir. Captain and Mrs. Duncan were on the other side of the ship, sir, just outside their cabin door."

"The smoke from the funnel was not blowing that way at all, was it?"

"No, sir; you see the wind was on the beam and all the smoke was going off on the starboard side."

"Now Capt. Clarke, please state to the court very distinctly whether you saw the approaching vessel with your naked eyes or whether you saw it only through your glasses."

"Now that you bring that point up, sir, my recollection is that I saw it only through the glasses."

"You are quite positive about that?"

"Quite positive, sir."

"What glasses do you use?"

"A fine pair of Admiralty binoculars, sir."

"They were in good condition and perfectly reliable?"

"Nothing finer on the coast, sir."

"And you had these in your hand when you entered the wheel house?"

"Well, now that you ask that question, sir, I believe I had lent them to Mrs. Duncan and she had not yet returned them. I just picked up the pilot's night glasses from the shelf, sir, and used them—they're a splendid pair, too, sir."

"Yes, Mrs. Duncan says that she had your glasses in her cabin at the time of the accident and handed them to you afterwards in the boat."

"Quite right, sir."

"And were these glasses the same ones that 'Dead-Eye' the pilot used?"

"The same, sir; there was only the one pair at the wheel."

"And did you hand them to him at the time?"

"Well, you see, sir, the junk was so near us that I didn't need them, so I just passed them over to him."

"What happened then?"

"He just had time for one squint at her. He screamed out 'Devil's Wings' or 'Devil' something or other and dropped them on the floor."

"What became of these glasses afterwards?"

"I haven't the slightest idea, sir; I presume they were stolen with the rest of the loot."

Sir William at this point turned to his Chinese valet and asked him to unroll from a silken handkerchief a pair of binoculars. Handing them to Capt. Clarke, he proceeded: "Does this look like the pair, captain?"

"They seem to be the same ones, sir."

"Now please oblige me by looking through them at the garden opposite the consulate and tell me exactly what you see."

The captain stopped to the window and, raising the glasses to his eyes, cried out in a voice that startled the assemblage: "Great Heavens! It's the devil's own junk again a-sailing through the trees!"

"Hand them back to me, if you please," said the consul, and unscrewing the larger lens in the right-hand tube he held up before the court a small piece of painted glass, exclaiming as he did so, "Gentlemen of the Court, I have the honor and satisfaction of presenting to you the original and only genuine phantom junk.

"Here it is, painted in almost microscopic proportions on this inner glass and any one of you can see it sailing through the trees of my garden—or up the streets of Shanghai—just as distinctly as the captain saw it that evening sailing down on him through Black Camel Channel.

"Gentlemen, the mystery is solved and it only remains for me to introduce to you now the one person to whom—more than to any other—we owe a debt of gratitude for clearing it up. Permit me to present to the court Mr. Wang Foo of Hong Kong, better known to the community as 'The Prince of Chinese Detectives,' who has consented to unravel the tale for you himself."

The consul's valet stepped forward to the desk, quickly removed a pair of bushy eyebrows with a corresponding mustache and goatee, lifted off a cumbersome wig with a servant's cap attached and unbuttoning a long blue house gown, retransformed himself into the famous visitor from the Southern colony of "Fragrant Waters."

When the court and the spectators had recovered from their surprise they instinctively greeted him with a round of generous applause, which Wang Foo most graciously acknowledged, and in a few terse sentences unfolded his story.

"Sir William and gentlemen of the court: I have just three important facts to lay before you. They illustrate, as usual, the fallacy—not to say the injustice—of popular inferences from a case of this kind and also the difficulty of the European mind in unraveling a tangling question when the Chinese are equally involved.

"My first and foremost pleasure is to vindicate the captain and his faithful pilot Ching (or 'Dead-Eye') from every lurking suspicion and reflection that may rest upon them. They are equally innocent. They are not users of opium or alcohol or drugs of any kind whatever.

"They are certainly not dishonest and even the hint that they combined to wreck the *Tien Pao* for the sake of the insurance is unworthy of those who made it nor are they victims of hallucinations. They imagined no 'subjective vision'—the junk they saw was decidedly objective, though made of delicate Chinese paints and not of seagoing timber.

"They simply saw what any of you, gentlemen, would have seen had you suddenly taken those glasses into your hands at that time.

"My second point involves a brief introduction into Chinese ideas of art little known as yet to Europeans. You have many of you seen the delicate snuff-bottles of crystal and of jade which are treasured so highly by our native collectors of antiques.

"The hand-painting is so minute that it requires a magnifying glass to bring out the details. In an ancient volume of our Empire they tell wondrous stories of these artists who were able even to picture an entire landscape in the center of a tiny crystal. 'Yiu Wei Fah Tai' is an ancient saying which refers to this: 'Through the minute we reveal the grand.'

"Many of the temples in the interior have sacred stones with tiny openings in them through which the devotees may behold the glories of a world beyond. In the case before us, the Temple of Nu Hai Wang (the Goddess of the Sea) has a stone of this kind through which the faithful may, by the payment of a moderate fee, behold the glories of the sea and the great junks that sail on it

"One of these paintings is that of a great Ningpo junk known as 'The Devil's Wings' with the three white arrows of death flying from her masks. It is really used to extort money for the temple. The great tablet over the gateway says, 'King Woo Tang Lai Yao Kwai Ling,' which is 'He who tribute never brings, will surely see the Devil's Wings.'

"Now, to see the 'Devil's Wings' being the very worst luck for a native sailor, he generally pays his tribute to the goddess promptly. A skillful duplicate of this painting of the great junk was inserted in the right-hand tube of the wheelhouse glasses and with a hasty glance would give exactly the impression which the captain and the pilot received.

"Who placed it there and what was his object?

"Gentlemen, I come to my third and last point. It has been my pleasure to exonerate the captain and old Ching—it now becomes my duty to point out to you the actual guilty party. He is sitting there in the second row of the witnesses' seats, and his name is Chang; he is the second pilot and known on board the *Tien Pao* as 'The Admiral.'

"He had the painting made and the glass cut to fit the binoculars. He had planned to hand them to Ching, the first pilot, at some convenient hour of the night and by making him see the junk frighten him into going to this temple as soon as he got ashore and making a liberal offering to the Goddess of the Sea.

"The captain coming in at the unexpected moment spoiled his plans for the Goddess and put the old *Tien Pao* on the reef, that is all. I suspected all this after my visit to the Temple with Ching and I found the glass on the floor of the wheelhouse while I was disguised as the consul's valet and so completed the evidence.

"Whether you can convict a man of wrecking a vessel when his only intention was to raise funds out of a fellow sailor for a celestial Goddess, gentlemen, is a delicate point of law that you—and not I—must decide."

"May I ask you just one question, Mr. Wang, please," said Inspector Gubbins of the police, as he rose to place the second pilot under arrest. "What special interest could Chang have had in going to all this trouble to raise funds for the Goddess? Was he specially devout?"

"No, not at all," replied Wang Foo, with a smile. "But you see his brother is the chief priest of the Goddess, and has charge of the cash receipts, and, as is usual in China, the family divides the proceeds!"

THE ABBOT'S BEADS

"WELL, AND WHAT'S THE MATTER with this poor old chap?" asked Dr. Cortelyou, the United States consul at Shanghai, of Dr. Evanstone, the surgeon of the American Mission Hospital, as they stopped in front of a cot in Ward No. 3, where a Chinese patient was groaning and struggling with his uncomfortable bandages. "He seems to be pretty badly damaged—accident, I suppose; was it on board ship or in one of the factories ashore?"

"'Neither, sir," replied the surgeon, "he was done up in a street fight not a block away from the consulate. The police rescued him just in time; if those brutes had had a few more whacks at him, he would have gone to the cemetery district, without having to stop at the hospital on the way."

"What was he, a thief? I know they beat them unmercifully sometimes when they catch them in the act. All Asiatics are a little inclined to favor lynch law, yon know, and the English consul told me last night that in their own system they believe in punishing crime on the spot where it was committed.

"So they will chain up a burglar to the door post of the house which he attempted to rob, and even hang up the head of a decapitated murderer over the entrance to his victim's home—a rather grewsome method of making the punishment effective, eh?"

"No, this patient wasn't a thief or a criminal of any kind, from our point of view. He wasn't even intoxicated. You will be very much surprised to know that the only offense of which he was guilty—

197

"The Abbot's Beads!" he exclaimed, "I have found them at last."

and it is a most heinous one to Chinese eyes—was of offering to his grandfather a cup of lukewarm tea!"

"What! You don't mean to tell me that for this trifle they fell on the poor fellow and put him into this condition; I can hardly believe it."

"It seems almost incredible, doesn't it? But it is an actual fact. His father pitched into him first, screaming, 'You've disgraced me, you unfilial wretch!' Then his uncle and his two brothers-in-law joined in and threw him out into the street. A gang of wharf-coolies passing by arrived just in time to vindicate the native code of honor by giving him a few extra blows with their bamboos, and then a foreigner driving by in his trap summoned the police and they brought him here."

"But please explain to me a little more. Wherein does the awful offense consist? Now I confess I don't like lukewarm tea or coffee myself, but I don't as a rule knock the waiter down and beat him half to death if the beverage isn't my exact temperature, do I?"

"Hardly, but you see we're living in another world here and our points of view are so radically different that what may be a very innocent thing in the West becomes a very serious thing in the East and vice versa."

Just at this point the surgeon's house-boy appeared with the chit-book and a visitor's card and interrupted the conversation; "Mas-si-ter, have got one piecee Chinee man your house side wantchee speakee you."

"All right, ask the gentleman to take a seat in the parlor and tell him I will be over in a minute"; then, turning to the consul and showing him the card, he added: "Here's just the man to tell you all about it. Our friend Mr. Wang Foo from Hong Kong is here in the settlement for a few days on business and I asked him to drop in for a cup of tea. You remember him, don't you? He's that wonderful man that solves all the Chinese mysteries for the police when they get beyond their depth."

"Why, certainly, he's the identical one that exposed that bogus miracle at the White Stag Temple last Winter when the Naval officers were there?"

"Come over and join us at the house and we'll put this question of the hot and cold tea up to him, while we're sipping a little of it ourselves."

Mrs. Evanstone received the little party at the surgeon's residence and after the usual greetings and compliments of the day, she took her place at the handsome samovar, which some of the doctor's Russian patients had presented him, and presided as the most graceful of hostesses over the tea table.

"Let me see," she said, turning to the native guest, "do you take yours with milk and sugar or with lemon? Or possibly you prefer it quite plain in real Chinese style?"

"No," replied Wang Foo with the most elegant of bows, "In all these matters I pride myself on being strictly cosmopolitan. According to your own proverb, when I'm in Rome, I do as the Romans do, so when I am in an American lady's home I take my tea as the American do, i. e., with milk and sugar and not even with a Russian lemon."

"Most complimentary and diplomatic! Now"—holding up the sugar tongs in the air—"shall it be one lump or two?"

"Well, modesty would dictate 'one' but a strict regard for truth impels me to say 'two.'"

"Two it shall be, then, and one little extra one on the saucer in case you find it isn't quite sweet enough for your taste."

"By the way, Mr. Wang," began the surgeon, "we have an interesting case in the hospital just now which the consul and I think you can throw a little light upon. It is nothing less than a patient who was actually beaten into a condition of insensibility by his family and his neighbors because he is said to have offered his grandfather a cup of lukewarm tea instead of one that was boiling hot.

"At least, that is the testimony that is given to me by the police and by the hospital staff. Now I know how particular the Chinese are about all their table etiquette and I appreciate their preference for the scalding hot beverage, but this is the first time I have ever known it to go so far as to cause actual physical injury.

"Don't you suppose that there is something else behind it all? Don't you suppose they have some other reason for attacking and beating this man and that the story of the offering of the lukewarm tea to the grandfather is only a blind? You are a person of very wide experience in these matters. Now just give us your judgment in the case. As a matter of fact, have you ever personally known anything as bad as this to happen?"

"O, yes, the cases occur all the time, but they do not as a rule, end quite so seriously. The Chinese are great admirers of—and practicers of—the doctrine of 'Blessed are the Peacemakers' and they usually separate the contestants in a quarrel before they come to actual blows."

"But just what constitutes the seriousness of the offense in the matter of the hot and cold tea, Mr. Wang?" asked Dr. Cortelyou. "I know how careful the Chinese are about civilities and courtesies, but why should a mere breach of etiquette or a matter of carelessness in as small a thing as a table beverage be regarded almost as a crime?"

"If Mrs. Evanstone will permit us to light our cheroots," addressing his hostess, who waved her fan in assent, "I think I can make that clear to you."

"O, I don't mind the odor of tobacco at all—In fact, I rather enjoy it," she replied. "Please go right on and if there is no objection I should like to stay and listen, too, for I've become quite interested in the case of this poor man myself."

"Well," began the Man of Mystery, "my people are Asiatics and you know that all over this great continent the laws of hospitality are much stricter in every way than they are in the Western world and to violate or disregard them constitutes a most serious offense.

"You have heard of the Arab and his tent and how his deadliest enemy is perfectly secure if once he can get inside and break bread and salt—well, very much the same idea pervades all the Far Eastern world. 'If the Rites and Ceremonies are observed'—as the Chinese quote—'then all is harmonious; if they are disregarded, then all is discord.' Eternal friendship or eternal hatred may hang upon the condition of the food and drink of which the host and the guest partake.

"The universal token of hospitality in China is the bowl of fresh made tea. It is everywhere placed before the guest, be he prince or beggar and be the place a palace or a hovel. To omit it, or to serve it in any other condition than boiling hot, is more than a breach of politeness; it is an insult which gives the deepest offense. What is a serious matter between friend and friend becomes infinitely more so when it is a case of an inferior to a superior, as of a pupil to a teacher, but it reaches the extreme in the case of a child to a grand-parent. From what I have learned of this man in the hospital, they would probably say of him, 'Kwai tien shang, kwai ti hia, kwai yin kwei,' i. e., 'He has insulted Heaven above and earth below and the spirits in the realm of shades.'"

"Good gracious! What an arraignment!" exclaimed the Consul. "Why, how could he possibly have been guilty of all this? How, by any human possibility could a cup of cold tea be an insult to Heaven and earth and everything under the earth?"

"It is just this way," continued the Chinese scholar: "Tea is one of the best gifts of heaven to man. There is just one proper way of preparing and serving it and every Chinese child is trained in it from infancy. To offer to any visitor a bowl of heaven's gift pre-pared in any but heaven's own way is simply a reflection on the gods above.

"Then, again, to violate the laws of hospitality by offering cool tea to a guest is to cast serious reflection upon the gods of the porches and the doorways, under whose protection he has crossed the threshold—so you see, the gods below are affected as well as those above."

"But the spirits in the realm of the shades, how about them?"

"That is the culmination of it all. That is the crowning insult to his ancestors and to Confucius and the Blessed Sages who taught us the doctrine of filial piety, for the guest in question was the man's own grandfather—his oldest living ancestor and the very last person, on this earth to whom he should have dared to offer a bowl of lukewarm tea.

"Now, taking all these things together, I think you can readily understand how the combination was enough to excite the family and friends to cast the offender out of doors, and the cries of 'Poo Hiao! Poo Hiao!' 'Unfilial! Unfilial! will always turn the passersby against the victim and they will be glad and ready to add their little quota to his punishment without inquiring into the merits of the case."

"And what chance is there of getting the family punished for half killing this poor wretch?"

"Very little, I fear, from a Chinese standpoint, for, however strong the foreign assessor in the Mixed Court might be for a penalty, the native magistrate would regard it as a case of culpable carelessness or of brutal disrespect to an ancestor—and in either case he deserved what he got."

"Well, Mr. Wang," said the consul, as he rose and extended his hand, "we are certainly indebted to you again, as we so often are, for helping us to get at the real reason that underlies so many of these doings. I can think of only one case that I ever personally witnessed that reminds me of this, and that was on the stage in a theatre in London.

"A poor sailor was eating his dinner in a restaurant and when he started to go out there was an altercation with the proprietor about the payment of the check, and from words they came to blows, and then the waiters and the whole establishment fell on him and beat him black and blue and threw him out onto the sidewalk, and when a kind passerby picked him up and inquired as to the cause, the poor man answered in broken words, 'I-I-a-a was-a-three-farthings-short!'"

When Wang Foo bade the surgeon goodbye, he started away in his jinrikisha toward the English Consular Gardens and in less than a quarter of an hour he alighted there and, paying off the coolie, crossed the park by one of the paths open to the public and, emerging into the native alley at the other end, soon found his way to the home of the basket maker from Hong Kong, which home supplied for him the place of a native hotel.

After the evening rice and the pipe of peace he started out again—apparently for an innocent stroll by the river's bank—and ere long reached the high brick wall which bounded the consular gardens. Here he paused a moment and, looking in both directions to be sure he was not being observed, he quickly removed his jacket of yellow and his gown of blue and turning them inside-out, changed their whole color and appearance, and redressed himself in brown and purple.

The blue knob on his hat was drawn out on its wire and a red one quickly slipped into its place, a long mustache and goatee fastened to his upper lip and chin and he reentered the park as a visitor from one of the up-river cities.

Even the surgeon's house boy, who took such an interest in his afternoon visit, would have been utterly unable to recognize him in the evening. (It was this self-same house-boy, by the way, that told Wang Foo all about the patient in the hospital, at whose bedside the consul and the surgeon were talking, and thus enabled him to form a judgment in the case before his host even introduced the subject.)

He sauntered along, over the Kong Kew Bridge and down by the old American Consulate, till he came to the gate of the Mission Hospital and, passing it, took a proffered seat in the gatekeeper's lodge. After the pipe and tea he inquired, quite casually, "The foreign doctor will not return this evening?"

"No, Venerable Sir," replied the keeper.

"And who is in charge here during the night?"

"Dr. Chang, his assistant, is in charge, sir."

"Please say to him that a visitor from another city would like the honor of meeting him" (slipping a good-sized coin into his palm).

"Alas, sir, Dr. Chang and the head nurse are both away at the bathing-hall, but the second nurse will escort you, if you wish to go into the hospital, sir."

"Thank you, I want very much to see if an old friend of mine is a patient here."

Duly escorted by Hoo Sing, the second nurse, Wang Foo entered the male Ward No. 3, and passed along from bed to bed, until he came to the place where the unfortunate victim of the "lukewarm tea" was asleep under his quilt. He paused and asked Hoo Sing about him, quite astonishing the nurse with his familiarity with the case and utterly disarming any suspicion he might have about a visit to the ward at this late hour of the night. "Poor chap," he said, "It certainly went hard with him for his unfilial spirit."

"It certainly did, sir."

"But my heart goes out to him now, for he certainly has suffered. I wonder if you couldn't just run down to the fruit seller's by the Hong Kew Bridge and buy him a dozen oranges and hide them away under his bedding for him? See, here is the money and a wine-tip for yourself."

"I ought not to leave the hospital alone, sir, when the doctor is away, but it won't be for very long, so I think I can risk it."

"Here, this window is very near the ground. I'll help you out and you can slip quietly down there without anyone being the wiser."

Suiting the action to the word, the nurse climbed out the window and crept away in the direction of the bridge, leaving Wang Foo alone in the ward. The moment he realized the situation he rose and looking very carefully about him stepped softly over to the last bed in the corner and leaning forward eagerly scrutinized the face of the patient. He was asleep. His face and skin were as yellow as the golden letters on the scroll above his bed. He was breathing slowly and painfully. On the wooden tablet his name was written, "Ting Tai Foo," and after it the significant words, "Poison—Unknown." The detective unfastened the upper buttons of his sleeping jacket and uncovering his chest revealed—stretching across from shoulder to shoulder—a string of seven round scars.

"The Abbot's Beads; The Abbot's Beads!" he exclaimed, "I have found them at last."

He started and looked hastily around, but no one had heard him and not a patient seemed to be stirring. He retraced his footsteps and, bidding the gatekeeper goodnight, turned sharply around into the adjoining street. Summoning the first two jinrikishas he bargained with them for a very special duty, which was no less than to assist him in returning a patient to his home from the foreigner's hospital—a duty they are always glad to undertake.

He hurried with them to the window through which the nurse had gone for the oranges; it was but the work of a moment for him to push the two coolies through it and to point them to the bed where the poison victim lay soundly sleeping.

In an instant more they had wrapped him up in his colored quilt, passed him out through the window and were dragging his jinrikisha through the back streets of the Settlement in the direction of the Chinese City gates.

When Dr. Evanstone made his rounds through the hospital on the following morning, he came to bed No. 11 in the corner of Ward No. 3 and noticed that the patient was missing! Dr. Chang and the two nurses all disclaimed any knowledge of the escape and the gatekeeper swore that no patient had passed through the door— there was only one conclusion, namely: he had vanished through the window!

"But he was too weak to walk," said the surgeon to his assistant, "to say nothing of attempting to climb out of a window."

"Yes," was the reply of the Chinese deputy, with the blandest of smiles, "but you see it is getting near the Chinese New Year season now and all the patients' friends want them back home—and, if they can't come themselves, why their friends and relations just come and bring them, that's all. Every hospital in China has the same experience. Shall we enter him as 'Discharged and cured'?"

"No, sir," replied the American, rather irritated at the question, "we will enter him simply as 'Vanished.' I will enter myself as 'Cured,' and if this thing occurs again when you are on duty you will enter yourself as 'Discharged.'"

That afternoon, Dr. Evanstone met Mr. Wang Foo strolling through the English garden. The latter greeted him with:

"Well, Doctor, how is our poor unfilial friend today?"

"O, he is getting on nicely, but the chap in the next bed to him— a mysterious poison case that I was most anxious to treat and watch—jumped out the window last night and took French leave. The nurses tell me he went home for New Year's. Isn't it a little early in the season for that sort of thing, Mr. Wang?"

"Well, yes, unless he came from a distance, and they all like to get home early, you know. What was the case? Opium, as usual, I suppose."

"No, not at all; some drug or other that he had taken that turned him yellow as gold. We couldn't get a word out of him, so I had to make all my diagnosis by dead reckoning, as the sailors say."

"Too bad that you couldn't go on with the case, wasn't it? Well, perhaps he will turn up again, they sometimes come back after New Year's, if they think the hospital has been good to them. Would you know him again if he did?"

"Yes, I could spot him out of a thousand."

"How so? The foreigners usually say that their native patients all look so much alike that they can hardly tell one from the other."

"Well, this chap had a string of scars across his chest. They looked as If they had been made with old copper cash by some native doctor. They were so regular that I nicknamed him at once 'Old Necklace' and I know I could pick him out anywhere."

"You don't remember who brought him to the hospital, do you?"

"No, it's impossible for me to remember those things without referring to the Record Book—but, now that you speak of it, I believe he was picked up in the street very early in the morning, quite unconscious and with a piece of paper pinned on to his gown which said, 'Please take me to the foreign hospital.'"

"Well, his coming, then, was about as mysterious as his going, wasn't it?" remarked Wang Foo with a smile, as he bade the surgeon good night and continued his walk through the park.

THE LAMP WAS BURNING LOW in the inner chamber of the Tao Tai's Yamen in old Shanghai, where two officials were leaning over a table and carefully scrutinizing a number of papers unrolled before them.

"Your Excellency," remarked the Secretary, "these letters show that so far nothing has been found in the up-river cities, although most careful search has everywhere been made. Here are reports also from Hang Chow and Soo Chow and they are all to the same effect. I still believe that he will be found hiding somewhere in Shanghai, for, as you know, they think they are safer here than anywhere else in the country. They are lost in the mixed multitude here and can easily escape detection."

"How long has Wang Foo been at work here now?"

"He arrived on the third day of the moon, this is the seventeenth, exactly two weeks tonight."

"Well, what is his latest idea? Has he any definite clue?"

"Nothing that he has given out, so far, but, as your Excellency knows, he is a man of few words and very reticent and doesn't as a rule commit himself until he is very sure of his whole position."

"Have the European police made a thorough search through all the pawnshops and rookeries in the Settlement for the stolen beads?"

"Yes, but the difficulty is that no one is able to give them an accurate description, for no one has ever seen them."

"True, that adds to the mystery. We must wait a few days more and see if anything further develops."

The above conversation between the Tao Tai and his secretary had reference to the head of one of the most dangerous band of counterfeiters the Chinese Government had had to deal with. After many months of unrelenting labor, most of the members had been apprehended and some of them summarily punished, but the ringleader was still at large and the provincial authorities were holding the Tao Tai responsible for his whereabouts.

The latter, after exhausting all other means, had sent to Hong Kong for Wang Foo and the great detective had now been some two weeks at work upon the case. All that he had to go upon was a very meager description of the man, which had been wormed out of his confederates by torture and a placard which was found tacked to the door of the Tao Tai's apartment in the Yamen. The placard bore these words:

> "Wei Jin Yoong Yao Chien Chao,
> Choo Tze Choo Ting Yeu Pao."

Which might be freely rendered as follows:

> "He who makes coin for human needs
> Will surely wear the Abbot's beads."

As all criminals are generally fond of jewelry, His Excellency concluded at once that the head counterfeiter was wearing a valuable rosary, probably purloined from some neighboring temple, and, in due course of time, would seek to dispose of it at some pawnbroker's in the city.

A very thorough search was accordingly made by both the English and the Chinese police of the temples and of the pawnshops, but, although several necklaces were unearthed, nothing was recovered that could with any propriety be called "The Abbot's Beads." No temple treasury had been robbed—what other kind of beads could possibly be referred to?

It was while passing a sailor's tattoo shop near the Japanese wharf that an inspiration came to Wang Foo, which opened an entirely new line of search. His eye was attracted by the sign and its peculiar wording:

"Why pay out your money for jewels of silver and gold.
When I can adorn you with those that never grow old?"

This was surrounded by cheap pictures and prints of rings, watches, pins, necklaces and glittering jewels tattooed on the human frame. Why might not the "Abbot's Beads" be painted or tattooed or even cut and burned into the neck of the man he was seeking? He thought it all out that night, and the very next day began his search for the "beads." How and where he eventually found them, has been already told above.

"But what made you think of looking for him in the Mission Hospital, Mr. Wang?" inquired Inspector Gubbins a few days after the capture, as they were having a friendly chat and smoke over it at Headquarters. "That's about the last place to expect to find a Chinese criminal, isn't it?"

"Yes and no. If they or their friends have ever been treated by a foreign surgeon, they are almost certain to go back to him in time of trouble, for they know it's their only chance of life.

"You see he had evidently two companions, and, as is often the case, when the time of danger came, one stood by him and the other turned against him. The friend was the one who pinned the paper on his gown saying, 'Please take me to the foreign hospital,' the enemy was the one who attempted to poison him and who put the placard on the Tao Tai's door."

"But why should they make their notice so formal and ambiguous? Why go to all the trouble of putting it into poetry?"

"Ah, my dear Mr. Gubbins, that's just the difference between East and West. 'Whatever is worth doing at all is worth doing well,' we say, and there is no reason why a notice of a thief to his friends shouldn't be in good poetry—that is, provided he can write the poetry, is there?"

"Why, I suppose not. I've even heard that in some Asiatic countries, when a man intends to commit suicide, he spends hours, and even days, in composing his farewell to the world. I suppose that means that he wants lots of pity and sympathy and all that sort of thing after it's too late to give it to him, eh?"

"No, not at all. It simply means that the law of courtesy and grace holds right through unto the end. There's no reason why one shouldn't go out of this world in as refined and as becoming a way as possible, is there?"

"How beautiful and dignified were the old suicides of the East! Contrast the silken cord of China, or the hara-kiri sword of Japan with the horrible and repulsively vulgar blowing out of one's brains with an American gun. Would any person with an artistic taste hesitate between them?

"It reminds me of the classic:

"'What is perfect propriety?' asked the disciples of Confucius.

"'To withdraw as gracefully as one enters,' replied the Master."

THE CORAL BUTTON

CRACKLE! CRACKLE! CRACKLE! Bang! Bang! Bang! went the firecrackers which the coolies were carrying in front of the wedding sedan-chair proceeding along Queen's road in Hong Kong. It was such a common everyday occurrence that, outside of the usual pleasant sensation associated with the noise and the fire and the smoke, it did not attract any very special attention from the native passers-by, but two European gentlemen, evidently out for an afternoon stroll, stopped to comment upon it.

"Sounds mighty like the old-fashioned Fourth of July at home, doesn't it?" remarked Col. Harold Westinghouse, the newly arrived Consul for the United States, to Capt. John R. Marshall, late of New Bedford, Mass, and now acting agent for the American river-steamers to Canton.

"It surely does," replied the latter, "and you notice that the Chinese small boy takes just about as much delight in it as the American one used to do—that is, before a lot of pious old fogies got scared and took his powder and crackers away from him."

"They don't seem to scrimp themselves at all; why, that fellow must have half a dozen packs tied on to the end of that fishpole there, and he is setting them all off—one right after the other."

"I wonder what the real idea of the thing is, anyhow? It can't be just simply to make a noise. The Chinese are too thrifty and prudent and saving to waste any of their hard-earned money just on an empty noise. You mark my words, there's philosophy in their

"Why don't you see
that one is right and
one is left, just like a pair of shoes!"

madness. I believe these hard-headed people have some theory about it that you and I don't understand at all."

"O, I suppose it's on the same principle as the joss-money they buy and throw overboard every time the ship starts. It helps to give good luck for the voyage and to keep the devil away. I asked our ship's compradore about it a trip or two ago. Says I to him: 'Ah Sam, what for Chinaman he throw all that joss-paper in the sea every time ship sails, eh?' 'B'longee velly good joss,' says he; 'Chineeman talkee plenty piecee debbil have got in air all samee velly hungly. He wantchee chow-chow lice but no got cash, s'posee he no pay him plenty paper money, debbil velly angly sendee plenty wind and lain and makee that sea velly lough. Ship no can go ploper, savee?'"

"O, I see," said the consul, with a smile, "it's just a kind of a fair weather insurance, as we would say."

"Yes, that's about the size of it," replied the skipper. "These hobgoblins—or whatever they are that they believe in—say to these poor dupes: 'Here now, you pay up so much cash before you start, or we'll make it mighty unpleasant for you when this ship gets out to sea.'"

"But of course it isn't real money they throw overboard?"

"Not on your life. It's just the cheap counterfeit stuff you see them selling in the shops. You can get about $500 worth of it for 10 cents, my boy tells me."

"And do they think the devils in the air don't know the difference between this and real money?"

"That's what it looks like. But that's only one of the many ways they have of fooling them. However, it's too big a subject for you and me to attempt to unravel. If you should try to get at the inside of any of these superstitions we'd be over our heads before we knew it. I just leave them alone and simply say, 'Joss Pidgin,' and that covers it all."

"Yea, even in the short time I've lived here, I've discovered that 'Joss Pidgin' covers almost everything the European doesn't understand about the strange religious ways of this people. But see! Here comes just the man that can tell us an about it"—extending his hand to Mr. Wang Foo, the famous Chinese detective—"we'll refer the whole matter to him for explanation. Mr. Wang, the captain and I were just talking about firecrackers and wondering what the real secret of their constant use and popularity among the Chinese is.

"There's no subject connected with your people that you cannot enlighten us poor Westerners upon and we will feel grateful for any light you can throw on this."

"Delighted to serve you in any way that I can, gentlemen," replied their Chinese guest in his usual cordial and very courteous manner, "but don't stop here right in the road. Across the way is the tea-hong of my old friends, Long Tuck & Co; they have a broad and spacious veranda there at our disposal; let us sit down and be comfortable."

When they had found three comfortable rattan chairs on the cool brick veranda and had sipped the tea which Long Tuck & Co's compradore placed before them, Wang Foo opened his cigarette case and offered each of his friends a roll of the famous old English "Three Castles."

"You are inquiring about the philosophy of the fire-cracker," he began. "Well, gentlemen, to be candid with you, there is a certain philosophy about it, though we hardly ever dignify it by that name.

"The theory—If theory I may call it—is simply this: the Chinese believe that the air about them is filled with all sorts of little spirits that float about like the motes in the sunbeams and have to be supplied with food and clothing and the necessities of life just as if they were material creatures of flesh and blood. In addition to the ordinary tribute which they expect from all passers-by upon the streets, they levy special taxes, as it were, upon all special occasions, such as festival processions, weddings, funerals, etc. This is what the people resent and the fire-cracker is their means of showing it and of securing immunity from the unjust demands. Whenever a procession starts down the street, the spirits flock together and attempt to block the way.

"This means that they must be got rid of and pushed to one side and the firecracker does it most effectively by stunning them with its short, sharp report, thus clearing the road and the air and allowing the procession to pass in peace."

"You mean the crackers knock those little demons senseless, but don't actually kill them? Is that the idea, Mr. Wang?"

"Precisely so."

"Well," interrupted the consul, "what are the big crackers for? I see that every now and then they set off one of these."

"Ah, that brings up a very interesting point," replied the host, as he leaned over and deposited his cigarette ash on the tray, "regarding the organization of the forces of the invisible world. In the religion of the Western world, angelic forces—both good and bad—have their ranks and their degrees, have they not?

"The demons in the Christian Scriptures when asked their name replied, 'Our name is Legion.' It is exactly so in the Chinese conception. The spirits of the air are divided into regiments and companies exactly as the soldiers are in the native army. They are similar to the grades in the armies of Imperial Rome, having their hundred men under a centurion and their thousand men under a chiliarch. Now inasmuch as an officer is much more important and valuable than a private, it will naturally require—so the people reason—a larger and stronger firecracker to stun him.

"That is why at every hundredth cracker they insert a large one to stun the centurion and at every thousandth a still larger one to stun the chiliarch."

"So they really knock the whole regiment down flat, do they not? Officers, private and all? And when they recover consciousness again it's too late to catch them. That's the idea, is it not?"

"Exactly so. And that explains why they do not set them off in the little square packs that you use in America. Those are only made for export; we do not use them here. Those 'fish-poles,' as you call them, enable us to hang a whole string of crackers in the air and weave-in the officers in their proper rank and places.

"That is why we call it 'Fang Pien' or 'cracking the whip,' don't you see? Now, tell me how many American boys who use fire-crackers have ever heard of the Chinese idea of using them?"

"Not one in 50,000, Mr. Wang," replied his friends in unison, as they rose to depart and thanked him for his explanation.

The Consul drew forth from his pocket a handsome silver cigarette case and, offering one of the perfumed Turkish rolls to the detective, said as he did so, "I want you to try one of these, sir; they are the very genuine thing; just arrived from the sacred city of Mecca and made by the most famous manufacturer in the city of Mahomet the Prophet, sir, not one of them to be had for love or money in all Hong Kong, I can guarantee that.

"These were presented to me by the captain at the British surveying ship, just back from a cruise to the Red Sea and along the shores of Arabia. Light one of them now, sir, and if you enjoy it as much as I do, I will ask you to accept a small bar of them with my compliments."

Wang Foo reached out his hand and drew one of the delicately perfumed rolls of Turkish tobacco from the case. As he did so, he suddenly started and, looking at the case intently, remarked to its owner; "Why, that's rather a singular coincidence, isn't it? You and I seem to carry our little smokes in the identical kind of holder, do we not?"

The Consul took the two silver cases into his hand and holding them side by side and comparing them, remarked, "Well, Mr. Wang, if they were human beings I should certainly put them down for twins, for even their own parents would have a job to tell them apart.

"That's quite unusual, isn't it, in a country where everything is made by hand? I've always understood that no two pieces of ivory or silver or anything of that kind were ever exactly alike. In fact, it is quite impossible ever to got a real duplicate, as so many European shoppers find out to their disappointment. How about that, Mr. Wang?"

"You are quite right, Mr. Consul, our native workmen rather pride themselves on the fact that no two products of their skill are ever exactly alike. There is resemblance, but no identity.

"We Chinese dislike the cold, hard, mechanical duplication of artistic wares—the kind you turn out by hundreds to Birmingham, for instance—we say it violates the whole law and system of Nature.

No two stars in the sky, no two birds in the air, no two flowers to the field, not even two human faces among all the millions at mankind are ever identically the same."

"Well, then, how do you account for the fact of these two cigarette cases being exact duplicates, the one of the other."

"I beg your pardon, sir, they are not duplicates, though at first sight they might appear to be so. There is a striking and a most important and significant difference, when once your attention is called to it. Look! Do you not see it now?" And as he spoke the words he held the two cases up to the light "I must confess it is too much for me," remarked the consul as he shook his head. "Please point it out to me."

"Why, don't you see that one is right and one is left, just like a pair of shoes! Look at this one; the coral is on the right, isn't it? Now look at the other; the coral is on the left."

"So it is. Why, it's strange I didn't notice that in the first place. How did it happen to catch your eye, Mr. Wang?"

"Well, you see it struck me as rather unusual that the two cases should be so very much alike, and knowing that when that happens it is nearly always because they are rights and lefts, I at once suspected that these were two separate parts of the one whole. If I place them together now"—suiting the action to the word—"you will notice that they open like a hinge, as you say in the unpoetic West, or, as we say in the poetic East, like the two corresponding shells upon the seashore."

"You mean, then, that these are really parts of one set? In a word, they belong together and should never have been sold separately, sir?"'

"Of course, that sort of sentiment doesn't appeal very much to the average tourist mind, but no Chinese—and, I may say, no Japanese, either—ever would have knowingly separated them. There is a deep and mysterious significance in the symbol of the double shells which nature has joined together and ill-luck nearly always follows the man who attempts to separate them. Perhaps some day when you have a little leisure, I may be able to explain this to you more in detail. We haven't time to go into it now."

"Good afternoon, then, Mr. Wang, and thank you again for giving me a very interesting tale to tell Mrs. Westinghouse when I reach home. She will take a special delight in hearing all about it, for you see she gave me that cigarette case for a present last Christmas morning."

"You don't happen to remember just where she bought it, do you—but that is hardly a courteous question for me to ask—"

"O, that's all right, as long as our curiosity is aroused—why, I suppose she bought it at one of those Cantonese shops in Queen's Road where she usually goes. At any rate, I'll ask her tonight and drop you a line if you care to know."

"I should appreciate it most highly, sir," remarked Wang Foo, as he shook the consul's and the captain's hands and bade them the politest "Good afternoon."

The next morning a uniformed messenger with the chit-book of the American consulate knocked at the outer gate of No. 5-5-5 in the alley of the Red Cloud, just off the avenue of Fragrant Waters. Old Chang, the gatekeeper, admitted him, bowed him to a seat, produced the tea and pipes and, after a few preliminary greetings, took the message and delivered it to Wang Foo in the upper chamber. The latter opened it and read as follows:

"Consulate of the United States
    Hong Kong.
"Dear Mr. Wang—Referring to the sliver cigarette case about which we were talking yesterday, I find that Mrs. Westinghouse purchased it from a silver dealer who came to the consulate one day and exhibited his wares in the drawing-room. He claimed to represent one of the largest establishments in the colony, but, strange to say, she has never been able to locate him. She inquired of all the servants, but none of them remember seeing him before or since.

"I am afraid this chit is not very satisfactory, but it is the best I have been able to do for you. Very cordially yours,
        "Harold Westinghouse."

He laid it down upon the table, signed the chit-book and re-turned it to the messenger. Then, closing the door, he took out of his table drawer the cigarette case and holding it up said to himself as he lighted one of the "Three Castles": "So, So! The left-hand silver shell with its half of the sacred coral button was sold to the consul's wife by an unknown dealer, was it?

"That makes a most interesting link in the chain. The old abbot and I will have a very pleasant evening together over this," and stretching out his long chair of carved bamboo, the Prince of Chinese detectives closed his eyes and set himself to thinking and thinking while the wreathing smoke floated upward to the rafters.

AMONG THE MOST TREASURED POSSESSIONS of the family of His Excellency Chang, the Viceroy at Canton, was the famous Coral Button of the Mings, which had actually been worn on State occasions by His Imperial Majesty Kwang Hoo and had come into the keeping of the Changs through their being descended from the old State Treasurer at Nanking.

His Excellency had worn it at the midnight ceremonies in the Temple of Confucius and the following morning when his secretary was carefully folding it up in its wrapper of yellow silk, preparatory to storing it away in the official vault, he suddenly discovered to his utter dismay that some skillful thief had spirited it away and left a very poor imitation button of cheap red glass in its place!

In fear and trembling he communicated the fact to his master, who immediately called for his hat-of-state and personally verified the theft. In place of at once notifying all the officers of the Ya Men (or Courthouse) and instituting a general alarm and search for the missing jewel, the Viceroy decided upon just the opposite course. Calling the secretary into his inner office, he closed the doors and drew the curtains, "Yu Kai" ("Crystal Ladder"), he said, in the sternest of voices and with the most threatening gestures, "this is the most serious thing that has happened in the Ya Men since we came here, but not a human soul must know it.

"I warn you not to breathe a word of it to anyone. We must recover it at all costs—and the only safe and sure way to do so is by the utmost secrecy. Someone from within has done it, for no one from without could have had access to it. It has all been carefully planned and carried out right under our very eyes, and we must be 'silent and sagacious,' as the sages say, before fixing our suspicion upon anyone. You understand me and promise to obey?" Within three days after the discovery of the theft, word had been quietly conveyed to Wang Foo that His Excellency wished to consult him on a matter of the utmost importance and would be glad to have him come up to Canton at his earliest opportunity. As it was necessary to avoid even the slightest suspicion, could he not come in some suitable disguise? A sentence of nine words in which the fifth and sixth words could indicate the particular dress would be expected as an answer.

Wang Foo, who appreciated this native mode of conveying a secret correspondence, mailed the next day to the Viceroy a slip of red paper, without any heading or signature, and containing merely these words:

"Tou Shu Tik Yiu King Shiu Tou Tzo Mang."

(The scholar with his spectacles repairs the defects of nature.)

His Excellency duly received it, marked mentally the fifth and sixth words, "spectacles—repairs," and knew that ere long the most skillful detector of crime in all the Empire would knock at his door in the disguise of a vendor of glasses. And he was not mistaken.

"Tell the second gatekeeper," he said to his personal servant as he arose from his morning rice, "that if a traveling optician should happen to come along today, I have a pair or two of spectacles that need attention."

"It is already done as the Great Man says," was the reply; "we humbly announce that the repairer of glasses is sitting in the outer court."

"Bring him to my inner apartment without delay!"

"The Great Man speaketh well—it is already done according to his august wishes."

"I can fit Your Excellency's glasses much better in the darkened room than in the strong light of day," remarked the optician, as he motioned towards the inner apartment, and, gathering up his boxes and his tools, he followed the Viceroy into the secret chamber.

When all the coast was clear, Wang Foo and Chang the Viceroy sat down quietly over their tea and pipes to discuss the mysterious vanishing of the Coral Button of the Ming Dynasty. All the circumstances of the loss and its discovery were gone over and the named of all the possible culprits were softly whispered between them, as also the different means that might have been used to dispose of it. The detective asked his usual careful and leading questions and made copious notes in his little leather-covered book. One important thing was not mentioned until the end of the interview, namely, the Coral Button was in two pieces, fitting so perfectly together that the joint was never noticed and held in place by a delicate and almost invisible wire of gold—the imitation one of glass was simply one solid piece.

Who had taken them? How had he been able to do it? What disposition had he made of them? These were the three uppermost questions in Wang Foo's mind as he sat on the forward deck of the returning steamer and saw the net of suspicion and guilt drawing closer and closer around the form of "Crystal Ladder" the secretary.

"Good morning, Mr. Westinghouse," said a Chinese caller as the hall-boy ushered him into the office at the Consulate.

"Ah! Good morning, Mr. Wang," replied the Consul, as he rose to greet his visitor. "What new and interesting discovery have you got to report this morning? You know I have come to look for something startling now every time I see you coming down the path to the office door."

"You flatter me, sir. I have nothing especial to report on, but I have come to ask a very peculiar and a very special favor of you and"—looking significantly in the direction of the Consular residence—"of your good wife, sir."

"Well, what may it be? Always delighted to accommodate you when I can, you know."

"It is simply this: I have come to ask you to allow me to purchase of you the silver cigarette case which Mrs. Westinghouse gave
you for Christmas."

"You want to have it go with yours, then, to complete the set,
do you?"

"O, not at all, sir; I shouldn't presume to make the request for
a purely personal reason or for any selfish motive whatever. As a
matter of fact, I am not making the request for myself at all, but
for an old and very dear friend, from whom the articles were stolen
and who is willing to pay almost any price to have them back again."

"Well, of course. Mr. Wang, neither Mrs. Westinghouse nor I
wish to be the receiver or purchaser of stolen property, and if you
are quite positive as to the facts, why here is the case now, and you
can take it away with you for exactly what we gave for it. I presume you will add your own to it so as to make the set complete,
will you not?"

"Most certainly, sir, and I am more indebted to you than I can
express."

"It wouldn't be proper for me to ask your friend's name, would
it?"

"Perfectly proper for you to ask it, sir, but, I regret to say,
absolutely impossible for me to answer. It is a matter that involves
the honor of a family of very high standing and I am bound to
inviolate secrecy."

Wrapping the cigarette case carefully up in a handkerchief of
yellow silk—after having shared with the Consul the last two rolls
of tobacco which it contained—Wang Foo handed over on the spot
the full value of the purchase and hurried back to his home in Red
Cloud Alley.

Early in the evening the old Abbot arrived from the Temple of
the Queen of Heaven and ascended to the detective's upper sanctum, where he saw the two silver cases lying next to each other
upon the table and Wang Foo reinserting the two corals in their
settings, from which he had very carefully removed them.

"You see, Venerable Father, they are both here," he exclaimed.
"Your theory was quite correct. Instead of trying to dispose of them

separately, he had them made into ornaments for use at the meetings of 'The Society of the Double Shells,' one of the worst and most exclusive gambling hells that have ever disgraced the colony."

"Yes, and probably stole them in the first place to pay his debts to some of the other members and then begged them to remain in the Club Room as ornaments for fear of detection if they were disposed of outside."

"No doubt of it, and that of course accounts for their being made up into cigarette-cases, which would be very popular with the *jeunesse doree* who patronize the establishment. The Cantonese bar-boy who sold the pawnbroker the one which you obtained was undoubtedly the reputed agent of the silver establishment who disposed of the other to the Consul."

"When are you going to make your final report to His Excellency?"

"I take the day steamer for the city tomorrow."

"May the blessings of all the Buddhas be with you as you break the news to him."

"Venerable Father, your prayers and benedictions shall, as always, be my consolation and protection."

"You have done a good work and the Island of Fragrant Waters is well rid of a curse that has sent many of its finest men to the bad."

WANG FOO ON HIS TRIP needed no disguise when he entered the Viceregal Ya Men. His Excellency was waiting to receive him as an honored guest and after the preliminary courtesies of tea and smokes they passed together into the inner apartment and the doors were closed.

Wang Foo unwrapped the package of yellow silk which he drew out of his sleeve and, laying its contents before the astonished and delighted officer, said, with the most gracious of bows: "I have the honor to return to your Excellency the famous Coral Button of the Mings!"

"I knew it! I knew it!" cried the Viceroy. "I was certain from the beginning that Yu Kai the Secretary was the guilty party. Clever rascal! And to think of his doing it right under my own roof and while acting as my own most trusted friend and helper! Let me seize him at once and denounce him before all the Ya Men." He rose to open the door—

"Stop, Your Excellency," interrupted Wang Foo, "do not put a hand on Yu Kai."

"And why not, pray?"

"Because he is absolutely innocent and is now, as always, your faithful and devoted secretary."

"Who is the thief, then?"

"The thief, Your Excellency, for you must now hear the painful truth, the thief is none other than your eldest son, Wing Choo, who stole the Coral Button, substituted for it a cheap glass imitation which he procured at some curiosity shop, carried the original with him to Hong Kong and sold it to his companions at the 'Double Shells Society' to pay his gambling debts."

"His gambling debts at the Double Shells Society! Then, alas! My suspicions as to his trips to the Island have been only too true."

"Quite so, Your Excellency, and his friends, thinking they would be a valuable asset and ornament for their club, had them made into cigarette cases for the use of the wealthy members. A dishonest bar boy stole them from the hall and disposed of them to parties outside, that is all."

"How unfilial! How unfilial!" exclaimed the aged Viceroy as he raised his arms into the air and implored the mercy of Heaven on the son who had so miserably failed to reach the moral standard of the Sages. "How unworthy of the Master and the Teachings are we all! To think that the grand old name of the Double Shells, the symbols of Eternal Friendship, should sink to adorn a gamblers' den! For doth not the ancient poem say:

> "As shell to shell is bound and clasped
>   Upon the ocean's beach,
> So hand to hand and heart to heart
>   True friends to friends do reach."

THE EXECUTIONER'S SWORD

"Now, REMEMBER, DEAR, whatever other curios you buy, don't fail me on the executioner's sword. I must have the genuine one—the real grewsome kind, you know—all stained with the bloody gore of the pirates and murderers and all that sort of thing. It will be the greatest ornament in the armory. Don't let the guides fool you with any cheap and bogus imitation."

This was the farewell charge of Mr. Hawthorne Chester of Worcester, Mans, to his wife, whom he was leaving behind in China for an extra month's tour in the East, while he was hurrying home in answer to an urgent business cablegram.

"Why, what a terribly bloodthirsty individual your better half must be!" remarked her dear friend and companion, Miss Pinkerton, to Mrs. Chester as they took their seats on the company's launch that had carried the "goodbye party" out to the departing Pacific Mailer. "Just to think of any man asking his wife to bring him home a ghastly thing like that!

"It reminds me of an Englishman that I saw bidding goodbye to his wife in Egypt, and what do you suppose his last message to her was? Why, just this: 'With all the rest of that antiquity trash, dear, don't forget the baby mummy!' It was bad enough to speak of all those beautiful jewels and relics as 'antiquity trash,' wasn't it?—men are such unappreciative creatures, anyway, you know, my dear—but to calmly ask her to bring home that horrid, cadaverous bundle of dried-up human flesh and bones under the name of the 'baby mummy' was just one too many for me.

The sword, dripping with human blood, was floating in the air above her.

"You'll pardon my saying it, but just for the moment it made me reconciled to—I might have truly said thankful for a condition of single blessedness. No husband of mine would ever ask me twice to act as a freight carrier for that old dead and disgusting stuff."

"O, my child," replied Mrs. Chester, with a good-natured smile (she called her friend, Miss Pinkerton, "child" out of a sort of patronizing affection for her and sympathy with her in her loneliness), "you're entirely mistaken. He's the tenderest and gentlest creature in the world.

"He wouldn't hurt a mouse. His own mother used to say that when he was a little boy he wouldn't pull the wings off a fly. This is just a little innocent hobby of his, this collecting terrible weapons of all kinds to hang on the walls of his den in the attic which he calls his 'armory'. He's been buying them up ever since before we were married.

"He's got it just covered with guns and pistols and swords and knives and daggers, to say nothing of Cannibal Island war clubs and frightful things they beat out each others' brains with. He loves to tell you that every one of them is genuine—"

"Just what does he mean by that remark?"

"Why, that every weapon there has killed somebody—or tried to, I suppose."

"How perfectly awful!"

"And nothing disappoints him more than to have some visitor ask him about something that isn't in the collection. He just worries about it until he gets it. That's the reason he's so crazy about a Chinese executioner's sword.

"You see some old tea merchant from Boston, who had lived many years in China, told him that would be the greatest thing in all the 'armory' and, in fact, was the only really important thing he lacked. You see, if only we could have gone and bought the actual sword there and then; but that miserable cablegram spoiled it all."

"And so, manlike, he has left the unpleasant duty for his wife, has he?"

"Tut, tut, my child, you don't understand. It isn't an unpleasant duty at all; it's just a joy to me to gratify that little hobby of his

and add a little something to his 'den.' Why, I don't feel any different about buying him a sword than I do about buying him a new
pipe or a tobacco box. My only anxiety is about it's being absolutely 'genuine,' as he says. Of course, I can't go up to Canton and
actually see their heads chopped off myself—"

"Merciful heavens! I should hope not," interrupted the astonished companion.

"So I'm obliged to rely on the consul's finding me some thoroughly reliable party who can do this for me. He thinks the *Bennington* will be going South next week and, if so, Lieut. Ward, who
is a most charming man and an old personal friend of our family, I
know will take a day or two off and do this little favor for me."

IN PERFECT FULFILLMENT of Mrs. Chester's expectations, the U. S. S.
Bennington did sail for the South the following week; Lieut. Ward
did get a few days' leave, he did go up to Canton and he arrived
there just in time to join a party being formed at the consulate to
witness a native execution. Two globetrotters from Chicago, a British colonel from India, a Dutch Naval officer from Java and himself constituted the group of Europeans who stood patiently in the
little rough court in the center of Canton, which has seen the shedding of more human blood than many a battlefield. A motley crowd
of curiosity seekers filled one end of the court, while those who
were unable to offer the customary fee to the soldiers on guard
were kept outside a rough picket gate.

The other end of the yard—the center being reserved, like a ring
in a circus, for the actual entertainment—was occupied by a number of potters who were placing their hand-made clay jars on strips
of straw matting to dry in the sun, and who seemed utterly uncon-
cerned at the impending tragedy which was about to take place in
their midst. Suddenly a cry arose from the crowd, "Lai Liao! Lai
Liao!" (They have come! They have come!), and from the adjoining narrow alley a procession of soldiers and lictors with guns and
old-fashioned spears approached and entered the enclosure. Following them came eight wretched coolies bearing between them in
bamboo baskets the four condemned victims of the law.

The latter were unshaven, unkempt, ragged, and filthy beyond words. Half-dazed by narcotic wine which their friends had bribed the jailers to give them, they seemed perfectly listless and indifferent to any fate that was in store for them.

The coolies stopped and at the word of command from the white-buttoned magistrate, who sat calmly smoking in his sedan chair, they dumped the contents of their baskets out on the ground with no more ceremony or feeling than they would have shown had they been so many bricks or stones.

The executioner, a fat, coarse kind of creature with a perfectly impassive face, stepped out of a little hut at the end of the yard, bearing in his hand a significant sword. It was of ancient Chinese make, carved with curious symbols on the hilt, double-handled, and its long wavy surface showing the marks of the recent grinding that had sharpened it for the work of the day. He bowed respectfully to the magistrate and received from his deputy a paper with a list of names.

"Only four today, Your Excellency?" he inquired.

"Quite correct, four only," was the calm and stoical reply.

"Fang Ling Pien!" ("Line them up!") cried the bearer of the "sword-of-mercy" to his assistants, who proceeded to place the criminals on their knees in a row about four feet apart, their feet securely chained together and their arms fastened behind them. The Lord High Executioner bowed once more to the Mandarin Master of Ceremonies and took his place at the head of the line. He raised the blade into the air, grasping it firmly with his outstretched hands—

"Sak! Sak!" ("Kill! Kill!") said the voice in the chair between the puffs from the pipe. The assistant grasped the arms of No. One and jerking them upward threw his head and neck straight forward. The sword fell and with unerring aim it lopped off the life of the pirate, whose quivering body fell forward into a pool of crimson blood. "One!" shrieked the crowd as they all clapped their hands—not in approval of the headsman's skill, as the European spectators all supposed, but to frighten away the evil spirits who always hover about such scenes.

"Quick work, that, eh?" remarked the Indian colonel.

"Mighty lively," replied the tourist from Chicago. "Did you notice how the crowd checked them off as the heads fell? Reminds you of the old days of the French Revolution, doesn't it, and the old ladies who knitted at the foot of the guillotine and kept tally on the unfortunates? But, look! What's that old chap dressed like a priest doing with those biscuits?"—pointing to a figure bending over before them and dipping some little cakes out of a basket into the stream of human blood that was trickling at their feet. "Another horrible superstition, I suppose?"

"Him b'longee velly good joss," explained Choo Loo, the guide in charge of the party. "S'posee some man gettee velly sick, he chow-chow dat cakee, velly soon gettee more better. How fashion him joss-man can savee."

"Well, isn't that the horrible limit?" turning to the lieutenant.

"It certainly is—but I must hurry up and get that sword now before the old man disposes of it to someone else. I see he's washing it and putting it away in his cabin."

"What do you suppose he will want for it, if he sells it at all?"

"I have no idea, but I'll start him on a couple of Mexicans and see what he says."

Taking the guide to one side he instructed him to negotiate the purchase and Choo Loo disappeared in the direction of the cabin.

"Velly solly," he began as he came back, "dat execution man no wantchee sell. He talkee him fadder hab dat swordee plenty year."

"O, that's an old yarn. Every old dealer in Asia tells the same tale. You just go up to him and show him five brand-new Mexican dollars and bring me back the sword, see?"

After a prolonged discussion, which rather irritated the remainder of the party, who, having gratified their morbid curiosity, were now just as anxious to get away from the cursed spot as they had been to reach it, Choo Loo reappeared and whispered in the lieutenant's ear that $5 was hopeless, but $10 would salve over the wounded feelings of the son at parting with the ancestral treasure. The money was handed over, the sword carefully wrapped in yellow paper and deposited under the seat of the sedan.

"You guarantee that this is the correct one with the blood stains all on it?" inquired the purchaser.

"My can se'clure," was the confident reply. "Number one sword—hab gottee plenty bloody."

Unwilling to risk any possible loss on the way or in the native customhouse, the Naval officer very sensibly placed the purchase in the hands of a personal friend, who delivered it the following week to the anxious Mrs. Chester at Shanghai.

"Well, now that you've actually gotten the grewsome thing at last, I suppose you are perfectly satisfied," remarked Miss Pinkerton of Boston to her friend and fellow-traveler as the latter was exhibiting the sword of Canton to a little party of friends at afternoon tea on the Astor House terrace.

"I am sure Hawthorne will be more than delighted with it when he once gets it into the den," replied her charming hostess, "but, do you know, though I am not in the least superstitious, I am really beginning to believe that this is a kind of a hoodoo, as many strange things have happened since I've had it in the trunk there."

"What, for instance?" asked Mrs. Cortelyou, the wife of the American consul.

"Well, you see it's been here just eight days now. The first day it came, my jinrikisha ran into another one and nearly killed an old coolie who was crossing the street. Then, two or three days after that, the hotel got on fire right in the corridor where our rooms are.

"Then, last Friday, I lost my purse in the consular gardens and, most significant of all, the night before last the sampan which was taking Capt. and Mrs. Winslow back to their steamer after dinner upset in the river and nearly drowned them—and the sword was the very last thing they laid eyes on when they left the hotel. I am actually beginning to think that perhaps it would be better for me to ship it home to Hawthorne by express instead of carrying it around with me—but, then, you know, I shouldn't like to have it hoodoo him if I wasn't around, should I?"

"I certainly would send it away, Mrs. Chester," continued Mrs. Cortelyou. "It really seems perfectly spooky to have it lying around.

Why, I couldn't sleep a wink at night if I thought that awful thing was in the same room with me."

One by one the guests departed, taking their little pony-traps for the drive along the Bubbling Well road, the one famous recreation and breathing spot of Shanghai, and Mrs. Chester rang the bell for the boy to remove the tea tray. He entered just as she was wrapping up the sword, and his eyes nearly started out of his head when he saw what she was doing.

"Here!" she said, "boy, just help me wrap this up, please."

"Velly solly, missee, my no can."

"No can, why, what do you mean?" she inquired in astonishment, for it was the very first time that the obliging Tack Sing had ever hesitated to do her instant bidding. "You're not afraid of it, are you?"

"Yea, missee, you please 'scuse me, I talkee tlue, too muchee 'flaid, my no can touchee, velly bad joss."

"Why, you superstitious old thing you, what do you suppose it is? It isn't going to hurt you."

"My can savee, my can savee," was the reply of the thoroughly frightened boy. "B'longee 'sclusion man sword, all time choppee Chinee head offee, so fashion. 'Spose my touchee, all same gettee sick, p'laps go makes die. No can."

And with this reassuring remark to his missee, he disappeared with the tea tray through the lattice work door, leaving her alone with the object of Chinese horror.

She took it up and made up her mind there and then that it was the very last time she would touch it until it got safely to her husband's den in Worcester. As she held it in her hand for a moment, it seemed to her, for the very first time, to assume a new and horrible shape!

The old blade brightened up and the blood spots seemed to grow crimson again and actually begin to trickle along the steel! She dropped it on the table in horror and instinctively closed her eyes—when she reopened them the sight that met her gaze was too awful for words.

The sword, dripping with human blood was floating in the air above her and spirit hands seemed to be seizing it and striking downward blows with it, while ghostly voices shrieked "One! Two!

Three! Four!" The atmosphere grew thicker, a strange sepulchral odor as from a tomb long closed seemed to rise up through the very floor and mingle itself with clouds of incense, while dying groans and demon yells echoed on every side.

She felt herself choking and, putting her hand to her throat, cried out with all her remaining strength. "Murder! Help! Help!" and fell unconscious to the floor!

"But, doctor, is this a usual thing? Have you ever known cases of it among European residents before?" asked Miss Pinkerton late that evening of Dr Hall-Clayton, as he was bidding her goodnight after making his patient, Mrs. Chester, as comfortable as possible.

"O, bless your heart, yes, many of them. They often get it from going to the Chamber of Horrors in the Buddhist temples or other terrible places that no European lady ought really to visit—but you can't stop them, you know; the more repulsive it is, the more attractive it seems to be—or perhaps from seeing some group of lepers or loathsome Chinese beggars.

"I have known cases where they didn't visit any place or see or touch anything, but simply listened to some grewsome tale from someone who had been there, and that was enough to set them off. You see, Mrs. Chester had heard the full account of the execution from Lieut. Ward—who really ought to have known better than to repeat the details to her—and then, after talking it all over with her friends this afternoon at tea, the houseboy gives the finishing touch by conjuring up all the native horrors of it, and, of course, as soon as she is left alone, she begins to see the sights and hear the sounds all over again and—away she goes! There you have the whole story in a nutshell."

"But it won't leave any permanent injury, will it, doctor?"

"O, no, not at all, but we shall have to keep her as bright and cheery as possible these days, and," he added with a good deal of emphasis, "we must see that she gets out of this wretched country as soon as possible and help her to strengthen up her nerves."

"And what about the executioner's sword that caused all the trouble? Don't you really think we ought to dispose of it?"

"She must never lay eyes upon it again—husband or no husband—she can't stand it. Just give it to me and I will dispose of it to some tourist or other and write Mr. Chester my reasons. He will understand at once. He surely doesn't want to break up his wife's nerves just for one old relic less in his den, does he?"

Miss Pinkerton took the package containing the sword from the table to hand it to the surgeon. It seemed remarkably light; she unrolled it and, to their mutual surprise, it was empty! Its contents had vanished into air!

"Why, that's surpassing strange," remarked the surgeon, "It can't have gone out of the room. Let us search for it." Suiting the action to the word he searched every nook and corner of the apartment, while the over-inquisitive Miss Pinkerton took advantage or this excuse to investigate carefully all the contents of Mrs. Chester's trunks and wardrobe, but not a trace of the weapon of death could be found.

"Ah! What's this?" said the surgeon, as he picked up a mysterious looking piece of Chinese red paper from the floor and, unrolling it, read as follows: "Sak Jin Hwai—Ji Sho Kwai."

"What does all that mean, doctor? You understand Chinese perfectly, don't you?"

"Madam," he replied, "no European, living or dead, understands it perfectly, only a few of us know a little about it. These words, as nearly as I can decipher them, mean:

"'The Executioners' Guild has claimed its own.'"

"The Executioners' Guild! Why, what can that be?"

"I haven't the slightest idea; some native mystery, I suppose. We'll have to get the police and the missionaries who know their tricks to help us unravel it. One good thing—the sword has gone and I hope forever." And with this he bade his patient and her amateur nurse a final farewell.

A few days later he was chatting with the proprietor of the hotel on the Astor House steps and happened to mention the matter of the paper and its inscription. The host smiled and merely remarked: "Well, if the Executioners' Guild has claimed its own, I guess they've got Tack Sing, too, for he disappeared the same afternoon that Mrs. Chester was taken ill, and no human being around here has laid eyes on him since."

"What do you think has become of him?"

"My dear doctor, I've long since given up trying to fathom their mysterious ways. I just let them go—it saves time and good brain power. In short, as our English friend says, 'I don't think!'"

INSPECTOR GUBBINS and Chief Detective Morehead of the Shanghai Police had had several conferences with the members of the American Mission regarding the robbery at the hotel and the kidnapping and murder of the unfortunate servant.

From them and from the Chinese members of the force they had obtained information that led them clearly to the following conclusion, viz: The sword which Lieut. Ward had purchased for Mrs. Chester was not the personal possession of the Canton Executioner, but was the property of a secret organization known as "The Executioners' Guild," who were enraged at the sale of it to the foreigner and who determined at any cost to recover it.

They had evidently traced it as far as Shanghai and there had lost track of it until the afternoon when Tack Sing, the hotel-boy, caught the first glimpse of it at the tea party and refused to help put it away.

Returning to Mrs. Chester's room in answer to her cries for help and utterly distracted by seeing her lying unconscious upon the floor, mingled fear and excitement led him to do exactly the opposite thing from what he intended. He seized the sword, wrapped it hastily up, and rushing out of the room with it, before he gave the alarm or made any effort whatever to assist his unfortunate "Missee," never stopped unto he had tucked it safely away under the mattress of his bed in the garret, or in some other convenient hiding place.

Returning to the apartment he rung the bell violently and shrieked down the hallway for the other boys to come to his assistance. Equally paralyzed with fear at seeing the foreign lady—as they supposed—dead upon the floor, they refused to touch her and ran to call the proprietor.

Tack Sing rushed by them and down the stairs, crying as he did so, "Missee go makes die, me go hossipital side catchee doctor man!" That was the last that was seen or heard of him, and, as the ablest native detectives could find no trace of him in all the settlement, the natural conclusion was that the "Executioners' Guild" had probably drowned him in the river.

"And is there no chance of my recovering it?" asked Mrs. Chester of Dr. Cortelyou, the consul, as she sat in his office a week or so after the robbery. "My husband will be so disappointed."

"Inspector Gubbins gives me very little hope, madam, because, as he says, when these things get into the hands of secret societies and the like, they have all sorts of mysterious ways of hiding them, and then they take advantage of all the superstitions of the people and threaten them so severely if they divulge anything that it's really impossible to get a word out of them."

"And do you suppose they really kidnapped Tack Sing and drowned him in the river or anything horrible like that? He was such a nice boy and I feel awfully conscience-stricken about it. Dear me! If it only hadn't been for that foolish fainting fit of mine, this would never have happened. And it seems so strange to accuse him of stealing the sword when he was scared to death at the sight of it and wouldn't even put his fingers on it."

"Well, madam, the Inspector is not positive about the drowning or the murder, because his body has never been recovered, but he and the Chinese officers all feel that that is probably what has taken place. A secret organization like the "Executioners' Guild" wouldn't stop at anything to accomplish their object you know. And as to the taking of the sword, the missionaries tell us that under excitement and fear the natives will often do exactly the opposite thing from what they originally intended. Haven't you noticed that when a native starts to cross the street from north to south and you frighten him by screaming at him from your jinrikisha, he will immediately turn around and go in the opposite direction?"

"Yes, I know they are easily disconcerted."

"They most certainly are," replied the consul, as he rose to show his visitor to the door.

THE EUROPEAN COMMUNITY at Shanghai, consuls, police, residents, tourists, missionaries, one and all, would still be in blissful ignorance—as they so often are in Chinese matters—of the whereabouts or final disposition of Tack Sing and the executioner's sword, had the ever-watchful eye of Wang Foo at Hong Kong not happened to see a little account of the occurrence in the Shanghai *Daily News*.

Although not requested officially to take up the case, he had for his own pleasure and satisfaction decided to follow the evidence and the conclusion arrived at by the police was to him very far from satisfactory. He had talked it all over with his old friend the Abbot at the Temple of the Queen of Heaven and had followed it by a trip up the river to Canton and a careful inquiry from the inner circles as to the so-called "Executioners' Guild," which mysterious organization, he was obliged to conclude, existed only in the imagination of the authorities at Shanghai. He decided to take a trip on his own initiative to the great northern seaport.

"I am here, Mr. Inspector," he said to the chief as he greeted him one morning at headquarters, "not because you have sent for me, but simply for my own personal interest in the case of Tack Sing, the hotel boy, and the theft of the executioner's sword."

"Well, you are of the same opinion as we are, of course, as to the 'guild,' and their getting away with him, aren't you?"

"You must please excuse me from expressing any opinion on the case until I have been able to go into it thoroughly and we meet—shall I say two weeks from today?"

"Just your old way, Mr. Wang," said the Inspector with a smile, "but it shall be as you say. Two weeks from today, then—and may all good luck be with you!"

As the great detective, clad in the simple dress of a Cantonese gentleman, sat in one of the tea-houses kept by a fellow townsman that evening he overheard, at an adjoining table, fragments of a conversation between a group of young clerks who wore evidently employees in the new Government Post-office. There was nothing specially that interested him until, as they rose to go, the one that sat nearest to him whispered to his companion, "Goodbye, old head-chopper. I'll see you later at the Choppers' Club." Just a little meaningless phrase to the other patrons of the establishment, but one of the deepest significance to Wang Foo, for it proved the golden link in the chain of evidence and conclusion that he had for several days been working out in his own mind.

The Inspector and Chief Detective Morehead were eagerly awaiting him on the appointed morning at the head office. After the ceremonious closing and locking of the doors and windows and the lighting of cigars, the disclosure began: "Do you know, gentlemen, what postage stamps are called in Chinese?"

"Beats me," answered Morehead. "I always say 'stampee,' but I suppose that's only pidgin, isn't it?"

"Quite so. The proper term is 'men's heads' and the Chinese have named them that because the heads of the various sovereigns on them have no apparent bodies attached to them, and look like the chopped-off heads of native criminals. The clerk who sells the stamps at the Post-office is known to his cronies as the 'head-chopper'—in other words, gentlemen, the executioner."

"Not a very complimentary allusion to the King, is it, sir?"

"Pardon me, gentlemen, I have just a word more. There is a little club of Post-office clerks here—all of them from Canton—that is known among themselves as 'The Executioners' Guild.' Having in a moment of frenzied excitement stolen the sword, Tack Sing was at a loss to know how to dispose of it; confiding his dilemma to a friend he heard of the guild and presented it to them as an ornament for the club room, where it is hanging peacefully over the mantelpiece.

"So much for the sword—Tack Sing is temporarily employed as janitor of the club, and, eating and sleeping within, he has escaped any public attention. There has, you see, been no murder, no kidnapping and no intentional theft, for the man was practically out of his head when he took it and consequently not amenable to the law. 'Blind to his doom,' would describe him in the words of Confucius."

THE CRYSTAL GLOBE

"GENTLEMEN, YOU CAN TAKE MY WORD for it, the Chinese are the very best and easiest people in the world to trade with if you only understand them and are willing to do an honest business with them," remarked Mr. Wilson Greggs of the Great Western Trading Company to an interested group of visitors sipping their afternoon tea on the veranda of the Hong Kong hotel

"I've been dealing with them off and on for over 20 years and I know what I am talking about. You've got to have a first-class article to start with, and the goods must always be up to the samples for if they once suspect that you are lowering your standard you are gone.

"Then, you've got to have a nice-sounding chop or trademark that they can easily pronounce and that has some good luck in it to gratify their little superstitions, and, lastly, you have got to have a fair fixed price that you never under any circumstances vary from, and the trade and goodwill of the Chinese are yours.

"Now, Dr. Burroughs, you've lived a long time among them and speak their lingo and all that and know them even better than I do," he said, turning to the Mission surgeon, who had just joined the party. "You'll bear me out in this statement, I am sure, won't you?"

"With pleasure, Mr. Greggs," replied the surgeon; "you have stated the case very accurately, and I congratulate you upon your grasp of the situation. Unfortunately, a great many European and American merchants fail to understand these points in the

Before the excited priest could stop him, he flooded the room with a torch-like glare

Chinese nature, and consequently they allow the trade to slip right through their hands.

"In the years that I have been here I could give you a long list of the firms from abroad who have come out here and flourished for a little while and then gradually their custom has fallen off and passed into the hands of others, and they have finally given up in disgust and gone home. They've developed a very bitter feeling against the natives and say it is impossible for any decent European to deal with them, and all that, when all the time it was simply their own fault and no one else's. If they had really understood the nature of their customers they could not only have kept the trade, but have had it grow larger every year. However, this is a very large subject, this matter of international trade, and if I should go into it to any extent I am afraid I should keep you gentlemen here all the rest of the day."

"You spoke of the trademark or 'chop,' Mr. Greggs," interrupted one of the tourist group. "I have heard it said that this is really the all important point with the Chinese and that a wisely chosen and popular chop really goes further with them than even the quality of the goods. Have you found that this is so?"

"Well, I should hardly say that it was the most important thing, but it certainly goes a very long way with them toward selling the goods, doesn't it, Dr. Burroughs?"

"It most certainly does. But, as I said a moment ago, this is a very large subject—it would fill a volume in itself—and the full story of it has never yet been written for Europeans. I may say, however, as an indication of the value that they place upon it, that a large Chinese firm will spend days and weeks of time and many hundreds of dollars, if necessary, in selecting just the right chop for an article before placing it on the market."

"It practically corresponds, then, to careful and elaborate advertising in our countries, doesn't it?"

"Yes, and it practically takes the place of public advertising, which the Chinese do not care very much about. Let me give you just one little illustration of the value of a name in a case that came under my own observation a few years ago. The lamp trade, as you all know, is one of the most important in this country, and with the lamps, of course, there goes a great importation of chimnies and globes.

"There is naturally not very much variety in the matter of the chimnies inside, but there is an endless variety of choice in the outside globes, because these, in the native mind, correspond to the glazed paper coverings of their old-fashioned lanterns, about which they are very particular. Now there happened to be two English dealers in glassware in the very same block on Queen's road, and both of them filled their windows and showcases with the handsomest patterns of lamps and shades.

"At first the tide of native customers seemed to flow about evenly into the two establishments, but gradually the gentleman on the left, whom we will call 'Brown,' found his list of customers growing shorter and shorter, while his neighbor and rival, whom we may call 'Jones,' rubbed his hands in delight at the sight of the constantly increasing number of his patrons. Their stock in trade was so nearly alike and the arrangement of the goods in their windows so very similar that the European mind was at a loss to account for the shifting of the tide, especially as the prices were identically the same."

"What then was the secret?" inquired one tourist on behalf of a much interested and listening circle.

"Why, it was simply this," replied the surgeon with a smile; "Brown was content to have the large Chinese sign in the window simply say in its golden characters. 'Crystal Globes,' while Jones, who had been wise and crafty enough to consult an old missionary on the subject, advertised his wares by the striking title of 'Dragon Bubbles.'"

"Well, what of that? What could the difference signify? Why should they run after bubbles rather than crystals? Is it simply because they are human like the rest of us and, as the poets and philosophers tell us, we all spend our lives really in chasing bubbles!"

"O, no; that's the Western idea—not the Eastern—and you mustn't make the popular mistake of putting Occidental thought and reason into the Oriental brain, for that's what causes three-quarters of all the trouble between them. The difference lies just here: a globe of crystals or glass is to the Chinese mind simply a piece of inanimate and material nature, a cold, dead and lifeless thing like the rock or sand from which it comes—beautiful and attractive, but not alive or capable of communicating life or any attendant blessing to mankind.

"On the other hand, the bubble formed from the foam in the mouth of the dragon—himself the king of nature and embodiment of all its forms of life—is not only a beautiful and living thing in itself, but conveys to its fortunate possessor the vivifying qualities of all the animal kingdom. So you see, to have hanging from the ceiling a lamp-globe that bears the name of the 'dragon bubble' would convey infinitely more good luck to a native home than all the 'crystal globes' in the world!"

"Remarkably interesting and clever story, that!" exclaimed Maj. Perkins from Bombay, as he laid down his cheroot and drew out of his pocket a notebook. "I'll just jot it down here at once before I forget it. By Jove! You can learn something new here every day. Just as you can in India, don't you know. 'Dragon Bubbles.' Very good! Very good! I'll not forget that in many a day, not I. And now, gentlemen, as it's a very warm afternoon, I suggest we all have a little liquid refreshments and imagine we see genuine dragon bubbles sparkling on the soda, eh?"

He rang the bell for the boy, but before giving him the order for the liquids, he thought he would just get his view on the subject, and so he said: "Boy, you can savvee dragon bubble?"

"Yes, my can savvee."

"Talkee him b'longee velly good joss, eh?"

"Chineeman talkee him number one good joss."

"You thinkee Hong Kong side can catchee?"

"S'posee some piecee joss-house makee sell glassee, look see all samee. Chineeman he buy, no can get house fire, no can get sick, gettee plenty lich, can catchee cash buy licee."

"General protection all around, eh?"

"My savvee joss-man he talkee so fashion—some piecee man talkee all same fool pidgin."

"Well, hurry up the sodas now, boy, and have them cold and sparkling."

After the ever-popular and refreshing beverage of the Far East, the little party broke up and wandered off toward the tennis club and the boathouse, the two favorite cooling-off spots of the colony. They had not noticed at all a quiet Chinese gentleman who had sat in a large wickerwork chair just beyond them on the veranda, and who, although apparently deeply absorbed in the mysterious contents of a native volume, had been a most interested listener to all their conversation. After the last one had departed he rang the bell for the boy, and addressing him in his native tongue, said: "At what temple on the island are they selling the dragon bubbles now?"

"The elder-born asketh well, but the ignorant little servant knoweth not."

"You told the foreigner just now that you know, for I distinctly heard you."

"The honorable elder-born must have misunderstood the question of the ocean-man."

"Not at all; I understood it perfectly."

"Great and august is the learning of the elder-born that he understands the language of the ocean-man so easily."

"Waste not thy flowery terms on me, nor scatter jade-stone compliments in the pathway of the sages' humblest scholar," replied Wang Foo, the famous Man of Mystery, as he took the boy into the farthest quiet corner of the veranda and, opening out the Japanese screen that stood there, concealed them both from the eyes and ears of all observers.

He seized him by both wrists and holding him with the grip of a vise, looked straight into his eyes and said: "Ah Ling, I know exactly who you are. You are from Pow Tai village across the bay, for your accent tells it. The information that I want is for the Mandarins. You know the native proverb well: 'Keep out of the clutches of the law!' Now tell me at once what I want to know, or before the moon is three days older the wooden cangue will be about thy neck." He tightened his grasp on the wrists of the trembling Ah Ling, who now was wriggling like an eel—

"You know it, tell me quick!"

"I do not know; I do not—"

"Liar! You do. Which temple is it? Quick! or I will—"

The houseboy fell upon his knees, gasping as he did so: "Yuek Tai Tai, Yuek Tai Tai" (the Moon Goddess, the Moon Goddess). But spare me, O merciful Master, for the vengeance of the Queen of the Night follows those who reveal her secrets."

"You are protected on condition of absolute silence until we meet again. You shall speak when I call upon you—until then, you are as dumb as the stone image of Poo Sak. You understand?"

"The Master hath spoken well, the stupid servant understands."

Wan Foo released his grip and, raising the trembling boy to his feet, gave him a significant look that said in unmistakable terms: "Remember now, you disobey me at your peril," and pushing the screen aside, passed out onto the veranda and disappeared through the doorway into the hall.

Hailing a waiting jinrikisha, he ordered the coolie to take him to the Red Cloud alley, and, descending at the foot of the incline, he walked to the gateway of No. 5-5-5, where the old matron, the "Venerable Grand One," was waiting to pour out the bowl of scalding but most refreshing tea. He sipped it gladly, and calling for the water-pipe and tobacco, ascended the little staircase to his quiet study and chamber of rest "So! So!" he remarked to himself as he stretched himself out on the bamboo couch, "the Moon Goddess' Temple is selling the dragon bubbles again, eh? The cross-eyed priest must be up to his old tricks. We shall have to look into it and stop him before he does too much harm."

A DAY OR TWO AFTER THE SCENE between Wang Foo and the hotel boy the whole community of Hong Kong was thrown into a state of the most intense excitement by the report that a European child had been kidnapped! Little Donnie Goodwin, the 4-year-old child of

Mr. and Mrs. Goodwin of Victoria terrace, had disappeared from the care of his amah while playing with some other European children in Cricket Ground Park, and not a trace of him could be found.

They were too far away from the water's edge for him to have fallen into the harbor, and as it was only a minute or two before he was missed he could not have wandered down any of the neighboring streets.

The police, who were diligently assisted in their search by the naval and military authorities—to say nothing of the scores of civilians who hurried to offer their services to the department— were therefore reluctantly driven to the conclusion that the child had wandered away for a moment into the roadway and there had been suddenly seized and thrown into some passing jinrikisha or sedan chair by the kidnapers and was now being concealed in some outlying section of the colony and probably held for a ransom.

Meanwhile Mr. and Mrs. Goodwin, the parents, were driven almost to distraction by the news of the loss of the child and the conjuring up of every terrible suspicion regarding the disposing of him. The frantic mother kept crying out "They will kill him! They will kill him! My darling boy, they will drown him, they will burn him! I shall never see him again!"

But her condition, heartbreaking as it was, was really no more pitiable than that of the poor Chinese amah, who, rolling on the nursery floor in paroxysms of uncontrollable grief, kept shrieking! "Take me! Take me! Stab me, kill me, eat me if you wish, but bring back my boy."

There was no more faithful or devoted native servant in the entire community, and it was no exaggeration to say—and the oldest residents well knew it to be true—that she would willingly have given her life to have saved the child, for such things have actually happened in the history of European life in the Far Eastern world.

Of course a large reward was immediately offered for the apprehension of the thieves and the return of the child.

Sir Wayne-Evington, the Governor of Hong Kong, called personally with Lady Evington at the Goodwin residence and after tendering his sympathy and promising every assistance on the part of the authorities, headed the subscription list with a very handsome sum, which was multiplied a great many times by the amounts offered by the various societies and organizations in the colony.

It was remarkable to see how the tragic event drew out the sympathy of the entire populace, without any distinction of race, creed or nationality. The consuls of all the different countries, officers of the garrison and of the naval and mercantile marine, the bishop and all the various missionaries, the heads of the Mahometan and Parsee guilds, either called in person or sent their cards and kindest inquiries.

It surely was the little "touch of nature that makes the whole world kin." But among all those who expressed their horror at the occurrence and hastened to tender their sympathy and assurances of help, none surpassed the Chinese themselves. The consul came in person with all his staff, and was followed by the heads of the various guilds and firms and leading citizens of the native community, who vied with each other in expressing their detestation of the crime and requested the privilege of being allowed to subscribe to the reward.

Among the first of the red cards to be presented by a native servant at the Goodwin door was that of Wang Foo, the detective, who accompanied it by a personal note of assurance that he would leave no stone unturned in his efforts to cooperate with the authorities and to bring the villains to justice, and begging Mr. and Mrs. Goodwin—which many others had forgotten to do—not to give up hope of securing the child's return until every effort had been exhausted.

In accordance with the foregoing promise, he called at once at the Department of Police and on being ushered into Inspector Wallace's private office greeted him with: "Mr. Inspector, this is the time when I have anticipated you. My general custom, as you know, is to wait till the department sends for me and requests my services, but this is a case that touches the whole community so vitally—and one, I may say, in which we all feel that we cannot help too willingly or too promptly—that I have token the liberty of coming down here at once to offer my services to the authorities. In other words, as you say in England. 'I am yours to command.'"

"Well, Mr. Wang, you certainly were never a more welcome visitor at this office. Please take a seat and help yourself to a cheroot out of the new box there."

The Inspector rose and closed the doors and windows—his customary precaution when anything of a specially private nature was to be discussed in the office. He then continued: "You have read the account in the papers; now, what is your theory? Is it a case of kidnapping or of simple 'disappearance,' as the reports call it? Where is the little chap and who spirited him away? What is your solution?"

Wang Foo removed his round Chinese cap and laid it on the table (this he would not have done in a Chinese presence, but he sometimes allowed himself what he called his "European privilege" when he was alone with a friend from the West); it seemed to relieve the pressure on the brain and enabled him to pass his right hand two or three times across the brow as if to rub away the headache or the wrinkles. He looked up after a moment and answered: "Mr. Wallace, I have no solution whatever—that is, as yet

"I never have at first you remember. Like the sign in Weston's drug store around the corner, I may say, 'I take time and care in preparing all my solutions.' I expect to begin some of these chemical brain processes tonight however, and you may hear from me in a day or two. In the meantime I shall be grateful to you for a copy of the case as you have drawn it up, if you can spare it."

"This is the only one I have—take it and return it promptly, please."

"You shall have it back safe and sound before the office opens in the morning, sir," replied the Prince of Detectives, as he accepted a roll of documents, gratefully, from the Inspector. "And, remember, if anything turns up during the night and you need my help. Just send for me without a moment's hesitation. Your head chair-coolie knows my house very well, and I will see that Old Chang, the gatekeeper, sleeps with one ear open to listen to possible midnight knocks."

"Thank you, Mr. Wang, and remember, I shall look eagerly for that solution of yours tomorrow or next day. I am very anxious to know how will fit in with mine."

"With yours? By the way, what is yours in a word? Was the report in the evening paper correct?"

"Quite so, sir; It seems to be a clear case of kidnapping and very carefully planned and carried out, as most of them are. The villains evidently knew all about the dally life of the family and the exact time when the amah would bring the child to the park, and while she was chatting and gossiping with the other amahs, as they always do, they evidently enticed the child out to the road for an instant and tossed him into a waiting sedan chair and rushed him off.

"It must have been a sedan because you see that is closed, while a jinrikisha is all open and they would surely have been seen. We shall probably get some anonymous letters tomorrow demanding a fabulous ransom and threatening to mutilate the poor child in some way if we don't pay up. It's awful to think of, but 'bandits is bandits,' as Morehouse says, whether they're in Italy or China. However, we hope for the best. Good night, Mr. Wang."

"Good night, sir, and many thanks for the solution, which will be helpful to me in compounding mine."

It was late in the evening when the old Abbot from the Temple of the Queen of Heaven arrived at Wang Foo's residence and passed at once into the upper chamber where the Man of Mystery was waiting to receive him. Old Chang brought up the tea and pipes and after the preliminary warming-up they proceeded at once to the subject before them.

"Are there any new developments since the morning?" asked the Master of the Temple.

"None that I know of," replied the host. "See, here is the Inspector's report, containing everything as far as they have gone. I will read it over to you, translating as I go," suiting the action to the word, "Now, what do you think of it?"

"Well, it is the natural conclusion of the Western mind. The Inspector feels that is the way it would have been done in Europe and consequently the way it has been done in China—but that does not follow at all, as you very well know, I can recall but one case of kidnapping of a foreign child in all the long years that I have lived in Hong Kong, and that was done by a gang of drunken Portuguese sailors who were ashore on a spree and who carried the child away to the ship more for a lark than for anything also.

"No, no, it requires too much care and trouble and expensive preparation—for they always require well-paid confederates—and the risk of exposure and detection is far too great for the ordinary gang of thieves and villains to undertake it.

"Of course, there have been stealings of native children, but that is a very different proposition. I do not believe this is a case of kidnapping at all—that is simply a theory and nothing more—there is not a grain of evidence to prove it or even suggest it. Had there been, you may be sure that the amount of the reward would have already tempted some one of the party to turn State's evidence, for the walls are covered with the posters and thousands of handbills have been printed and distributed through the native quarter. The child has disappeared and we must find him, that is all."

"Yes, venerable father," answered the detective thoughtfully, "that is all, as you say, but it is a very puzzling and complicated 'all.' We do not seem to have even the shadow of a clew, and there is nothing for us to do but to wait, as the English say, until something or somebody turns up. By the way, you know that our old friend, the cross-eyed priest at the Temple of the Moon Goddess, is up to another moneymaking scheme?"

"What! Old 'Cross-sights' at it again? What is it now? A miracle of some kind, I warrant. Jewels falling from Heaven, or something of that kind?"

"Well, you hit it very nearly; it isn't jewels from Heaven this time, but it's the next thing to it. The sacred foam from the mouth of the heavenly creature is being sold for medicine under the old name of 'dragon bubbles.'

"He's keeping it very quiet and only selling it to the inner circle now—for fear the local mandarin will want a heavy commission—but he is making a good thing out of it, as I accidentally learned from the hotel boy, who I believe acts as his local agent for the devotees in the colony. I am going across the bay to the temple tomorrow to make a personal investigation and see whether it is serious enough to report to the Tao-Tai. I will report to you in the evening."

"It is well, it is well that you go, and may the blessings of all the Buddhas be with you!" was the farewell benediction of the old visitor as Wang Foo bowed him out to his waiting sedan-chair.

The following morning Old Chang accompanied his master as far as the Central Wharf, where he took the steam ferry for the opposite side of the bay and, having safely landed at Kow Loon, engaged a sampan with a sail to take him to the second inlet beyond, where a well-worn road of stone led up to the Temple of the Moon Goddess. Disguised as a wandering old peddler of books, he attracted no notice from the temple attachés nor did his presence at the inner shrine—into which he had gradually forced his way—arouse the least suspicion on the part of "Old Cross-Sights," who was there in person arranging little pyramids of glass balls in front of the gilded wooden figure of the goddess.

"Venerable Father," he said with a carefully assumed air and tone of rural and unsophisticated innocence, "what may these treasures be that you are hoarding so carefully?"

"These are none other than the foaming bubbles from the mouth of the Dragon King. The grandest and most potential medicine that ever came to mortal man. Stir but one of them in a basin of boiling water, it will dissolve into a thousand fragments and he who drinks of the precious fluid that remains will be blessed with all the virtues and protected from every ill that mortal flesh is heir to.

"These little globes are the children of the great parent globe that hangs yonder above the Goddess' head—the crystallized bubble of the sacred foam. See! It has a thousand—" He stopped abruptly in the middle of the sentence, startled at a cry that seemed to come from the inner room behind the shrine.

He dropped the last globe that he held in his hand, shivering it into pieces on the temple floor, and with a wild shriek drew aside the sacred curtain and rushed into the dark space beyond. Wang

Foo followed close behind him and drawing a bunch of matches from his pocket-case suddenly struck them, and before the excited priest could stop him, he flooded the room with a torch-like glare.

Why did he start back? What was the sight that met his eyes? What was it lying there upon the matting? A child! A European child! Pushing the priest roughly aside, he seized the little figure in his arms and dashed backward with it into the daylight.

Yes! One of the greatest surprises, but one of the most joyful experiences of his life, there, soiled and dirty, hungry and thirsty, but absolutely unharmed, was the lost child for whom the whole Island of Hong Kong was searching!

"Who brought him here?" he asked in excited tones of the now thoroughly frightened priest. "Tell me, you cross-eyed villain; tell me quick."

"They brought him, they brought him in the box—" he stammered out. "He carried me the sacred crystal in his hands—the dragon bubble, the dragon bubble! He was the messenger of the Goddess!"

Terrifying the priest and his attendants and holding them back at the point of his revolver, Wang Foo retreated down the stone roadway to the water, and finding a sampan waiting he deposited his tired burden on the mats and ordered the coolie to row for all his life to Kow Loon.

In less than an hour Mrs. Goodwin was clasping her lost Bennie to her heart and all the colony of Hong Kong was rejoicing with the happy parents.

IN THE STATEMENT which Wang Foo made to the Inspector and his deputy that evening he explained the disappearance and the mysterious finding in the Temple across the Bay. It seemed that Bennie, playing with some other children in the park, left them and wandered off by himself alone to the driveway.

Just as he appeared there two old coolies, carrying a large empty box on a bamboo, stopped to rest and smoke. As often happens, they were so tired that, before they knew it, they had fallen asleep on the grass by the roadside. The child, seeing the empty box and thinking to play "hide-and-seek" with his fellows, had climbed into it and pulled the cover over himself and while hiding there the coolies had picked him up and carried him along.

Noticing the difference in weight they had put the box down at the corner of the street and, uncovering it, had discovered Bennie within. Their first thought was to lift him out and summon assistance, but—and here is the strange part of it all—seeing the English policeman approaching and hearing him calling them to move on, they became thoroughly frightened, and, covering the box over again, picked up the bamboo and hurried away with all speed to the water.

Fearing further trouble here, they jumped into a sampan with their burden and started across the bay.

"Let us take him to the Temple of the Moon and put him under the protection of the Goddess," they said, and so to the temple they went and presented the child to the priest, who swore them to secrecy and sent them back with the empty box.

"But what made Old Cross-eyes think he was bringing the dragon bubble?" asked the Inspector.

"Why," answered Wang with a significant smile, "Bennie was carrying a glass ball in his hand which his amah had given him to play with."

THE TEMPLE GONG

"WELL, BROWNLOW," said Inspector Gubbins of the Shanghai Police to his chief assistant, "what do you make it out to be, an accident or a regular old case of incendiarism?"

"Looks rather queer for an accident to start out in about four different directions at the same time, doesn't it?" replied the captain, as he proceeded to take off his rubber coat and cap cover and brush the cinders and dust off them; "and they can't work off the old-fashioned excuse about 'carelessness' this time, either. I know these chaps are awfully careless about fire, but even Chinese carelessness doesn't burst out in four distinct spots at exactly the same time, does it, now?"

"No, that's true. There might have been one or two careless coolies smoking in the godown (warehouse) when the watchman wasn't looking—"

"Or, just as likely," interrupted the captain, "the watchman himself when the English quartermaster wasn't looking—"

"Yes, but hardly four of them in four different parts of the building, eh?"

"Hardly. No, sir, you can be sure that thing was all carefully planned out beforehand and those four fires started by some kind of slow match concealed in the cotton and arranged so as to get a good old headway on before we could get an alarm turned in. It's incendiarism pure and simple, that's what it is, sir, and now I suppose it's up to us and the department, as usual, to find out who the firebrand was."

The conflagration to which our two officers were referring had taken place about 11 o'clock in the evening in the old godown of MacMillan & Co, near the lower Australian Wharf, and before the alarm had been given and the foreign engines and firemen had been able to respond, thousands of taels' worth at valuable goods had been destroyed.

The curious circumstance, as the captain said, was that it seemed to break out in four different places at almost the same moment of time. The first alarm was given by the native watchman at the godown of the Australian mail, adjoining MacMillan's on the north: the second by a jinrikisha coolie, who was passing up the street on the south and saw smoke curling out from under the eaves; the third by two old women who were having their goodnight tea on the second-story veranda of the house across the way on the west, and the fourth by the deckwatch of the Ning-Po steamer lying in the stream almost directly east

When the police and firemen arrived they found the iron doors and shutters to the windows all intact and apparently securely locked, so that they were obliged to break a passage in for the hose with axes, and this it was that made them conclude at once that the fire had been started some hours before and must have been actually smoldering when the godown was closed and fastened up for the night at sunset.

It was no very strange occurrence for a fire caused by carelessness to smolder on for several hours and finally burst out into flame later in the night; indeed, the Chinese dropping of hot ashes from their pipes in between the cotton bales generally produced this result; but for four different fires to burst out simultaneously in four different parts of a building looked to everyone as if something far more serious than carelessness had been at work, and the entire foreign community on reading the account in the papers next morning agreed at once with Capt. Brownlow in his conclusion.

The agents of the English and French insurance companies, with a promptness and courtesy characteristic of the Far East, at once set their appraisers and adjusters to work, and in a very few

They had watched him
purchase four long coils of
powder-paper slow fuse.

days Messrs. MacMillan & Co received from them checks to cover their loss in full, and arrangements were made to rebuild the burned out godown.

So far so good, but Inspector Gubbins had not yet been able to report to the British consul that either he or any member of his force had laid hands upon the incendiary; nor had they been able to solve the mysterious question as to what purpose he had in committing the deed. The Chinese detectives on the force, very naturally, concluded that it must be a case of hatred or revenge, and so, after due consideration with their chief, they started a very careful inquiry among all the employees and attachés of MacMillan & Co as to any possible cause or motive for such a retaliation.

Their efforts, however, seemed to meet with very little success. They could not find that the firm had recently dismissed any of their native employees, nor that they had reduced their wages, nor that they had inflicted any hard and unjust rules upon them, nor that any European connected with the establishment had ill treated or abused a native—any one of which actions might have given rise to a feeling of bitterness or resentment—but they found that, on the contrary, everything seemed to have been going along in a most harmonious manner.

Last of all they took up the question of religion, including various native customs and prejudices, against which they know the European was apt to protest and stumble and so start trouble and opposition, but even here the firm seemed to have been entirety innocent.

They had not objected to the burning of incense and the offering of idol money to the wharf-god, under due precautions; they had not compelled any man to work upon a native holiday; they had granted the usual number of absences for grandparents' funerals and other ancestral ceremonies and had yielded very generously to all the little native requests which the compradors included under the general all-embracing term of "joss pidgin"—in fact, they had got along together most satisfactorily and smoothly.

As the senior member of the firm expressed it: "A little oil on the wheels doesn't cost very much, and it makes all the machinery go smoother."

Sidney C. Partridge

"Well, Sam," asked the Inspector of his head Chinese assistant (mistaking the popular native name of "Life" for the English abbreviation of Samuel, which most Europeans do), "what does your part of the force think put the fellow or fellows up to it? What grudge did they have against the white man this time that led them to try to get even with him by setting his godown on fire?"

"Me no can savvee just now," was the laconic reply. "S'posee bime-by can catchee. My tinkee b'longee two tlee piecee man have do. Just now he velly glood fliend, no talkee. S'posee bime-by he makes fight, one piecee man come talkee my, one piecee man go lun away—all time so fashion."

"Ah! I see; you mean that as long as the gang holds together they'll keep absolute silence, but just as soon as a row breaks out between them some of them will turn State's evidence and inform the police, just to get even with the rest of them, eh? That's about the way they do things at home and in other countries."

"My tinkee so fashion."

"I guess you're about right, my friend, as the American consul says, and about how long is it before they come to this falling-out?"

"No man can talkee tlue, but two weekee more b'longee big Chinee feastee, all samee water-joss him catches birthday, plenty piecee wharf-coolie dlinkee sam-shu get dlunkee, bime-by makes fight."

"Well, we'll wait and see what turns up after the holiday; in the meantime, keep a sharp eye open for any evidence from other quarters, see?"

"My can s'clure," was the assurance of the faithful Sam.

THE OLD FIRM OF MACMILLAN & CO that had been for so many years a well-known name in Shanghai and the other ports had recently dissolved, following the death of the last of the MacMillan family, and the good will of the establishment, together with the firm's name and their Chinese chop of "Mel Lang," or "Beautiful Wave," had been sold out to a Eurasian relative named Peasley and his Portuguese friend, Rodero.

Being naturally most anxious to keep up the trade of the old house and to continue the good will of the Chinese, they had made very few changes in the native staff, and so, as far as the general public was concerned, the firm of "Mel Lang" was still doing business at the old stand by the Australian Wharf, where they had been for so many years and where every jinrikisha puller and cargo coolie knew the address.

Messrs. Peasley & Rodero decided to offer the customary reward for the arrest of the incendiary—not from any very high motive, but largely to keep themselves in good standing at the Merchants' Club and with the foreign community generally—and so they inserted the following advertisement in the local papers, both foreign and native:

REWARD!
The sum of five hundred Mexican dollars will be
paid by us for information that will lead to the arrest and conviction of the party or parties who set
fire to our river godown on the night of July 17.
MacMillan & Co,
(Chinese chop "Mel Lang")
Whang Poo Road.

In less than three days after this had circulated freely all over the settlement and was being discussed at every teashop from the Customhouse to the International boundary, two native visitors sought out the person of Sam, the detective, and put in a claim for a share of the reward by giving him what they considered a very important clew.

He listened carefully to all that they had to say and then reported it to his superior officer, Capt. Brownlow. The testimony was to this effect, via: They had seen Nam Tuck, the night watchman employed at the Australian Wharf just to the north of MacMillan's, enter a native shop on the Whang Poo road on the evening of July 18—the night before the fire—and had watched him purchase four long coils of powder-paper slow fuse, such as are used by natives during the long Summer nights for lighting their pipes.

To be sure, he might have been perfectly innocent in the purchase, but the date and the hour and the exact number of the fuses looked very suspicious, and so the web of circumstantial evidence began gradually to weave itself about him and to point to him as having concealed the rolls of slow-burning paper in the four different corners of the godown on the day of the conflagration.

Brownlow reported the matter to his chief with the result that it was decided to place the unsuspecting Nam Tuck forthwith under arrest, and to put him through an official grilling before he had any chance to confer with his friends or cronies. The native officers found him at his home early the following morning and he was securely locked in a cell at headquarters before breakfast.

When he was brought up for the preliminary investigation, Inspector Gubbins thought it would be well for the British vice consul to attend and to bring his official interpreter with him. (For although the consul was a proficient Chinese scholar, he spoke only the northern mandarin tongue of Pekin and would have great difficulty in understanding the local dialect of Ning Po of Shanghai.)

The interpreter being away on a vacation, the consul brought in his place Archdeacon Wiggins of the English Church Mission, who not only spoke the dialects like a native, but who, from his long residence among the people and intimate knowledge of their ways, was always of invaluable assistance in unraveling these international tangles. It was a cause of intense relief and gratification to Nam Tuck—to say nothing of his astonishment—to find himself in the presence of a foreigner familiar enough with his own tongue to converse with him directly, and so, after a little hesitation, he told the archdeacon his story and the latter in turn repeated it in English to the foreign officers.

He acknowledged the purchase of the fuses on the afternoon of July 16, remembering the exact date by the fact at on that day he had drawn three strings of brass cash out of the "well" (a dry hole in the ground where the Chinese conceal their money), and also acknowledged the exact number of four.

He explained, however, that he intended them only for the purpose for which he always used them, that was to light his pipe during the night and to keep away the mosquitoes.

"Please ask him how he came to buy exactly four—no more, no less," said Inspector Gubbins, turning to the Archdeacon; "that's not the usual native way of selling goods, is it? I thought they always sold them in packages of 10, corresponding to our dozen in England."

After a lot of chattering back and forth between the missionary and the prisoner—which seemed to Brownlow long enough to have asked the question 10 times over and to have answered it in 10 different ways—the missionary said: He bought just four because that happened to be all the cash that he had brought with him in his girdle.

"He says the shopkeeper, who knows him well, will gladly testify that he buys them there regularly and either singly or in packages of 10 as a rule, but sometimes in odd amounts if he doesn't happen to have the cash. He denies all knowledge of the origin of the fire and swears that the very first he knew about it was when he saw smoke and flames bursting out under the roof on the northern side and ran out into the street to summon the foreign policeman."

Further questioning on the part of the officers and the visitors failed to bring out anything further from the watchman or to shake in any way his direct and simple testimony. It was thought best, however, not to release him at once, so he was remanded to his cell for further safekeeping and the consul returned with the archdeacon to the office.

As soon as it became known in Heavenly Moon alley that Nam Tuck had been arrested and taken away by the police, the entire population of that row of native buildings gave way to screams of excitement and crowded around his family's doorway to learn the why and the wherefore.

His wife and mother were discovered rolling on the floor and tearing their hair, while the children were alternately weeping and yelling and running about in every direction. The venerable Choo,

the "Old Father of the Alley," as he was affectionately called by its
denizens, immediately took charge of the situation and began to
quiet things down. When order had been partially restored he sat
himself down in the high seat in the room and, after a sipping of
the tea and a whiff or two of the pipe which a kind neighbor had
provided, he gave it as his counsel that a committee from the alley,
consisting of the mother, the eldest son and two respectable residents, should proceed without delay to the head office of the Australian Wharf and there protest against Nam Tuck's arrest and
demand his release.

His age and position secured immediate compliance with his
advice and the "committee" waited in due order upon Mr. Bellsize,
the head manager of the Australian Wharf, at his office. He listened very respectfully to their story and complaint and, assuring
them of his complete confidence in Nam Tuck and of his intention
to do everything in his power to clear him of suspicion, he handed
them over to the compradore for tea and refreshments and, calling
his own jinrikisha, ordered the coolie to take him to Police Headquarters.

"What's the meaning of all this, Gubbins?" he began, as he was
ushered into the private office. "Why have you pounced upon my
night watchman and locked him up without a bit of evidence? He
hadn't any more to do with that MacMillan fire than I had—not a
bit, and you fellows know it, too. But I suppose, as usual, you had
to make a scapegoat of somebody and so you listened to the first
fellow's yarn that came along and grabbed an innocent spectator.
It's a way you police fellows have."

"Calm yourself, Mr. Bellsize, please, and take a seat," replied
the Inspector. "You are entirely mistaken in saying that we have
arrested an innocent man without evidence. We have a very well-
defined case against your watchman and I may say it is growing
stronger every day."

"O, you have, have you? Well, I should like to hear it. What is
it, pray?"

"Why, simply this: there is no question but that the fire was
started by someone who concealed four lighted fuses in the godown
during that afternoon. Now we have positive evidence that Nam

Tuck, your watchman, went to a shop nearby on the day before and purchased four just such fuses—"

"Fuses? Do you mean those slow-burning mosquito punk things the coolies burn during the night?"

"Exactly so. Now we have further evidence that he went to MacMillan's godown during the afternoon of the 17th and loitered around there some time, where he had no particular business—"

"Well, what of that? Haven't you been long enough in this country to know that the Chinese beat the world on loitering around and having no particular business?"

"Wait a minute, please. I come to the most damaging evidence of all. Two of the cotton-bale coolies swear that they heard him say to the second compradore: 'The old godown is about finished and if a good fire or typhoon would only come along and finish it, it would be a relief. The walls are utmost ready to fall over into the next yard.'"

"Somebody gave them a couple of dollars apiece to say that, I'll warrant."

"Well, you can think what you like about it, but with these different points we have a chain of evidence that is really stronger than many on which good people have been convicted in England."

"I don't agree with you at all," remarked the irate manager, as he rose to depart, "and I'm going to have a good long talk with the consul at the club tonight over the whole matter."

"That's your blessed privilege as a free and enlightened Britisher," answered the Inspector, as he bade him good afternoon.

Mr. Bellsize had hardly gone down the steps when Capt. Brownlow knocked at the inner door and entered with a smile of distinct satisfaction upon his face. "Well, we've got it at last," he began.

"Got what?" inquired the much-interested chief.

"Why, got the remaining link in the chain against the watchman. You know the only thing we really lacked was a cause or motive for the burning. We've got it now, and what do you suppose it is? Its the same old story: Sam has just discovered that Nam Tuck's brother is the man that sold the bricks to build the now godown. He burned it to get the brother a job!"

"It surely looks that way," replied the satisfied Inspector.

"OF COURSE, THE EVIDENCE is all circumstantial, but it generally is, you know, in these native cases," said Consul Clayton to Mr. Bellsize as they sat on the upper veranda of the Shanghai Club and talked over the matter of the MacMillan fire.

"Well, what will they do with the poor chap now? Drag him into the native city and torture him, I suppose, until he confesses?"

"That is the usual procedure, but the magistrate must first make up his mind that he is guilty. You see he practically makes up his mind and decides the case beforehand on the evidence submitted to him; the torture is simply to compel the prisoner to confess, for the native law requires the confession before the penalty can be inflicted."

"And what, pray, may the penalty be in such a case?"

"Probably decapitation, for arson is a capital crime."

"Heavens! Do you mean that there is no possible way to save Nam Tuck from being killed like a common murderer?"

"There is only one person in all China, that I know of," slowly and thoughtfully replied the consul, "who could possibly be of practical help to you."

"And who is that, pray?"

"That is Mr. Wang Foo of Hong Kong."

"Is he a native lawyer?"

"Yes and no—he is practically lawyer and judge and jury all combined, though he holds no official position. He is a marvelous expert in the matter of unearthing Chinese crimes and is known as the Prince of Chinese Detectives. If any human being can get at the bottom of this thing he is the man."

"By Jove! I think I remember him. Wasn't he the chap that exposed that hotel poisoning case a few years ago?"

"The very same, and I advise you to send for him at once. He won't intrude, however, unless he is officially invited; so you had better go and see Gubbins and get him to wire down in the name of the department and he'll almost surely be here on the next mail from the Island."

Mr. Bellsize lost no time in following the consul's advice and in less than a week's time Wang Foo, the "Man of Mystery," found himself once more in Shanghai, with his time and services placed at the disposal of the British authorities. He went into the whole case thoroughly with the Inspector and the captain, and of course talked it all over from a native standpoint with the Chinese portion of the force.

He visited the scene of the fire and made careful notes of the inside of the godown and of the exact spots from which the alarm was first given, and he was unusually particular to inquire the exact moment when the different persons in question first saw the smoke and the flame. He even took the trouble to go aboard the Ning-Po steamer and look up the record of it on her logbook.

He called on the disconsolate family in the Alley of the Heavenly Moon, representing himself as a private citizen much interested in the case, and found out all that he could regarding Nam Tuck and his relations to the parties in the godown next door. In a word, he made a very thorough investigation of all the circumstances surrounding the case, and then took a quiet evening off, in the home of his old friend, the basket maker from Hong Kong, to think it over carefully.

"Yes," he said to himself, "It certainly looks at first sight like a very clear case against the watchman. First, you have the motive, which was to get rid of the old building and secure the contract of the new bricks for the brother; then, second, you have the fact of the four smoldering fires inside; then, third, you have the purchase of the four fuses on just the day before, and then, fourth, you have Nam Tuck's own expressed wish that a fire would come along and 'burn the old thing down' as he stood in the godown on the very afternoon of the 17th! Yes!

"It's a clever piece of work that the foreign police have done and a pretty close net of evidence that they have woven about him, but they have got to draw it just a little tighter before they can convince me that he actually committed the crime.

"There are just four 'buts' or 'mays,' as I prefer to call them, that deserve our fair consideration. First, he may have made the remark about wishing the old building burned down just as innocently as anyone else might have made it; second, he may have used the four powder-paper fuses just to light his pipe and drive away the mosquitoes, as he says; third, he may have had a brother in the brick business without any thought of the fire; and, fourth, the fire may not have been started from paper fuses at all, but from something else which the police may never have thought of."

He lighted his little cloisonné pipe and, taking out a copy of the *Classics* from his trunk, he soon forgot this present world of suspicion and of crime and found himself wandering once more in the delightful glades of Confucius and the Disciples and breathing with them the refreshing air of divine philosophy and the uplift of mortal life. So reading, he fell asleep.

He was awakened from his slumbers by the loud beating of a brazen gong in some building just behind the basket-maker's home. He opened the shutters and looked out into the darkness and listened.

The sound came again, louder than before, and it seemed to be accompanied by some monotonous chant as of a number of voices singing a dirge. His curiosity led him to put on his gown and jacket and to pass down the stairs, out into the street, and around the buildings into the neighboring alley.

He found that the sounds came from a little temple where a group of aged priests were having some kind of religious ceremony. The doors were closed, but the cracks were wide enough for him to see clearly all that was going on inside.

Some half a dozen of them were standing around a shrine which they had placed in the center of the room and before the idol of which clouds of incense were rising to the roof. Above the shrine, hanging on brazen chains from the rafters, was a beautiful gong swinging slowly through the air, as if it had been struck with spirit hands.

He read the great characters painted upon it, "Shen Low'" ("The Spirit Gong"), and over the shrine he saw this scroll:

> "He who can strike the Temple Gong
> Will surely his earthly life prolong!"

He returned to his room and in the morning asked the basket maker about it. He found it was a little Ning Po Temple with a number of devotees who came to it frequently in search of health. The gong, he learned, was of an adjustable height and could just be touched by the tips of the visitor's fingers, the priests raising and lowering it by concealed pulleys behind the screens.

The patients were all profound believers in its virtue, for, like so many of its companions in the pagan world, it had most assuredly fallen at one time from heaven. There was just one other secret, which he learned from the old tea-man across the way from the temple gate, which even the basket maker did not know and that was that virtue of the life-prolonging gong could be transmitted to invalids at home and to criminals in prison.

The process, which was rather expensive and supposedly secret, was to have a prayer written on a piece of sacred paper bearing the image of the gong and then to have it rolled up and thrown into the air until it struck the edge of the brass and thus absorbed its virtue. It should be taken and thrown at the head of the person whose life was to be prolonged, while the thrower cried out: "He has struck the temple gong! He has struck the temple gong!" All of which was carefully noted by Wang Foo in the little leather notebook in his sleeve.

Some 10 days afterwards a company of gentlemen met the inspector of police by special invitation in his private office. Among them were the British Vice Consul, Mr. Bellsize of the Australian Wharf, and Messrs. Peasely and Rodero of the firm of MacMillan & Co, besides Capt. Brownlow and several English and Chinese detectives.

When all were seated Inspector Gubbins rose and said: "Gentlemen, I have invited you here this morning to listen to something of the deepest interest and concern to us all from the lips of a man who has no superior in the matter of the unveiling of Chinese mysteries. I have the pleasure of introducing Wang Foo of Hong Kong, better known as the Prince of Chinese Detectives."

What Wang Foo said, condensed into a very few words, was as follows: "Gentlemen, on the seventeenth of July the godown of

Messrs MacMillan & Co was, as you know, mysteriously set on fire and much of its contents destroyed.

"Suspicion happened to fall upon one Nam Tuck, the night watchman on the adjoining wharf. He was proved to have expressed a desire to see the old godown burn, to have been in it on the day of the fire and to have purchased four fuses with which (supposedly) to fire it, and, moreover, he is known to have had a material interest in the destruction, because his brother runs a brickyard and sold the material for rebuilding.

"Circumstantial evidence is strongly against him, but I propose to show you now that he had nothing whatever to do with it. More than this, gentlemen, that godown was never set on fire by a Chinese, but by a European!"

The company started and looked at each other in surprise. He continued: "The four fires, as shown by the times of the alarms, were started in the exact order of the European points of the compass, viz.: North, South, East and West.

"Now, no Chinese would ever do that: he would always start—no matter whether his deed was good or evil—with the Asiatic order of 'Tung, Si, Nam, Pek,' that is, 'East, West, South, North.'

"The moment I was certain of this order my suspicion lighted on Messrs. Peasely and Rodero, the latter member of which firm is not unknown to the police in Hong Kong. Inspector Gubbins, at my suggestion, had their houses searched, and complete outfits of fuses and slow matches—as he will himself show you—were discovered there. Gentlemen, I will not detain you longer, the story is a very brief one: Messrs. Peasely and Rodero set their own godown on fire to secure their very heavy insurance.

"The reason you did not suspect them was because they concealed themselves behind the good name of one of China's oldest and most respected firms, which makes their action more contemptible in the eyes of both East and West. You remember what Shakespeare says about the man who steals a good name; the sacred literature of the Orient is full of the self-same sentiment."

"Brownlow," said the Inspector, "bring in the prisoner and let us honorably release him in the midst of this company."

The captain motioned to an officer, who returned in a moment with the figure of Nam Tuck. Mingled fear and joy played across his countenance as he heard of his release.

"What is that piece of paper sticking to your forehead?" asked his employer, Mr. Bellsize.

"I think, sir," he stammeringly replied, "that I must have been struck with the Temple Gong!"

THE INCENSE BURNER

"Ching ying tak fok! Ching ying tak fok!" ("Make it a thousand dollars more! Make it a thousand dollars more!") shrieked out old Sam the compradore as he stretched out his long bony arm toward the center of the table and deposited there, in front of the censor of the game, a fat roll of Hong Kong bank notes.

The sleek and oily receiver of money took the roll from the gambler's hand, but before he said a word in acknowledgment of its receipt he laid out every separate bill before him, examined its surface carefully through his rough horn spectacles, held it up to the light, peered through it—as if suspicious of its interior structure—rubbed it between his thumb and long-nailed fingers and then deposited it in a n old -fashioned iron-chest, which he held securely between his knees.

Sam hai ching cheng tak fok" ("Sam truly adds a thousand more") he cried to a pock-marked cripple bending over an open account book at his side, and the latter promptly noted down the fact in the column under the name of the brave and reckless Sam. "Come now, Hop Hoy," he said, addressing the central figure of an interested group on the other side of the ring, "where's that valiant spirit of your ancestors of which you and your family are always talking?

"You're surely not going to allow a beancake to balk a lump of sugar that way, are you?" At this outburst of native wit the assembled crowd broke out into loud and good-natured laughter, recognizing at once the pointed allusion to the fact that the party

"Where did the prize-fight take place?"
asked Wang, as he siezed his wrists
in his grasp of steel.

named was a dealer in sugar, while his opponent was a shipper of the ever-popular beancake.

Now, ridicule—even in its most good-natured form—being something which the Chinese mind cannot tolerate, the remarks of the cashier, especially his clever reference to the ancestors, at once called forth from the excited Hop Hoy then retort. "By the noble spirits of my ancestors I will 'sweeten the mixture' with $1200 more."

And, suiting the action to the word, he drew from his sleeve the requisite amount, which disappeared in regular order through the opening in the cover of the iron chest

These two were the largest wagers of the evening on the spirited contest being waged between two local champions of the manly art in a carefully guarded cellar some ten feet or more beneath the surface of one of Hong Kong's crowded alleys. Of course there were smaller bets, even as low as the twenties and the tens and the fives, but no copper or brass was admitted in the moneyed transactions of this most aristocratic club—even the current Mexican silver having been tabooed and the minimum limit placed at a five-dollar note.

"We are all ready for the next and final round of the night," said the master of the bets, as no more money seemed forthcoming. "Whenever His Majesty shall give the word," addressing a pompous and brutal-faced individual who occupied the most prominent seat in the circle.

The "King of the Contest," as he was known to all the patrons of the establishment, bowed in acknowledgment and replied, "In accordance with the ancient customs and in obedience to the traditions of our ancestors, we will first pay our tribute to Tik Yok Wang, the third ruler of Hades, who presides over all the gods of the cellars. Let the candles and the incense be lighted and the wine and rice cake a be presented!"

"It is already done as His Majesty has commanded," replied Sung Ling, who acted in the capacity of doorkeeper and acolyte.

"Then let the honorable trial of strength begin!" announced the King in his most majestic tones, "and may the August decree of Heaven decide between the merits of 'Spotted Back' and 'Yellow

Legs.' (Loud cheers from the backers of these two champions greeted the royal remarks.) Are the red lacquer clamps firm beneath the waists—"

"They are! They are!" shrieked the room in one great chorus.

"Then all is ready, GO!" and with the word, "Spotted Back" and "Yellow Legs," stripped of every rag of clothing and held only around the waist by the clamps of the polished red lacquer, flew at each other and, grappling in an awful struggle for life or death, seemed to be trying to tear each other limb from limb, as they revolved around in the narrow arena—not of boards or of sand, but, as always in these contests in China—of baked, and polished porcelain.

The battle was brief but very bloody and in less than live short minutes "Spotted Back" was lying a crumpled mass upon the floor and the conquering "Yellow Legs," who had jumped upon his victim and was kicking out his few remaining sparks of life, had actually to be dragged off of him and lifted bodily into the air by the spectators who rushed into the ring.

His Majesty rendered the official decision—though that was hardly necessary under the circumstances—and amid the intensest excitement the iron chest was unlocked by the cashier and the full amount of the wagers, less, of course, the deduction of the usual percentage for expenses, janitor's wine-money and offerings to the cellar-god, were paid over to the lucky supporters of the victor.

One by one they retired from the scene of the conflict, passing out in single file through a dark and narrow passage into an adjoining cellar, where a pile of innocent-looking empty oil-boxes revolved on a pilot like the circular doors of a London bank, and up through the kitchen of a coffin-maker's shop and so out into a twisting alley and at length into the open street. There was no formal oath of secrecy as to the location and what took place there, but there was even a still stronger bond of silence, a sort of tacit and mutual understanding that the vengeance of the gods of Hades— to say nothing of the "foreign-devils' patrol," as they dubbed the English police—would surely light on the head of the unfortunate one who breathed a word of it outside. Under these circumstances there was naturally no public advertising of the periodic contests, but there were certain bulletin boards on the street corners where private tips as to the approaching dates, etc, were announced in ambiguous terms which conveyed exact information to the initiated but left a very different impression on the unsuspecting public—and the police.

For instance. "Yellow Legs will be in the market an the 19th of the moon" or "Spotted Backs will be for sale on the 20th" could refer equally well to Canton ducks and feathered game for the kitchen or to a coming prize fight in the secret cellar.

INSPECTOR WALLACE of the Hong Kong police was sitting quietly in his office overlooking the blue waters of the harbor, when the boy on duty appeared at the door with the card of the Rev. Herbert Smalltree of the Union Mission and after presenting it to his chief was told to show the visitor in.

"Mr. Inspector," began the missionary, after he had accepted the proffered seat and had declined the equally courteously proffered cigar. "I come to see you this afternoon because my conscience bids me, do so. I have hesitated for some time, because I dislike to stir up any trouble—especially with the Police Department, for which I have the greatest respect—but I feel that the time has now come when it is my religious duty, both as a Christian man and a resident of this community, to report to you that a very serious breach of the law is going on continually here, right under your very eyes and without any apparent effort being made by the authorities to stop it."

"Indeed! Well, that is rather a serious charge against us, Mr. Smalltree. May I ask to what you refer, sir?"

"I refer to prize-fighting, Mr. Wallace, and prize-fighting of the most degrading and brutal kind. I spoke to my friend Lord Dubbins, of Aberdeen—who, as you know, is visiting to the Colony—about it yesterday and he promised to bring it to the attention of Government House when he called there today."

"I am sorry that you did not report it to me, sir, before you allowed it to reach the ears of the Governor, because it may make serious and quite unnecessary complications. Tell me now exactly the facts as you know them, being very particular, please about names and places.

"Just when and where did this 'prize-fight,' as you call it, take place? You have made a charge against this department. Now, sir," continued the Inspector in a much more serious tone, "I demand that you produce your proofs and make it good, or else apologize for it and withdraw it."

"That is just the trouble, sir," replied the Rev. Smalltree, "we do not know the exact place or even the exact date."

"You do not know the place nor the date?"

"Unfortunately not, sir; all we know is that the fight took place— and that a number of similar ones have taken place recently—and that up to the present time not a single line has appeared in the public papers of any attempt on the part of the police to arrest the participants or to stop it."

"We do not publish all the transactions of the Department in the public papers, you know, until we think it wise and expedient to do so. Publicity of this kind sometimes acts as a very serious bar to getting justice done to the case. Where do you imagine these fights take place?"

"Well, sir, when my attention was first called to them, I though they probably took place in some native enclosure just outside the international boundary, but I now am quite certain that they are being carried on in some secret spot here in the Colony."

"Quite impossible! Utterly absurd, sir!" exclaimed the Inspector as he brought his closed fist down with an emphatic blow upon the office table. "There isn't a secret hiding place on all the Island of Hong Kong that could possibly hold a crowd gathered for a prize fight.

"I know they have their little 'rabbit-tunnels' as I call them, where they burrow under the ground and dig out a little hole for two or three to gamble in—we smoke 'em out of these every now and then—but the idea of their having a regular arena hidden away somewhere is quite impossible. I repeat it sir, quite impossible! But what is your evidence—that's what I want to get at—produce it, if you have any."

"The evidence, sir, is of a hearsay nature—"

"Ah! That's just what I supposed; some foolish native story, I'll warrant!"

"Wait a moment, please; the evidence is, I say, of a hearsay nature, but of a kind that I have implicit confidence in—"

"Well, out with it, then. Who concocted the yarn?"

"It is no yarn at all, Mr. Inspector," replied the Missionary slowly and very seriously. "It is the testimony of a tried and trusted assistant of mine, whom I would trust as soon as I would the oldest European in the colony."

"Well, what's the tale?"

"Listen! Coming down from Canton on the night boat last week, he occupied a cabin next to two travelers who kept up a running conversation until after midnight, and, the partition being full of cracks, he couldn't help overhearing a good deal that they said—"

"Eavesdropping as usual! My gracious, the curiosity of this people!"

"Well, sir, you know Europeans sometimes hare a little curiosity themselves; but to proceed, he kept hearing phrases like these: 'They certainly fought like demons.' 'The place was packed with their supporters.' 'They were clinched to a death grip,' 'They actually had to pull them apart,' etc., etc. Now, if that doesn't indicate fighting of the most brutal kind, what does?"

"It certainly looks that way, Mr. Smalltree, but there isn't a word there to indicate that the fight took place on English soil—it might have been in any country town in China."

"Wait a moment, please, that isn't all. I am just coming to the important point. They also said, several times, 'What if the devils' patrol had broken tin upon them and caught them in the act?'"

"You are quite sure they said that?"

"Quite positive, sir, and you know what that phrase refers to, do you not?"

"I believe my Department is honored with that title," replied the English officer, with a smile.

"Yes, sir, and it could never refer to any other place than just this Colony, because in Macao, which is Portuguese; they wouldn't have to 'break in.' They do all that sort of thing right out in public and the police generally look on and rather enjoy the scene. It was here and nowhere else."

"Well, something of that kind may have happened just once in a very small way; but what makes you think and say that it is still going on?"

"Because he overheard them say, 'Twice every moon, twice every moon', which makes it clear that it is a regular performance. And, in addition to the brutal exhibition of the fight, it is probably one of the very worst of our native gambling hells, for they kept continually referring to the size of the wagers, which ran up into the thousands.

"Now, there you have the whole story, sir. I give it to you exactly as it came to me, and I think it is high time that you set your native detectives at work upon the case."

"I will just note down in writing an outline of this," remarked the Inspector as he rose and reached for his desk pad, "and Capt. Brownlow and I will talk it all over this evening.

"There may be something in it and there may not—for Lord knows, you can hear something new is going on in this queer land every day you live—but, at any rate, we want you and all the good residents here to know that this department is doing all in its power to keep the moral tone of the Island high. Good afternoon, sir!"

"Good afternoon and thank you," answered the reverend gentleman as he passed out into the courtyard.

That evening the two English heads of the police force spent a quiet but interesting hour in discussing the complaint of the missionary and in wondering whether it could be possible that a contest of this kind had actually taken plaice in their midst and been so carefully and so successfully concealed.

"Goodness knows. It may be," laconically remarked Brownlow, "for all you and I know to the contrary, they may be slugging each other now right under this very private office, 30 foot or more under ground, and you and I a-sitting here in blissful ignorance, as the poet says."

"Hardly that," replied the Inspector, "for these headquarters are resting on solid granite; but it's just possible they may have burrowed a larger tunnel than we've found yet under some other part of the town. Do you remember the day we opened up that old drain by the Post-office and found a whole gang of them buried there like moles, sleeping off the effects of the opium?"

"I do, indeed, sir, and the wonder was how any human beings could have survived it, for it surely was worse than the old Black Hole of Calcutta in the days of the Mutiny."

"Dr. Bradlaw of the Church Mission Hospital tells me as how he believes they can get along with less fresh air than any human beings that ever lived. Says they not only close up all the windows in the hospital, but actually stuff up all the ventilators and airholes with bits of paper, so that not a breath can get in."

"You're right, Brownlow, I don't believe our laws of life and oxygen apply to this portion of the human race. Well, as to this prize-fight story, I suggest we get the ideas of the native staff upon it and see what they think of its possibilities."

"Right you are, sir, and here's hoping that if they have dug right under us they won't think it worth while to put dynamite to the tunnel and blow us all up, sir."

"O! They'll never do that."

"Why not, pray?"

"Why, don't you remember that old Kang, who was on the force two years ago, explained to us that the Chinese considered that a terrible waste of time and strength; just to dig a tunnel for the sake of blowing it up, even if it did send the 'foreign devil' with it into the air?"

"Yes, I believe he did, sir."

In accordance with the above agreement the native staff of officers and detectives was taken into consultation, but they didn't give the story much credence. They agreed that it would be well nigh impossible for a gathering of that size to take place regularly without its leaking out, and, besides that, prize-fighting was really a Western form of amusement, for which the Celestial had not yet any very great fondness.

The whole affair would probably have been allowed to quietly die out, had not the persistent Mr. Smalltree taken it upon himself to intrude into the sacred precincts of Government House and repeat to Sir Arthur Wayne-Ervington the report of Lord Dubbins of Aberdeen. This led His Excellency to send for Inspector Wallace and to insist upon a thorough and exhaustive search being made as to whether anything in the nature of a prize fight could have actually taken place in the colony—under ground or above ground—without the knowledge of the authorities.

The Inspector, in his dilemma, naturally turned to his best and most helpful friend in the matter of unraveling crime, and so that evening found him by appointment in the upper room of No. 5-5-5 in the Red Cloud Alley, smoking a soothing cheroot in the armchair of the great Wang Foo, the Prince of Chinese detectives.

WANG FOO LISTENED LONG AND PATIENTLY to the Inspector's story, making his usual careful notes in the well-worn leather note-book from his sleeve.

"You are inclined, then," said the Inspector, "to place considerable credence in the Christian teacher's story?"

"Yes, decidedly," replied the detective, "you see, testimony of that kind is always of great value, because it is unintentional. The passengers in the adjoining stateroom could have had no object in concocting a falsehood of that kind. It was simply a recalling of a scene of which one of them had been a spectator and which the other already knew about.

"What leaked out was simply what went through the cracks of the partition. There was unquestionably a fight, and a fight of a very brutal nature, accompanied by very heavy betting on the rival candidates. It also looks very much as if it was something that took place regularly from the remarks. 'Twice in every moon.' It is also very clear that it must have been in some place where foreign officers would have been liable to interfere, and of course this could not have been on native soil.

"However"—here he spoke very slowly and thoughtfully—"we have no right to immediately jump at the conclusion that it was in Hong Kong, for there are other possibilities. The Rev. Mr. Smalltree's criticism of your Department in therefore hasty and consequently quite unfair."

"I am glad to know you feel that way about it, Mr. Wang. It relieves my mind. People are very quick to accuse the police of negligence, when all the time we may be doing the very best we can, but we are simply groping in the dark."

"I quite understand that, Mr. Wallace, I have suffered from the same kind of criticism myself. Now, you will be good enough to let me have my usual 10 days or two weeks to go into the matter thoroughly, and, in the meantime, if anything turns up, I will let you know. Venerable Grand One!" he cried to the aged matron in the lower hall. "Renew the tea ere the honorable guest departs. Old Chang! (addressing the gatekeeper) Have the horn lantern lighted and show the Ocean Mandarin's chair safety to the Alley's mouth."

"It is already done as the Grand One orders!" came back simultaneously from the native servants, as the Inspector rose to bid his genial host "good night."

SEVERAL DAYS HAD PASSED since the interview in Wang Foo's room in the Red Cloud Alley and while nothing new of any value had come from the police, our Chinese detective had gleaned several points of interest from a close cross-questioning of the native teacher.

While he had not been able to extract from him the actual names of the combatants—for these, in spite of his careful listening, he had been unable to catch—he had made sure that one of them was spotted or scarred on the back, probably from smallpox, and that the other was lame (a rather strange handicap for a fighter in good trim, if true) or bow-legged.

This he gathered from the teacher's repeated assertion that he heard one of them alluded to as "Old Crooked Legs." This wasn't very much in the way of identification, but at least it was something, and he took it with him on the evening that he went to the Temple of the Queen of Heaven to talk the case over with his old friend, the Abbot.

After the usual ceremonial greetings and the hot tea and pipes, they sat down in the inner curtained apartment and Wang Foo unfolded the evidence in detail, pausing every few moments to see whether his Venerable Father grasped the point and what his comment upon it would be.

"And you haven't been able to identify a single one of those who were present?" he asked.

"Not positively, but he alluded to one of them as 'sweetening' the wagers, which leads me to suspect a dealer in sugar."

The Abbot thought for a while and then said: "It is not likely that any one of them was new at the game, especially those who played the very large stakes. It must have been one who had learned the trick at the foreign horse races.

"We will inquire carefully tomorrow and see if we can trace any sugar merchant who won or who lost heavily at the native booth during the May season at the Happy Valley Course. This may give us a valuable clue."

"A brilliant thought, my Venerable Father!" exclaimed Wang Foo, "and one well worthy of your careful and suggestive mind; we will act upon it without delay. Once having secured him, we can, by proper means, force out of him the names of others and then we shall be on the fair way to discover the 'Cripple' and the 'Pock-marked' and locate their secret meeting place."

They talked and talked well on into the night, but even with all the evidence they had neither of them seemed to be satisfied in his own mind that the fight had actually taken place in the Colony.

"It is too new, too new," repeated the Abbot, as he bowed his guest toward the door. "Our people have their own vices, as we well know, and unfortunately they are learning others from the ocean men (foreigners), but it is far too early in our history for them, I believe, to have gone into this sort of thing. Not yet, not yet—some day, perhaps. Alas! but not yet, thank the Buddhas!"

A day or two's careful inquiry among the jockeys and pony-boys at the race course stables—made by Wang Foo in the disguise of a peddler of lottery tickets, of which article they were liberal purchasers—revealed the fact that Hop Hoy, the sugar dealer, was the most liberal patron of the betting booth at the last Spring meeting, and both Wang Foo and the Abbot felt sure enough of the identity to inveigle him into the temple and there to supply the Chinese "third degree."

"Where did the prize fight take place?" asked Wang, as he seized his wrists in his grasp of steel and looked straight into his startled eyes.

"What prize fight!" exclaimed the astonished Hop Hoy. "Prize fight? Why I never attended a prize fight in my life. That is the ocean man's game; we Chinese have no such vice."

"The prize fight between a pockmarked man and a cripple," said the detective, "You know, you wretch, the one where you 'sugared' the pile with a thousand dollars. You know; out with it, quick!"

"A pock-marked man and a cripple? I do not know what you mean," he protested.

"Yes, the fight between 'Spotted Back' and 'Old Crooked Legs.' Where was it? Tell us quickly," interrupted the Abbott, "or by all the Buddhas, the vengeance of the Queen of Heaven will fall upon you."

"'Spotted Back' and 'Yellow Legs'!" (the sound of "yellow" closely resembling "crooked") cried the trembling man and a sudden ray of light spread over his face. "Why, that was—"

"Whisper it! Whisper it!" said Wang Foo, "whisper it to the Venerable Father; speak it not aloud, for the very walls of the temple have ears."

Hop Hoy leaned forward and whispered into the Abbot's ears a few short words. The effect was perfectly electrical. The Venerable Father started back in astonishment, then smiled, and finally broke out into a laugh and exclaiming, "We might have known as much!" himself whispered the mysterious words to Wang Foo, upon whom they produced the very same effect.

The secret was all out now, the confession was brief, but complete, and all that remained was for Hop Hoy to personally conduct the great detective to the underground arena and for the latter in turn to make the same revelation to Inspector Wallace and the police—if he thought it wise so to do.

Old Chang, the gatekeeper, made a special trip to Police Headquarters the following morning, bearing a precious sealed document from Wang Foo to be delivered to the Inspector in person. It contained these significant words:

"My Dear Mr. Wallace—All is up. We have discovered the ring where the bloody contest took place; have secured the principal witness and also the person of the victorious 'Yellow Legs.' I regret to say that poor 'Spotted Back,' his opponent, is still suffering from his injuries and unable to appear, but we have made it impossible for him to escape.

"It is a little unusual, but native ideas of justice and propriety demand that the criminal shall be transported in a wooden cage. We will produce him at headquarters at noon today, and I shall be glad to have you invite His Excellency and Rev. Mr. Smalltree to be present when he is carried in. The cage (which we have brought from Canton) will be carefully covered while passing through the streets, so as not to excite the public—especially the Europeans, who might not understand it. Very cordially yours, Wang Foo."

"P. S.—You might include Lord Dubbins in the party if he is still in town."

It was just five minutes to 12 when Hong Kong's famous detective alighted from his sedan chair and passed into the private office of the Inspector.

The invited guests were all there. It was easy to see that they were awaiting with the deepest interest—not to say anxiety—this exposure of the prize fight in their midst, and were wondering at the audacity—even of Wang Foo, with all his prestige—of transporting, a criminal in an old-fashioned punishment cage through the streets of the civilized British colony. He was formally introduced and arose to address them.

"The prisoner, the prisoner!" they all cried in unison.

"Yellow Legs and the cage! Where are they! Haven't you brought him?" eagerly inquired the Inspector, beginning to fear a disappointment.

"Gentlemen," said the Man of Mystery, as with a sweeping gesture he produced a little paper package from his silken sleeve, "behold the criminal and the prison!" he unwrapped before their astonished eyes a tiny willow cage and in it a yellow-legged chirping cricket!

"What means this pleasantry and why do you trifle with us this way?" asked the Governor as he arose and addressed Wang Foo.

"Your Excellency," replied the Detective with the most courteous at bows, "this is no pleasantry, it is the simple unvarnished truth. Listen to me, I beg you, for a moment. This whole thing is an illustration of the mistake of applying a European conception to an Asiatic transaction.

"A contest of strength—a true fight if you wish so to call it— takes place in your midst and you spring at once to the conclusion that the combatants are of course human beings. This does not follow at all in China. I have listened carefully to every word of the evidence and there is not a syllable from end to end that does not apply as well to an insect as to a man—read it over yourselves and acknowledge that I am correct.

"Every Nation has its own form of prize fighting; bulls in Spain, bears in Russia, crocodiles in Egypt, cobras in India—everything from quadrupeds to insects—crickets in China, the last and least harmful of all. It is only in civilized and refined Europe and America that these brutalizing contests are taken part in by human beings."

"By Jove! You know, that is really most mysterious and interesting," was Lord Dubbins' response on behalf of the assembled company.

"MR. INSPECTOR," REMARKED WANG FOO, as he called at the office a few days after the denouement, "I want you to accept this little gift in memory of your first real Chinese prize fight," unwrapping, as he spoke, a delicate package of yellow silk.

"What is it, pray?"

"It is a little incense-burner of bronze. You see, it is a cricket! And here are five sticks of incense—the sacred Chinese number of good luck—to go with it. One is inserted in either eye, one in his head, one in his mouth and one in the middle of his back. Light them some time after a long and weary day's work and you will find them most refreshing. They will purify the atmosphere."

"Thank you most heartily. Mr. Wang," replied the Inspector, as he gratefully accepted the gift. "I shall feel most happy, as the Immortal Dickens said, always to have a cricket on my hearth!"

"Yes," answered the Disciple of Confucius, "it is similar to the sentiment in the great *Book of Poetry*:

"Chirp! Chirp! Little visitor,
Always welcome to our home."

THE BUDDHA'S WAND

"THEY'RE OFF AGAIN, and a fine lot this time" said Mrs. Cortelyou, wife of the American Consul at Shanghai, to her friend and guest, Mrs. Marsdale of Boston, as they sat in the "Consuls' Row" on the grandstand at the race-course. "I do hope my husband's pony will win something this time, for he takes such a pride in the few American firms being able to hold their own with the English, you know."

"Yes, indeed," answered Mrs. Marsdale. "I am sure he is most loyal to his country in everything. He enters into all the port sports so enthusiastically—I wish all our American consuls did the same— and he is always 'on top', as they say, with the stars and stripes. By the way, which firm is it that he is interested in now?"

"Why, Farnsworth & Co., don't you know, blue and white, the colors we are wearing now—"

"We?"

"Why, certainly, my dear; didn't he pin that ribbon on you before we left the house?"

"I am afraid the good man forgot it!"

"Thoughtless creature! Just like him—the truth is his head was so full of ponies that he would have walked out without his helmet in all this broiling sun if I hadn't looked after him. You must forgive him, for I know he had the colors all laid out for you on his office desk. Here! You just take mine—" unpinning a handsome badge of blue and white ribbons from her dress and fastening it on her friend.

"Nonsense, my dear child," protested Mrs. Marsdale, "the idea of the Consul's wife being seen at the race without her colors! What

He turned a complete
somersault over his head,—
and landed safe and sound
upon his feet!

will people think of you?" But Mrs. Cortelyou insisted on making good her husband's forgetfulness, and there was nothing to do but to yield.

"And what do the words 'Foo Sang' mean," inquired the former as she noticed the gold stamp on the ribbons; "some wonderful and mysterious Chinese charm, I suppose; the Orient is all so quaint and interesting."

"Oh, no, that's only the Hong's (firm's) Chinese name. The native's can't pronounce 'Farnsworth' or any of our foreign signs, so they just select some happy and high-sounding phrase and transact all their business with us through that; it saves so much time and trouble. I believe it means "Fortunate Life', or something of that kind."

"What a happy idea!"

"Yes, or 'How appropriately felicitous', as they would say in old Boston, wouldn't they?"

"Wall, I suppose Beacon Street would be inclined to express it that way, perhaps," answered Mrs. Marsdale with a smile of loyalty for her New England home.

"Watch them! Watch them through your glasses, dear. See! They're at the quarter-post already—no, it's the half, and the blue and white is leading!"

All eyes were now turned in the direction of the flying ponies and their brave riders as they rounded the further side of the course. The whole grandstand seemed to swing around the circle with them. What a picturesque sight it was, and where in the world could one witness such a gathering of varied people, faces and costumes! European ladies with all the newest creations from Paris, London, Vienna and Madrid; in the rows of seats behind them brilliant colored robes from Calcutta, Bombay and Batavia, worn by the wives and daughters of those fortunate Orientals who from their prominent position in the community were able to claim a quasi-equality with the Western world; and in the adjoining "annex" all the hues of the rainbow reflected from the robes of the Chinese patrons of the white man's sport. Suddenly a sharp cry of excitement rang out. 'Foo Sang has fallen! The blue and white is down!"

as between the half and the three-quarter mile posts they saw the handsome gray Mongolian pony, whose jockey wore the popular colors of Farnsworth & Co., stagger for a moment and then fall with his rider, a crumpled mass upon the turf. There was a rush of policemen, surgeons, officials of the course and citizens toward the spot where the accident occurred, the pony—just breathing his last—was hastily dragged to one side, and the jockey, stunned but fortunately not seriously injured, was carried to the nearest shelter and given due medical treatment.

The Incident was soon forgotten by the assembled crowd and ere long the bell sounded for the second race and everything went on merrily as before. The third and fourth passed off successfully without any accident to horses or riders and after a short intermission for the inevitable afternoon tea, preparations began to be made for the fifth. In this one the Americans were again especially interested for the first and fifth were the only ones in which the firm of the Farnsworths had entered their ponies.

"And who is riding for you this time?" inquired Mrs. Marsdale as she saw the Consul and his friends leading out the new batch of ponies and the blue and white prominently among them.

"Why, it is Mr. Pierce, the brother of the first jockey, and, they say, equally as good a rider. They call them 'The Eurasian Twins' because they are almost exactly alike—not even the Chinese can tell them apart. They are fine fellows, both of them; sons of old Captain Pierce, who was in the coast service here for years. They've been riding for Mr. Farnsworth ever since we have been here, and they have the reputation of being absolutely honest, that is—" answered Mrs. Cortelyou with a questioning smile—"absolutely honest for jockeys, and my husband trusts them implicitly."

"And how is the other poor fellow who was thrown? It's a wonder to me he wasn't killed upon the spot."

"Oh, he's doing splendidly, and the doctor says he'll be all right in a day or two. Fortunately, you see, he fell quite clear of the pony and just rolled over and over on the soft grass there."

The conversation of the ladies was interrupted just here by the sounding of the second bell, and in a few minutes more the shouts of the assembled thousands of natives announced that the ponies and their riders were off again around the course. Now came the strange and startling thing: at almost the identical spot beyond the half-mile post where the wearer of the blue and white was thrown in the first race of the afternoon his twin brother's pony suddenly reared and came within an ace of repeating the accident. His jockey, however, clung with a veritable death grip to his mane and neck and when the animal leaped into the air and then fall upon his knees he turned a complete somersault over his head and landed, like the trained acrobat in the circus, safe and sound upon his feet!

"Merciful Heavens!" exclaimed the Consul, who had only just joined the ladies, "they're trying to kill another one. That's the second fall today and"—raising his field-glasses to his eyes and gazing steadily in the direction of the accident—"can you believe it, it's our own blue and white again! Excuse me, ladies. I must go and see Farnsworth at once," as he rushed down the steps of the grandstand.

His Excellency, the Tao Tai of Shanghai (who was always an honored guest of the Race Club at the Spring Meeting, and who was standing by the side of his official sedan-chair, surrounded by his staff and by the usual out-riders and attendants with red umbrellas and banners) happened to be looking through his glasses also at this identical moment and seeing the pony throw young Mr. Pierce, exclaimed: "Hai ya! Ma tao liao jen" ("Alas! The horse has thrown the man.") This was enough to start a perfect whirlwind of excitement among the Chinese, who began running in every direction, repeating the cry. "Ma tao liao jen! Ma tao liao jen!" and it required all the efforts of the English police and the native lictors with their long bamboos to restore order and quiet. "Shen mo ma? Shen mo ma?" they kept inquiring. ("Whose horse? Whose horse?") At first nobody seemed able to definitely answer the question, but soon a native officer came running back from the other side of the course, crying out: "Ching pak, ching pak. Hwo chi kwo hong Foo Sang!" ("Blue and white, blue and white! The Flowery Flag (American)

Kingdom's firm Foo Sang.") this was the signal for a most sympathetic outcry of "Ko Shi! Ko Shi!" ("How sad! How sad!") from the multitude, for the American firm was easily the most popular with the natives of all those represented on the course that afternoon.

Standing by the side of His Excellency, the Tao Tai, was a tall Chinese gentleman, who appeared to be acting for the moment as interpreter between this dignitary of the government and the newly arrived Consul for France, Colonel Francois DePuy Valette. He was not in official dress, but one could see at once from his attitude and bearing and from the deference paid him by the Consul and the Tao Tai, that he was far more than an ordinary civilian. It was also quite evident that he had more than a mere passing acquaintance with the two officers from East and West for whom he was acting as the go-between.

"A most extraordinary circumstance—most extraordinary!" remarked the Consul, "that the two riders of the same firm should be thrown in the same afternoon."

"Most extraordinary, indeed!" replied the Tao Tai.

"If this were in France I should begin to suspect foul play of some kind, there is so much trickery in our Western racing, but out here in the Far East, where everything is so informal and where the firms know each other so well, and all run their own ponies, I have never thought of such a thing."

"It is just possible that with the introduction of Western sports there may be coming-in the ocean-man's ways of fraud and wickedness, though as High Heaven knows, we have already enough of our own to contend with, sir, as our mutual friend, Mr. Wang Foo, will bear me out," commented the native ruler of the port.

"Alas, what Your Excellency says is only too true," replied the famous detector of crime—for it was none other than he who was acting as their interpreter—"and something that happened at the last autumn races in Hong Kong leads me to believe that the Western trickery of which you speak is not unknown in our Southern Colony."

He had hardly uttered these words when a stout individual clad in robes of the most elegant and expensive silk and wearing the

large horn goggles of the well-to-do merchant class, pushed his
way by them and motioned to some waiting coolies to make ready
his sedan. He was muttering to himself as he passed—evidently in
a state of considerable irritation and anger, "Tien Ming puh shi!
Tien Ming puh shi, pei tak Foo Sang." ("It is not the Decree of
Heaven, it is not the Decree of Heaven, he was discharged from
Foo Sang!"} These remarks were lost upon both Colonel Valette
and the Tao Tai; the former did not understand them and the latter
evidently did not distinctly hear them, but the trained and ever-
careful ear of the man who stood between them caught them and
did not forget them, and so, when he reached his quiet lodging that
evening, they found a place in one of the leaves of his note-book,
where they were securely hidden away for any possible future reference.

THE COLUMNS of the *North China Daily News* of the following morning contained this rather striking paragraph:

SINGULAR ACCIDENT AT THE RACES
Suspected Foul Play
"We deeply regret to have to chronicle a most unfortunate, and at the same time, a most mysterious
occurrence at yesterday's races. Two of the ponies
from the stables of our esteemed American firm of
Farnsworth & Co. (Chinese hong-name Foo Sang)
fell suddenly in the middle of the first and fifth races,
just near the three-quarter-mile-post, and died almost immediately. They were being ridden by those
well-known young men, the Messrs. Pierce of Hoo
Lang Road, than whom none are more highly esteemed in the entire club. Mr. Alfred, who was in
the first accident, was very severely shaken-up and
was for some time unconscious, but we are happy to
say had no bones broken and is rapidly recovering.
His brother, Mr. Eugene, escaped in a remarkable

manner by turning a complete somersault over his pony's head and landing on a soft piece of turf.

"The double occurrence at almost the identical spot led Mr. Farnsworth to have a careful examination made by the stewards of the course, but nothing was found that could have caused either of the ponies to stumble there and all the other riders of the afternoon passed over it in safety. The only conclusion was—and this was the generally expressed opinion at all the different clubs last evening—that there had been some vicious foul play and that deadly poison of some kind had been administered in both cases with the above results. This may have been done in some way by the jockeys themselves or it may have been administered in the stalls by someone who secretly worked his way in there. As Dr. Aubrey, our well-known veterinary surgeon is making a careful postmortem of the ponies under the direction of the Department of Police we reserve any further comment until his report is made public, especially as we desire to shield the Messrs Pierre, to whom this is naturally a very painful experience, from any possible opprobrium."

Wang Foo purchased a copy of the above edition the very first thing in the morning and clipping the article carefully out compared it with the notice in the leading Chinese papers They were practically the same in their substance and purport, though of course elaborately drawn out and clothed in all the flowery expressions of the native editor. Not a word in any of them, however, though he read every column through slowly and carefully, that would point to anyone, foreigner or native, as the actual guilty party, which fact seemed rather to disappoint him. The more he thought upon the case the more interesting—because the more involved—it became to him, and so taking out his little traveling writing-case he sat down and, rubbing the ink-slab up and down the stone tablet, after the manner of the true Chinese scholar, he repeated over as he did so the well-known words of Confucius, "As we polish and then grind! As we polish and then grind!" and dipping his brush in the carbon fluid he began a little letter to his home in Hong Kong, which conveyed to them the news that it might be the middle of the moon or more before he would set sail for the Island of Fragrant Waters.

He had a real and genuine problem before him in unraveling a case of which he had had the unusual advantage of himself being an eyewitness. This was more than worth to him the extra trouble and expense of a stay in Shanghai and he immediately set his thinking faculties to work, determined to work out at last some plausible theory before he should confer with his old friend, Inspector Gubbins of the police.

Four distinct questions naturally outlined themselves before him: First, was it an accident or a premeditated crime? Second, if a crime was it poison or some other form of deadly injury? Third, who was the guilty party? And fourth, what was his object in committing it, financial profit or merely the gratifying of some deadly hatred and revenge? As incidental to all this, he would of course take a delight in securing the identity of the mysterious personage in the silks and goggles, whom he had overheard rejecting the theory of the "Decree of Heaven" as he rushed past him by the Tao Tai's side. "Yes," he said to himself as he sipped his cup of evening tea in the upper room at the home of his old friend, the basket-maker. "yes, I have certainly a few days of very attractive work before me, and I had best begin, as the Sages taught, by 'bending my attention to what is radical'. 'Kwun Tze woo pen,'" ("The Superior Man observes the root") and so saying he blew out the little bean-oil lamp and fell asleep on his bamboo pillow.

WHILE THE MAN OF MYSTERY, as Wang Foo had come to be known by his European friends and admirers, was quietly working out his own theory unknown to the outer world or Shanghai, Inspector Gubbins and Chief Detective Brownlow had not been idle in their efforts to clear the Pierce brothers and fasten the poisoning—for such Dr. Aubrey, the veterinary, had unhesitatingly declared the crime to be—upon the head of some native or, possibly, European rascal. Among other suggestions, amid the many that had come to them from members of the Race Club and other interested residents, was one that was brought to them in confidence by an old racing hand from abroad and which appealed to them by its very ingenuity. Major Weltman, of Sidney, described to them a case he had personally known in which a jockey was bribed to mortally injure a pony in an Australian race. A subtle and quickly acting poison was concealed in one of his spurs, the star of which, instead of revolving as usual was soldered firmly to the shank. In it was concealed a hollow needle connected with a metal tube, so that when it was plunged into the horse's side from the rider's boot the poison was injected into his veins and soon did its deadly work. The whole thing was afterward exposed in the Sidney papers and the spur and needle are new on exhibition in the cabinet of the chief of police there.

"It would be a magnificent theory for us to go on, sir," remarked the thoughtful Brownlow to his superior officer, after listening to the Major's story, "but for one fatal defect—"

"And pray, what might that be?" interrupted the Australian visitor.

"Why, simply this," answered the detective. "I find, on careful inquiry, that at the last meeting of the Race Club Committee, steel spurs were ordered off, and nothing but these little 'bamboo ticklers,' as the Chinese call them, were allowed to be worn this season!"

"I am afraid the spur theory won't work this time, Major," added the Inspector with a smile, "however successful it may have been in Sidney."

"Yes, I'm afraid not," replied the Major, as he rose to leave; "you chaps will have to find some other form of devilish ingenuity—for that's what it is and that's what I call it, devilish, nothing leas. I'm an old racing man myself, and I tell you the man who will deliberately plan to injure a horse and kill man is—well, hanging's too good for him, that's my opinion, gentlemen. Good morning!"

As the days passed on, public opinion began, pretty generally, to clear the Pierce brothers of any complicity in the case and the firm of Farnsworth & Co. indeed completely exonerated them.

There was not a particle of real substantial evidence against them and nobody could even suggest any motive for the act. They were on perfectly good terms with their employers and the stakes—even the largest of them—wagered on the Shanghai port races were not large enough to induce them, or indeed any other jockeys, to undertake a risk like that which might be taken in some of the great race meetings in Europe. In a word, people came to the sensible conclusion that "the game wasn't worth the candle," as the saying goes, and so the efforts of the police and others interested were turned to the discovering of some "ma-foo" or horse-boy in the stables, who out of hatred to Farnsworth & Co., or if not that, out of pure maliciousness or deviltry, had committed the crime. But here was again the mystery: how could any mere ma-foo have had the knowledge of such a deadly poison? Where could he have obtained it and how could he have timed it so that it took effect exactly in the middle of the race course—and twice over on the same afternoon? Ordinary injuries could be accounted for, perhaps, but not anything as subtle and skillful as this. It must have been the work of some scientific man, and the ordinary employees of a racing stable were certainly not in that class. Who was it, then?

All Shanghai got to asking itself the question and all Shanghai was obliged to confess that it had to give up the problem—all except one, a quiet visitor from Hong Kong, who was secretly working out its solution, for Wang Foo could not brook the thought of a failure.

"Whom do you suppose I met upon the Bund to-day?" asked Dr. Cortelyou, the American Consul, of Inspector Gubbins, as he met him at the gate of the British post-office. "Why, none other then our mutual friend, Mr. Wang Foo, the great solver of international difficulties!"

"You don't tell me he is actually in town; he generally drops a card in on me when he passes through the Settlement. I wonder what he's doing here?"

"Oh, he said he was just back from a little trip to Peking, where he'd been doing some government work, I believe. I laughingly asked him if he ever investigated veterinary cases as well as human ones; for I was going to suggest that he might help you out with the Foo Sang case, you know, and he said quite significantly that he once studied up a case of villainy in the Hong Kong racing stables! I was just a-going to add that we had a good one here all ready for him when he—but see, sure as you live, here comes the very man now!"

Mutual greetings were of course in order and Wang Foo promised the Inspector that he would call for a friendly chat and smoke at headquarters that afternoon. He suited the action to the word, and upon admitting to Mr. Gubbins that he had been doing a little studying of the poison case on his own account, he drew from his sleeve the well-worn little leather note book, and with closed doors and windows, confided a considerable portion of its contents to him.

"You don't mean to say that you actually believe them to have it?" asked the Inspector in a tone of mingled surprise and curiosity.

"Believe them," answered Wang Foo, "I know them to be the ones, and I am now only just waiting to satisfy my own mind about one little extra bit of evidence, before I hand the whole thing over to you and Captain Brownlow. In the meantime, I think we can be mutually helpful. If you will look up carefully, for your own satisfaction as well as mine, the present whereabouts and daily doings of the personage I mentioned and then," he added in a tone of great satisfaction, "as my old friend, the American Consul at Hong Kong used to say, 'By the great Horn Spoon! We've 'cotched 'em this time, sure.'"

Just who the mysterious parties were to whom our friend the great detective was referring will appear in a very short time; in the meanwhile let us accompany him to the famous teahouse of The Golden Pheasant, where, in the innocent garb of a native attendant, he was waiting, and not in vain, for the appearance of Hung Tak Fong, the compradore of Jones and Mullins, the shippers. The latter soon arrived with a party of friends, and it was only a very few minutes before Wang was able, by the skillful use of a system of words and exclamations—known only to the Chinese mind—to turn the whole flow of conversation to the subject of the races and the supposed poisoning of the two Farnsworth ponies. He listened with all the attention that he possessed, carefully passing the trays and tea-bowls over to another servant (who had been paid in advance to stand close by and receive them) and never allowing himself to get more than two or three feet away from the table and from the person of the aforesaid Hung Tak Fong, whom he had easily identified as our old friend with the goggles and silks. The latter soon fell, quite unsuspectingly, into the trap which the detective had laid for him, and repeated again and again the very words, "Pei tak Foo Sang, pei tak Foo Sang," which he had used that day at the race course and which seemed on their face to mean, "He was discharged from Foo Sang, he was discharged from Foo Sang." Why did Wang Foo start and look so intently at Hung's companion from Foo Chow? Why did he listen so carefully to the latter's comment on this remark? Why, simply because he quoted the old legend of the "Wand of the Buddhas" and added most significantly, "The gods must indeed have been very angry that day to have struck twice in the self-same place." A slight change of accent had revealed the double meaning in the words and Wang Foo realized that what he had understood to mean, "He was discharged from Foo Sang" was really. "He was beaten with the Buddha's wand!" And so one of his very first theories—and one still firmly clung to by the native and foreign police—namely that the poisoner was a discharged employee of the Farnsworths', vanished sway like the rising aroma from the smoking tea!

A few hours later he again sought the ear of the Inspector. "Have you ascertained beyond a doubt, sir," he asked, "just who approached the ponies and touched them or patted them as they were being led out?"

"She was the only one, Mr. Wang, and they allowed her that privilege only because she was a lady, sir; you see their rules are very strict. Just to prevent tampering with them in any way. They even watch them carefully all day and all night before they race them."

"You said 'she,' did you not? You're quite sure of this?"

"Absolutely positive, sir."

"Then we are all ready for the exposure in the morning—but stop! We had better have a private interview with Mr. Farnsworth first, had we not? When he hears the truth, you know, he may wish for personal reasons to hush it up and keep the whole thing quiet."

"Right you are," answered the chief. "I will write him a chit at once and we will have him here this very evening."

The above conversation explains the brief notice in the *Daily News* of the following morning to the effect that:

"We are authorized by the Inspector of Police to state that the Messrs. Pierce. Jockeys for the firm of Farnsworth & Co., are now proven to have been entirely innocent of the suspicion of haring tampered with the latter's ponies at the late Spring races and so also are the Chinese ma-foos, whom we are very glad to clear of the charge. It has been discovered that the poisoning was the malicious work of a foreign visitor who, we are glad to say, has left for Europe by a recent mail and so closed forever a most unpleasant incident in our midst."

AT THE INTERVIEW, with closed doors, in the Inspector's office that evening, Mr. Farnsworth listened to the joint explanation of Wang Foo and the police. It was briefly this: Both the ponies were poisoned with a preparation of strychnine, which had been administered to them in capsules concealed in lumps of sugar! The person who did it was Madame de Roderigo, sister of a prominent merchant from Macao, who had come up from that Southern island to attend the Spring races at Shanghai. She was a notorious gambler and on the way up the coast had relieved an American passenger of several thousand Mexicans by her dexterity with cards. On his refusing to pay the last stake, she had risen in her anger and sworn, with all the hatred and vengeance characteristic of her mixed blood, to get even with him by injuring the first American she met on getting ashore. While staying at the Astor House, she had met Mr. Farnsworth's brother and had accepted an invitation from him to visit the firm's stables and inspect the ponies—and there and then she had plotted the crime. Obtaining the drug from a Portuguese physician, under the pretext of wishing it for poisoning her dogs, she had concealed it in a lump of sugar and given it to the unfortunate creature just as his rider mounted him, figuring carefully on its deadly effect before he could finish the race. Gloating over her success with the first race, she became bolder and repeated it with the second!

"Thank heavens! She is out of the place!" exclaimed Mr. Farnsworth as he rose to thank the two officers and begged them to avoid any further publicity and hush the whole matter up.

"Yes," replied the ever courteous Wang Foo, "as the great Master says in the closing words of the *Analects*, 'as to an unpleasant odor, one may truly say that the very best thing is to forget it!'"

THE GOLDEN LOTUS

"Now, do tell me, Captain," remarked Miss Atherton of Lowell, Mass., to the venerable Dan Collins, commanding the Canton river steamer *Kiu Kiang* on her nigh trip to Hong Kong, "aren't all those little puffs of smoke that we see arising from the sampans and river junks coming from the boatmen smoking their evening opium pipes? I'm so interested to know"—of course she was, for the fact was she was traveling as the correspondent of one of Boston's most popular papers, though she had never publicly announced it to the rest of the passengers.

"No, madam, not at all," replied the gruff old sea dog, "that's a very popular idea with globe trotters, but it's all a mistake. I'm glad you asked me, for If you hadn't, you might have gone home and written it down in your book on the far east, just as a lot of the rest of 'em do who only stay out here three weeks and then know it all. Most fools, they say, will believe anything you tell them, but the globe-trotting fool is the worst of all, for he doesn't even need to be told. He'll just put down anything he seen for gospel truth, he will. And the fellows who draw the pictures are just about as far off as the ones who write the books. Judging from what I saw the last time I was home—every one of them makes the Chinaman's cue grow out of the middle of the top of his head, when no China-man ever born had his cue grow anywhere else but out of the back of his head; just look at my table boy there, if you don't believe me. No, madam, as I was a-saying, those little curling columns of smoke are from cooking their evening rice and not from smoking

" WATCH THAT FELLOW ON
THE LEFT HERE , HE IS
JUST BEGINNING. "

opium at all. Opium doesn't make any smoke, does it, Mr. Wang?"
addressing a dignified Chinese gentleman seated near them at the
table.

"Very little, if any," answered the native passenger (who was
none other than the famous Wang Foo or prince of Chinese detectives, traveling in the European saloon). "What little is visible probably arises from the smoking wick of the little bean-oil lamp the
habitues use, the drug itself is volatilised and gives forth its strong
characteristic odor as they inhale it, but certainly not smoke in
any such quantity as you see it now arising from the river boats.
Capt. Collins is quite right, madame, as he generally is on these
Far Eastern questions—you see, he is quite an old resident now
and understands us very well," accompanying this last celestial
compliment with a most gracious smile and bow which went
straight to the heart of the old New Bedford skipper.

Miss Atherton was more than pleased and surprised at Wang
Foo's explanation; she was simply dumfounded at his English mas-
tery and his scholarly vocabulary (with its flawless accent), which
not only surpassed anything she had ever yet heard from a
Chinaman, but—to tell the plain and honest truth—most everything
she had heard from her fellow-countrymen in the east, not except-
ing a few American consuls! She could hardly wait for dinner to
be over before she rushed up to Captain Collins, just lighting his
cheroot on his way to the bridge, and begged him to introduce this
remarkable personage to her. "Why, captain," she said, "I never
really dreamed there was a Chinaman living who could speak
English like that!"

"Well, there ain't very many of them, I can tell you that, ma'am.
And what's more, he knows exactly what he's talking about, too,
which is more than you can say of a lot of these that are educated
abroad and just come back here and chatter off a lot of big words
like parrots. Now, if you really want to know anything about China
and the Chinese—I mean the truth, not the globe-trotter stuff they
pick up from the hotel-boys and the rick-saw coolies and put in
the magazines and the books—he's the very best man in all this
empire for you to got acquainted with."

Wang Foo was duly presented to Miss Atherton and her party and it is no exaggeration to say that in less than an hour they had really learned more about the middle kingdom and its people and customs than the miserable so-called "guides" had been able to give them in a week. "And now, ladies and gentlemen," he said, as they were about to leave the deck where he had been pointing out objects of interest, "If you really want to see opium smoking; and don't mind a little inconvenience, we have the golden opportunity right here and now. The native passengers have all finished their evening rice and after their customary siesta they are beginning to light their pipes and 'pass to the land of pleasant dreams' as they say, and if you will follow me I shall be very glad to escort you to the upper deck and explain the system to you. They are smoking in the open air there and you will find the atmosphere much less oppressive than in the crowded native saloon."

Delighted to have the opportunity, they all gladly followed Wang Foo up the starboard companionway and, with the captain's permission, passed through the iron grating which on all river steamers still shunts off the native passengers from the Europeans. (They noticed the Manila quartermaster standing there on guard, fully armed, and the significant boiling-water hose right at hand, ready for instant use in case of any mutinous or piratical outbreak, for these old-fashioned precautions still have to be taken as long as robbers and pirates conceal themselves among the passengers). What a sight there met their eyes! Stretched out for a distance of over 200 feet or more were rows and rows of what at first sight appeared to be bags of rice or logs of wood, but which on nearer inspection turned out to be human beings. They were lying just as closely to one another as they could without actually touching and all of them absorbed in the process of preparing or inhaling the drug and apparently entirely dead to the outer world.

"Just follow me, please, and step carefully over them," said their guide, suiting the action to the word—some of the party hesitated— "Oh, it's all right," he said, reassuringly, "they won't mind it at all as long as you don't actually step on them or kick over the trays."

Stopping at a convenient vantage ground near the top of the paddle box, he began. "You notice that everyone is lying on his side, generally the left, so that he can have his right hand and arm free to handle the pipe, and is facing the little lacquer tray. Now look carefully and you will see that each tray contains four articles, vis., a little oil lamp, a small pill box made of black horn, a set of long steel knitting needles and a bamboo tube about an inch and a half in diameter and a foot and a half in length—"

"Just let me jot that down, please," said Miss Atherton, as she drew out her little notebook, "there's still light enough to write by and it's so interesting. I don't want to miss a word of it. There! I've got them all four down, now, please go on Mr. Wang."

"Let me describe these articles separately," continued the detective; "the oil lamp has no chimney, you see, but is covered with a little glass globe about three inches in diameter—made very thick so that the heat will not crack it—and in the top of this is a little opening that is just above the tip of the flame and through which the smoke and hot air escape. The pill box, as I call it, is the little receptacle made of horn which contains the opium; this is about the consistency of thick molasses and is made of this material because they believe it will preserve the drug and not affect its flavor—"

"It is awfully expensive, is it not?" interrupted one of the party.

"Oh, yes, it runs all the way from silver to gold, as they say. Of course, there are all varieties and values, from the comparatively reasonable article raised in Yun Nan to the golden fluid that is imported from Patna. What they are using right here upon the dock is the poorer quality, as all of these are steerage passengers. Down in the private cabins below us, you will find a much more expensive variety. Now, the knitting needles—I always use that term in explaining the process to Americans, because it makes it so much clearer—are simply long steel points which are used to dip out the opium from the pill-box, and the long bamboo tube is, of course, the pipe itself. Look at the one right next to us, here. You see it is closed at the shorter end and has a small perforation at the longer end, which generally consists of a copper cash fastened in there and gratifies a native whim of 'breathing through money' as they say. About a quarter of the way from the end, of where the mouth-hole would be in an old-fashioned flute, you will notice the bowl. This is made of red pipe-clay and is completely closed over with the exception of a tiny opening a little larger than a pinhole right in the center. So there you have the apparatus, now for the trick! Let us watch this fellow on our left, for he is just beginning. First, he lights his little lamp and adjusts the wick to just the proper height, then he dips one of the needles into the pill-box and stirring it around draws out a little ball of the drug; he spreads the ointment over the top of the bowl right around the edge of the opening and than holds it over the lamp. Now, watch him! He puts his lips to the cash-opening at the end of the pipe and as the hot air volatilizes the opium and it fills his bowl, he slowly draws the heated mixture into his lungs and the pleasurable sensations begin. He quickly forgets the world and all its troubles and wanders around in a native paradise of undiluted happiness! I hope I have made it clear to you— "

"You most certainly have," replied Miss Atherton, tendering to Wang Foo the appreciations of all the party, "and now permit me to ask you just one more question. Which do you consider the greater curse, opium or alcohol?"

"Well," thoughtfully and slowly said the detective, "that is, of course, one of the leading questions which is often put to us by our American friends, and I do not believe, speaking after many years of careful observation, that a positive and decisive answer can be given to it. The slavery and degradation is about the same in either case, whenever the poor victims get really under the spell. There is, however, a difference in the form of the effect, if not in the degree. Alcohol will lead a man to commit violence and crime on others; opium rather to deceit, dishonesty, sneaking theft and the more degrading forms of self-destruction. The drunkard will beat his wife and children and starve them for his drink; the opium smoker will not attack them, but he will sell them—body and soul—for his drug. As our friend Capt Collins says, 'You can take your choice.'"

"And is there really no cure for it? That is one or the questions I was told to especially ask when I came to China."

"In answer to that I can only say that, while there is an enormous traffic all over the east in the so-called 'opium cures'—many of which are only the drug under another name and most of which are frauds and deceits—it is the general testimony of the ablest physicians that, unless the cases are taken at their earliest stages, mere medical treatment alone is useless. Speaking as a very humble Confucianist, I join hands here with my friends the missionaries from the west, and say, in the name of this great moral teacher of the east, there is really no hope for the opium smoker except in his spiritual regeneration."

A WEEK OR TWO AFTER WANG FOO's meeting with the American party on the Canton steamer he was passing along Queen's road in the latter part of the afternoon, when he was suddenly hailed by a lady in a passing jinrikisha. "Oh, Mr. Wang, Mr. Wang!" she cried, "Just a moment, please, just a moment—" The coolie turned the little vehicle sharply in toward the curbing, lowered the shafts and allowed Miss Atherton to step over them onto the sidewalk. "It is really almost rude for me to stop you in this unceremonious way," she said, "but I am so anxious to have you help me on a little matter of translation. You know, after that wonderful explanation you gave us of the opium smoking on the steamboat, I don't feel that any of my information is really authentic unless it has your endorsement—but what is that jinrikisha coolie saying, and why does he look so upset at me? I haven't done anything wrong to the poor man, have I? You know I feel humiliated enough to make a draught horse out of my fellowman, without doing him any further injury, that's the reason I always pay them double what they ask."

"Oh, nothing of any serious consequence," replied Wang Foo; "he is simply grumbling to himself because you stepped over the crossbar instead of over the shafts. They have a little idea—perhaps you would call it a superstition—that if the passenger does that they will have bad luck for the rest of the day; that is all."

"Is that really so? Well, please explain to him for me that I didn't know anything about it and that I wouldn't have hurt his feelings for the world. Shall I give him some extra money—"

"No, please don't do that; you are largely overpaying him as it is, and any extra gift simply makes it all the harder for the next European passenger that rides after you," and, turning to the mumbling coolie, he rattled off a few yards of his native tongue, which had the perfectly magic effect of turning his wrath into smiles and making him bow almost into the dust at the feet of his "Venerable Father."

"You must excuse my not removing my native hat, Miss Atherton," he concluded, "but you know you are in China now, and here the laws of courtesy are exactly reversed and true politeness requires that gentlemen remain covered in the presence of ladies and—their other superiors," he added with a smile

"Oh, yes, indeed, that is one of the little 'topsy-turvy' things I have already noted in my diary," she replied.

"And now what is it that I can have the pleasure of doing for you?"

"Why, just this," drawing from her little handbag a folded piece of native yellow paper; "we have been visiting the Temple of the Golden Lotus on the other side of the island and have had a most interesting day of it. The old priest in charge of the shrine showed us everything and when we came away he insisted on writing this Chinese charm for me and told me it would bring me good luck as long as I lived. I have been waiting until I could find someone who could give me a perfect translation of it, for I know it must be something full of oriental mystery."

"Have you not shown it to any one else yet?" inquired Wang Foo, as he took the paper from her hand and carefully unrolled it.

"Well, only to the hotel room-boy, who is acting as our guide, and of course all I could get out of him was a lot of that miserable pidgin-English jargon about "Missee, him talkee b'longee velly good joss. All samee lotus flower climbee down-side go topside. Him glow mud, by 'me' by all samee water, den must come outside look see. Missee all samee so fashion."

The Man of Mystery broke into a gentle laugh at the room-boy's attempts to interpret the Celestial poetry "Yes," he said, "it certainly is a most cumbersome and unsatisfactory medium of translation and expression, but he did the best he could with the means at his command. This is a poetical quotation in which the lotus is taken as the emblem of human progress. I will read it to you just as it stands:

> "'Yiu huk too,
> Ching sui tao
> Tung choy chui,
> Ching lien jak.'

"You see, it is very brief and condensed, consisting of only twelve words in all, written in four lines of three characters each. Of course, I could not attempt to give you a satisfactory version right offhand here on the road, but possibly I can improve a little on the room-boy's efforts. Let me try:

> "'From the dark earth,
> Through the clearer water
> To the air and light,
> The Golden Lotus ever
> Pushes its upward way.'"

"There. That isn't very much, but it is the best I can do on the spur of the moment." As he spoke these words, a strange look of mysterious inquiry—amounting almost to suspicion—came over his face, which fortunately escaped the lady's notice, "it really requires to be considerably expanded to give it a satisfactory English rendering, so, if you will kindly allow me, I should just like to take this paper home with me and I will return it to you at the hotel tomorrow, with something a little better than a mere roadside version."

"Oh, thank you so much, nothing would please me more, I am sure. It is most kind of you to take all this trouble. It is a perfect

little gem of poetry, I know; one could see that even from the room-
boy's pidgin."

He assisted her into her jinrikisha and directing the coolie to
take her to the "Ocean-men's Inn," waited until she was safely
around the curving street. Stepping into the shadow of the neighboring alley, he took the paper out of his sleeve, where he had temporarily secluded it and began to scrutinize the handwriting. "The
slight curving of the left downward stroke. The shortening of the
cross lines and the peculiar seal script in the character for lotus'—
it is he. Villain, thy penmanship hath betrayed thee," he repeated
to himself as he folded it carefully up and placed it between the
leaves of his little leather wallet. "Miss Atherton," he said, as he
turned and looked westward in the direction where her jinrikisha had
vanished, "you did a far better day's work than you could possibly realize when you visited the Temple of the Golden Lotus. You have laid
the department of police—and indeed the entire colony—under a most
lasting obligation," and turning eastward along Queen's Road, he
hastened to his modest home in the Alley of the Red Cloud, antici-
pating a most interesting evening of developments.

INSPECTOR WALLACE of the Hong Kong police was just sitting down
to a quiet dinner with his family, at his little stone home on Peak
terrace, when the house boy entered with a note in a Chinese envelope and, laying it on the table in front of his master, announced
that "One piecie coolie man waitchee kitchen side, talkee he tankee
you pay him answer chop-chop."

"Well, I wonder what's up now?" remarked the Inspector, as
he took up a table knife and opened the envelope (the aforesaid
house boy nearly putting his neck out of joint in his efforts to lean
over to one side and glance at the contents also), "It's a pity they
can't send all this sort of thing to the office and not bother me
with it at the house." His attitude quickly changed, however, when
he saw the familiar round handwriting of his friend Wang Foo and.
sending the boy for a piece of chit paper, he quickly dashed off an
answer. The burden of his reply was simply that he would be
pleased to see the former at headquarters at 10 o'clock the following

morning. Old Chang, the gatekeeper—for it was he who was waiting and sipping tea in the kitchen—took the note which the house
boy brought him and, lighting his little horn lantern, started back
on his way down the hill, reaching his quarters at No. 5-5-5 just as
the chair bearers deposited the sedan of the old abbot at the outer
gate.

"You have brought the papers with you?" anxiously inquired
Wang Foo, after the preliminary tea and pipes were over, and they
had both ascended to the quiet precincts of the upper study.

"Yes, they are all here," replied the abbot, as he drew from his
sleeve a yellow packet and proceeded to unfold it. "See! Here are
the three letters, and the torn piece of the revolutionary procla-
mation and the paper cover of the book with his signature on it,
and the two receipts for the guns and powder and three personal
cards. We may lay the last aside, for they are probably not in his
own individual hand."

"And what is the final result of your examination? Just how
would you recognize his characters?"

"By these three things—to be sure there are more, but these
are quite enough—by the curving of the left strokes, by the shortening of the cross lines and especially by that peculiar seal-script
in the upper part, of the lotus. Look! Do you not see that the four
strokes are really reversed?" said the abbot slowly and distinctly,
as, holding a dry pen in his hand, he pointed out every one of these
individualities to the careful and ever-watchful eye of the detective.

"They are the same, then, that you noticed when first we went
over them?"

"Yes, exactly the same, with the added point of the reversed
crown of the lotus."

"And with these you feel that we could identify the writer?"

"Beyond the shadow of a doubt, anywhere in all the empire."

"Venerable father," said Wang Foo, as he took from his secret
drawer in the desk the yellow paper with Miss Atherton's verses
upon it, "look carefully now at this and tell me what you think of it."

"The curved left stroke! The short cross lines and the reversed
crown above the lotus—in the name of all the sacred Buddhas now

at once, it is he! Tell me, where did you get this paper and when? It is a streak of fortune of which we little dreamed."

Wang Foo related the story of his introduction to the American party on the steamer, the scene with the opium smokers and the later meeting with Miss Atherton on Queen's Road and the finding of the poem.

"You think then that he is still in hiding on the Island—possibly in the Lotus Temple or somewhere on the other side?"

"Possibly, but that is all that we can say."

"And just how can we best apprehend him?"

"Ah, that will be matter for the utmost tact and secrecy. We must move most carefully and slowly; for the slightest breath of a suspicion that we are on his tracks—and he is gone."

As Wang Foo said this, he rose and lighted the farewell pipes. The two smoked for a while in silence, then, making the secret sign of the brotherhood in the air with their lighted matches, they concluded arrangements for another interview and bade each other good night.

At precisely 10 o'clock on the following morning Inspector Wallace received the great detective in his inner office and learned from him of the suspected presence in the colony of Ching Lien (or Golden Lotus), the leader of the recent riot at Swatow, for whom the police, both native and foreign, in all the ports had been zealously hunting for several months. "You say that you have good reason to believe he is here, Mr. Wang; tell me just where you think he is hiding and we will have the native staff ferret him out," said the chief.

"Considering the slippery nature of the individual—for no one seems to have been able to lay hands on him—I think we shall be able to work with a little more certainty, Mr. Wallace, if you will be good enough to detail two of your best native detectives to assist me quietly for a few days. I have worked out a plan for apprehending him, and, if I may modestly say so, I think I can carry it to success."

"I will put Sam and Chang, my two best men, at your disposal for a week," replied the Inspector, "and I will see that they report to you for your personal orders this very afternoon. Keep in close touch with me, please, and let me know the moment anything important turns up, and my best wishes go with you!"

"Thank you very much, sir," said Wang Foo, as he rose and bade him good morning.

Two DAYS LATER Sam and Chang, the detectives, appeared at the gate of the Temple of the Golden Lotus—the former in the garb of a jinrikisha coolie and the latter in the long blue robe of a European house boy—and sought an interview with the priest in charge. To their surprise, it was almost immediately granted. Chang then produced from a native wallet the identical yellow paper which Miss Atherton had given to Wang Foo, and, representing himself as the personal servant of the foreign lady, said that she had sent him for another copy of the beautiful poem, as this one had unfortunately been torn. The old priest hesitated for a moment, but on having put in his hand ten new shining dollars which they said she had sent as a gift, took his pen and inkslab from the shelf and adjusting his ancient spectacles, proceeded to copy the verses from the paper before him, little dreaming who the parties were to whom he gave them, or how closely the hand of the law was hanging over him.

Following out to the minutest detail Wang Foo's instructions to them, Sam and Chang returned at once to his house with the new copy of the poem for which he was most eagerly waiting. At last he had it in his hands, the final link in the chain of evidence that would convict Golden Lotus, now masquerading as a priest in the very temple from which he was named, of being the much-sought-for leader of the late port riot! He would have the same two officers repeat their visit to the temple on the morrow and arrest him there and then. He left his assistants in the lower hall and ascending to the upper chamber, closed and locked the door. He adjusted his crystal goggles and unfolded the paper before him. He could hardly believe his senses! Not a curve in the left strokes, not a flaw in the cross lines and the crown of the lotus was not reversed! It was absolutely the handwriting of another individual! Sam and Chang were again closely questioned as to any possibility of mistaken identity, but there was none. The priest was positively the same one that gave the paper to Miss Atherton; he remembered the visit and the incident perfectly—strangest of all, he made not the slightest effort to conceal it—and the two detectives stood right over him and watched every stroke of the little brush as he wrote the copy. The priest was the priest, no doubt about that, but he was not the Golden Lotus, and if not, how did he happen to present the foreign lady with a poem which both Wang Foo and the old abbot were ready to swear was in the chief rioter's hand? He stretched himself out on the couch of carved bamboo, and, half closing his eyes, began to think it all out. When he awoke it was with the fixed determination to personally visit the temple and trace out for himself the history of the mysterious paper; so thanking Sam and Chang for their services and pledging them to secrecy, he allowed them to return to headquarters.

WHEN THE ROOM BOY at the hotel answered the call bell from No. 65 a few days later he found Miss Atherton concluding a bargain with a native jeweler and vainly trying to write her out a receipt for her purchases. "Here, boy," she said, "I want you to help me. This poor man says he can neither read nor write, though he is sharp enough at a bargain and has a wonderful head for figures. I have written out a bill here in English and I want you to put the Chinese characters opposite each article, so that my friends at home will be sure I bought them in China."

"My no can litee velly good, misses," modestly protested the boy.

"Oh, I am sure you can do it perfectly well," she insisted, and he proceeded to draw a little writing case out of his sleeve. The jeweler watched him carefully as he traced the characters on the bill, and checked the articles off on his fingers, one by one, vis.: A silver necklace, a jade-stone pendant, a pair of napkin rings and, last of all, a brooch with a golden lotus—as he finished the last word, the jeweler drew from his sleeve a silver whistle and before any one knew what was happening blew a long, shrill blast. As he did so, the doors of No. 66, the adjoining apartment, flew open and Sam and Chang, the detectives, rushed in and seized the astonished boy. The game was up and Ching Lien the Golden Lotus was at last in the hands of the police.

"What does all this mean?" inquired Miss Atherton in utter astonishment, as Inspector Wallace and Capt. Morehead entered the room from the hallway, after courteously knocking.

"Why, it means that you have unconsciously rendered us a very great service by enabling us to apprehend a most dangerous criminal," replied Wang Foo, as he removed from his head the wig and beard of the supposed native jeweler. "We have traced him through his handwriting. We supposed at first that he was masquerading as the priest, but we afterward discovered that he wrote the poem at the priest's request, hence the slight delay in the arrest."

"What a remarkable thing," said Miss Atherton to the man of mystery, as they sipped a quiet cup of tea on the porch after the excitement was all over, "and what a strange contrast to his beautiful name. You know I've been thinking of the words of the poem and how he should have risen from dark obscurity like the lotus and pushed his way upward to the higher and purer and better, things of life—whereas he seems to have just reversed the process and fallen lower and lower into the depths."

"Ah, that explains the wonderful significance the Chinese place in their ancient chirography," answered Wang Foo, "and why they love to tell fortunes from their writing. The peculiarity of this man's script was that he always—no one can tell you just why—traced the character for the lotus with its crown reversed, and so, you see, the whole trend of his life was downward and not upward, or as we say:

"Fang tao ching lien." ("He turned the golden lotus upside down!")

THE YELLOW JACKET

"Yes, it is practically the same old three-card monte game that we used to see played on the sands at Coney Island when we were boys," said Dr. Upham of the American Hospital at Ningpo, to his friend, Dr. Forties of Philadelphia, as they stood on the old stone bridge at Shanghai and watched a native juggler entertaining the passers-by.

"You see he has three bowls and a little ball of toasted rice which he passes from one to the other. 'Now you see it and now you don't,' as they say, and the trick is to guess just which bowl it is under—and, as usual, though he places it there right under their eyes, the man in the crowd that bets on the 'sure thing' generally gets it wrong."

"Why, that's nothing but the old 'thimble-rig' that they used to play on the tourists when I was a student in Edinburgh," answered the famous American surgeon. "The man used to have three thimbles on a board and a little green pea which he rolled around until it got under one of them and then you had to guess which one it was under.

"You don't mean to tell me that they've got that same old trick out here in China—I suppose he picked it up from some foreigner in one of the ports, they seem to catch on to our bad ways even faster than they do to our good ones."

"No, not at all, the Chinese had that for years—I might even say centuries—before we ever dreamed of it. If there is any such thing as one nation learning it from another, then surely we got it

316

"THE INSPECTOR LOOKED
NERVOUSLY AT HIS WATCH."

from them and not they from us, like a thousand other ingenious ways of humbugging your fellow-men, that I could tell you about if I had time, but I really have to believe that we don't get these things from each other, but it's a sort of general cussedness that's in our human nature and so it just crops out wherever we happen to be—"

"Ah! I see, the little touch of Nature that makes the whole work kin, eh?"

"Yes, or one of the little links of fellow-feeling that joins the West to the East—but just watch this chap. I want to see how he does it; you'll find that there's a peculiar element in it here that you never saw at Coney Island in your boyhood days."

"And what's that, pray?"

"You'll smile when I tell you, but it's religion!"

"Good Heavens! Doctor, not religion in a three card-monte game!"

"The same—but I'll modify it a little for your benefit by just calling it superstition—now watch him."

The two surgeons stood in the midst of the curious but very good-natural crowd on the bridge while the juggler continued his talk, Dr. Upham's perfect familiarity with the local dialect enabling him to interpret the apparently meaningless jargon for his friend from abroad.

"I see with great pleasure," he remarked, not dreaming that his words were understood, "that we have in the distinguished audience of mandarins and literary gentlemen two famous visitors from across the ocean"—at this the crowd chuckled and laughed—"who have been recommended to this marvelous performance by His Excellency the Tao Tai, knowing that it is the most wonderful sight they could witness in our ancient Empire.

"My! How the crowds will gather around them in their distant ocean-kingdoms when they tell of what they have seen here today!" (More laughter from the crowd and a voice which cried, "Say! Ocean-Mandarin, do you have anything like this in your Honorable Kingdom?") "Now I will roll the little rice-ball around until it goes under one of the bowls. Ah! There it is! Goodbye, little traveler, until some great and wise philosopher before me comes and finds you out! Twenty brass cash of the Ming Dynasty to the fortunate one—what! No bids? Thirty, forty, nay, I am bold and reckless today, 50 coins to the prince among you who overturns the right bowl!"

He paused and looked about him, took off his dilapidated hat, scratched the head that was beneath it and then tapped it several times with a ragged fan. No one being bold enough to come forward and speculate, he continued, "Ah! I know someone who is waiting to tell me just where that little rice-ball is. My little Poo Sak (Idol) knows. I'll just ask him," and running his hand up his ragged sleeve he drew out an old and battered image of a native divinity and held it up in both hands before him.

"This is Foo Shen, the God of Wealth, who bestows his riches on all who implore him. I'll just pay my respects to him and then he will whisper his secret in my ear." Bowing low three times he rattled off a long string of unintelligible words to the wooden idol and then placed its lips close to his loft ear and listened for a moment. "Ah! He says he knows—he never makes a mistake—it's under the middle one. Behold it!" He lifted up the center bowl with an elaborate circular gesture of his arm and held it high in the air toward the gaze of the astonished spectators—there was absolutely nothing there!

"What! You lying rascal," he exclaimed, instantly changing his voice and manner to the idol. "I'll teach you not to deceive people that way after all the rice and cake and wine they've given you," and to the infinite delight and amusement of the natives, but to the astonishment, horror and utter disgust of the foreigners, he deliberately boxed the ears of the little poo sak and, returning it to the sleeve from which it come, said, "Go back up there and go to bed."

Dr. Forbes could scarcely believe his senses. "Is this all the respect they have for their idols?" he asked of his companion, "that they will devoutly pray to their gods in one moment and then deliberately turn around and castigate them in the next? Why, I never heard of such a thing in my life and if I hadn't actually seen it I could never have believed it."

"O, that wouldn't surprises you at all if you had lived any length of time among them," answered Dr. Upham, as they continued on their walk across the bridge and over through the streets of the French Concession. "It is just one of those peculiar little anomalies of the whole idolatry system.

"It is a curious blend of abject fear and ridicule. Sometimes when the skies are fair and everything is propitious, you will hear them speak in almost distrust of all their native gods, and then, the first moment that trouble and disaster comes, off they rush pell-mell to the temples and get down on their knees."

"Well," said the visitor, pausing thoughtfully for a moment, "perhaps after all they are not so very different from many people in the Western world. You know the story of the atheist who stood on the ship's deck arguing with his fellow passengers against the existence of God and sneering at their religion generally, and then when the ship suddenly struck a rock was the first man down on his knees."

"Yes," answered the Mission surgeon, "it recalls the old saying, doesn't it, 'When the devil was ill, the devil a monk would be—when the devil was well, the devil a monk was he!' This dear old human nature of ours is pretty much the same all the world over."

"I haven't a particle of doubt but that if his house should get on fire tonight, or thieves should rob him, or any disaster overtake him, that, old juggler would be down on his knees before that very same idol whose ears he so vigorously just now boxed in our presence. 'China is China,' we say, but I can tell you that if the Chinese weren't very human under all these native disguises, I wouldn't be here, that's all."

They were interrupted just at this point in the conversation by two French policemen, who were rushing across the street to stop an incipient fight among the wheelbarrow coolies at the mail wharf.

There was the usual amount of shrieking and yelling and the throwing of sand at each other from a convenient neighboring heap and the hurling of all kinds of curses back and forth until the air was a rich Chinese blue, but no actual blows or personal injuries. The two officers quickly picked out the ringleaders and seizing them by the cues drugged them off to the nearest station and the crowd melted away as rapidly as it had gathered.

Just as they crossed the canal into the British Concession they saw standing there Dr. Cortelyou, the American consul, and Inspector Gubbins of the police.

"Good morning, gentlemen," said the former, "I want you to meet the chief of our 'guardians of the peace,' as we call them at home—though I believe our friend Dr. Upham already has the pleasure—we were just looking across into the French Settlement and watching the disturbance. The Inspector here tells me that it's a part of the barrow-coolies' trouble that has been threatening for some time and may break out into serious proportions at any moment, though so far the authorities on this side seem to have things under very good control. Isn't that so, Mr. Gubbins?"

"Yes," answered the officer. "I am thankful to say it hasn't come to any general row yet, though we have had several beginnings down at Jardine's and the Japanese wharves that might have proved serious if we hadn't nipped them in time. You never can tell, however, what these things may grow to, especially around the native holidays when they lay off work and take to drinking sam-shu."

"What is the trouble?" asked Dr. Forbes, "is this a 'strike,' as we call it at home, for higher wages—or just what is their grievance?"

"Well, sir, it's partly the same and partly different. They're all greatly upset because the authorities are charging them 10 cents more for their licenses than they did last year—"

"What! You don't mean to say that they would threaten to start a riot for the small sum of 10 Chinese cents? Why, that's only about a nickel in our American money—"

"Yes, I know, sir. It certainly seems ridiculously small, but you must remember that the wages of these men is ridiculously small also. As my deputy, Capt. Brownlow, says: 'Brass cash to them is dollars to us, and they can live on what any white man would starve on.'

"Then, again, they're awful sticklers for a fixed custom. They don't like to change, and when you once give them a settled figure for anything, why it's almost impossible to alter it. As my old houseboy says: 'Chinee man no likee Melican man all time too muchee changee. S'pose he catchee one plicee, more better he stopee long time dat side, more better look see. All time dat changee pidgin too muchee bobbery.'"

"Ah, I see, part of the old conservatism of the East and the general disinclination to change, eh?"

"That's it, sir. It's just like that little sampan that you see yonder a-sculling that native passenger across the river. My native officers tell me that the price is just the same that it was 500 years ago—they might just as well have said a thousand—and if they attempted to raise it even one small cash, there'd be such a protest and a row that the sampan-man's life wouldn't be worth living.

"But the real grievance just now, sir, is all over this threatening on the part of the Municipal Council to compel them to grease the axles of their barrows and stop this everlasting squeaking that is so annoying to the Europeans."

"But that seems to me even more petty than their row over the few extra cents for the license and then, I can't understand why the opinion of a few wheelbarrow coolies should be so important a matter, either one way or the other. We wouldn't think anything of it at home—"

"Quite true, sir," added the Inspector, as he turned to enter his pony trap, which was waiting at the curb for him, "but we're not at home now and you must remember that we have practically no trucks or drays here and that we are dependent on these thousands of barrow coolies to handle all the freight that passes in and out of Shanghai, so you see it's a serious question, sir. We are practically in their hands and they can do us thousands of pounds of damage if once they make up their minds to it."

His Excellency, the British Minister at Pekin, was just bidding his colleague from France good-night, after a friendly rubber at the club, when the latter said: "By the way, anything further from that anticipated trouble at Shanghai?

"I have word from our Consul General that they are beginning to feel a little uneasy in the French Concession and some of the ladies are so nervous that they are talking of sleeping aboard the warship, and so the captain has sent a marine guard ashore to reassure them."

"O, I don't anticipate that it will really come to anything, Shanghai is the best protected place in the Far East, except possibly Hong Kong. They have a splendid police force and the volunteers can be called out at a moment's notice, and, besides, there are always two or three men-of-war lying in the upper and lower reaches of the river."

"But then there's the arsenal, you know, just above the city, and two or three thousand native 'braves' there might be induced to join the rioters if they saw a good chance for plunder, might they not?"

"Not likely under Chang, the present Tao Tai. He's a clever fellow and he knows that his moneyed interests demand that he stand in with the European authorities just at present. Why his 'squeeze' on the opium alone last year was worth fifty thousand taels to him, they say, and you may be sure he'll do all he can to protect the Custom House and the rest of the Settlement.

"If worst comes to worst, why he will just distribute a thousand or two among the ringleaders and the discontents and that will make it all right. They have their own ways of adjusting these things, and, so Sir Harry, my esteemed predecessor used to say, they can always control their own people when they really want to."

At the British Legation a little group of individuals deeply interested in the keeping of peace and friendly relations between China and the European powers had been discussing the news from the South. The American Minister and two of his oldest missionaries were there, as was also the English Bishop with his Chaplain and Archdeacon and two leading heads of large mercantile establishments.

The military and naval attachés were unfortunately both away on a hunt in the Western Hills. After a general revue of the situation and a discussion of what had taken place on similar occasions in the past, his excellency the Minister expressed the opinion very decidedly that a prompt and strong display of armed force was the only way to handle it.

"Quite true, Your Excellency," answered the bishop. "I believe in the upholding of law and order as much as you do, when the outbreak actually occurs, and my 15 years as naval chaplain have taught me the wisdom of prompt and decisive action in all such cases. Old England has won a great name for herself in these Eastern lands by her display of armed force, but I am sure you will agree with me that she has won a far greater name for herself in India and other places by her high and exalted sense of justice and her willingness to listen to both sides of the case.

"Prevention—yes, sir, an ounce of prevention is well worth the pound of cure. You and I, sir, representatives of the Government and the Church, are not only sent here as teachers and protectors of the people, but we are here for a much higher reason also, namely, to secure the good-will of this great Nation and cement and strengthen the friendly relations between us.

"We may easily overawe and shoot down a few hundred of these poor coolies in the streets of Shanghai when they protest, in the only way they know how, against what they consider our ill-treatment of them, but the consequences will be far more serious and lasting than we imagine; and the permanent interests of British trade, let me assure you, gentlemen (turning to the merchants present), will be damaged thereby a great deal more than they will be helped."

"What do you suggest, then?" inquired the Minister, who had hardly given a thought to this side of the question, but who knew in his innermost heart that this might seriously affect the permanency of his position when the facts would be eventually brought up in Parliament.

"I suggest that we use every effort in our power to right this grievance, if it is a grievance, and to adjust the matter by a just and equitable compromise. I believe this can be done and thousands of taels of damage avoided without the crippling of trade or the shedding of unnecessary blood."

"And just how will you do this?"

"We Europeans cannot do it alone. We must call in to our aid the very best and wisest of the Chinese, assuring them of our honesty and allowing them to suggest the way that will best appeal to the native mind."

"Do you not think that looks like humiliating ourselves?"

"On the contrary, it will raise us in their estimation far higher than we realize. Am I not right, gentlemen?" (turning to the American missionaries).

"As old residents in China, Your Excellency, we can assure you that the Bishop is absolutely correct," they answered in one voice.

"And who is the one person among the Chinese to whom you would entrust this delicate mission?" inquired the minister.

The bishop thought for a moment or two and then conferred with his colleagues. "The first and the very best person that we can think of," he answered, "is Mr. Wang Foo of Hong Kong. He knows his own people and our people probably better than anyone on the coast and his standing is such as to secure him instant respect. They will listen to him quicker than to anyone else, and he seems to have an almost magical power over them."

"He is a Christian, I suppose?"

"No, Your Excellency, he is a devout Confucianist of the highest type, and that is one reason why I take especial pleasure in commending him to you."

The result of the above conference was a telegram sent that very night from the Legation to the Consulate in Shanghai, instructing them to confer immediately with Wang Foo as to the best means of adjusting the threatened revolt of the wheelbarrow coolies.

"You must remember, sir," said the great Chinese detective, addressing the British consul, who had just joined Inspector Gubbins and himself at headquarters in Shanghai, a few days after his arrival from Hong Kong, "that this matter of their greasing the axles of the barrows is not only a question of the expenditure of a few cash for the lard—"

"O, I see," interrupted the consul, "it's a matter of their religion, like the greasing of the cartridge that started the mutiny in India—"

"No, not at all. In this particular case it doesn't happen to go against a religious prejudice as it did in that," answered Wang Foo; "It's a matter of the white man coming and taking away a native consolation and enjoyment which has been theirs for ages."

"Why, what consolation can they possibly find in that awful 'squeak, squeak' that racks the nerves of every European in the settlement?" asked the Inspector.

"That 'squeak,' as you call it," answered Wang Foo with a smile, "is to his ears the sweetest music in the world. It is the cheery voice of the bird which sings to him as he wheels along and lightens both his heart and his burden. You take it away and you make his life just so much drearier and his load, which is heavy enough as it is, just so much harder for him to lift and push along."

"Is that really what they believe?" asked the consul.

"It certainly is, sir. Why, haven't you ever noticed the farmer when he goes out to plow his little field here? He takes his little kite with him and puts it up in the air and fastens a tiny whistle to its tail, and then as he plows it sings and whistles to him and cheers him on with its bird-like note."

"Why, yes, I've often noticed the kite, but never heard the music," smiled the consul.

"Perhaps that's because your English ear is not attuned to their harmonies, sir, or discords, as my friend, Mr. Gubbins, would call them, I suppose."

"And do you mean to tell me that all their hard feeling toward us is just on account of that little thing?"

"Little to you, sir, but not to them, and there is just the differ-ence. Why should the white man for whom the coolie toils and labors day in and day out begrudge him the little cheer of his barrow's song? That is the way he looks at it, gentlemen, and that is what he resents. Why do you make his burden heavier than it is? Do you not see the point?"

"And do you think they will refuse to obey the order if we try to enforce it?" asked the Inspector.

Wang Foo looked thoughtful and serious. After a moment he spoke. "They may, if they can secure concerted action. It may eventually come to a serious race riot unless it is handled judiciously, and that in the end means bloodshed, which we all should so bitterly regret.

"You may carry your point by force of arms, but what is the use? You have antagonized the most patient and faithful set of laborers in the world and stirred up a bitter race prejudice which it will take years to live down. Is it worth it? Gentlemen, it is not!"

IN THE SHEDS AROUND the Temple of Kwan Foo Chee, the god of war, just beyond the British Settlement limits, a great concourse of barrow-coolies were listening to the words of a leader and exporter. "Our Lord of the Yellow Jacket," he said referring to the token of nobility which adorned the great wooden image of the divinity, "shall decide the great question for us."

"Shi, Shi," they all cried; "hwang ma kwa Lao Ye yao ting!" ("Yes, yes, our Venerable Lord of the Yellow Jacket shall decide it!") "If by the midnight hour of the first day of the feast the ocean-map does not relent and restore us the sweet music of our wheels, then he will draw his great bow and shoot the arrow of his wrath into the ocean-man's streets and fire." Great cheers greeted this sentiment and all pledged their heartiest loyalty and support.

The meeting was about to break up in an uproar, when a solemn and venerable bearded figure arose and bade them wait. The traditional veneration for age compelled a listening and the beard swayed them with the power of magic. "Listen, my children," the unknown voice began, "to a few words of ancient counsel—"

"Yes," they cried, "go on old White Beard, let us hear what you have to say."

"The ocean-man is the best friend you have in the world. Who fills your bags with cash and your bowls with rice, is it not he? Why do you foolishly do that which throws away your livelihood? Why are you angry at him for doing that which he does not understand?

He knows nothing of your old traditions or the customs of your ancestors."

At these words the crowd grew suddenly quiet and began to listen as he went on. "His ocean-ear cannot hear the sweet music of your barrow-wheels; to him it is only that awful discord of which the Sages wrote. You should pity him—not blame him. Let us go to him and explain to him. His heart is great in kindness and after his religion he observes the five great relations, of which the Master spoke. I ask you to agree to pay the extra tax and request the ocean-man to allow you to keep the cheery music of your wheels."

"The old White Beard has spoken well!" they cried. "We will send him to the ocean-man to intercede for us."

"I will go and speak for you," he answered, "but still, the Yellow Jacket must decide it. Behold! At midnight on the second day, the 16th of the moon, if our Lord shall draw his great bow and shoot his fiery arrow through toward the streets of the ocean-man, then our cause is lost; but if he shoots it toward the native villages across the river to the East, then our cause is won. We will pay the extra cash and he will yield the greasing of the barrows."

"Golden words! Golden-words!" they exclaimed, "we will watch for the shooting of the arrow of the Yellow Jacket!" as the meeting broke up and the old white-bearded orator vanished as mysteriously as he came.

JUST WHAT DREW the hundreds and hundreds of the barrow coolies to the river's bank on the second night of the Chinese feast, very few if any of the Europeans in the settlement imagined, and just what they were chattering about as the hands of the Customhouse clock approached the hour of 12 they neither knew nor cared, but to the watchful eyes of Wang Foo, the Consul and Inspector Gubbins, who were secretly observing them from the tower gallery, they presented an interesting and most significant sight.

"It lacks but one minute of 12 now," said the Inspector, nervously looking at his watch. "Mr. Wang, the safety of this settlement is largely in your hands; I hope you will not fail us."

"I never fail," was the slow and quiet answer of the great detective.

They heard the whirring of the wheels in the clock chamber beneath them. One! Two! Three!—suddenly a gleam of light shot out from the opposite side of the river and a long and slender line of fire streamed across the sky toward the East. "Yellow Jacket is shooting," came from a thousand throats.

"Yes!" cried Wang Foo, "Yellow Jacket is shooting," as he grasped the outstretched hands of his two companions, "and he is shooting away from the Settlement! Gentlemen, the danger is over; there will be no riot in Shanghai."

THE SHANGHAI *DAILY NEWS* of the 17th of the moon announced in its headlines:

> "ALL DANGER OF A RIOT OVER!
> "The Municipal Council has wisely decided to withdraw its proposed order compelling the wheelbarrow coolies to grease their wheels, on condition of their agreeing to pay the extra tax for the license. We trust the European residents will not object to this trifling annoyance, which seems to have stirred up so much native feeling.
>
> "It is a very small concession to our faithful laborers, upon whose services the handling of the business of the Port is so largely dependent.
>
> "They will all return peacefully to their work on the morrow."

"A little compromise after all does no harm," remarked the Inspector to Wang Foo, as he read the notice from the paper; "it oils the wheels of life, as the grease does on the wheelbarrows, does it not?"

"Yes," answered the detective with a smile, "and it certainly is not expensive. The fifty dollars that I gave to the sailor who fired the signal rocket from the roof of the temple was very little compared to the safety and welfare of the city. As the old Chinese saying goes—

> "'Hwo Chia Pien,
> Pao Hwa Chu.'
>
> "('The cost of harmony is little.
> Its results surpass our words!')"

THE FATAL TEA CHEST

"By the way," remarked Col. Clifford, the new American Consul, to Capt. Florence of the Pacific Mail, who had brought him over from San Francisco just a few months before, as they were having an afternoon smoke on the porch of the Hong Kong Hotel, "I heard a very funny story today about the Chinese idea of why we put our flags at half-mast—perhaps you already know of it. If so—"

"No," answered the old Pacific skipper, "I don't believe I do. I have listened to their queer tales for years, and nothing that they do or say ever surprises me, but I don't recall just this one. Let's have it."

"Well," modestly continued the consul, "I can't begin to do proper justice to it, because, you see, I haven't been here long enough to become adept in this 'pidgin English,' as they call it, and it really must be told in pidgin to be appreciated. It was given to me by my friend Bradshaw, the surgeon of our hospital in Canton, and he gets it off perfectly. It was so good I made him say it over several times and I just wrote it down and committed it to memory. He himself overheard it on the steamer coming down last week, so I can vouch for the absolute accuracy of it."

"O, you don't need to garnish up the truth at all to have it funny in this country, I assure you. Things are ridiculous enough just as they are."

"I begin to believe you, captain, from what I hear and see every day, but here goes the story: Two Chinamen, one from Canton and one from Hankow, were conversing together on the upper deck and,

331

"He Has Carried the Mysterious Tea-Chest"

as you know, the dialects of those places are so totally different that they have to write on paper to make themselves understood, unless they happen to have acquired some knowledge of pidgin, which, in this instance, was happily the case. Noticing a flag at half-mast on a German steamer lying in the stream, the first one turned to his friend and asked: 'What for Melican man he putchee dat flag middle side? No got top-side, no got down-side, b'longee middlel how fashion dat? My tinkee him no got 'nough lopee.'

"'You no tinkee ploper,' replied his companion, 'plenty lopee have got. Dat talkee sailor man go makee die. Melican man go makee die, s'pose he b'longee velly good man, must go top-side all samee flag; s'pose he b'longee velly bad man, must go down-side all same flag. S'pose he *pletty good* man must stop middle-side all samee flag.'"

"Well, that's pretty good philosophy, isn't it?" smiled the captain, "even if they do get the Germans and American flags confused, eh?"

"O, a trifling distinction like that between the two foreign countries doesn't trouble them in the least—all white men look alike to them and 'Melican man' does duty for almost anything here."

"When you're very, very good and die, you go to the place that begins with 'h,' up above: when you're very, very bad, you go to the place that begins with the same letter, down below—that's it, ain't it?—and when you're only pretty good, they don't know which way you go, and so they just leave the flag in the middle of the mast! A good yarn that. I must try to remember it for the smoking room going home on the next trip."

"Yes," answered the consul. "It certainly is a good illustration of their reasoning about us. As my old friend, Hapgood, the pilot, says, and he's been out here well nigh on to 40 years, 'Everything we do is strange to them, from the time we get up in the morning till we go to bed at night, and their explanations would fill a library.'"

"Thank you," said the captain, as he rose to go, "for a very good story. I'll make a note of it—as old Cap'n Cuttle used to say in Dickens—'and when any man goes to Davy Jones' locker aboard my ship, I'll do a little inquiring into his morals before we do any flag-hoisting,' eh?"

As the consul rode along in his jinrikisha, on his return from the hotel to the office, he suddenly came upon a great crowd of people at the corner of the Kow Loon wharf and saw at once that an accident or something had taken place and that the foreign and native police were trying to push the ambulance through the excited throng. "What's the trouble, Mr. Wallace?" he asked, recognizing the tall, soldierly form of the Inspector of police, "any one injured?"

"Just a wharf-coolie fell suddenly dead, sir, as he was a-carrying a couple of tea chests off the steamer. Seems to me to have been heart disease of some kind, for he was gone in less than two minutes. We're taking the body to the coroner, sir, down there below the warehouse."

"What is the crowd so excited about? I see they are all crying out something and pointing across the harbor? They don't think anybody murdered him, do they?"

"O, no, sir; they're just objecting to our taking him away before the old priest from the temple across the water comes and takes a look at him. They're great at that sort of thing, but it would never do for us to leave him there; there'd be 1000 or more of them there in less than a half an hour's time, sir, and it would block all the unloading in the port for the rest of the day. Besides that, we're just a little afraid of a stir-up among the wharf coolies, for this is the fifth case we've had inside the week and that's quite unusual, sir," added the Inspector, as he bade the consul good day and hurried the ambulance along the waterfront.

Just at the corner of the wharf, as he was turning into Prince Albert road, Col. Clifford recognized one of his own coolies from the consulate, who evidently was taking the deepest interest in the proceedings and jabbering away with all the lung power at his disposal. He couldn't understand a word of what he said, but he seemed to be repeating the same words over and over again. He took out his notebook and pencil and made an attempt to jot them down. They sounded like "Tow low wow chow shang" to him as nearly as he could catch them, so "Tow low wow chow shang" they went down in the book, and he determined to ask his interpreter just what they meant.

"Is Mr. Choo in the office?" he inquired of the servant when he entered.

"My tinkee have got," was the laconic reply of the hall boy.

"Tell him I would like to see him for a moment in the inner office."

Mr. Choo promptly appeared, clad in the long blue gown of the Chinese scholar, which he had adopted immediately on his return from his school days in England.

"Mr. Choo," the Consul said, motioning him with all courtesy to a chair. "I have jotted down some Chinese words here which I heard on the street and I shall be very much obliged if you will kindly translate them for me," showing him the page of the note-book. Choo slowly adjusted the inevitable horn spectacles (worn more for their impressiveness than for any real aid to vision) and spelled the words carefully out:

"Tow low wow chow shang." He repeated them over several times and then said. "May I ask where you heard these and in what connection?"

"You can't catch them, then, right offhand, can you? I am afraid my Chinese isn't very smooth as yet."

"Well, you see, sir, just a very slight difference in their sound to your ear makes a very considerable difference in their meaning. They may mean a number of things; for instance, if you heard them in a restaurant, they would probably be, 'Serve my meal upstairs'; if you heard them in a tailor shop they might be, 'Cut my coat a little higher,' but if the circus was in town they would be, 'Take me out to see the elephant.'"

"Good gracious!" exclaimed the colonel, "you don't mean to say you can got all those different ideas just out of those few words—"

"That is one of the distinctive peculiarities of the language, sir, and it is rather difficult to explain it to Europeans, as they have no system of tones to correspond to it. May I not ask again, sir, just whom you heard utter the words?"

"Why, certainly, it was one of my own coolies, down at the wharf there."

"Well, if you will send for him, sir, we can get at it in a moment."

It took over an hour for the coolie in question to saunter home again, and when he appeared he was promptly summoned into the office. After being assured that he was not to be disciplined or punished in any way, he relaxed and showed a willingness to speak.

"What were you calling out at the wharf, with the rest of them?" asked the interpreter.

"Tao liao ngao cha siang," was the instant reply. Mr. Choo turned to the Consul and said, "The words are perfectly clear now, sir; they mean simply, 'He has carried the mysterious tea chest!'"

"Carried the mysterious tea chest! What tea chest, and who carried it, and where and when?"

This question on the part of the consul was the signal for a dialogue between Choo and the coolie that seemed almost interminable. Finally the explanation came, and it was this: There was a curious superstition on the part of the cargo coolies that in every five thousand chests of tea brought down from the interior to the foreign wharves there was one, the handling of which would certainly prove fatal to its bearer, unless he had promptly paid his devotions and his due to the goddess of the tea shrine. This was the inexorable penalty which she demanded of her children who neglected her. Five victims in a week at the Hong Kong wharves had conclusively proven the truth of this to the native mind, and they had naturally supposed that the one whom the consul saw was the sixth. To make assurance doubly sure, however, they always sent for the old priest from the temple across the harbor to officially give his judgment. The foreign coroner and the doctors might give all the opinions in the world as to the cause of death being apoplexy or heart disease or anything else—this did not make the slightest difference to those who devoutly believed in the tradition of the fatal tea chest.

"Thank you, very much, Mr. Choo," said the colonel, when the former had finished his explanation. "It is certainly most curious and interesting, to say nothing of its mystery, and adds another chapter to my collection of articles on 'Strange Beliefs of China and Its People.'"

"HAVE YOU HEARD of that sad occurrence at the Kow Loon Wharf a day or two ago?" asked Lady Wayne-Evington, at Government House, of her friend, Mrs. de Pugh Tompkins of Adelaide, as the boy brought in the polished brass samovar and placed it in front of the silver tea tray.

"Do you mean about the poor man who they say fell dead because he carried a fatal chest of tea? Why, my husband read it to me out of the *Daily News*. Strange, wasn't it?"

"Poor things! They remind me so much of the natives in India with all their curious superstitions. Why, do you know, when I was visiting my sister, Lady Morton, at Madras, she just put my poor head full of these stories day after day."

"Yes, I have often heard of the strange beliefs of the Hindoos and their fatalistic ideas. Sometimes, you know, they may grow to very serious proportions, unless they have European officers over them who thoroughly understand them and know how to handle them—that's the blessing of our new civil service and its training for the men right on the spot."

"Yes, indeed; why, do you know, one of the oldest missionaries in Madras told me that every native patient that dies of cholera in the English hospitals is supposed to be a tribute demanded by the great god Vishnu; a sort of penalty that they must pay for allowing the white man to come in and govern their country! And yet, the greatest blessing that ever happened to the land was when we took it over and began to rule it."

"Shall it be sugar or lemon in your cup?" interrupted Lady Evington at the moment.

"Sugar, if you please—"

"One, two or three?"

"Three, I think, of those dear little lumps; why I haven't seen anything so delicate since we left Paris—where *did* you get them?"

"Why, they came in a case of French delicacies which the departing Consul sent to my husband a few weeks ago—"

The Governor himself entered at this moment, and, after greeting the guests, sat down by Mrs. Tompkins' side and joined them in the conversation about the accident.

"Yes," he said, "it is a strange and mysterious occurrence, and if it was only one case, it wouldn't amount to anything and would soon be forgotten. The trouble is, however, that this is the fifth within a week, and Inspector Wallace tells me that the wharf coolies are becoming quite excited about it and may strike and refuse to work at any moment."

"Well, there are surely thousands of others who will be glad to take their places, my dear," broke in Lady Evington. "Are there not? Why, there seem to be so many of them waiting around there with their bamboos that one can hardly count them; and they all look so poor and hungry that it's quite pathetic."

"Ah, that's just the difficulty in the case. You see, the Chinese are very clannish, and though it is true they don't have the iron-bound castes that give us so much trouble in India, yet they have all sorts of guilds and local and provincial distinctions and every gang of laborers seems to have some special privilege which no other one can take away from it without a serious row. My esteemed friend, Mr. Wang Foo, explained all this carefully to me last night—I sent for him, you know, because I consider him the very best-informed man on all native matters and he has a wonderful faculty of making Chinese problems clear to the European mind—he says that the handling of tea is entirely a separate matter from any other kind of cargo, and the ordinary wharf coolie would not be allowed to touch a chest of it. The loading and unloading of it has been a sort of monopoly for years in the hands of a gang of coolies from a northern village above Canton and they resent any interference with their inherited right."

"And do you actually mean that this free and enlightened British colony is not free to employ any one it likes to do its work and unload its ships?" inquired Mrs. Tompkins in a tone of thorough British patriotism. "Do we allow ourselves to be dictated to by bodies of native laborers?"

His Excellency Sir Wayne-Evington was just a little ruffled at this outburst from his Australian guest, but kept himself under perfect control and, soothing his nerves with a cup of delicious tea, quietly and politely answered: "My dear Mrs. Tompkins, permit me to explain that after you have resided a year or two in the colony among these people, you will understand some of these things much better than you possibly could now, even though I should give you the most careful and detailed explanation. We are not here to antagonize them but rather to try and live in peace and harmony with them and to build up our international commerce. Those who have lived longest among them and who know them best assure us that this can only be done by conciliating them when no great principle is at stake. I believe this most thoroughly and have tried to act up to it over since I came here. The coolie is as hard working a slave of his fellow-man as you will find anywhere on earth, toiling from daylight to dark for his few small coins. He is a necessity to us, we are absolutely dependent upon his help. Why should we object to his doing his work according to his own native ideas, which have been his inheritance for centuries? You cannot change and overthrow Oriental traditions in a year—or even in a number of years—it is a slow and painful process of training and education, and requires unlimited patience and faith, as our good dean told us, you remember, in his sermon last Sunday at the Cathedral. Do you see that large blue flag flying over Jardine & Co's hong there?" rising and leading Mrs. Tompkins toward the front window; "notice the words, 'E Wo,' 'Just and Harmonious.' That's the carefully chosen business sign of the oldest and largest firm in the colony, it is known and quoted by the Chinese all up and down this entire coast, and represents in a remarkably significant way exactly the attitude that all representatives of our British Empire ought to assume."

An orderly suddenly appeared at this moment with a dispatch for the Governor; so he was obliged to excuse himself and leave the ladies to continue the conversation or turn it into channels of a more congenial and social nature.

IN THE QUIET OF THE UPPER ROOM at No. 5-5-5 in the Red Cloud Alley, Wang Foo, the man of mystery, was engaged in a deep and earnest conference with his old friend and counselor, the abbot of the Temple of the Queen of Heaven.

"And you say there have been five already?" inquired the latter, as he passed the pipe from his right hand to his left, and leaning back in his chair, slowly exhaled the blue smoke through his nostrils.

"Yes, Venerable Father," replied Wang Foo, "your golden words are truth itself. There are exactly five already and we may at any moment hear of the sixth."

"It must be stopped at once! It will never do to let it reach the eighth or the results may be most serious. You know how they all regard our sacred number, and those tea coolies from Kwang Kien are very bigoted and difficult to handle when once they get excited. That is the very worst district in all the Canton province."

"What does my Venerable Father advise?"

"You must see the priest of the old temple across the harbor and find out from him, without his suspecting it, just how the situation stands and what compromise can be arranged. He seems to have gotten into their favor by some means—probably he comes from the same district—and his word will go farther with them than any others."

"And then?"

"Then you must see the Inspector and possibly the Governor and explain to them the significance of the numbers and the risk of a disturbance if any more are allowed to die."

"And then?"

The Abbot looked around the room, listened for a moment to be sure of their perfect security and privacy, and then, leaning over toward his host, whispered a few short sentences into his ear. Wang Foo started a little, but at once resumed his composure.

"Do you think it possible?" he asked.

"Not only possible, but absolutely certain," replied the venerable father, as he sipped the parting tea and rose to go.

"It shall be as you say, then," said the host, as he called for old Chang to arouse the sleeping chairmen in the courtyard.

The following morning Inspector Wallace welcomed the detective by appointment into his private office, and together they discussed the situation.

"You know me well enough, sir, I am sure," began Wang Foo, "to realize that I am no alarmist, but I should fail in my duty to you and to this community if I did not warn you of the serious consequences that are likely to arise from this smiting of the tea coolies at the wharf. These men, as you perhaps know, are not our fellow townsmen, but come from a turbulent district in the north and are very clannish and superstitious. The old people among them are densely ignorant and prejudiced and still bitterly oppose the export of tea—which they think is the sacred beverage given by the gods to China and its people for their exclusive use—and when they hear of the series of deaths at the wharves here, it will be a comparatively easy matter for their leaders to stir them up to trouble."

"And what then?" asked the Inspector, becoming more and more interested in Wang Foo's story.

"Why, then they might strike and refuse to work or to allow any other coolies to work, and turn around and before we could stop them they would pitch thousands of dollars of tea over into the harbor—"

"Like our American cousins in the old days at Boston, eh?"

"Yes, and, as far as their minds are concerned, with even a much better reason. This would not only mean a great financial loss to the buyers and shippers and a serious injury to British trade, but, what to my mind is far more serious, it would strike a blow at British prestige in this colony, from which it might take years to recover, sir."

The result of this interview of Wang Foo with the Inspector, which lasted considerably longer than either of them had anticipated, was that the latter promised to have a private counsel with his Excellency the Governor and to report to Wang Foo's residence immediately any further fatalities at the tea wharf. That evening a coolie from police headquarters handed in the official chit book to Old Chang, who promptly carried it upstairs to his master. He took out the enclosed note and quickly tore it open. It contained only this brief sentence:

> "Dear Mr. Wang—Number 6 was stricken just before dark.—Inspector Wallace."

He signed the book and handed it back to Old Chang, saying as he did so, "See that the bearer has boiling tea and a pipe before he leaves and slip two extra bits (10-cent pieces) of a dollar into his hand from me, before he passes out of the gate." There was no time to lose, and Wang Foo made all his preparations for the morrow before he turned in to rest, feeling more deeply than ever the responsibility that circumstances had laid upon him of being, as the old master, Confucius, said of Yang Loo the Faithful, the "Harmonizer" between the opposing people. Yet under all the burden he was supremely happy, for was it not written in the pages of the Great Teaching, "The ideal gentleman and scholar is he who devotes his learning to make the people understand."

Three important interviews must be had, the first with the Governor, the second with the tai pan (head of the firm) of Jardine's, and the third with the old priest across the river. All three bore a direct reference to the problem before him, which was to put on end to the smiting of the wharf coolies by their carrying of the fatal tea chest. He was fortunate enough to secure a few private moments with his excellency and to obtain from him an introduction to Mr. Gregory, the head of Jardine's, with whom he was closeted for over an hour, and from whom he obtained something that he very much needed for the successful carrying out of his plan. It only remained now for him to see the priest, and to this he devoted the afternoon.

Infinite tact and an intimate knowledge of his people and their ways secured for him at last what very few others would have been able to obtain. Appearing in the disguise of an aged gentleman of wealth, he ingratiated himself into the old priest's confidence and finally the latter confessed to him that he had received a payment of 20 Mexicans for each trip that he had taken across the harbor.

"There are just 20,000 chests more to be loaded," said Wang Foo; "that means four possible deaths from carrying the fatal one. Four times 20 is 80, and 20 more for good luck makes 100. See! Here are 100 new and shining dollars if you finish your trips and sign the paper which I ask."

The old priest's eyes sparkled as he saw the coin; he hesitated for a moment—but this was sure, and the trips across the harbor might not be—he went for his ink slab and the temple seal, and ere long the great detective stepped again onto the ferryboat with the coveted document up his sleeve.

WHEN INSPECTOR WALLACE took his seat at his desk in the morning he found lying there a chit in the familiar round script of Wang Foo. Just how and when it was delivered there nobody seemed to know, but the office coolie insisted that it was there when he swept out the room in the early morning, so it must have been delivered into the hands of the night watchman before daylight. He opened it and read as follows:

> "My Dear Inspector Wallace—Please put your mind at perfect ease about the tea coolies at the wharf. There will be no more deaths from the fatal chest while this season's cargo is being landed. I personally guarantee it.
>   "Faithfully yours, Wang Foo."

"Wonderful man, that!" he exclaimed to Moorhead, his deputy, who had just entered the room.

"Who?" asked the interested arrival.

"Who? Why, who should it be but our friend Wang Foo? Here, just cast your eye over that," as he handed him the chit.

"Well, all I have to say is, that if any living man can guarantee anything about these chaps, he's the one. But, at the same time,

Chief, I'm not a-going to leave that wharf unguarded until the very last chest is landed, mark me, guarantee or no guarantee. 'Seeing is believing,' I say, in this country, and nothing else is, as far as I am concerned."

When Capt. Morehead reached the wharf a little later he found everything going along merrily and smoothly and the native officers whom he had sent ahead of him scanning with great satisfaction a large placard of yellow paper with characters and seals which unknown hands had affixed to the central wharf post at the break of dawn.

"What's all this?" he asked of Sam, his native assistant. "More trouble brewing? I hope not."

"No more trouble," answered the smiling Sam. "He talkee bobbery all finishee. No. 1 jossman speakee all piecee tea coolie hab' pay ploper joss money, no more man makee die."

"O, that's it, is it? The old arrangement of the Italian bandits, I see; no more robberies and murders for this season, because all travelers have paid the proper 'squeeze,' eh? Well, I guess we'll have a sharp lookout here just the same and keep the ambulance handy when No. 7 reels over," was the captain's only comment on the interesting document

The day passed away in quietness, however, without any accident, and so did the next and the next. The last package of the valuable cargo was safely landed, the wharf coolies received their last cash and their usual bonus and prepared to return to their homes without any more demands upon their lives to pay the toll of the fatal tea chest

"This Colony of Fragrant Waters—I am using its poetic Chinese name out of compliment to you, Mr. Wang—is once more deeply indebted to you for leading it out of a very delicate complication," said His Excellency to the detective, as a little company gathered in the drawing room at Government House.

"Not to me alone, sir," modestly replied their Chinese guest, "but to yourself and to our esteemed friend, Mr. Gregory, of Jardine's, without whose hearty co-operation I could never have accomplished this result."

"And are you ready now to reveal to us the secret of that guarantee that you promised?" asked Inspector Wallace. "I've been waiting for that, you know."

"With pleasure, gentlemen; it was just this way, you see: I found there were exactly 20,000 chests still to be landed, and you remember I explained to you their superstition about the fatal tea chest in every five thousand; this made a possibility of four more deaths. It was most important to keep it from reaching the number eight, for that is a number of very special significance. The deaths, I found out from my good friend, the coroner, who kindly took me into his confidence, were all of very aged men, who were in no condition to stand the very heavy strain. The tea chests, I incidentally ascertained from the wharf weighers, were extra heavy this year on account of the difference in the boards and the native lead on the inside, and this made an extra risk. Now, there were just 200 of the coolies who carried these chests, and my friends, the doctors from Mission, who also kindly assisted me, picked out 50 of them who were superannuated and liable to drop dead at any moment; the others were all strong enough to stand the strain. I bought off these 50 by giving them all double pay for two days' work which they didn't do, so, you see, I was quite able to authorize my guarantee. The placard from the temple completed the guarantee by allaying the fears, which was on important element in the case. This was a little extra expense, but my good friend, Mr. Gregory, who so generously furnished the wherewithal, will agree with us, I am sure, that it was a very small and most justifiable outlay to secure the peace and good will of the people and to make more popular than ever that grand old sign of our leading firm:

"E WO"—"Just and Harmonious!"

THE DRAGON'S CLAWS

"Now, MY DEARS," said Mrs. Cortelyou to her friends, the Misses Coplestone of Boston, as they sat on the veranda of the Consulate sipping the delicious Hankow tea, which the compradore had just presented to the family, "If there is any other very special sight that you would like to see while you are here in Shanghai, be sure and let me know, and I am sure my husband will be delighted to arrange for it; that is, if the time and the place are suitable."

"O, thank you so much," replied the American visitors together, "I am sure that is most kind of you and of him. We really almost hesitated to ask any such favors after what we heard about consuls and tourists aboard ship—"

"What, what was that? What terrible things are they saying about us now?" inquired the wife of our country's representative, with a curious smile.

"Well," said the elder of the Coplestone sisters, not without a little hesitancy, "they told us that all our consuls out here in the Far East look upon tourists—or 'globe-trotters' as they call them— as nothing but annoyances who take up their time, and sometimes their money, and put them to all sorts of trouble and inconvenience and then go away without so much as even saying 'thank you' for their pains."

"That really is unfair to both sides. But it only goes to show that there are all kinds of tourists in the world and, I suppose also, all kinds of consuls. I believe it is entirely a personal matter

The financial manager ---took out the enclosed coin --chinked it --and entered the name of the giver in the marriage ledger

and we must learn to discriminate between individuals and not condemn an entire class.

"I have certainly found that true among that much-abused circle whom we send out here as missionaries—and whom I heard the ship's officers abuse all the way from San Francisco to Shanghai—some of them are among the most cultured and charming people I have ever met, and there are some, again, whom I should not care to cultivate a very intimate acquaintance with."

"We are so glad to know you feel that way, for we had the very same experience."

"My husband and I came out here expecting to find all our American residents ladies and gentlemen and to treat them accordingly, until they proved themselves to the contrary. We have made the same rule for our tourists.

"We try to treat them all with equal courtesy and do everything for them that we can while they are here—my husband, the consul, in the office, and in our home—and most of them, I am proud to say, appreciate it, but, of course, there are some who are never satisfied and who utter all sorts of complaints if they cannot have just what they want at the moment. I suppose that is part of an official life in almost any quarter of the world."

"Yes, I am sure it is," replied the ladies.

"Why, would you believe it, a party of tourists not so many weeks ago actually found fault with my husband because during the few days that they were in port he could not take them to see a Chinese execution! Just as if the American consul could control the Chinese Department of Justice and have heads chopped off at any date to suit his own convenience! How utterly unreasonable!"

"How absolutely awful! Well, my dear Mrs. Cortelyou, neither my sister nor I were thinking of any such grewsome sight as that, I assure you. What we had in mind, was something of a very different and a very pleasant nature; we wanted to ask if your good husband could possibly arrange for us to attend a Chinese wedding. That is one thing we specially set our hearts on when we left home."

"I cannot promise with certainty any definite date," replied their hostess as she refilled their teacups, "for I don't suppose these people can get married to order. However, if you are going to be some time in the Settlement, I am quite sure he can secure the privilege for you through our good friends at the American Mission, for he has done so several times before. I will speak to him about it the first thing when he comes home this evening."

"That is perfectly lovely of you both," exclaimed the guests as they rose to continue their afternoon drive along the river.

"WHAT ARE ALL THOSE AWFUL SHRIEKS and howls? I suppose the poor creatures are returning from a funeral, are they not?" asked a party of English travelers of the British consul's interpreter as he was escorting them through some of the native streets.

"Oh, no, quite the contrary," he replied as he stopped the jinrikishas for a moment; "it's a wedding and they are bidding farewell to the bride."

"The bride! Why, what's the matter, is she being torn away from her family against her will? Please stop a moment and explain it to us—"

"Neither against her will nor in accordance with her will," explained the interpreter, "for, you see, a Chinese bride has no will of her own at all. She is betrothed to her husband-to-be when she is a child and her own wishes are not consulted at all.

"All these matters are arranged in a business way by the go-betweens. When the lucky day is fixed by the fortunetellers for the wedding, she is securely locked up in that great red sedan-chair that you see just disappearing around the corner there, and her family follow her to the center of the street and then bid her good-bye."

"What? Do you mean that they do not go with her to the wedding?"

"Certainly not. Her own father and mother cannot even see her married. Not a single member of her family 'receive cards' as we say in England."

"What is the idea of such a heathenish custom?" asked the leading lady in the party.

"Why, simply this: She is supposed to die to her own kith and kin and to become a living member of her husband's family. Her mother may go to see her at the end of 10 days and she may revisit her family at the expiration of a month."

"And those poor, broken-hearted things are weeping at the loss of their child; how pitiful!"

"Don't waste any unnecessary sympathy on them, I beg you," replied the apparently hard-hearted interpreter. "Of course they have the natural feelings and instincts common to humanity, but three-quarters of all that weeping and howling is all put on as part of the ceremony. That is the correct traditional thing for them to do, and tradition rules everything in China."

"What an awful mockery!" exclaimed the ladies.

"Not at all from their standpoint. It is simply following out the old maxim of Confucius, 'Wan shi yiu ting lee' ('Let everything be done according to the established rites'). You will understand this all much better after you have been in China a little longer," and turning to his jinrikisha coolie he said: "Kwai kwai! Tao pao ma ting!" ("Hurry up now to the race-course!")

The bridal procession which had so interested our English visitors was wending its way slowly through the crowded streets to the home of the happy bridegroom, who in this case happened to be Mr. Lang Choo, the scribe of the American translator at the Poo Tung Arsenal.

This relationship had been the fortunate means of securing an invitation through the consulate for the Misses Coplestone to attend the wished-for ceremony, and they had been already waiting nearly two whole hours for the bride to arrive. Finally the crackling of thousands of firecrackers announced that the suspense was over and the great sedan, carried by four bearers, was safely deposited in the reception hall.

The go-betweens produced the key, lifted out the bride and escorted her to the ceremonial room, where she was positively identified by the raising of her thick red veil. This ended their official duties, and the ladies took charge of the rest.

At the central door of the house the bridegroom received his honored guests. He wore full official robes (his privilege for three days) and bowed low several times to every arrival. At the last bow a small packet of red paper was quietly slipped into his sleeve by each guest, and this he passed over without word or comment to a friend seated at a table just behind the door.

The financial manager—for such he was, really—carefully unwrapped each packet, took out the enclosed coin, checked it to make sure of its genuineness and entered the name of the giver and the amount in the marriage ledger. It interested the Misses Coplestone to learn that wedding presents in China do not consist of silverware or jewelry, but plain hard cash and that the amount received is so carefully calculated beforehand that it is supposed to just cover the expenses of the wedding feast, which begins in the forenoon and lasts until midnight. (Bogus coins, counterfeits, etc, are promptly returned to the giver for exchange the following morning!) They also jotted down a number of other things in their notebooks in which the Celestial ceremonies differed very radically from those in Boston.

They found, for instance, that the religious service, if such it might be called, consisted simply in the master of ceremonies calling off the titles of all the groom's ancestors for a number of generations back and asking the bride to accept them as her own, which she very promptly did, not by speaking, but by having two old ladies bow her head for her. The same two gracious females bowed her head all through the day for her and also moved her hands and feet, the bride to their eyes being merely an automaton, who could neither speak nor move of her own accord.

They also learned the interesting fact that there was no such thing as a wedding journey, that being to the Chinese mind the height of insanity—if their minds could even conceive the thing— that after three days and nights of feasting and drinking the groom's mother took charge of the house and the daughter-in-law became her slave and that then the one momentous question was how and where to borrow money enough to meet the remaining expenses. After the wedding banquet, where, to their surprise and regret the ladies and gentlemen all dined separately, they returned to their hotel, dazed and mystified by all that they had seen, but quite reconciled to the thought that they had been brought up on the Western Continent.

The following morning they did what all globe-trotters most innocently do; they gave a full account of it to the room-boy when he brought in the morning tea-tray. "What do you call a wedding in Chinese, boy?" they asked.

"Hob got plenty diffelent name," was the answer.

"Well, we want a nice poetical one. You can savvy poetry?"

"B'longee all same sing-song, my can savee."

He thought for a moment and then wrote on the paper which they handed him the following couplet:

> "San tien foo,
> Pak nien koo!"

"And what does that mean?"

"Talkee all samee thlee day velly happy; eight year velly solly."

(The Consul's interpreter explained to them later in the day, however, that the popular synonym for a wedding, 'Three days of happiness; eight years of misery' did not refer to matrimonial infelicity, but simply to the combined struggles of both parties to pay off the wedding debts!)

AT EXACTLY EIGHT O'CLOCK in the evening, on the fourteenth day of the eighth moon, all Shanghai was startled by a low rumbling sound, followed by a loud booming report like the crashing of nearby thunder. Thousands of natives ran out into the streets, crying at the tops of their voices: "Ti tseng! Ti tseng! Lao lung chi lai chek!" ("The earthquake! The earthquake! The old dragon is waking up!"), referring to the popular belief that this convulsion of Nature is caused by the arousing and stirring of the great dragon who sleeps just beneath the ground.

Many Europeans who were just sitting down to their dinners rose and rushed out on to the verandas. "Yes, it's an earthquake, sure enough," said an old resident from Japan at the hotel. "I've felt them for so many years I never mistake them."

"Well, you're mistaken this time, all right," replied another voice from the adjoining room, "that isn't any earthquake; that's an explosion up there at the arsenal. Just look at that red glare away to the south and the column of black smoke. Someone's blown up the powder magazine, that's what they have."

And sure enough, that's exactly what it was, as the papers announced to the world the following morning—not the main magazine, but a smaller one some distance away from the central buildings and containing only a moderate supply of old-fashioned native powder. "Fortunately no lives were lost except that of the watchman on duty, of whom not even a trace has been found," the *Daily News* said in its brief notice, adding that "His Excellency Chang Tao Tai has ordered an immediate and thorough investigation."

The article in the *Chinese Evening Herald* (printed in the native tongue) was slightly differently worded and ran as follows:

"Singeing the Dragon's Claws."

The explosion of the smaller fire-medicine storehouse (powder magazine), at the Poo Tung Arsenal last evening unfortunately destroyed a part of the beautiful Dragon Garden which was laid out by the uncle of our present Tao Tai, and which outlined in its paths and rockwork the entire body and limbs of the famous creature.

The small stone building containing the fire medicine was clasped in the claws of the left front foot and today is a shapeless ruin. The work could not have been accidental, for the building is isolated from all the others; it must have been the evil deed of someone who had a grievance against the authorities or some of their employees. Whoever he be, we warn him that vengeance will surely overtake him, and we bid him remember the words carved on the ancient stone:

"Who singes even the smallest claw,
Will surely feel the dragon's wrath."

When Dr. Powell, the American translator of military and naval books, returned to his office at the Arsenal on the 20th of the month, his scribe, Lang Choo, failed to put in an appearance, although the week of absence which his employers had given him for his wedding had more than expired.

"He waited for him one, two, three days and then the importance of his work urged him to send his house-boy to his home, just outside the French international boundary. The boy returned late in the evening with the astonishing news that Lang Choo had been arrested by the officials from the native city!

"My velly solly, but must talkee tlue," he said, "dat old Shanghai Mandalin have send yamen-lunner catchee he, s'posee thlee day more before time."

"Sent the yamen-runners to seize him! Arrest him in the very week of his wedding! Why, good heavens, boy, what has he done?"

"My no can savee," replied the boy, who began to show the inherent native fear of any complication with the law, even to merely giving private testimony; to his own master, "more better you askee policee man, he can savee all ploper.

"My b'longee house-boy, no can savee Mandalin pidgin, so please you 'scuse me," getting more and more frightened every minute that he spoke.

Dr. Powell sent to the nearest stand for a jinrikisha and hastened to consult his friend Dr. Cortelyou, at the Consulate. Fortunately he found him at home, just looking over his latest papers by the morning mail.

"I am very sorry for you, Doctor," he said, after listening carefully to the translator's recital of the arrest and imprisonment of his scribe, "but I am really afraid there is nothing I can do for you. You see it is entirely a native case, as he lived outside the settlement limits and the only foreign connection with it is that you paid half his salary.

"The city officials are very jealous of any interference with their own prerogatives and if I should send a dispatch to the Tao Tai and ask him why he had arrested a man on his own native heath, he would in all probability tell me—of course most politely—that it was absolutely none of my business."

"And isn't there any way that I can even find out what crime he is charged with?"

"Well, you had better see Inspector Gubbins and have him get at it through some of his native officers. I guess that's your only chance."

Early the next morning, Dr. Powell reported the case to the Inspector, who, turning to his report book, said: "Why, if he's employed in the arsenal, they've probably arrested him for some connection with the magazine explosion."

"The magazine explosion?" exclaimed the doctor in utter astonishment, "why, what on earth could he had had to do with that? He's a quarter of a mile away from the building in the first place and doesn't have anything to do with the machinery or gun or ammunition departments. It's perfectly absurd."

"It may seem so, sir, but you never can tell where their suspicions will land, they're so different from us. And, I must say, they do sometimes hit it very straight when we go all astray. However, I'll just call in Hoo, my best detective, and ask him if he has heard."

Hoo promptly appeared in answer to the Inspector's summons and saluted his chief and the visitor in a semi-military fashion.

"Hoo, why have the yamen-runners grabbed Lang Choo, Dr. Powell's scribe at the arsenal?"

"Chineeman all talkee he have makes burn fire medicine house, have spoiled garden, too muche bobbery, dlagon all same velly angly."

"Well, there it is, you see," said the chief, turning to his caller, "it's just as I supposed. They've run him in for that explosion and now that they've once got him they'll probably torture him into some kind of a confession and then finish him up. You see it's this dragon superstition that makes it so complicated.

"If the magazine had been anywhere else it wouldn't have been so bad, but unfortunately the beast had it right in his left claw and so it will go mighty hard with the poor chap because they all believe that the fire scorched the creature and made him perfectly furious. Then, again, sir—I'm sorry to say it, but I know it's true, and so do you—they're always apt to be harder on the man that's in foreign employ. It's sort of prejudice that they don't seem able to shake off."

"Quite true, Mr. Gubbins, and I can also understand now why they were all so mysteriously quiet about it out there at the arsenal. Probably every clerk in the department knew it and yet not one of them breathed a word to me about it."

"A strange fear of being drawn into it in some way, I suppose. They are as afraid of letting their opinions be known as the French were in the old days of the Revolution, eh?"

"Just as bad, or even worse. But can't you possibly think of any way in which I can help this poor chap. I believe he is just as innocent as you and I are. They're only making him a cat's paw, that's all. How can I possibly reach the yamen and the officers who have the case in charge? I am willing to do anything and to spend a half year's salary if necessary."

The Inspector shook his head as he rose to bid the doctor goodbye, then stopped for a moment and said: "You might try Wang Foo—he's the only man I know that can get at it for you." Explanations as to who this mysterious personage was, where he lived and how he could be reached followed in due order, and in less than a week Hong Kong's great detector of crime found himself once more in the English Settlement at Shanghai, listening to the reports of the Arsenal case and thinking and planning his investigation.

"TELL ME ABOUT OLD WING, the watchman," said a visitor from Canton to the soldier who was showing him about the Dragon Garden and pointing out the ruins of the powder house.

"He was a quiet, queer old fellow," answered the guide, "he's been here for a good many years and didn't talk much to anybody. He lived in a kind of a little hut that he built for himself just outside the iron door of the magazine. There are all sorts of stories about him, some even say that he was very rich and hid his money away in powder kegs there to avoid suspicion."

"And you say not the slightest trace of him was ever found after the explosion?"

"Not a particle, sir."

"And has the place all been carefully searched?"

"Yes, sir, and the very ashes raked over."

"And you say, do you not, that he always carried the old bunch of brass keys in his girdle?"

"Yes, sir, I've often seen them."

"Oh!" exclaimed the visitor with deepening interest, "what were they like?"

"They were large old-fashioned ones, sir, two of them were as long as my hand and had curious teeth in them that curved up like pincers. Old Wing himself used to call them the 'dragon's claws,' sir."

"And not one of the keys has been found or even a piece of them?"

"Not one of them, sir. Many thanks! Many thanks!" as he stretched out his palm for the silver pieces which the visitor offered him, "and may lucky stars guide you all along your way!"

"And are you on duty here at night also?"

"Yes, sir, there are two of us always sleeping in the guard-house yonder."

"I should like to come out and see the ruins and the garden in the moonlight some evening, if I may," adding another coin to his already very generous gift, "perhaps on the 24th, if the weather should be fine."

"Just come in before the outer gates shut, sir, and have a cup of tea and a pipe with us, and stay as long as you like, sir."

The visitor thanked him and passing through the long rows of bamboos that led the way into the Arsenal Gardens, remounted his jinrikisha, and after a long ride through the suburbs entered the house of a basket-maker from Hong Kong, and appeared once more as his old friend Wang Foo.

Missing very much the valued companionship and ever-wise counsel of his colleague, the Abbot, whom he had left at home, he had to do all the thinking for himself and it was well on toward the quiet hours of the morning before he finally reached his conclusion, which was briefly this, viz: Lang Choo was perfectly innocent, there was no doubt about that. The officials had simply arrested him to save their faces before the higher authorities and had selected him as their victim because he happened to be in the foreigner's employ.

The only shred of evidence they had against him was that he was away from home at the time of the explosion and consequently might have been at the powder house, and the fact that the other scribes in the department had overheard him say that "the old building was only an eyesore, anyway" and "It would be no loss to have it out of the way." Second, Old Wing, the watchman, could never have disappeared as completely as they supposed.

Some portion or trace of him would have been found by the hundreds of searchers who scoured the ruins and the Garden and the large brass keys would have certainly remained as a very tangible proof. Old Wing was alive and well! No doubt about that, either. Did he fire the magazine himself with a slow match of some kind, or did he hire someone else to do it for him? And, most interesting of all, what was his object?

He must be found at any cost and found at once—that was the task before our Man of Mystery, and while he knew that the finding of the traditional pin in the haystack was easy compared to tracing a stranger in the wilderness of Shanghai, he resolved to undertake it without delay. Every teahouse and resort in the city was watched by himself and the native detectives whom the English police had placed at his disposal, but up to the morning of the twenty-fourth day not a sign of him had appeared.

He then decided to make use of an ancient superstition, which now, as often, proved the key to the solution. Placing his trusty revolver in the specially constructed pocket in his sleeve, and tucking away a pair of handcuffs in his girdle, he called a jinrikisha and at sunset hurried away toward the Arsenal Garden. There he found his friend the soldier and whiled away a pleasant hour or two in his cabin before beginning his evening stroll and meditation in the Dragon's Paths.

Finding a quiet and secluded spot near a bamboo fence behind the ruins he sat down, and making himself comfortable took out from his sleeve an ancient roll, and unrolling it carefully scanned it by the dim light of his pocket lamp. At last he found the place of his search and read the words over carefully and slowly to himself.

Yes! There was no mistaking it. "Ten days after the commission of the crime the conscience of the guilty one is smitten by the avenging gods and he will return to the scene to view it o'er. If not apprehended then he may make good his escape forever!" he rolled it up again and put it back. "It is one chance in a thousand," he said to himself, "but I will take it." Listen! What were those sounds that reached his ear? Footsteps!

His heart beat rapidly as they drew nearer. They were not coming from the direction of the arsenal, but from a little country path outside the wall. He saw a head and shoulders appear above the bricks and in a moment or two more a solitary figure stood before the ruined powder house.

Raising both his hands to the sky he moaned out the words, "Shao liao lung wang sheng ti! ("Alas! I have burned the sacred body of the dragon king!") In another instant he was in the iron grip of Wang Foo, who, seizing him from behind, threw him like a trained wrestler to the ground, and before he could recover his senses or even utter a scream, Old Wing lay there helpless with the steel handcuffs on his wrists!

WHEN HE CONFESSED IT ALL before the district magistrate, it came out that he had brooded so long over a supposed injury and insult to his family on the part of his employer, the manager of the arsenal, that he had decided to explode the magazine and trust that the penalty would fall on his enemy's head for a neglect of duty—but he utterly miscalculated, for it fell instead on the innocent head of Lang Choo.

"One question more, before I release you," said the magistrate to the scribe; "where were you at exactly 8 o'clock on the evening of the explosion? I should like that answered for my own satisfaction. Can you prove an alibi?"

"Absolutely and to the great man's complete satisfaction. Mr. Wang Foo knows perfectly and will have pleasure in telling you."

"Where was the prisoner at that hour?" inquired the magistrate, turning to the detective.

"He was making a ceremonial call upon two American ladies at the hotel, your honor, and thanking them for their attendance at his wedding. Thus, as your honor sees, it was absolutely impossible for him to have been anywhere in the vicinity of the arsenal."

"It is enough, the prisoner is released and the court is cleared!"

AT THE LITTLE FOREIGN DINNER PARTY which Mr. Lang Choo gave at his home to celebrate his return from the yamen, there were just four guests, Dr. Powell, Wang Foo and the two Misses Coplestone. Out of deference to their expressed wishes, Mrs. Choo, the bride, waived the strict laws of native seclusion and joined her guests at table.

"What a wonderful experience we have had! How misfortune and fortune in turn have woven our lives together in a way that we never could have forgotten! And how very much we all owe to you, Mr. Wang!" said the elder sister to the great detective, when the feast was over.

"Not at all," modestly replied Wang, "I have simply been able to do a little international harmonizing, which, after all, is the supreme pleasure of my life. And now, ladies, I want you to accept a pair of little brass curios for your mantel-shelf at home.

"They may serve to recall us all to you when you are far away again from China and the East." He drew from his sleeve, as he spoke, a little roll of yellow silk, and opening it, handed to Miss Coplestone the old pair of brass keys which formerly had locked the iron door of the powder house. "Only," he added as a caution, "you must be very careful not to let them get too near the fire, for you see what I have had engraved on them:

"The Dragon's Claws.
"Who singes even the smallest claw,
Will surely feel the dragon's wrath!"

THE MIRROR OF THE SHINTO GODS

"IT SEEMS VERY STRANGE INDEED, Colonel," said Capt. Goodfellow (secretary to his excellency, Sir Evington Beecham, governor of Hong Kong), as he took his seat by the side of Col. Oliver Hopkins, the newly appointed American consul, "that with all Inspector Higgins' skill and ingenuity he hasn't been able as yet to throw any light upon that robbery at the hotel two weeks ago."

"Yes," answered the consul, as he opened his Cantonese silver cigar case and handed the British official one of those rarest luxuries in the far east—a genuine Havana. "You know, ever since I landed here I've been admiring your splendid police force and my office staff have told me story after story of their clever ways of detecting crime and exposing the crooked ways of the 'wily celestial' and yet, here is the very first case that comes to the consulate, and they seem absolutely helpless. By the way, there go Mrs. Tucker and her daughter now." He pointed across the road from the club veranda. "Charming people!—you've met them, of course?"

"Yes, indeed: Lady Beecham presented me at the garden party last Tuesday. Sorry they are not going to make a longer stay in the Colon, but they are sailing on the Rangood Mail a week from Saturday. Globe-trotting, you know, and they want to do Burmah and Mandalay and all that sort of thing so as to get to Calcutta before the holidays. Lovely girl that! Pity she's leaving us in that frame of mind, though. They say she's all broken up over her loss and wants to go back to California on the next American boat. But

361

A CLOUDLIKE FRAGRANT SMOKE
CAME OUT OF IT AND SPREAD
OVER THE FACE OF THE SILVER
MIRROR.

they've got ten days yet, you know, and Higgins will surely get something definite for them in that time—if he doesn't, then I shall begin to lose faith in the force myself."

"Well, how about that mysterious native detective that seems to get at it when all others fail?"

"You mean Mr. Wang Foo?"

"I believe that's the name. He's great at unraveling that sort of thing, isn't be? My interpreter and secretary both think he's a wonder."

"Well, he certainly is. Scotland Yard hasn't anything finer in its entire outfit. As you say, we may have to fall back upon him yet."

"So Miss Josephine wants to turn around and go home, does she?" said the consul, with a significant little smile paying over his face; "and all on account of the loss of one curio when travelers sometimes have a whole trunk full stolen—well, all I have to say is that she's a cute little thief herself—"

"A thief, sir? You surely don't mean to reflect upon her honesty in—"

"Only in the line of something infinitely more valuable than oriental curios, captain, and that is human hearts! Lieut. John Barrington Wetmore—who is temporarily acting as my vice consul, you remember—hasn't, as yet lodged any definite complaint with the police, but, 'just between you and me and the lamppost,' as we used to say in Ohio, that attractive young man has been missing a very vital part of his make-up for some two weeks past and (drawing the words out slowly) though I've never prided myself on being anything of a detective, I rather think that the article in question will be discovered in Miss Josephine's possession."

"Lucky dog! He'e to be congratulated on his loss! Now if he can only prove as cute a little thief on his part as she has on hers, and steal the corresponding treasure for his own, why I as judge will dismiss the case and say fair exchange is no robbery. Let us wish him success!"—raising his glass from the bamboo table as he spoke.

"Success to both our juvenile criminals," answered the colonel. "And here's hoping that Inspector Higgins may be as successful in apprehending his thieves as we have been in finding ours."

The entrance of the inevitable club boy with the chit-book at this moment concluded the interview, and the two gentlemen took the waiting jinrikishas for their respective offices.

DR. MELVILLE PATTERSON was, by general consent, the leading physician in Victoria colony, Hong Kong, and his long experience in treating tropical diseases—to say nothing of the various little upsets that are apt to afflict the visitor to that "Island of Fragrant Waters"—made him the one to whom Mrs. Tucker and her daughter naturally turned for professional advice in this case of a nervous collapse. It was just before the afternoon tea hour on the day in question, when his card was brought to their room by the hotel room boy.

"There's the doctor now, Josephine," said the anxious mother, "and I want you to be a good girl and tell him the whole story from beginning to end." The daughter rose from the reclining Manila chair in which she had been retting on the veranda and, passing through the screen doors into her own apartment, answered. "Just a moment; mamma, till I make myself a little more respectable."

Was it entirely accidental that her room. No. 324, was directly opposite the Peninsular Shipping Company's building? Was it entirely a matter of chance that the second story of that building was being occupied by the offices of the United States consulate? And, furthermore, had the fates ordained that at that particular hour of the afternoon the handsome acting vice consul should be leaning over the railing, just above the narrow street, and allowing his eyes to wander across to the verandas of the hotel? Perhaps yes, perhaps no, for the fates themselves are quite accidental at times, you know. At any rate, the fact remains that Miss Josephine took far more than the necessary few moments to make herself presentable for the doctor's visit and her pulse beat with considerably more activity than the normal worry over the theft alone would have called for. (All this, of course, while quite unconscious of the fact that the room clerk of the hotel had shown Lieut. Wetmore just a few days before, the exact location of No. 324 on the diagram.)

Dr. Patterson, with charming grace of manner and with that wonderful tact which some physicians possess, had made his fair patient feel perfectly at her ease, and so, sentence by sentence, she told him the story of the robbery and the cause of her collapse. In a word, it was this: Just before leaving Japan they had been invited by one of the oldest missionaries in Nagasaki to attend a little picnic at one of the old Shinto shrine near its sacred mountain, and had spent a most delightful day. Their host had explained to them about the ancient faith of the people, and with an old native priest had been their guide through all the precincts of the temple. Miss Tucker, while apparently interested in it all, was especially fascinated by the story of the silver mirror of the Shinto gods—that mysterious disk of polished silver, in which if one only gazes long and silently enough, he will see the image of his inner life and read the deepest secrets of the soul. She had been reading much at home about the mystic ways of eastern devotees, about cloud-visions and crystal-gazing and mirror-worship, and all that, and now here was the ideal embodiment of it all. She set her heart upon obtaining a genuine "mirror of the gods," and determined to place herself in the proper frame of mind to enter into its secret revelations.

Alas! This was one of the cases where all the influence of friends and even the almighty power of the native dollar proved ineffectual—for not a single dealer in the port had one for sale, and although the missionary pleaded for her in the most fluent Japanese, the old Shinto priest and his fellows at the shrine were as obdurate as the stone images by the wayside. She was almost heart-broken. However, even Shinto priests sometimes relent, especially when they have a few duplicate treasures hidden away in the inner shrines—and just before the *Nippon Maru* sailed for Shanghai the following morning, the old priest himself knocked at her cabin door and announced that he had fortunately discovered a most efficacious mirror in an unused part of the inner court, and he was willing to let her have it (on the pledge of her inviolate secrecy), for about five times its normal value. Money being no object when the secrets of one's soul are for sale, the purchase was promptly sealed.

Now for the mysterious disappearance; she had brought it safely to Hong Kong and had kept it locked securely in one of the inside compartments of her wardrobe trunk. It had only been taken out a very few times to show to admiring friends and had always been carefully locked away again. About a week ago she was explaining it to some visitors from the consulate, and laid it carefully on the table by the tea-tray, rolled up in its covering of yellow silk. After her guests were gone she turned to pick it up, and, to her horror and utter dismay, the yellow silk wrapper just crumpled up in her hand—it was absolutely empty, the mirror had vanished!

"Yes, doctor, I would rather have had them steal all the rest of my baggage and leave that alone. Don't try to cheer me up by telling me that I can buy another one just as good. No other mirror in the world can be to me what that one was. I hope I am not wickedly superstitious, but that had become part of my innermost life. I spoke to it and it answered back more clearly than the cleverest ouija-board—it seemed to contain my other self and to reflect back to me my future. I not only feel lost without it, but I am utterly broken-hearted and all interest in my eastern trip is gone."

"Now, don't worry, my dear child"—that was always Dr. Patterson's fatherly way—"we're not going to palm off anything else on you at all. We're after that original mirror and we're going to get it and you are surely going to see your own dear self in it—and anything else you want to see there—before you leave this port. We've got the finest police in the world here, if you know anything about Inspector Higgins, and if he don't catch the thief, why, Wang Foo will, so there you are. Now, in the meantime, I'm going to send you up 3,000 feet into the air for a good change and rest, see? You just leave all your trouble and worry down here in the settlement for ten days, and away you go this very night up to two nice rooms that I have for you and mother in the sanitarium an the peak."

The two ladies promised implicit obedience, and, after writing out a little prescription for overwrought nerves, the doctor bade them goodbye.

"But who is Wang Foo that you say will help us?" asked the patient as the door stood ajar.

"Oh! Wang Foo? Haven't you ever heard of him? Why he is the great Chinese man of mystery who unravels all tangled affairs for us. What he cannot find isn't worth the finding."

"And he is clever at catching hotel thieves, is he?"

"Why, ladies, that's his very specialty—but you know we must give our own officers every chance first, otherwise it wouldn't be fair to them."

INSPECTOR HIGGINS AND DEPUTY BROWNLOW were closeted together at headquarters and comparing notes on the disappearing of the Tucker mirror. "Of course," began the chief, "the hotel boy who brought in the tea things is our first thought. He seems to have been the only outsider who entered the room between the time Miss Tucker unlocked the trunk and the time she missed the article. Has he been properly grilled?"

"Most thoroughly," answered the deputy, "but we haven't made much out of him. You see, in the first place, he is one of the oldest houseboys in the settlement—been in the hotel ever since it was built—the manager and everybody else swear by him. They say they'd as soon suspect their own sons as suspect Ah Ling. Now, you know as well as I do, chief, that it isn't this kind that does the stealing; they're always the newcomers that try on that sort of game."

"No one could have crept quietly along the veranda and slipped it off the table, could they?"

"We thought of that, too, chief, but the table wasn't in a place where even the longest Chinese arm could have reached in from outside. We measured the distance carefully when the ladies showed us the apartment."

"Well, what does the head hotel boy say about it? They're awful shrewd at ferreting out their own native tricks, you know. They'll see far further into these things than even the sharpest of us Europeans will."

"Yes, and you know they have the honor of the hotel boys' guild at stake, so that they have a sort of gentleman's agreement that they won't do any kind of stealing from inside themselves. No, whoever the thief was, you can be quite sure he climbed over the wall from outside, as we used to say at home."

"And the only Europeans in the room besides the Tuckers were Col. and Mrs. Hopkins and Lieut. Wetmore? You are quite positive of this?"

"Absolutely positive."

"Well," remarked the chief as he rose and took his cap from the wall, "you can't really suspect an American consul of robbing his own countrymen, now, can you?"

"Hardly," chuckled the deputy, "that would be as bad as the old judge we used to read about who picked the pocket of the prisoner in the dock as he was a-passing up to the bench."

"Brownlow! This is a Wang Foo case, and the sooner you and I acknowledge it the better."

"Right you are, sir," and they parted—the deputy to his home and the inspector to No. 5-5-5 in the Red Cloud alley. "Hung Yuin Loo, Woo Pack Woo Shi Woo," he cried to the jinrikisha coolie at the gate. "Allee light, my can savee Massiter Wang Foo all ploper," replied the puller (swift of foot but light of garment,) as he sped rapidly down Queen's Road to the native quarter of the city. Fortunately the famous detector of crime was at home, and when Old Chang, the gatekeeper, drew back the wooden bolts of the courtyard gates and ushered the foreign visitor in the venerable, grand one hastened to announce his presence and to set the kettle boiling for the inevitable tea.

"Well, Mr. Wang," began the Inspector, "I suppose it is hardly necessary for me to tell you why I have come. We are in trouble over a case, and we need your usual valuable assistance."

"Not the case of Miss Tucker's mirror, is it?"

"The same, sir, and I've come to have a quiet talk with you and to find out if you can offer us any further suggestions, sir."

"My time and service are always at the disposal of yourself and the department, Mr. Inspector," replied the most courteous host, as the venerable grand one appeared with the tea tray and cakes, "and I consider it a very great compliment that you have taken the trouble to call upon me in person. Refresh, yourself, I beg you, with a cup of hot tea, and then we will have a quiet smoke and meditation over it in my private den upstairs—which is literally somewhat nearer heaven than this damp ground-floor reception room. Lao Tal Tai"—addressing the venerable grand one—"kwei kak niung tsz si tsai pao jih tsa fak tien shing! (For the attendant of our honorable guest, let the hot tea be immediately poured and the sweet things of the heart be offered!)" The ideal Chinese gentleman never forgets the waiting-servants of his visitors.

"These, I feel quite sure, are genuine," continued Wang Foo, as he drew from the drawer of an inlaid cabinet in the "Quiet Glade of Reflection" to which they had both ascended, a silver box of tiny Manilas, "for my esteemed young friend Lieut. Wetmore of the consulate brought them directly from the factory in the Philippines. By the wav, he is a remarkably fine young man—quite different from many of the consular officials whom I have known—you have met him, of course?"

"Oh, yes, sir, I've had quite a number of talks with him. You see, he's the one that first called us to the consulate to tell us about the robbery. He seems to take the loss of the mirror almost as much to heart as Miss Tucker herself; in fact, Mr. Wang, as you know our English and American ways so well, I don't mind repeating to you what I said to Mrs. Higgins at our home last night, and that is this: He's as much interested in the young lady herself as he is in the loss of her property, perhaps even more so!"

"Ah! Then there is a little romance interwoven with the case, is there? That, of course, makes it much more interesting for those who are trying to solve it. I am delighted to know that you have received that impression, for, to tell you the truth, I received it myself very vividly the afternoon of Lady Beerham's garden party. And now that you have done us the honor to confide your impression to me, I will return the compliment and add another of my own, and it is just this: Miss Tucker's interest in the vice consul is just as real and vivid as his interest in her, though she is sweetly unconscious of the fact that she has let out the secret to any one. As one of our ancient poets says:

Hwa tzs si tien shiang
Tao yao tek jih sheu.

(The flower will reveal its sweetest fragrance
Even to the hand that tries to pluck it.)

"But to return to the details of the case"—taking out the yellow leather notebook and preparing to make some entries. "I shall have to ask the privilege of my usual week's time. I shall postpone my visit to his excellency the governor of Canton and I shall request three interviews, viz.: One with yourself and Deputy Brownlow, one with Mrs. Tucker, the mother, and one with Miss Tucker alone—however reluctant she may be to grant it. There will, I need hardly say, be other interviews and with other parties whom I do not name now, but these three I am going to ask you to be kind enough to arrange for me at the earliest possible date. I will drop in at headquarters just after tiffin tomorrow. Shall we say 2 o'clock sharp? Thank you. And now for about a dozen very leading questions before you go. Mr. Inspector, your answers to which shall not only be absolutely confidential, but as I jot them down in my notebook they will be in my secret system of Chinese stenography, absolutely meaningless except to the sacred circle of the five initiated ones."

When the Inspector finished his answers and rose to leave, Wang Foo's Chinese cap of woven silk covered all the leading facts of the robbery. Within the next few days Wang Foo was granted the privilege of the three interviews which he had requested of Inspector Higgins; and his courtesy, and gracious manner with the ladies and, last of all, his deep personal interest in the case had made for him a new circle of admiring friends.

He, of course, visited the apartment where the afternoon tea had been served and had Miss Tucker go over with him carefully every detail of the consular visit. He examined the room, the walls, the doors and windows and made a minute inspection of the veranda with its exits and entrances. Yet, though he did not spare his questions at all—his piercing eyes seeming to penetrate into every nook and corner—there was an entire absence in him of that rough and sometimes very annoying inquisitiveness with which detective officers conduct such an examination in western lands. He appeared rather in the role of an interested personal friend, and thus led the ladies to avoid all suspicion of being cross-examined by the police and to tell the story as naturally and freely as they would have to any member of their own immediate family.

What pleased Miss Josephine more than anything else was his sympathetic inquiry about her visit to the shrine at Nagasaki, and about the way in which the mirror of the gods was finally secured. He drew out from her many of her own thoughts about crystal and mirror gazing and more than charmed her with his unfolding of the oriental conception of these and other esoteric mysteries.

"If you will pardon my saying it, Miss Tucker, I believe that from my standpoint as a child of the far eastern world, I am privileged to enter more feelingly into the sense of your loss than are my friends of the Hong Kong police force—splendid men and officers though they be. They would be rather inclined to measure it by the money value of the curio than by its inner worth to you. What to you—as to so many of my own people—seems to be the secret message of the spirit of the mirror or the crystal, is to them merely a reflex of your imagination, a subjective sensation, not very far removed from superstition. But to you, Miss"—and here his voice became gentle and almost hushed—"to you I know it means that if your mind and heart"—he spoke this last word very slowly—"are pure and trustful as the silver surface of that sacred mirror, you will find there your other self, your better self that will guide and mold your life, reflected in the polished metal, is it not so?"

"It is so! It is so, Mr. Wang; you have spoken to me as no other person has. You seem to know and understand that to which they are all blind. The deep secret longing of my life is hidden there, in that mirror of the ancient gods, and until it flashes itself out to me, I am little better than a wanderer over the face of the earth. Oh! sir, find it and restore it to me if you can. Never mind the punishment of the thief—forgive him, pay him anything he asks, but bring my treasure back to me."

"Be restfully happy, Miss Tucker; east and west are joining hands to help you. If we cannot pledge success, at least we can always hope for it. As the sages said of old:

"'Pang Wang King Chien tak tao tien tso.'

"They mean." said the man of mystery as he bowed his way toward the door and raised his long hand upward, "they mean just, this:

"Hope is the golden arrow that uplifts us to heaven's throne."

"ONE PIECEE COOLIE, my no savee what side he comee, have pay dis chit my side talked you must look see velly chop-chop," remarked the jinrikisha man as he handed Inspector Higgins a carefully sealed document the following morning at his home. He tore it open and read these words:

> "My dear Inspector:
> "We have found the thief and recovered the mirror!
> Preserve absolute secrecy and come to my home.
> "Wang Foo."

He finished a hasty breakfast and started without delay for the "Quiet Glade of Reflection" at No. 5-5-5 in the Red Cloud Alley. Wang Foo was awaiting: him and they ascended to the quiet upper room.

"You don't mean to tell me that you have this double good luck—" began the Inspector; "tell me who he was and how he got a hold of it. Brownlow is as anxious to know as I am."

"Did he come with you?"

"No, sir, I came here straight alone from home; I haven't even been to the department yet."

"Good! These words are for you and me alone—not for any other human ears as yet. We can't afford to take any risk by an advance exposure. Now, Mr. Inspector, listen carefully to me, for there is something much more than a mere curio at stake here. You have absolute trust in me, have you not?"

"Absolute, Mr. Wang."

"Then listen carefully, ask no questions and carry out my instructions to the letter. Tomorrow night at exactly 9 o'clock I want you to bring Mrs. and Miss Tucker, Col. and Mrs. Hopkins and"— he added in a most emphatic and significant lone—"young Lieut. Wetmore to a little entertainment which I am planning for them at the Temple of the Queen of the Sea. Present the invitation in any language that you please, but make it perfectly clear to them that it will be well worth their while to attend, as I have very important information to give them concerning the robbery. My directions may seem very strange to you and my orders rather peremptory—but obey them and all will be well; disregard them and all is lost!" So the interview ended and the chief returned to his office for the duties of the day.

At a few minutes before 9 o'clock the following evening, a row of official jinrikishas drew up before the residence of the United States consul on the terrace overlooking Queen's Road. They were waiting for the party that was just rising from dinner—the same five persons whom Inspector Higgins had been commissioned to invite to the temple. While the older members were putting on their wraps, the two younger ones strolled out onto the porch and stood for a moment gazing at the beautiful scene spread out in the moonlight before them. The long curving sweep of the harbor, the myriad lights in the settlement just beneath them, the shipping of every name and kind, the thousands of paper lanterns on the native junks and sampans and the flashing of the red and green signals from the towers of Low Loon all helped to form the dazzling panorama that unrolls nightly before Britain's rocky isle of the Pacific.

"Miss Tucker," said the young lieutenant, as he turned and looked for a moment into her face, seeming to gather new inspiration and strength for his thoughts from the vision that opened before them, "is it true that you are sailing on the next Indian Mail for Rangoon?"

"That depends very much on the events of this evening," she answered, very deliberately. "I may and I may not. But why do you ask?"

It certainly was a broadside, but he recovered in an instant from the shock. "Why do I ask? Why do I ask?" he stammered. "Why, just because this Island of Hong Kong is going to be a dreadfully lonely place without you, that's why."

"Oh, you really think so, do you?"

"I certainly do. And one question more, please, do you really believe all this stuff about the mirror of the gods that you and your mother are always talking about, and all this ouija-board nonsense about seeing your future affinity in it?"

"Not my affinity, if you please, lieutenant, much more—my divinity!"

"You really believe this?"—the doors were opening onto the porch—

"I most certainly do!"—the party were coming out now.

"Then," he cried, "may all the Shinto gods at once send their blessings on Wang Foo!"

"Happy sentiments," echoed the consul and Mrs. Hopkins, who now had joined them, "so say we all of us! And now for the Temple by the Sea."

Arrived there they were welcomed by the great detective himself and ushered into a beautifully gilded banquet hall where a literal feast of the Chinese gods awaited them and sweet music—of the kind rarely heard by European travelers—filled the air with its melodies. Two other guests joined them at the temple, and they were none other than our friends Higgins and Brownlow of the police. When that hour which in the western world is known as "coffee and segars" finally came, Wang Foo arose and, addressing the company in a few well chosen words of welcome, thanked them for the honor they had done him in being his guests for the evening.

"And now, my friends, it is time for the great denouement. I propose by the kind help of the Shinto gods—" addressing these latter words to Miss Tucker, who blushed in response—"to do just four things, viz.: First, to expose a thief; second, to restore a stolen property; third, to heal a broken heart, and fourth, to reveal a brave but modest hero. Such is the sum and substance of my little drama, which you will agree is quite a modern 'thriller.'

"Lieut. Wetmore, will you be kind enough to raise me, sir!" The handsome young officer instantly obeyed. Then, turning to Inspector

Higgins, Wang Foo said: "Mr. Chief, behold your robber and your villain!" It would have been hard to tell which face, the Inspector's or Miss Tucker's, bore the more astonished expression at these words. They were about to speak, but Wang Foo motioned them to silence; putting his hand inside his capacious silken robe, he next drew forth the original mirror of the gods and stepping over to the young lady's chair, placed it gracefully in her outstretched hands. "I now have the pleasure of restoring to its owner a borrowed—not stolen—treasure, and of healing a broken heart and restoring a case of shattered nerves—"

"With a much better medicine than mine!" cried Dr. Patterson, who by previous arrangement entered the room just at this moment.

"And now, as the closing scene, I want to reveal the brave but modest hero." As he spoke these words Wang Foo drew from his sleeve a jade-stone vial, and opening it, a cloud-like fragrant smoke came out of it and spread over the face of the silver mirror. "Miss Tucker, if you will look carefully and trustfully into its surface now, the future and the affinity will be revealed!" She held it up in spite of herself, and there, clear and distinct as in a photographic frame, were the pictures of the lieutenant and—"His bride to be!" they all cried out together.

"I KNEW AT ONCE," REMARKED WANG FOO at the consular dinner which took the form of an engagement party, "that either the consul or his assistant had taken the mirror and I thought I had better charge the younger man with it at once. He made an open and frank confession to me, and pledged himself that as Miss Tucker had vowed to see in it the face of her 'future,' he proposed to paint his face on that mirror before any other man had a chance. He slipped it under his coat while the ladies were talking, and I naturally promised to help him by some Chinese invisible colors which the contents of the vial eventually brought to light.

"Every magician must have a confederate, you know, and I now must expose our mutual friend. Dr. Patterson as having consented to play that role.

"He saw with the trained physician's eye how completely the idea of the fortune-telling mirror had taken possession of the lady's mind, and he agreed with me as to the only perfect and permanent cure. That cure having now been accomplished, we make our homage at Miss Tucker's feet and humbly ask forgiveness for all our wicked ways! For, as the great master said:

> "He who heals s broken heart,
>   Of Heaven's reward shall have a part."

THE ENCHANTED BASKET

RATTLE, RATTLE, RATTLE DOWN the beautiful Shanghai water-front went the jinrikishas over the Hong Kew bridge and along the Bund toward the long row of foreign banks near the Nan King road. "Ho Lan Yin Hong! Ho Lan Yin Hong! Aw Saw Dik! Aw Saw Dik!" cried the hotel-boy who was acting as guide to the party of three Americans—("To the Dutch-Asiatic Bank! To the Dutch-Asiatic Bank! Hurry up! Hurry up!") The coolies increased their already rapid pace and in a very few moments more deposited their burdens at the gateway of a pretentious looking building, from the flag-staff of which floated the tri-colored flag of the Netherlands. "All three piecee man can waitee this side little time," said Dr. Williams of the China Navigation Company's medical staff, quite ready to exhibit his knowledge of pidgin-English to the later arrivals, and turning to the lady and gentleman who accompanied him, added: "Here we are. Now we will all go in and divide the spoils."

They passed up the steps and entered the bank, where the assistant compradore (or native cashier) received them at the counter and took their cards into the manager's office. "That looks all right, doesn't it?" said the surgeon as he pointed significantly to a handsomely framed notice on the inner desk—

TICKETS
of the
Royal Dutch Lottery of Batavia cashed here.

"Happy dreams over,
our new-found wealth!"

"Now the only question is: shall we take it in sovereigns or bank-notes or silver? Let me see—ten thousand dollars divided among three, that is about three thousand, three hundred and thirty-three apiece, with a little extra change thrown in, doesn't it?"

"It certainly does," answered Miss Olivia Spencer, who, with her brother Jack, formed the remainder of the trio, "and I congratulate you on the excellence of your mathematics. I think I will take mine half in bank-notes and half in gold—you know I just love the sight and feel of gold: I can't help it. I caught it in California— but none of those awful 'chop dollars' for me, if you please. Why, it would take an extra jinrikisha to carry the load, and then, the very thought of all the people that have been handling them is enough to give you the creeps, anyway."

"And you. Jack? What shall we say for you?"

"Notes, old man, and notes only; I want to have that old-fashioned American feeling of a 'fat roll' in my pocket, you know."

Harry Wagenpool, the genial Dutch manager, appeared at this moment and greeted his customers with real East Indian courtesy. "First of all, ladies and gentlemen," he said, knocking the ashes from his Sumatra cigar, "I want to extend to you my hearty congratulations on winning the third prize. And to assure you that the directors of the Royal Lottery will be especially pleased to know that it has gone to a group of Americans. We are anxious to have our institution better known in your part of the world where"—he smiled broadly as he spoke the words—"I believe there still lingers a little of the old-fashioned prejudice against raising a government's income by these means. Please step into the inner office and we will call the head compradore at once." When all were seated he touched a bell, and the long-gowned Celestial immediately responded. "Talkee Compradore come this side just now!" The vision bowed and vanished as silently as he came.

"You have the ticket with you, of course?"

"Oh, yes," answered Miss Spencer promptly, "it's right here in my little bag."

"And the number is—?"

"Thirty-six-thousand-and-one. And here is the special telegram from Batavia, which reached us before the papers announced the lucky numbers this morning."

"Quite right, quite right, and the third grand prize is yours." Then, addressing the native cashier who had just entered in answer to the summons: "Compradore, please cash this order for ten thousand dollars for the visitors."

"Velly good," bowed the corpulent Ching Pow, "wantchee all notee? Some goldee, some silliber, how fashion?"

"Oh, only about a hundred dollars in silver," spoke up Dr. Williams, "the rest in notes and then"—pointing significantly toward the vault behind the glass partition—"you might give us three of those nice little bags of new sovereigns you always keep in there for your special friends."

Ching Pow withdrew to the inner sanctum, where his brother Celestials were chinking the coin. He was gone but an instant when he rushed back with a look of surprise and anxiety on his usual placid countenance, and startled the manager and his guests with the exclamation: "Dis ticket him no good, my have pay dis money one piecee Chineyman dis morning. S'posee some man he hab makee stealee!"

"What on earth do you mean?" cried Mr. Wagenpool, rising from his seat and snatching the ticket and order from the compradore's hand. "You say you've already paid this number? Go back there and get me the other ticket at once!" Then, calming himself, he turned to the party: "There may have been some serious mistake here on the part of the native staff—although they are always over-particular with their customers—but we will have it corrected at once "

"Why, what can it possibly be?" exclaimed the lady, "there certainly are no duplicate tickets and these people, with all their cunning ingenuity are surely not able to forge one?"

Ching Pow reappeared with a book and two pieces of paper which he laid on the astonished manager's desk. Sure enough! There was the unmistakable evidence before them: ticket number thirty-six-thousand-and-one had been presented at the native counter fully three hours before: the cash had been duly paid to the holder Ting Sang and the bird and the prey had vanished together!

"My friends," said Herr Wagenpool, after he and his customers had examined the papers, "I am bound to confess that we are the victims of a very clever forgery—the very first in all my experience here—we will summon the Police Department at once."

"A pretty serious affair, this," remarked Dr. Williams as the party rose to take their departure. "And who, may I ask, has to bear the loss in the case, we or the Royal Dutch Lottery? That's the all-important question to us."

"Ah, that will have to be determined by the Consul when the police make their report. The bank can pay only one ticket and the evidence must determine which is the genuine one and which is the forgery."

"And are we to leave our ticket with you now?"

"Yes, the police must have possession of them both."

"Well," remarked the surgeon, "in order to make sure of future identification I will just put my private mark on ours," and drawing a little vial of iodine from his pocket, before the manager could stop him, he painted with the little brush in the cork the initials "A. R. W." right across the face of the ticket.

RIGHT ACROSS THE WIDE NAN KING ROAD with its twinkling lights, and in toward the north where the Tea House of the Ancient Sages entertains its hundreds or nightly guests, there passed that same evening a solitary figure clad in the long blue gown of the scholar and followed by a coolie bearing on his bamboo two commonplace bundles of matting. They turned at the corner by the Tea House and elbowed their way through the narrow Alley of the Genii until they came to the rear entrance of one of those handsomely-gilded shops which front on the Ho Nan Road, and which are known all over China as places where lottery-tickets are bought and sold. There were no lamp-posts in the alley and they had almost to feel their way along. There were no distinguishing signs or numbers on the doors and each house looked exactly like its neighbor. When they stopped, the leader felt with his hand across the stone lintel and muttered to himself: "No, not here, it must be next door." He went a few paces further and felt the stone again. This time his fingers went into a crack and out of it he drew a long brass key. "Ah, it is here!"

"Put the bundles down and I will carry them in," he said to the panting coolie, who was mopping his brow with a very ragged piece of white cloth.

"The venerable master speaketh well," was the reply, "and. now as the night is dark and the way is long and the burden is heavy, I know the master will not begrudge his servant a few extra cash."

"We bargained for a hundred and fifty, did we not?"

"The master's words are truth itself, but the extra pipe and bowl of tea are not amiss."

"Hold out thy hand: Behold the extra ten—and now begone!"

He waited until the coolie had disappeared, and then placing the brass key in the ancient lock he opened the door and dragged the two bundles into the courtyard. Leaving them there in safety, he ascended three small wooden steps and knocked upon a closed wooden shutter: first, three knocks, then two, then one. He waited a moment and then he heard the bolt drawn from within. The shutter was opened cautiously. "Have you brought it?" asked a mysterious voice. "It is all here," he replied, "come out and help me carry it in." A small door opened and a figure emerged (bowed over with the apparent weight of years, he was really physically afflicted—none other than "Cripple Ching," the well-known vendor of chances) he attempted to lift one of the bundles, but it was too much for him. so he untied it and took out carefully twenty rolls of rough brown paper and carried them, five at a time, into the house. They closed the door and the shutter and both sat down at a table. A small and very smoky kerosene lamp shed a dim light from a shelf above them. Cripple Ching began: "All went well as I directed? You took three thousand in gold, three thousand in notes and the rest in silver?"

"Exactly so," replied the faithful confederate Lang Shin ("Twin Stars," so called from two star-like frost bites that adorned his cheeks). "Here is the gold and the notes," placing the bags and rolls upon the table: "and here are the forty packets of a hundred dollars each."

"And the compradores suspected nothing?"

"Nothing at all—they simply overwhelmed me with congratulations and thanked the Buddhas that I had won it and not the while man."

"Ah, that is as it should be, but it is fortunate that you got there early, for some miserable foreigner is almost sure to bring the other ticket before the day is over. And you took it all to the Baptist Mission and hid it in the storeroom until night?"

"Yes, exactly as we planned."

"Then, by the aid of all the Buddhas, we will count it all over once more and place it in the Well of Heavenly Blessings for safe keeping."

Suiting the action to the word, Twin Stars and Cripple Ching went over every coin and note and then, wrapping them all carefully up, they lifted a worn piece of matting from the floor and opening a trap-door concealed by the dust, deposited the treasure in a deep hole in the ground and covered up all traces of their crime.

"Now that all is successfully accomplished," said the Cripple with a sigh of relief, "what do you say to a fresh bowl and a pipe at the Tea House of the Ancient sages?"

"It would be most refreshing after this hard and dangerous day's work," echoed Twin Stars.

"Yes, we will drink the health of the Royal Batavia Lottery—and then to happy dreams over our new-found wealth."

So they passed out together through the living-room into the gilded shop with its mirrors and carvings and scrolls and all the paraphernalia of the lottery dealer—out into the street under the great golden sign of the establishment—

"MIAO LAN TZE"
(The Enchanted Basket)

INSPECTOR JOSEPH MCARTHUR of the Shanghai Police looked across the table at his deputy, Captain O'Keefe, as they sat in secret conference in the private room at Headquarters, and pointing his finger significantly at the lottery tickets that lay before him, said: "Well, Cap, it's a mighty clever piece of work and no mistake. Now the first question is: Were they made here or abroad?"

"Oh, sir, you can take my word for it, they were made right here in the Settlement, and what's more, they were made by their own people. You see they're so sly and secretive and suspicious that they wouldn't let the tickets go out of their own country for fear they'd never get them back."

"I believe you're right—and now the very first thing is to search every printing house in Shanghai and find out whether they have any press that will do this kind of work. Put Ah Sam and his brother at it: they're our best native officers, and they'll ferret it out quicker than ever we could."

"Beg pardon, Chief. I put them at it yesterday morning and they report that there's only one possible place where it could be done, and that's up at old Dr. Donaldson's. He's just fitted out his place with a lot of new machinery from home."

"You mean the Baptist Mission Press up by the French Bridge?"

"The same, sir."

"Well, I think you and I had better just go up there quietly this afternoon and have a private interview with the old gentleman before the natives begin to get suspicious and hide things. Come around two o'clock and we'll hire a couple of public jinrikishas on the Bund, and mind, no uniforms, just citizen's clothes."

"Right you are, sir."

Early that afternoon the two officers called at the Mission Press and were courteously received by Dr. Donaldson in his study. They explained the object of their visit and ended by asking if it was possible that the tickets could have been printed—of course without his knowledge—at his establishment.

He looked the papers over very carefully by a strong light and finally said: "Well, gentlemen, it is an excellent piece of lithographic work, and we have, I believe, the only new press in Shanghai that is capable of it, but you must remember that there is something even more necessary than a press for doing this kind of thing, and that"—pointing to a group of workmen in courtyard—"that is the printer! There are only two men in our whole outfit who are really what you could call skilled lithographers, and I know them so well that I wouldn't suspect them for a moment. Besides this, I superintend all this kind of work in person and it would be impossible for them to put any matter on a stone without my knowing it at once. No, gentlemen, the Baptist Mission Press is not responsible for this fraud; you will have to look elsewhere."

Inspector McArthur, however, was far from being satisfied with this statement of the manager and insisted on accompanying him to the pressroom and in putting him through a regular third degree, and, evidently to his great annoyance, included his two native assistants in the process. "Where did they spend their nights? Who kept the keys to the pressroom? Was it not possible for them to duplicate the stone?" etc., etc., until his little notebook was quite filled to overflowing with memoranda; then he and the deputy respectfully took their leave.

"Well, Captain, what do you make out of it?" he asked when the two officers once more returned to the seclusion of the Chief's private room

"Believe me, sir, that 'Charles' and 'James' as he calls them—the missionaries being accustomed to give English names to their employees, especially if they are converts—are a sly and tricky couple. I think it would pay us to inquire a little more deeply into their whereabouts and various doings. You see the old gentleman will believe anything those fellows tell him, and how does he know but that they have false keys and get into the pressroom at night and work this sort of game while he is asleep?" So for the next two weeks a careful watch was kept over Charles and James, but their comings and goings were as innocent as those of any Chinese lambs, and at the end of that time the police were reluctantly obliged to confess to Herr Wagenpool that they were as much the dark as at the beginning. "Well, gentlemen," he said, "you have evidently come to the end of your rope. Have you nothing else whatever to offer?"

"Nothing except Wang Foo," was the Inspector's reply.

"Wang Foo? And who is he, pray?"

"The famous detective at Hong Kong."

"You mean the one who recently recovered the Governor's stolen jewels?"

"The same, sir."

"Please wire for him to come at once. Make him the most liberal offer you please and tell him to spare no expense."

That same evening Old Chang, the gatekeeper at No. 5-5-5 in the Red Hand Alley handed a piece of yellow paper to his master in room above. "Tien pok, tien pok, chin lien kwai, chin lien kwai!" (A lightning message, a lightning message, please read quickly!) The man of mystery opened it, perused it carefully, then rang the bell for the Venerable Grand One and said: "Prepare the honorable baggage—I sail in the early morning for Shanghai!"

"Now, Doctor," said Miss Spencer, as she added another lump of sugar to his dainty little teacup which he held out beseechingly before her, "you really must control your trembling nerves or you will be dropping your cup and saucer and decorating this hotel verandah with fragments of porcelain, and"—she added with a significant smile—"that would be worse than losing the lottery-ticket, wouldn't it? perhaps you are drinking too much China tea; they say, you know, that it is apt to make new comers a trifle shaky at first."

"Miss Olivia," answered the blushing young man, as he promptly steadied his arm and so avoided the threatened crash of the porcelain, "do you really notice that I am a little nervous today?"

"You most certainly are."

"And do you really, in your hear: of hearts, think that it is nothing more than the Batavia Lottery and the China tea that causes it?"

"Why," she added, with that sweetly innocent but very deep look that has played over the countenances of the daughters of Eve since the very first day of a mortal man's proposal, "why a what else can it be?"

"What else? What else?" he repeated as he drew his chair nearer to her side—and inwardly thanked the gods that her brother would be gone at least another ten minutes—"why nothing else, of course, except just my own foolish self and, a-n-d you."

"And me? Oh, yes, I see. Of course, it was all my fault. If I hadn't said half-jokingly to you and Jack that night, when the hotel-clerk offered us the ticket, 'Let us all three take a share in it!' why we shouldn't have gotten into all this entanglement, should we? And you wouldn't have been obliged to run over here every afternoon to tell me how the case was going on, would you?"

"Oh, I really didn't mind that at all. In fact, I've actually enjoyed it so much so that I've mustered up courage to come over here today and ask you to share—"

"Another lottery-ticket with you?" (Did he notice that she very deftly, as she said these words, slipped a little doily over a paper novel that lay on the table beside her, and just in time to prevent his reading the title if he had looked that way?) "Another lottery? Why, that would just even-up the account, wouldn't it. I inveigle you and Jack into the Royal Dutch game and then you turn around and suggest a similar risk to me. First Eve tempts Adam and then Adam returns the compliment by a similar temptation on his part— isn't that it?"

"Well, yes, it does look a little that way, but this isn't that kind of a lottery. I m-e-a-n it isn't that kind of a risk, don't you see?"

"Anil where does poor Jack come in on the risk? We couldn't leave him out, you know."

"Oh, he won't be left out, but he won't have exactly the same kind of a share in the game that you and I have. He will come in all right"—and he actually did so that very instant as he burst into his room and called out to the verandah to save him a hot cup of tea.

"Miss Olivia," said the young surgeon, making a desperate effort to save the last few moments before the brother's appearance from his room, "you really didn't give me time to finish my sentence. What I tried to say to you—in fact, what I have been trying to say to you ever since we first met, is simply this: I want you to share my life and my home and my future with me, and to take me for whatever risk I am. Are you not willing to venture it?"

She did not answer at once, but reaching over to the table she gently withdrew the white doily that covered the novel and pointing to the illuminated title on the cover said, after a moment: "Perhaps it would be well to settle the lesser before attempting the greater." He picked up the book and read the words carefully. They were startlingly clear and distinct: "Marriage, the Great Lottery of Life."

Jack's appearance on the verandah at this moment turned the conversation into the commonplaces of the day, and after a few moments the surgeon rose to depart, more determined than ever to secure the two great prizes of his life, viz.: Miss Olivia and the Batavia gold!

WHEN THE CHINA MERCHANTS' PACKET *King Loon* (or Golden Dragon) discharged her passengers at the Hong Kew wharf, among them was a dignified native gentleman who created somewhat of a sensation by the fact that both the English Captain and the First Officer came down from the bridge and shook him cordially by the hand as they bade him good-bye. "Here's hoping to have you with us on the next trip, Mr. Wang."

"Thank you, gentlemen; it is always a genuine pleasure to travel with you."

He hailed a jinrikisha and also a wharf-coolie. "Nan King Loo. Pak Yien Kai. Tien Loo Mian. Hong Kong Lan Tze Poo!" (Up The Nan King Road and the White Cloud Alley to the Shrine of the Heavenly Gong and the shop of the Hong Kong basket-maker.) After a cordial greeting from his old fellow-townsmen and a quiet night's rest under their hospitable roof, he started out early the next morning to find his friend, Inspector McArthur, and from him and the deputy he heard the full story of the double ticket and the consequent loss of the third grand prize of ten thousand dollars. He also had lengthy interviews with Herr Wagenpool and with Miss Spencer and Jack and the surgeon, and then he and the Department went out with a dragnet to try to find the criminal.

By the end of the week their mutual investigations seemed to point more and more directly to the combination of Charles and James at the Mission Press. There was no doubt that they were skilled workmen and perfectly capable of lithographing a duplicate ticket, but the difficulty was to establish the proofs of this particular crime. Nor had any trace whatever beep found of the mysterious person by the name of Ting Sang who had actually taken the money away from the bank. Scores of wheelbarrow coolies had been arrested and questioned, but none could give any account of the disappearance of the treasure. At last the missing link in the chain was discovered, and this is how it happened: Late one night Wang Foo was returning from Headquarters, and being worn out with the work of the day, he fell asleep on the seat of his jinrikisha and only awoke when the coolie deposited him at the door of "The Enchanted Basket" in the Ho Nan Road. "I told you to take me to "The Temple Basket," he said to the runner, that being the sign of the shop of his friend. "Miao Lan Tze, Miao Kan Tze!" Then it suddenly dawned on him that the words for "temple" and "enchanted" being almost identical in sound, his runner had quite naturally mistaken the one for the other. Recognizing the shop as one where lottery-tickets were offered for sale, he decided to enter and interview the proprietor. The doorkeeper ushered him to a seat and in a moment the form of Cripple Ching appeared.

There was an unmistakable something in his face that immediately aroused the detective's suspicions and he decided to take the chance of an evil conscience and boldly accuse him of the theft. After the formalities of the tea and pipes he turned suddenly upon him and seizing his arms with both hands, he lifted him bodily to his feet, and looking him through and through with his piercing eyes, said: "Cripple Ching! Lead me instantly to the place where you concealed the money!"

"What money?" asked the astonished proprietor of The Enchanted Basket, struggling to free himself from the iron grasp.

"What money? What money?" repeated Wang Foo, feeling the power of his threat beginning to work, "why the ten thousand dollars that you cashed on ticket No. 36001 of the Dutch Lottery. Give it to me instantly or we will summon the police and tear up every board in your floor."

"I didn't forge the ticket! I didn't forge the ticket!" cried the terrified cripple. "It was genuine and I bought it and paid for it."

"Never mind that; we will prove all that later—show me the money or in come the police, and straight to jail you go!"

He led the way into the inner room, lifted up the torn piece of matting, uncovered the "Well of Heavenly Blessings" and there lay the notes and the gold and the silver just as he and Twin Stars had hidden them! The latter individual entered the room just at this moment, climbing down the ladder from the loft above. Wang Foo ventured one more chance. "Ting Sang!" he cried, and the luckless Twin Stars, looking into the barrel of the detective's revolver and seeing that escape was impossible, surrendered himself as his prisoner.

"IT LOOKS VERY MUCH as if The Enchanted Basket was like a magician's hat," remarked Inspector McArthur to Wang Foo, as they compared their final notes in the office, "it contains all the goods we are looking for, and more besides. We've got both the villains and the money, and now all we want is the man who forged the ticket: perhaps he's hiding down somewhere in the basket, too. You can guarantee Ting Sang belongee all same Twin Stars?" he asked of the native officers whom he had summoned into the room.

"My can seclure all ploper," was the answer; "dat bank compladore hab come dis side two thlee timee talkee he."

"Then," he added, turning once more to Wang Foo, "let us summon all our friends and proceed to Mr. Wagenpool's at once."

When all the party were assembled in the manager's office, including Dr. Donaldson, as well as Dr. Williams and the Spencers, our Man of Mystery arose, and tightly grasping a piece of yellow paper in his hand, thus addressed them: "Ladies and gentlemen, it has been a pleasure and a privilege to me to work in connection with Inspector McArthur and his splendid Department in unraveling this most interesting case; and I now present to you my report, which takes the form of three rather startling surprises, viz.: First, and perhaps most important to you who were losers, we have recovered every dollar of the ten thousand! Second, our suspected villains are entirely innocent! Cripple Ching bought his ticket honestly from the regular agency and Ting Sang cashed it honestly for him! Third, we have not found any trace of the forger—for the simple reason that there has not been any forgery—and Charles and James must be freed from all suspicion at the Mission Press! This telegram from Batavia will give you the needed information as well as the closing surprise."

He unfolded it and read as follows:

"To Herr Wagenpool, Manager.
"Dutch Asiatic Bank, Shanghai.
"Just discovered that by curious accident the numbering machine printed duplicate of ticket No. thirty-six-thousand-and-one. If too late to call them in, the Royal Dutch Lottery will have, in honor, to pay them both.

Kark Kringleson.
Government Agent."

It of course goes without saying that Dr. Williams did not allow any delay in the matter of interesting Miss Spencer in the larger "Lottery in Life"—as an actual fact, the exchange of the tickets, if such we may call the proposal and acceptance, took place on the steps of the bank and as Wang Foo smilingly remarked "they both drew prizes!"

And when, a few days after the wedding, the bride wished to select a name for their little bungalow on the Peak, to whom should she more naturally turn than to our famous detective, and what could he—or you or I or anyone—say, but to tell her to christen it "The Enchanted Basket."

THE TILE OF HEAVENLY BLUE

WANG FOO, THE MAN OF MYSTERY, arose from his evening meal and
took the fan and the steaming facecloth which the Venerable Grand
One had ready in waiting at his side. Thus cooling himself according to the custom and tradition of his ancestors, he said to the aged
matron, "I ascend this evening to the upper hall and will spend the
hours in quiet thought and meditation. Speak to Old Chang when
he returns and tell him not to open the gates to any visitors. He is
merely to receive the honorable cards and ask the gracious guests
to call again when the skies are brightening"—this being the old
Celestial term for "tomorrow." He walked for a few moments up
and down the stone-paved courtyard and then mounted the little
staircase to the floor above. He passed through his study, which
bore the significant name of "The Glade of Quiet Reflection," and,
unlocking a central door concealed by a silken curtain, entered a
dark apartment which adjoined it.

"The Grotto of Mystic Changes"—for that was the meaning of
the great golden symbols on the central roofbeam—was like the
secret chamber of the dreaded Bluebeard, a place which the foot
of the ordinary mortal never entered. Besides the great detective
himself none but the Venerable Grand One ever cross its threshold, and then only when it needed a periodic sweeping and clean-
ing, at which times her lips were regularly sworn to a silence more
stony than the Buddhist idols. It was none other than the sanctum
sanctorum where modern science, with all its various appliances
assisted the master in the solution of mysteries and the detection

"WE MAY HAVE TO SACRIFICE
YOU ON THE ALTAR OF SCIENCE."

of many a secret crime of the far east. As he lighted the little lamp that swung from the ceiling, its rays revealed a number of cabinets and shelves filled with rows of retorts, bottles, batteries, tubes and other apparatus of the chemist and the electrician, and, in the corner, a complete outfit for the development of photographic plates and films.

Wang Foo stepped to the table in the center of the room and, taking from it a wooden frame holding four glass test tubes, he held them up to the light and examined them critically one by one. "Ah!" he exclaimed with a tone of satisfaction, "we are getting nearer! we are certainly getting nearer—another forty-eight hours and all will be ready for the final test. Tube No. 1 shows the setting of the crust of wax already, but the solution is not dense enough; we must wait until we reach heaven's deepest blue and then—then. My poor little friend," turning to a little cage in the corner where a white rabbit was munching contentedly a leaf of cabbage, "we may have to sacrifice you on the altar of science." He carefully replaced the four tubes in their holders, and, extinguishing the lamp, passed back quietly into the study, where a number of important papers were waiting for examination.

"WELL, I'VE RATHER SAD NEWS for you, my dear," said Captain McAlpin of the Australian Mail to Mrs. Whitmarsh, as she greeted him at her bungalow on the Peak after his brisk walk from the tramway station. (He always took the privilege of his years and of his old acquaintance with the family in Melbourne to address the most charming young widow in Hong Kong in this way.)

"Why, Captain, what can possibly have happened?"

"My poor little 'Chop Sticks' is gone!"

"'What! Run away or stolen?"

"Worse—some miserable coolie has poisoned him."

"How very dreadful! Well, you must sit right down here by the tea table and tell me all about it."

The skipper laid his hat and cane on the bamboo lounge and, drawing a chair up to the tempting tea-tray with its toast and cookies said, "You know I called him 'Chop Sticks' because he was always such a lively little critter. That's the meaning of the word in Chinese, 'Lively children,' and he was just the liveliest little kid—dog though he was and not human—that I ever had as a passenger aboard my ship. Well, let me see. It was last Monday night that—"

"Why, that's the very day that you brought him up here in the afternoon," interrupted his hostess.

"Sure enough, the very day. Well, as I was a-saying, he began to act queer that very evening; wouldn't take his chow and all that; just lay in his little basket a-kind o' gasping like and breathing hard, and when I tried to get him to sit up he just ups in a convulsion and that was the end of him."

"Just like my poor little Trixy a month ago. How strange!"

"I got Doc Patterson to just run in and take a look at him, and he says, 'Cap, its poison and no mistake.'"

"Why, who do you suppose could here done it? He wasn't cross to the natives, was he?"

"Cross? Why, never, they were just as fond of him as I was. My room-boy actually cried like a child when he saw he was dead. No, no, it wasn't anybody on board the ship. I'm sure of that. Doc thinks he just must have picked up something in the street as he was a-running along."

"But how about my Trixy? He never went out unless I carried him in my chair, and he went just that way. And the Chinese just loved him, too, although some of the old residents told me when I first came here that they were actually so-clannish that sometimes a Cantonese house-boy wouldn't feed a Pekinese dog! Could you believe it?"

Just at this moment the aforesaid house-boy appeared with the chit-book and a message for Mrs. Whitmarsh. "Excuse me just a minute, Captain, while I glance at this." The visitor bowed and turned to the boy. "Yung Lung my watchee talkee you, how fashion you thinkee your missussee little doggie go makee die, er?"

"My no savee," was the always-ready and immediate answer.

"I know you don't 'savee,' but how fashion Chineeman he talkee? Cook, coolie, outside man, how fashion thinkee? Eh?"

The boy hesitated for a moment and then replied, taking good care to screen himself from every particle of suspicion: "Cook talkee

him chow-chow no ploper, suppose him dlinkee Melican man medi-
cine-water havee sick go makee die—my no savee. Chair-coolie
talkee b'longe joss pidgin—my no savee."

"Aha!" remarked the captain, relapsing for a moment into his
correct mother tongue; "Then there's a religious element in it, is
there? Some miserable old superstition, I'll be bound. I was afraid
of that, you know. Well—how fashion that joss pidgin?"

The boy looked carefully over toward his mistress to see that
she was out of hearing and then said in a low tone to his ques-
tioner: "Coolie talkee Hong Kong joss no likee Australee dog come
dis side. Plentee piece go makee die—joss all same chokee he?"

"Why, what a singular coincidence," exclaimed Mrs. Whitmarsh
as she laid down the letter and signed the chit-book. "Mrs. Wilkins
says that her two little Japanese poodles—you know she brought
them here to show, me yesterday—are dreadfully ill, and her children are just broken-hearted for fear they are going to die. I wonder if our good friend Dr. Patterson would mind just dropping in
and taking a look at them on his rounds—"

"Certainly. I'll stop there myself on my way down the hill and
send him up; perhaps he'll catch them in time," answered the skipper, as he bade his hostess good-bye and started off in the direction of the doctor's office—outwardly anxious to save the Wilkins'
doggies and inwardly "cussing the luck" that cut so short his delightful afternoon with the widow.

"Mrs. Wilkins has just been telling me about the loss of their two
dear little Japanese dogs," said Mrs. De Peyster as she joined the
group at Lady Beecham's side in Government Gardens; "isn't it just,
awful? Why, she says she thinks there is a regular plot on the part
of the Chinese to drive all foreign dogs out of the colony, and so
they're beginning to poison them on the sly, every chance they get.
(She did not notice that a dignified native gentleman standing near
by caught her remark and turned his footsteps in her direction.)
Mrs. Whitmarsh lost her Trixy a few days ago and I've just heard
from my husband that Capt. McAlpin told them at the Club Tiffin
that his little pet dog had been poisoned in the same mysterious

way. (The native gentleman seemed more and more interested, and, casually taking a little memorandum book out of his sleeve, jotted down a few rapid notes.) I wonder if Sir Evington has heard of it and what he thinks of it."

"My husband was speaking of it at breakfast this very morning." replied the wife of the governor, "and he said that while he had known of such things happening among the natives in India and Burmah, he couldn't really conceive of their happening in a civilized community like Hong Kong—but here he comes himself; let us ask him.

"We were just speaking, dear, of the poisoning of those little pet dogs, and Mrs. De Peyster seems to think that it's a general plot of the natives to drive them all out of the colony—"

"Nonsense! Nonsense!" interrupted the governor, "it's just one of those foolish scares that nervous citizens get into when two or three cases of anything whatever happen in the colony. It is true that several of us have lost valuable dogs within the last few days— and all of them apparently from poisoning—but this may be just an accidental coincidence, or it is possible that some servant or employee may have a grudge against their owners and have gratified it in this unfortunate way. I don't think we shall really hear anything more of it."

These reassuring remarks on the part of his excellency, however; did not prevent the excitable and talkative Mrs. De Peyster— who was always only too ready to believe anything bad on the part of the natives—from adding that she felt convinced that there was some religious superstition behind it, and that unless they took prompt measures to suppress it some ridiculous "joss pidgin" would end in the slaughter of all their pets, even to parrots and canaries. This opinion, certainly received some additional weight from a line or two in the next day's issue of the *Morning Press*:

"MYSTERIOUS DEATH OF VALUABLE DOGS
"The sudden death, apparently from poison, of a number of pet dogs in the colony has led to an unfortunate rumor that this is an act of revenge on the

part of some superstitious and vindictive natives, for some accidental affront to a sacred animal in a local shrine. We do not concur in this belief ourselves and we look to our respected Chinese fellow citizens to join with us in immediately correcting this report before it grows to a possibly dangerous proportion.

In the Quiet Glade of Reflection Wang Foo leaned over his table and carefully perused the English newspaper and its Chinese translation in the evening edition. He also looked over the notes which he had jotted down in Government Gardens. He touched the silver bell and the Venerable Grand One mounted the little stairs. "Lao Tai Tai, chow kan mung tik tao Tien Ju Wang Miao chuk, ching Lao Fu Tze king bang chik lee lai!" (Venerable Grand One, call the gatekeeper and tell him to go to the temple of the Queen of Heaven and ask the Venerable Father to come here this evening!)

"Hien Sang sho ting hao, Chu Jin tze hwa ee jing tso liao!" was the immediate response. (The elder born speaketh well; the master's words have already been obeyed!) In less than an hour the abbot's sedan-chair was deposited at 5-5-5 in the Red Cloud Alley, and, after the ceremonial tea and pipes, the two friends repaired for quiet conference to the room above.

Wang Foo began: "We are in some danger, Venerable Father, of more racial clashing in the colony, which we must take immediate steps to head off. You have heard of the poisoning of the dogs? If not, kindly cast an honorable glance at this," handing him a copy of the Chinese paper. The abbot adjusted his large round horn goggles and carefully perused the article. "Hung Miao. Hung Miao," he repeated to himself several times—("Local Shrine, Local Shrine"). "Ah! that can refer only to the sacred dog of the Llamas by the Macao wharf, concerning which the coolies are always so jealous. I wonder now if some thoughtless foreigner has stirred up their anger by insulting the idol; if so, we must make it good at once and quiet their feelings or the government will surely shut down on us, and then"—lowering his voice to a whisper—"away goes a large part of my temple income, for the llama dog always pays handsome tribute to the Queen of Heaven!"

"I do not really believe that anything of the kind has taken place at all," replied the detective, "but at the same time I am most anxious, as you, Venerable Father, so well know, to stop any such rumor at once and to do all I can to preserve the good feeling between the races that has made Hong Kong famous all over the east. We both remember that case several years ago, do we not, when we almost came to a riot down on the wharves, because a party of vulgar tourists threw their cigar stumps right at the head of this same sacred dog of the llamas? Well, we don't want that repeated."

"What do you advise?"

"My plan, which has been most carefully thought out, and which I now humbly submit for your approval is that we should both make a careful investigation of this thing, but that we should do it separately. I want you to pay a visit to the dog shrine—dropping in without notice and quite informally—ask the old priest how business generally is going, etc., etc., and note carefully his replies. Watch him closely to see if he is attempting to conceal anything, although I do not think he will do so, and if there is anything in this story of the foreign insult, either he or one of his servants will be sure to leak it out."

"And if it should happen to be true, what then?"

"Why, then you will naturally use every argument in your power to have it quieted down and ignored. As a loyal citizen of the colony you will plead for its peace and security; as a disciple of the sages you will quote the sublime words of harmony and good will; and lastly, you can phrase the financial issue, if you wish, by showing him how your mutual income would fall off should the government have to suspend all worship at the shrine."

"Fu tze yen tsung, yiu loong tze yiu seng!" exclaimed the abbot ("Wise are the words of the philosopher, and deeper than the dragon's pool").

"And I, on my part, will carefully go into all the details of the case, visiting the various foreign homes and interviewing the people, and we shall be ready to confer together again in about a week's time. Are we perfectly agreed?"

"'Their words and thoughts did blend as the twin sources of the sacred river!'—is it not so written in the analects?"

"Venerable Father, it is!"

And so the interview, ended, and old Chang swung back the outer gate to let the coolies carry the temple sedan to the roadway.

IT WAS WELL PAST THE USUAL HOUR of bedtime in Hong Kong when a somewhat dilapidated sampan sculled out into the harbor and headed for the opposite shore. Two dark figures crept out from under the mat-shed and stepped off onto the beach. Silently they wended their way among the crowded huts until they came to a crooked alley that led them at length to a small brick house almost hidden by the overhanging cliff. Over the door was an old Chinese sign, much the worse for wear, which announced that "Tung tik sui chi fak kwei kak," or, in our Anglo-Saxon tongue, that "Articles of brass and iron are here made for our honorable customers." After several knockings at the entrance it was finally opened and the two passed inside.

The apartment into which they entered was dim and dingy and bore all the usual signs of the native worker in metals. There was the bench with the tools and beyond it an anvil and a furnace and some clay retorts, and lying around on the rough board shelves were unfinished pipes and bowls and pincers and tongs such as are used in the humble Celestial home:

"You have brought the tiles?" inquired "Silver Star" (or "Ying Sing") of his visitors, "and they are three in all."

"Behold them!" they cried, as they unwrapped a couple of rough-looking packages from beneath their coats.

"And they are the genuine heavenly blue from the crown of the goddess?"

"There are no other like them."

"True! True!" cried Ying Sing, "I know them at once; they are priceless. The peach-blow glaze of the Mings is as nothing to this deep blue of the Tangs. I must copy it for my brass enamel. It will take three days and then you shall carry them back and replace them just where they were and the secret shall be mine. Here are your dollars and now begone! Three nights hence you return at the self-same hour!"

At the appointed night and hour Ying Sing's hired thieves awaited their master's bidding. They received back again the three heavenly tiles, the secret of whose wondrous color he had now discovered, and crossing back to the colony, they climbed over the back wall of the temple of the Queen of Heaven and replaced them in the large blue canopy over the head of the goddess, which her devotees called her crown. Yes! They certainly replaced them there, in spite of the fact that the very next day Ying Sing climbed up the ladder hanging over the side of the P. & O. liner in the harbor, with the those very same tiles concealed in a leather valise! But strange things happen in China.

Having eluded the customs officer, who was leaning over the rail smoking a cigar with the pilot, he slid quietly along the deck until he came to room 63, where he stopped and gently knocked. "Come in!" said a rather gruff voice. "Ah! It's you, is it? And have you brought the goods with you, as we say in the U.S.A.?"

"My hab got, all ploper."

"Well, trot them out, then," said Archibald Wilkins (the senior member of the firm of Wilkins Brothers, the most famous art dealers of Boston), "and if they're the genuine thing, you're the richest man that wears a cue on any sum-pan in this harbor."

Ying Sing opened the valise and unwrapped the cotton tags that concealed the treasures. Mr. Wilkins look the tiles and, holding them up to a powerful electric bulb (which he had substituted for the dim lamp of the cabin), examined them long and carefully with a powerful pocket lens. When thoroughly convinced that they were genuine "Tangs," he turned and asked, "Where did you get them? You are quite sure that they are your own family's heirlooms and that they have not been stolen from someone else?" Ying Sing was indignant, to say the least, and putting on a look of injured innocence that would have done justice to a Raphael cherub, answered, "My no b'longee tiefee, my talkee tlue, my blandfader he hab all same glandfader pay he—many hundled year hab got he home-side. S'pose you b'lleve, all light my can sellee oder man." The American apologized for his suspicion, and after the usual haggling Ying Sing slid over the side of the ship with a thousand in Mexican bank notes hidden away in his girdle, while the priceless tiles of heavenly blue reposed under lock and key in an inner compartment of stateroom 63.

It was, of course, not to be supposed that the article in the daily paper had escaped the eagle eye of Inspector Gubbins of the police, and he was naturally as anxious as any one to prevent an international row in the colony. He had called at once on the editor and had traced the rumor concerning the insult at the shrine to a native reporter. This individual, after being carefully questioned, admitted that he had no actual evidence to go on, but had gathered the story from the suggestions of a personal friend, who was none other than the afore-mentioned Yung Lung, the blue-gowned house boy at Mrs. Whitmarsh's bungalow.

"Now, what possible reason could the faithful Yung Lung have had for starting a tale of this kind?" was the question which the inspector put to Wang Foo when they met by appointment at headquarters to talk the case over together.

"What reason except his personal loyalty to his mistress—and his devotion to her dear little Trixy."

"How many European dogs have actually been killed, Mr. Wang?"

"Eight in all, sir," was the answer. "Well, now that we think of it, that is not such a very large number—"

"No, to be sure, it is not; but the trouble is that they all happen to be valuable animals and their owners are prominent residents."

"I wonder if we could get an accurate list of them anywhere?"

"I have made very careful inquiries and I have them right here in my notebook" (drawing it out from his sleeve). "There is, first, Mrs. Whitmarsh's Trixy and her friend Capt. McAlpin's Chopsticks, and Fuji and Yama, the Japanese dogs of the Wilkins' girls, that is four; then the two pointers belonging to Col. Yardley at the barracks, that is six, and lastly—and most important of all—the two Scotch collies which arrived for Lady Beecham by the *Glanmorgan*, that makes the eight, does it not?"

"Exactly so; and it was poison in every case, was it?"

"So every one thought at first, for people naturally jump at conclusions, but Veterinary Tompkins says now that the pointers really died of distemper, and the two little collies just couldn't stand the heat. That reduces the list, you see, to exactly four."

"And there is no doubt about the poison?"

"None whatever—the symptoms in each case were identical."

"Well," continued the inspector, after a moment's thought, "then there are just three questions for us to solve: First, what was the poison? Second, who administered it? And. third, what was his object? Our very next move, of course, is to get Tompkins to make an analysis."

"Sorry, but it is too late."

"Too late?"

"Yes, unfortunately, Trixy was sold by the houseboy to a beggar for his hide; Chop-sticks was tossed into the harbor as food for the fishes, and the Japanese poodles were cremated!"

"Cremated! Why, what in the world induced them to do that?"

"Well, you see, Mrs. Wilkins had told them that that was the custom in their native land and the children had both insisted that their pets must have a proper Japanese funeral."

"Did you ever—"

"There is one important factor that I think you have overlooked," interrupted Wang Foo.

"And pray, what is that?"

"Why, the place where it occurred. I have discovered that Capt. McAlpin always took Chop-sticks with him when he went to call on Mrs. Whitmarsh; that the Wilkins' girls had taken the poodles there to play the very day the doggies died, and Trixy, of course, was in the bungalow all the time."

"Then there is only one conclusion to all that, viz.: The Whitmarsh servants did it, and that slick Yung Lung of hers knows all about it!"

"It certainly looks that way."

"I think we had better arrest the whole gang in the morning—cook, boy, coolie, amah and all—and get the truth out of them by a proper native grilling; what do you say?"

"Better wait a few days longer; something new may turn up," was the carefully worded answer of Wang Foo.

AND SOMETHING CERTAINLY DID TURN UP a few days later when the captain paid another visit to the ever-attractive bungalow, and this time had the pleasure of introducing our famous detective to the widow. At his especial request she showed him over the little drawing room where the children had played with the poodles, and it was there that he first noticed her cabinet of curios and began to take a rather unusual interest in a beautiful blue tile which she especially prized.

"A genuine Tang! Mr. Wang," she exclaimed with delight, as she opened the glass door and brought it out. "You know, of course, that they are very rare and—" (she whispered the last words so that the ever-curious houseboy behind the screen should not hear)—"almost priceless. The only others in Hong Kong are in the Government Museum."

"And," Wang Foo added to himself, "in the canopy over the Queen of Heaven."

"It is an awful shame that it got chipped this way," pointing to a jagged edge, "but, I accidentally dropped it on the stone hearth the other day while showing it to the Wilkins girls—why! there's their mother now, just outside our gate; you must excuse me just a moment while I run out and pay my chin-chin to her" (Chinese for "How do you do?").

The genial captain insisted on accompanying her out to the sedan-chair—he would have been delighted to accompany her to the ends of the earth—and the thoughtless and tactless Mrs. Wilkins, who by general consent was the greatest matchmaker in the colony, had no more sense than to say: "Why! Capt. McAlpin. I declare! What a surprise to find you here! How long your ship is staying in port this time, isn't it? And isn't it strange that you are so fond of walking up this awfully steep road?" and then, with a most significant smite at them both together, she added. "I suppose I am still a little premature in tendering my congratulations, am I not?"

Left for a few moments alone in the room, Wang Foo carefully searched the floor with his flashlight and to his great joy finally discovered, under the cabinet, a few fragments of blue enamel that looked like little crumbs of colored candy. He eagerly gathered them up, placed them in a little purse in his girdle, and that night in the Grotto of Mystic Changes he began the secret chemical analysis with which our story begins.

"I have solved the mystery at last!" said Wang Foo to the Venerable Abbot, as they held their final meeting in the Glade of Quiet Reflection. "My little rabbit has died from the very same poison that killed the foreigners' pets."

"And the poison is—?"

"Just what I suspected: the Lan Ling Yu (Pearl of the Blue Dragon), the fatal berry described in the 'Deadly Secrets of the Tangs.' See! Read here!"—opening an ancient volume and pointing out a line to his astonished visitor—"this deadliest of poisons when mixed with the wax of the yellow Canton bee produces the glaze of heavenly blue."

"And I have solved the mystery, too," exclaimed the abbot, "none other than the thief who stole the tiles from the Goddess' canopy and then replaced them."

"No! Not the same, he replaced them with the counterfeits of poisoned wax. The genuine ones he sold to the foreign dealer."

"Then it was one of wax that the lady bought?"

"Exactly so, and the dogs playing in the drawing room and searching for bits of the children's candy, swallowed the fragments and so they died."

"Then Silver Star, the metal worker, is the villain?"

"He certainly is the guilty party. And now we have an illustration of the Master's words. 'The people of the west also have their sages,' for, thanks to western science, at which so many of our scholars sneer, we have saved our colony from trouble."

"Yes, and thanks to all the Buddhas, we have saved the income of our temple, for now the stream of cash will flow in steadily from the shrine of the Llama Dog."

WHEN THE AUSTRALIAN MAIL STEAMER, after a month or more in dry dock, finally steamed out for the south, some of the people were rather surprised to see the first officer in charge on the bridge and the well-known skipper a passenger in the cabin. But the bunting that decorated the ship from stem to stern—to say nothing of the fact that a Mrs. McAlpin's name was on the list of those sailing— told the story of a very happy wedding in Hong Kong Cathedral and the delightful prospect of a honeymoon in the southern seas. Among the many friends who came out from the wharf to say "Bon voyage" was Wang Foo, the solver of mysteries, arrayed in all his oriental glory. As he greeted them he placed in the hands of his old friend the captain a parasol of the daintiest silk and told him to open it and hold it over his bride, explaining as he did so that the ivory carving on the handle meant "The Cerulean Canopy of Our Goddess."

"Why! How perfectly lovely," she cried as she noticed its deep rich color. "I will christen it at once as my 'Tile of Heavenly Blue.'"

THE BUBBLING WELL

"Impossible! Quite impossible, I assure you!" said Sir Evington Beecham, Governor of Hong Kong, to Capt. Burling of the India Mail, as they paused for a moment on their afternoon stroll back from the golf links, "the idea of an intentional wreckage is preposterous. Why, Webb and the boatswain are two of the very best men we have in the service, and they've been in it for years. And they both know, just as well as we do, that it means imprisonment for life. Do you think they would take a risk like that and actually turn pirates—for that is what it amounts to—for the mere salvage from a coasting schooner? Never! I don't believe a word of it."

"Well, I can hardly credit it myself, but Barlow & Co., the owners, declare they have a perfectly clear case against them and swear they will prove it in the colonial court."

"Let them prove it, then!" was the emphatic answer of the governor, as he drove his walking-stick deep into the sand to enforce his opinion.

The subject of this conversation was an occurrence that had stirred the whole foreign community, and incidentally taken up a good deal of space in the columns of the local papers. It was briefly this: The English coasting schooner *Prince Edward* had sailed out of the harbor at dusk and had set her course for Formosa. Her cargo happened to be an unusually valuable one, consisting of several thousand pounds' worth of the choicest ginseng, the most costly of native drugs, which the Chinese shippers (for some unknown prejudice) had been unwilling to consign to the regular steamer.

"THE POLICE HAVE ARRESTED THE BRIDEGROOM!"

Every precaution had been taken to secure and protect it, and it was whispered that her captain and crew were heavily armed. All had gone well until midnight when she was approaching Pak Lao Ting (White Tiger Point), and then suddenly the light in the tower on the point began to flicker and grow dim—and finally, to the consternation of her skipper, sputtered and went entirely out!

A STRONG EBB TIDE was running at the time, and before she could be brought about, in the sharp turn that they have to make at the red buoy, she was swung close in to the headland and was thrown broadside on the beach. The native crew of eight men became panic-stricken at once, seizing the first things at hand—which happened to be the oars of the schooner's boat—jumped into the surf and shrieked to their gods to save them. The—four English sailors tried to cut the boat loose, but finding the oars gone, threw off their coats and started for the shore, which, fortunately, they all succeeded in reaching.

There being no apparent way of scaling the cliff, they decided that their only hope was in following the beach to the nearest village where they could secure help. Fortunately they found two of the native crew—the six others having fled—and holding them as guides and interpreters, they walked all night and half the following day, when they reached a cluster of fishing huts and there found food and shelter. When the government tug that was sent out from the port after their arrival there reached the scene of the wreck a few days later, the schooner was found intact, though badly battered, but every trace of her precious cargo had disappeared!

"Looted by Cantonese pirates," was what the papers said, and no one doubted it was correct—except Barlow & Co. and some government agents.

The revenue officers who accompanied the lighthouse inspector went at once up the steep path to the tower, and there they found Webb, the keeper, and his assistant (known as "The Boatswain") in a state of great trepidation.

"It wasn't our fault, gentlemen," they cried; "it wasn't our fault. Something went wrong with the oil and we've been these five days trying to light her up again. We surely have."

"And what's the meaning of all this?" inquired the Inspector, pointing to several large bundles of ginseng behind the door.

"That's what the boatswain and I saved from the wreck in the daytime, before the pirates got at her, sir," was his answer.

"And why are you trying to hide it?"

"We're not trying to hide it, sir; me and my mate just stowed it there for safekeeping."

"A likely tale, that! Well, back with you both to Hong Kong aboard the tug—these two new men will take charge of the light and you'll explain all this to the court."

Now, the charge of tampering in any way with a government lighthouse is, as every one knows, a very serious one to bring against an Englishman, but when to this is added the accusation that a light has actually been extinguished to cause a wreck, it becomes a capital offense. Yet Messrs. Barlow & Co., the officers of the schooner, brought this charge against Webb and the boatswain, and claimed that they had a budget of evidence to prove it. The case was simply this: They said that the two foreign and the two native keepers were in league with confederates in the colony who knew of the sailing of the *Prince Edward* with her valuable cargo, and who arranged with them to extinguish the light at the critical moment and thus throw the schooner on the beach. The ginseng was to be taken from the wreck on the following day and temporarily stored in the lighthouse until a junk which was hiding behind the headland could get it on board and then sail away to a pre-arranged spot. Here it was to be landed and carried away to an inland town to be sold, and a rich profit would accrue to all concerned.

There was great noise and bustle at the corner of the White Pearl Road and the Red Cloud Alley, where the largest Chinese drug stores were located. "Yiu mue leh lao Yiu mue leh lao?" ("What is the excitement?"), cried the passers-by as they stooped to look at the red festoons and hangings and lanterns and to listen to the firecrackers. "Pak yu tai pan hsiao jie pei ting!" ("The daughter of the proprietor of the White Pearl drug store is being betrothed!") was the answer of the crowd of chair coolies, who, having brought their fares to the doorway, were now regaling themselves with the free tea and tobacco which the happy host was always expected to furnish. Within the famous establishment of the White Pearl all thought of business had been given up for several days, in order to make suitable preparation for the auspicious event. The decorations were most elaborate and the music was at one moment weird and mournful enough to make one weep, and the next lively and thrilling enough to set one's feet a-tingling. Occasionally, of course, it would vie with the gongs and the firecrackers as to the greatest amount of ear-splitting noise, and it goes without saying that every one was talking at the top of his voice, as if to fill in any accidental notes of silence that might have been left by the music. As a matter of fact, from a dignified European standpoint, it was simply pandemonium let loose—but "pandemonium let loose" is, after all, only our crude and labored synonym for a real Chinese good time.

THEY CERTAINLY WERE HAVING IT. The entire store was transformed into a reception room and banquet hall and the guests were enjoying the "tien ti eng shing" (or "gracious, gracious gifts of heaven and earth") in both solids and liquids to their hearts' content. In the inner apartments the genial host and his good wife were receiving the congratulations of their many friends. Having spent many years in Singapore, where strict native customs are greatly modified by the European surroundings, the ladies and gentlemen of the party mingled much more freely together than they ordinarily would have done under the social code of Asiatic seclusion. Even the sweet and smiling "Chin Chee" (Azure Butterfly) appeared openly upon the scene and announced to Mrs. Hopkinson, who with a bevy of lady friends from the colony had been especially invited, that she didn't see any reason why the one person of all in whose honor the party was given should be hidden way in the background.

"No, indeed," replied the consul's wife, "you are the center of attraction now just as much as you will be at your wedding, and we should have been awfully disappointed if we hadn't seen you, wouldn't we, ladies?"

"We certainly would," was the answer that came back in chorus.

"And where is the fortunate young man? Aren't we to see him, too?"

"Ah! I am afraid not this time at least. That would really never do just here and now. We are several years ahead of the times, as you say, already, but to actually allow the prospective bridegroom to appear at his own betrothal party would be to take a fifty years' jump into the future. No, poor, dear boy, he is having to content himself with a little feast of his own at his room's, with a few college chums, you know."

"Yes, and all the time bemoaning his hard luck and the stupid old native conservatism that keeps you apart, I suppose."

"Well, we shall not really be separated so very long, for the wedding is only three months hence—which is awfully short for China—and, after all. we don't mind being a little Chinesey now, just to please our families and our friends, because, you see," and here Chin Chee blushed and smiled, "this is a truly-truly love match, and that makes all the difference in the world!"

Yes! It certainly did. And just how it came to be one of the "truly-truly" kind and not one of the old-fashioned, commercial-contracts was owing largely to Miss Julia DuBray, who had been Chin Chee's devoted teacher and guide and counselor and friend during her recent years at that wonderful school on the Hill, known as "The Victoria College for Chinese Young Ladies." Now if any one had called Miss Julia a matchmaker she would have instantly resented it, but at the same time she would have been obliged to acknowledge that she had done everything in her power to rescue her darling Chin Chee from the man the family had planned for her.

"Just to think of their throwing away a beautiful and accomplished girl like that on a miserable old drug-clerk who can't even speak a word of English, and who hasn't anything in the world but his money," she was wont to say, "when there's that splendid young fellow Yung Wing, just back in the colony from Harvard and simply waiting for a chance to make her the finest husband in the world!"

And so Miss Julia went to work to bring about the desired result. She worked long and patiently and never gave up her hope. She planned and devised various interviews with Chin Chee's father and mother and never missed an opportunity to sing her favorite pupil's praises to Yung Wing. And in the end she won out, as most persevering creatures generally do; and when she had finally convinced the parents that it was their solemn duty to the daughter to give her at least some little choice in the matter of her husband she felt she had dealt a serious blow at the whole commercial matrimonial system, The rest was easy; and after she had placed Chin Chee next to herself in the Cathedral pew on Sunday morning and arranged to have Mr. Yung Wing sit just across the aisle and accidentally meet them as they were passing out, why, all that remained was for her to pray the good Lord that, Chinese or no Chinese, it might he a case of "love at first sight"—and it was!

Now there may have been some happier guest at the betrothal feast than Miss Julia, but, if so, no one was able to discover her. There is only one word that can adequately describe her appearance and feelings, and that is "radiant"—yes, she was literally radiant. She was the one who had really brought it all about, and in the midst of all her magnificent triumph over ancient custom and tradition she plaited for herself a crown of personal satisfaction that she had brought these two young lives together.

"You dear, darling child!" she cried, as she literally raised the slender form of Chin Chee from the floor and clasped her in her arms, "I know I am kissing the happiest girl in all—" but whether she meant "Hong Kong" or "the whole world" nobody ever knew, for with a piercing shriek two of the woman servants burst into the room and exclaimed: "Sing boo tao liao sing lang! Sing boo tao liao sing lang!" ("The police have arrested the bridegroom! The police have arrested the bridegroom!") while the sweet little "azure butterfly" gently folded its wings and fainted away in its teacher's arms!

The report was only too true. Acting on the complaint of Messrs. Barlow & Co., the police had carefully watched the movements of Yung Wing and his companions in the shipping office, and had arrested all three of them at a little suspicious wine party, where they seemed to be spending more money than their salaries naturally allow.

"IT CERTAINLY BEGINS TO LOOK pretty dark for Webb and his mate," remarked Inspector Higgins to Deputy Brownlow, as they returned to headquarters after an hour or two spent in the crown advocate's office.

"It certainly does that," was the brief and ready answer.

"You see, it's clearly shown that Mr. Yung Wing and his friends visited the lighthouse a week before the wreck, and they probably made their bargain with the keepers then—"

"Yes; but why—if they wanted to be secret about it—why in the world did they allow them to write their names in the visitors' book? You saw them there in the book yourself, didn't you?"

"Well, that may have been just to avoid all suspicion. Sort-a keeping things going regular, don't you know."

"His honor didn't seem to put much faith in that story of theirs about the saving of those bundles from the pirates, did he?"

"No," replied the chief, "nor, as our old judge in Calcutta used to say, could you 'lubricate' his mind with that yarn about the oil going bad. Why, every barrel of that oil is drawn out of our own storage tank at the navy dock here, and inspected and sealed before it's put on the tender. It never is allowed to vary a particle from year to year—it's always the same. Now, if it had gone bad at any other time, or if it had burned low and flickered or gone out on any other night, when some other ship was a-passing, why there might be something to the story; but when it goes bad on that particular night, and just at the critical point when the *Prince Edward* is passing the buoy, why, it's pretty hard to make me or any other man believe it's all accidental."

"Well, how about 'number one' and 'number two,' the native assistant keepers; can they get anything out of them?"

"Not a word, nor anything out of the old cook, either, who seems to have slept through the wreck and 'to have cared much more for his kettles and his pots than he did for the depths of the sea,' as the old song goes. If they are really 'all in the game,' as the Barlows claim, why they've been threatened and bribed into silence and they'd die by slow torture rather than leak out a word." Taking out of his pocket a memorandum book, the inspector sat down at his office table and began to look over a number of notes, and turning to Brownlow, continued, "as far as we have gotten at present, I number our points as follows:

"(1) We know that the *Prince Edward* sailed on that night with her valuable cargo of ginseng and that in the middle of the night she was wrecked on White Tiger Point. When the relief tug readied her a few days later, her cargo was entirely gone, with the exception of the few packages that we discovered in the lighthouse.

"(2) Her skipper swears that the light went out just at the critical turn by the buoy. Both the keepers acknowledge this to be true.

"(3) Yung Wing and his two friends, who handled the shipping of the ginseng for the native druggists, were at the lighthouse a week before the wreck, and afterward were noticed to be spending money very freely.

"(4) The mysterious junk which anchored by the headland has not been entered at any port with a cargo of ginseng.

"(5) The lighthouse inspector and his officers examined the lamp and tested the oil and found nothing whatever the matter with either.

"(6) A careful searching of Webb's private locker revealed a roll of bank notes equivalent to nearly three years' salary hidden away in a little keg.

"(7) A copy of the *Daily News* picked up on the floor of the lighthouse contained a marked article on 'the enormous increase in the value of ginseng and the combined efforts of Chinese and Europeans to smuggle it front Hong Kong into the native territory.'"

He laid the book and his glasses down, upon the table, and taking a Manila cheroot from the box on his desk, he slowly struck a match and lighted it, then placed himself in a comfortable position by tipping his office chair back against the wall and blowing the smoke slowly and thoughtfully in the direction of the ceiling he remarked to his deputy, "Brownlow, old man, it doesn't require very much legal brains to weave a pretty good case out of that, does it?"

"No, sir, it does not. That is provided you believe in—and are willing in convict on—pure circumstantial evidence. For, when all's said and done, chief, that's exactly what we've got and nothing else."

"Well, perhaps something else will turn up—"

"Perhaps it will. I hope it will, for unless the old agent with the wig (alluding to the crown advocate) has got much more up his black sleeve than he has shown us so far, I'm not a-goin' in my own mind to convict two honest English tars—as I still takes them to be—of goin' into a Chinese wrecking game like this, even for a lot of their old ginseng."

At No. 5-5-5 in the Red Cloud Alley, Wang Foo, the man of mystery, was taking his customary evening walk in the little courtyard, when there came a knock at the outer gate and Old Chang, the gatekeeper, laying down his teacup and his pipe, threw back the bars and handed his master a little red chit-book. "Tai Ju Hsio Tang Lai," he cried ("It is from the College for Girls"). "Yao hwai sing! Yao hwai sing!" ("They desire an answer! They desire an answer!") Wang Foo took the letter, which was addressed in a lady's hand, and, opening it, read as follows:

> My Dear Mr. Wang:
> It is of the utmost importance that you come to the
> college tomorrow morning. Please name a conve-
> nient hour by bearer. Sincerely yours,
>   Julia Du Bray.

He thought for a moment and then writing "Nine o'clock, sharp!" on the edge of the page, he initialed the book and handed it back to Old Chang. Ascending the steps to the glade of quiet reflection, he made his preparations to retire, but before going to sleep he reread in the English and Chinese papers the evidence in the shipwreck case, in order that he might be quite ready for what he felt would most surely be Miss Du Bray's pathetic appeal to him in the morning. And she certainly did appeal to him with all the eloquence and persuasion in her power. It would not be an exaggeration to say that she really implored him—for her sake, for their sakes, for everybody's sake—to secure the release of Yung Wing and save dear little Chin Chee from a broken heart.

"It's all a mistake! It's all a mistake!" she said, rising from her seat in the school parlor and walking nervously up and down the carpet: "it's part of a Chinese conspiracy to involve him and his friends in disgrace. My own native teachers have told me so and I know that they're right. Why, Mr. Wang, that young man is just as innocent of this as I am."

"How do you explain his mysterious visit to the lighthouse then, a week or so before the wreck?" asked the detective.

"Why, that is as simple and innocent as anything in the world. Mr. Yang Loo, who was Yung Wing's classmate at Harvard, came from the village of Pak Lao just two or three miles back of the Point. His old parents and grandparents live there still and he goes back to visit them regularly every few months. This was one of his regular trips to his home and he naturally took his friend with him, don't you see? And as the foreign lighthouse is one of the curiosities of the place, they, of course, went out to see it."

"But how did they get admitted, when, as a rule, natives, unless in government employ, are never allowed to go inside the gates?"

"Why, they both spoke English so fluently that the head keeper couldn't believe they were Chinese at all. And then, of course, they sent in their foreign cards in the usual courteous way and he just let them in and treated them as he would any party of European visitors."

"Ah! I see," smiled the detective, "the benefit as well as the penalty of a foreign education!" Then, rising to go, he added: "Just one question more, Miss Du Bray, if you please—and I shall appreciate a very candid answer from you. How do you explain the apparent lavish expenditure of money by the young man so soon after the wreck?"

"That had nothing whatever to do with it. You know, even better than I do, Mr. Wang, how freely money is spent at betrothal feasts—"

"Yes, to be sure—"

"And when you think that this entertainment combined really the extravagances of both China and America, and that he and his friends celebrated in both native and foreign style for about a week, you can readily see that it cost a good round sum."

"It undoubtedly did, and where do you really think he got the money?"

"Well, wherever he got it, and I presume he borrowed, as usual, from his friends—I know he got two hundred Mexicans from me, which I was delighted to let him have for Chin Chee's sake—he certainly got it honestly and not out of any proceeds of the ginseng wreck. Shall I have your jinrikisha called, Mr. Wang?"

"If you please. And let me assure you that I will do everything in my power to clear up this very distressing mystery."

"Boy! What side have got Mr. Wang Foo coolie?"

"Just now hab got kitchen-side, makee smokee," replied the ever-faithful.

"You go catchee he velly chop-chop, talkee wantchee go home-side."

"All light. Can do." And in a few moments more the little two-wheeled carriage was rattling down the hill toward the Red Cloud alley. Once there, the thoughtful detector of crime betook himself to his quiet den and the long chair of carved bamboo. Stretching out in it at length, he lighted a delicate Manila cheroot, and opening the lattice-work shutters, allowed the cooling breezes from the harbor to play across his brow as he weighed the evidence of the morning's interview. Having been up rather late the night before, he fell asleep before he knew it, and was only awakened by the report of the noonday gun from the Peak as it echoed along the cliffs above him.

"Yes," he said to himself as he made a final examination of the various papers that lay on the table, "it is practically an ingenious case of circumstantial evidence. Everything can be satisfactorily explained except this one thing, namely: Who or what was it that caused the light on White Tiger Point to go out at that particular time? In brief, was it intentional or was it accidental? Yes, it all turns on that. The fate of Webb and the boatswain and the native keepers hang exactly in that balance—to say nothing of the future happiness of Yung Wing and Chin Chee. The crown advocate must be convinced on that point, and—he heaved a long sigh as he said it—it seems to be decreed by the Buddhas that I am the one to convince him! If so, then 'to work'! To work! Quickly!"

THE TEMPLE OF THE STARRY SEA was already reaping quite a harvest from the number of pilgrims at its annual festival. The priests, who had been parading around through the villages and hamlets for the last two months announcing and advertising the great event, were true to their promise that their patron goddess would provide a special miracle for the occasion and that the Sacred Well would surely "bubble." Among those who gathered for the sight were quite a number from the village of Pak Lao—and among them the old cook from the lighthouse, who was enjoying one of the sacred bamboo pipes as he rested by the side of his baskets.

"Ki Tien Chung Yao Jing Tai? Ki Tien Chung Yao Jing Tai?" ("At what time will the Well begin to bubble? At what time will the Well begin to bubble?") was the question that arose on all sides, as the crowd leaned over the sides of the old stone curb and intently peered down into the water. "Tsai Sam Tien Chung, Leu Yao Slang, Lung Hwang Lien Fak Chee!" ("At the stroke of 3, when the brass gong sounds, his dragon majesty will graciously breathe!") was the answer repeated in chorus by the priests, as they passed around through the assembly, tinkling their little bells and holding out their gourds for offerings of cash. (For to the Chinese mind, the bubbles, which rise to the surface of a well, are but the breathing of the dragon who sleeps below, and are controlled by him at will.)

Suddenly the gong sounded and the crowd surged forward with shouts of delight to witness the "breathing of his dragon majesty" (without even so much as a thought for the old priest behind the curtains of the shrine, who was exhausting his strength by blowing the bubbles down into the water through a long hidden tube of bamboo!). The attention of the people being drawn off, the cook rose from his siesta, knocked the ashes from the long pipe and started to carry it back into the inner apartment of the temple. As he did so the figure of a man who had been quietly smoking just behind him, suddenly arose and stepped rapidly forward to where the cook's bamboo carrying-pole was lying on top of the buckets. He lifted it off and quickly ran his hand down though the cabbages and other vegetables as if trying to find something concealed there. In a moment ha drew out an earthenware jug and, uncorking it, poured some of its contents into a bottle concealed in his sleeve and then promptly returned it to its place beneath the greens in the basket, without a single human eye but his own having witnessed the transaction, or having noted the fact that the label on the bottle was marked with a red letter "A."

The closing ceremonies on the evening of the "bubbling" of the Dragon well were of a decidedly different, though very interesting, nature. At precisely 9 o'clock the abbot himself appeared, in his most gorgeous vestments, and mounting a stand by the side of the well-curb, cried out, "Bring forth the Holy Rod and the Scoop and prepare the Flask of Jade to receive the Dragon Scum!" An attendant handed him a long slender rod with a small copper cup at the end, and the abbot leaning over, skimmed the top of the water in the well as an English dairymaid would skim a pan of Jersey milk.

What he drew up from it, however, was certainly not cream, but an unctuous filth with a decided flavor of dragon (or fish), which was poured from the Flask of Jade into a number of tiny bottles and sold at a fabulous price to the devotees, under the striking title of "Dragon Scum—a certain cure for every mortal ill." The same pilgrim who had investigated the cook's basket purchased a vial of "Scum," and, marking it with a red letter "B," stowed it away in the opposite sleeve from its fellow, remarking to himself as he did so, "Now for the Cave of Mystic Changes and the chemical analysis that shall establish the identity and prove that my theory is correct!" So Wang Foo passed one more night in the village inn and in the early morning returned to Hong Kong.

"I hardly think it will be necessary to carry the case beyond this private hearing," remarked Sir Evington Merchant to the crown advocate and to the Inspector of police, who with Wang Foo and a few others were met in the office of Government House. "Mr.

Wang's careful and accurate statements have covered all the facts. He has exposed the lighthouse cook as the real culprit and shown us that he stole the government oil from the carrying cans while the keepers were at supper and replaced it by a cheap native product that refused to blend and consequently put out the lights. The odor of the sperm oil appealed to the temple priests, to whom he sold it, and they resold it as 'Dragon Scum' at an enormous profit. There is no reason to question any further the stories of Webb and the boatswain—they seem to be perfectly true and the men are released. The schooner was undoubtedly looted by coast pirates and all these tales about a conspiracy between Yung Wing's office and the keepers have failed to be proven. There remains, however, one very strange circumstance yet to be explained and which makes the charge against the cook either a very light one of the theft of a gallon or two of oil, or a very heavy one of a deliberate attempt to wreck a vessel and loot the cargo. Will Mr. Wang explain just how the light happened to go out, on the very night that the *Prince Edward* sailed?"

ALL EYES WERE TURNED toward the great detective as he slowly rose and prepared to solve this crucial part of the mystery. "Your excellency and gentlemen," he said, clearly and without any hesitation, "I am glad that you have now given me the opportunity to introduce the Chinese solution, which a purely European mind might never have thought of. My people, as you may have heard, are very particular about the date of any important undertaking in life, and the calendar of lucky days from their favorite temple is always consulted. The strange thing is that this applies to evil deeds as well as to good, and the thief or the villain will consult his oracle just as much as the saint—"

"Something like southern Spain," interrupted the governor, "where the assassin asks the blessing of his divinity upon his efforts, before he sets out to murder—"

"Precisely so," continued Wang Foo, pleased with this endorsement of his words, "and in this case the good and the bad happened to agree upon the very same date. When Mr. Yang Loo, Mr.

Yung Wing's partner, was asked by him to select a lucky day for the sailing, he remembered the festival of his native village and fixed it at the time of the bubbling of the well. The cook, who consulted the soothsayer in the temple, naturally received the same suggestion and so they both fell on the 28th day of the Harvest Moon! There is your explanation, gentlemen, and it answers every point except the fact that the light went out exactly as the schooner rounded the buoy—which I believe to have been entirely accidental, and which, with a great number of the other mysterious things of life, I shall have to ask you to leave to Tien Ming, that is, to Chinese fate!"

"Mr. Wang," said Miss Julia Du Bray, as she rushed up to him on the evening of the wedding feast of Yung Wing and the charming Chin Chee, "these dear people really owe this all to you! The betrothal feast I claimed as mine, but this I yield entirely to you!"

"I am very happy to have been in any way the means of bringing this joyful evening about," Wang Foo modestly answered, "and I am only going to thank you now for the compliment by twisting your popular saying, 'All's well that ends well,' into a somewhat more celestial form and let it be—'All's well that bubbles well.'"

THE OLD COMPRADORE'S GOGGLES

"OF COURSE," REMARKED SIR ARTHUR DUKELOW, who had recently been appointed as Commissioner of Customs at the great port of Shanghai, "the Chinese are not yet up to the European use of sympathetic inks, or I should at once recommend that the usual chemical tests be applied to the letter. We often have to resort to that in secret diplomatic correspondence, you know."

"Quite so," replied the famous detective Wang Foo, who was closeted with him in the inner office of the Custom House, "but you see this native paper is not sized or stiffened at all and any acid or strong liquid applied to it would immediately destroy its texture and we should thereby lose our only chance of detecting the criminal."

"What would you suggest, then?"

His visitor thought for a moment or two, and then taking out of his sleeve a small magnifying glass, gave the letter a careful examination. Laying it down on the table again and leaning back in the large office-chair, he answered: "You are of course aware, Sir Arthur, that Chinese chirography has all the individual characteristics of European penmanship—in fact, a tolerably long acquaintance with both languages leads me to say that it has even more. Our people cannot only identify the person very easily from his writing, but some become very expert in delineating his character from the various light and heavy strokes which he makes with the brush. They claim to do that in England, too, do they not?"

The Only Object Visible Through the Openings Was the Old Brick House! Could it be Possible That the Two Lost Treasures Were Really There?

"Yes, I have seen some remarkable instances of it. Scotland Yard has, I am told, several persons in its employ who make him a special study."

"Well, I will ask you to do me the favor to allow me to take the letter away with me for a few days and submit it, in perfect confidence, to one or two friends of mine who pride themselves on being expert fortune-tellers in this particular line."

"It shall be as you say, Mr. Wang," and folding the letter up and replacing it in its red native envelope, he handed it over to him.

Now the letter in question had troubled the new Commissioner more than anything that had come to hit deck since his arrival in the port: so much so, in fact, that he had decided, after several conferences with Inspector McArthur of the Police, to ask Mr. Wang Foo, who happened to have to come up from Hong Kong and help them in the solution of the mystery, which up to the present had completely baffled the officials at Shanghai. The mystery was really three-fold, viz: First, who was the writer? Second, why had he sent it? Third, how had it come into the inside of a strongly locked desk? For when the office-boy handed the Commissioner his Chinese mail just before tiffin, the latter had counted them over carefully and they were just eight in number. He laid them together in a little pile on the center of his blotter—intending to open and read them on his return—carefully locked his roller-top desk and went down to the club, telling the aged and very sleepy boy on duty that he would be back in the course of an hour, and that in the meantime no one was to be admitted to the room. When he came back and opened his desk, what was his astonishment to find that another letter had been added to the eight already there and that they had been resorted and carefully arranged in three piles of exactly three letters each: Not only this, but there was a peculiar method in the arrangement, which indicated that the villain, whoever he was, had not placed them there by chance or mere accident. The center pile was laid exactly horizontally and parallel to the edge of the desk, while the two on the right and left side respectively sloped-up at an angle which made them correspond to the first three sides of an octagon—thus outlining the "Pak Kwah" or "The Eight Diagrams," the most famous of all the symbols in the Chinese mythology.

"Well, there is certainly method in this madness," exclaimed Sir Arthur, as he rang the bell for the boy. "Who have come this room side while I go tiffin?" he asked of the "boy" (as he called him, though his age must have been very near sixty).

"My can s-clure no man comes dis side, my havee sit dis chair all times," was the immediate response.

"When I go tiffin, have got eight pieces letter in my desk side—when I come back have got nine pieces! How fashion that, eh? You come look see!"

The boy turned his eyes toward the desk where the three piles of letters lay as yet undisturbed—one glance was enough, throwing both hands up into the air he cried: "Pak Kwah! Pak Kwah! (The Eight Diagrams! The Eight Diagrams!) B'longee joss-pidgin. No Chinee man he do so fashion. My talkee tlue, one piecee joss hab comee dis side do dis."

"In other words, then," smiled the Commissioner, "you and I have come to the same conclusion, namely: it is either ghost or joss, which practically amounts to the same thing."

The "ghost or joss" solution, however, was very far from satisfying the mind of Inspector McArthur, who regarded it as simply a piece of native villainy, with a little superstition thrown in—or "sprinkled over the top like sugar on a cake," as he felicitously expressed it, just to head-off any inquiries on the part of the servants. Wang Foo was clearly of the very same opinion, even though he had asked that the letters be replaced on the desk in exactly the position in which they were found, and had made very careful notes of it all.

ALTHOUGH THE MACPHERSONS had been already two seasons in Shanghai, this was really the first time they had ever been honored with an invitation from the Hunt Club to go on one of their famous runs over the country. It wasn't because Miss Florence lacked an appreciation of this most glorious Far-Eastern sport, but simply because her devoted and over-careful mamma had declared that she didn't propose to have her only daughter risk her dear life on the back of one of those "awful Mongolian ponies." This autumn, however, she had finally been induced to give her consent, but only upon the repeated assurance of Dr. Holloway, the American Consul, that he would himself select and try-out the pony beforehand and have his own daughter (who was reputed to be one of the best and most fearless riders in China) go on a preliminary run or two with the creature before the day of the hunt. So the afternoon of the November "meet" found Miss Florence securely mounted on Miss Holloway's favorite pony and galloping over the fields as freely and easily as if she were back on her grandfather's old farm in Vermont.

"How well you ride, Miss MacPherson; why, you're no more a 'griffin' than your pony is!" exclaimed young Anthony Lowder of the Maritime Customs, as he drew up alongside and politely doffed his racing-cap.

"Well, you know it isn't the first time that I was on a horse's back, Mr. Lowder, and after all, I don't believe these Mongolian animals are really a bit harder or more dangerous to break-in than many a plain New England colt."

"I don't think so either," replied the young officer, as they both slowed down their gait and gave their ponies a chance to get their wind again. "By the way, excuse my asking, but is your mother riding too this afternoon?"

"Mother! Why, you must be out of your head, Mr. Lowder, to ask such a question, Mother! She would no more trust herself in one of these saddles than she would in a balloon. No, indeed, she is probably on the Consular Verandah sipping Mrs. Holloway's delicious tea and wondering whether I am ever coming back alive."

"No! Not really?"

"Yes, indeed, she is, and even if the creature doesn't throw me into a ditch, or a Chinese canal, she is quite positive that some bandit or pirate will seize me and I shall be dragged off to a Blue Beard castle and there be tortured or murdered in some delightful Oriental way. Now, you don't really think there is any risk of that, do you?"

"Not as long as I am your gay cavalier—which I trust will be for the rest of the afternoon," replied the courteous young Englishman, who was being more strongly drawn to his new American acquaintance every time they met.

The conversation, as they rode along together, became more and more interesting—in fact, so much so, that ere either of them realized it, their ponies had wandered quite away from the scent and they found themselves suddenly at the entrance of a little village where a funeral procession with gongs and firecrackers was just passing out. The noise and racket startled the ponies and frightened them so that the riders were utterly unable to control them and they bolted in opposite directions. Miss Florence clung bravely to the reins and saddle and didn't propose to be thrown if she could help it. Fortunately there were no canals or ditches in the direction she was headed and after crossing a half a dozen diminutive farms she found herself on the Old Pagoda Road and going rapidly back to the Settlement. The "gay cavalier," however, was not quite so fortunate. His mount darted across the neighboring fields and in a few moments reached the edge of Pagoda Creek, where, stopping suddenly at the slippery bank, he tried to keep from sliding down into the water, but the incline was too steep for him and the animal, and they both rolled over to the very edge of the stream. The pony by a tremendous effort struggled out of the predicament and, freed from his burden, started on a beeline for the town, leaving his helpless rider bleeding and unconscious in the mud.

Fortunately—or unfortunately as the case might be—the accident was not unobserved. Two coolies, bearing heavy burdens on their bamboos, were just starting to cross the neighboring stone bridge, and dropping their loads, hurried to his assistance. They picked him up and carried him up onto the roadway. After a few moments consultation, they decided to take him to the only shelter in the vicinity, which happened in this case to be an old brick house about a hundred yards away and directly at right angles to the bridge. (This structure, by the way, was one of those old double arches, so common in that part of China, and rejoiced in the euphonious title of "The Dragon's Eyes.") They knocked at the door, which after a short delay was opened very cautiously by the aged occupant of the dwelling.

"Well, what have you there?" was the somewhat anxious inquiry.

"An injured foreigner whom we picked up on the bank of the creek," was the reply.

"Ah; a rider, I see"—pointing significantly to his boots and spurs—"why do you not take him back to the foreign city? I do not want him here, it serves him right for recklessly destroying our fields the way they do."

"Lao Ye Chuin Tse poo chi yiu shio, tak tan Tse yueh, lien ming yiu tien mang!" ("Venerable Father, that the superior man is not a utensil, we all know, but the Master said: 'Mercy brings the reward of Heaven!'")

The apt quotation from the Sacred Classics produced its usual magical effect upon the native mind, and the old man admitted them and had them place the Englishman on the rough straw couch, while he produced the customary tea and pipes. As they left, he drew out of his girdle two short strings of brass cash and—to their utter surprise and delight—handed the money to them with these words: "In the name of all the Buddhas, see that you speak of this to no man. Keep it a profound secret, for if it be known that he who dwells by 'The Dragon's Eyes' is sheltering the foreign tramplers of our fields, the vengeance of all the neighborhood will come down upon my head."

THE CONTENTS OF THE MYSTERIOUS LETTER which the Commissioner had entrusted to Wang Foo, and which the latter was examining carefully in his little upper room in the basketmaker's home, were as follows:

> "Two losses will be yours and two valued treasures will
> disappear: the golden earth and he who guards it!
> "You will search for them far and near, but you
> will search in vain. The sacred Buddhas will hide
> them from your mortal gaze, only he who looks

through the 'Old Compradore's Goggles' shall find
them and bring them back."

The *Daily News* gave the explanation of the second, when it
announced the disappearance of young Mr. Lowder, and a confidential interview with Sir Arthur in his private office revealed the
first, when he confessed to the great detective that serious thefts
of the most valuable opium (or "golden earth") had recently taken
place from the Customs pier in the most unaccountable manner.
Now what possible connection could there be between the two?
Only this, viz.: that some desperate and skilful thieves having succeeded in abstracting the opium from the storeroom on the pier
and fearing detection had deliberately kidnapped the Customs
Officer whose duty it was to guard it! Such was the inevitable conclusion to which the Inspector of Police had come when the facts
were made known to him.

On the other hand, there were three things against this: First,
Mr. Lowder was not one of the guards on the pier and had nothing
to do with protecting the opium except as the shipping papers, etc.,
passed through his hands in the office. Second, there could not
have been any pre-arranged kidnapping, for it was perfectly evident from Miss McPherson's testimony that his pony had run away
with him at the paper-hunt in the country. Third, the thieves would
not have been foolish enough to go to the trouble of announcing
the facts to the Customs, and of suggesting a solution by means of
"The Old Compradore's Goggles."

"Now, would they, Mr. Wang?" inquired Sir Arthur.

"Probably not, had they been Europeans, but being Chinese—
which all these circumstances most conclusively show them to have
been—that is exactly what they would have done. Mystification is
always part of their program; there seems to be a subtle fascination about it which they can't resist."

"But the letter is written in the future tense. You see it says,
'will disappear,' although it is put into my desk forty-eight hours
after the robbery and the kidnapping have taken place. Now how
do you account for that?"

Wang Foo hesitated for a moment or two and then replied: "Oh! That is only a skilful deception, intended to frighten you and make you think it was all planned-out before hand. They often do that."

"Well, what is your conclusion as far as you have gone?"

"I am only willing to say this at present, Sir Arthur, and I do not wish to have it go beyond the privacy of this office. I believe that there has been a 'row among thieves' as they say, and that a fight has taken place over the division of the spoils. The disappointed parties are determined to expose their rivals to you and the authorities, but instead of doing it directly, as Europeans would do, they are going about it in this roundabout manner. Now hearing of the disappearance of a Customs employee, they are trying to make you believe that they kidnapped him in revenge, and so when you catch them, they will have to suffer for a double crime, don't you see?"

"And what do you think is meant by 'The Old Compradore's Goggles?' Is that also a blind?"

"Perhaps."

"Is there any kind of a magnifying glass that the natives use that bears that name, or do you recall any allusion in the Classics in those words? I know how very fond they are of this sort of thing."

"I shall have to put on my thinking cap," replied his visitor as he rose to go. 'There are plenty of 'old compradores' in Shanghai, and they undoubtedly have plenty of 'old goggles'—perhaps we shall find a pair that fits this particular case."

The "thinking-cap" which Wang Foo put on that same evening would hardly have been recognised by the Commissioner—or indeed by any of his friends—for it was a complete and perfect disguise. He had entered his house as a Chinese gentleman and he had emerged later on as an ordinary jinrikisha coolie, having hired the outfit and the vehicle for double the entire evening's fare. He turned down the broad Nanking Road and passing slowly along the Bund, reached at length the jinrikisha-stand just beyond the Custom pier. Here he deposited his vehicle and after having refreshed himself with an oil-cake purchased from the old woman at the gate, coiled himself up between the shafts and pretended to doze away while awaiting his customers.

The great Customs clock struck "nine," "ten" and "eleven" before anything occurred to awaken his curiosity. From where he sat he had a perfect view of the pier and of the three native guards who watched over the opium storeroom. They appeared to be most faithful to their duty. No one was allowed to approach within ten feet of the gate and no sampan was permitted to touch that side of the pier—yet balls of the most precious opium had several times disappeared from that very room during the night. How had it happened? He watched and waited, and this is what his trained eyes saw: From across on the Poo Tung side of the river a little low craft put out and headed for the middle of the stream. Four paper lanterns hung from its sides and from its bamboo on its bow a string of firecrackers crackled and flashed, while the notes of a tiny brass gong floated across the water.

"There comes the 'joss boat' over to this side!" he heard the foreign policeman say to a passing sailor, "that'll be good luck for the incoming tide."

"They sure are great believers in that sort of thing, now, ain't they?" was the jack-tar's reply, as he rolled along the sidewalk.

"Chiang Wang Lai! Chiang Wang Lai! Hai Kwah Ma Tow Ching Foo!" said the guards on the pier. ("The River King is coming! The River King is coming! He will bless the Customs pier!") He saw it come nearer and nearer until it touched the pier and stopped right in front of the storeroom. It then swung around and made fast, with the stern several feet under the flooring.

The old priest on board greeted the guards, rattled off a lot of blessings to them, beat his brass gong and ended up by setting off another pack of firecrackers for which he reaped his reward, in a shower of brass cash which was liberally thrown into the boat. He finally pushed off and started to scatter further blessing along the river bank—but not until the other priest concealed in the stern had had time to open the trapdoor skillfully cut in the floor of the wharf and to remove from the storeroom three balls of Patna opium (worth almost their weight in gold) and stow them away under the floating shrine of the River King! That was the conclusion of jinrikisha coolie No. 946—otherwise known as Wang Foo—who watched the whole proceedings from his vantage ground, and his conclusion was absolutely correct, even though he was only using his natural eyes and had not put on "The Old Compradore's Goggles."

"Yes! This is the exact spot where we separated; I remember it perfectly," said Miss McPherson, as the searching party drew up at the entrance to the village where the ponies had been frightened. "He must have gone right off in the opposite direction."

"We had better divide into four parties from here, then," said Major Campbell of the Volunteers, who was directing the movements, "and scour all these fields thoroughly for hoof-prints—though I must confess it's awfully hard to trace them in this mud—and we will meet again at the old stone bridge they call 'The Dragon's Eyes.'"

"Right you are, Major," answered the Consul, who was acting as Miss McPherson's escort.

"What do you think can have happened to him?" she asked, more distressed than ever at their apparent failure.

"Well, he may have crawled away fainting and be lying on the edge of one of these fields—"

"Poor man! He might be dead by this time. Oh! It's too awful to think about."

"But I still feel very sure that some natives have found him and have concealed him in their home."

"Why, they surely would come and tell us if they had, wouldn't they?"

"They might and they might not, you see; they are so queer and superstitious that they might do the very opposite thing."

The parties searched until nightfall and finally were obliged to return to the Settlement with the object still undiscovered. Yes, they returned, but not all—for one rider on a very slow and old-fashioned Chinese pony stayed behind and resolved to spend the night in the country. Wang Foo came to a little village not far from "The Dragon's Eyes," where no one knew him or connected him with the searching party for the foreign rider.

"It is far to the great city, is it not?" he inquired.

"Aye, it is fully thirty 'li' from here," an old farmer answered.

"I am weary with my journey, and so is my steed. If you will permit me, I will share your meal and lodging with you and reward you in the morning."

"It shall be as the two Venerable Grand Ones say." So, with the consent of the aged grandparents, he made ready to spend the night.

The moon was almost at the full and being near the feast of All Souls, the children were allowed to roam about with their torches and little lanterns until far past the hour of bedtime. An inclination, stronger than he realized, came to him to follow a little party of them out toward "The Dragon's Eyes" and seated by the roadside, he watched them as they played.

Two of them ran over the bridge and stood directly opposite it where the creek made a sudden turn, while two of them stood on this side and, bending low, waved their lanterns through the arches to their companions.

"What do you call this game," he asked.

"Oh!" they replied, "we call it 'Kwan Lao Tai Pan Ching Tse.' Haven't you ever seen it before?"

Wang Foo started up suddenly and running down to the bank where they stood, looked through the arches of the old bridge. The reflection in the water made the two perfect circles of one of the old "spectacle bridges," and so they called the game "Looking Through the Old Compradore's Goggles."

He took one more glance—the only object visible was the old brick house! Could it be possible that the two lost treasures were really there?

He waited until the children were gone and then slipped quietly up to the door—there could be no mistake—was Anthony Lowden's voice!

It would have been folly to have attempted the rescue alone. He hurried back to the village. "The moon is so clear. I have decided to try to reach the city," he said, and saddling the old pony, he whipped him into his utmost speed and never stopped until they reached the gate of the American Consulate.

How the rescue party was quickly made up: how by midnight they reached "The Old Compradore's Goggles"; how they released Mr. Lowder, whom they found tied hand and foot to a bamboo bed; how they arrested the old man and took him to the city; how they discovered the hiding-place of the stolen opium in the inner room— all this was told in a leading article in *The Daily News*, but it still remained for Wang Foo to unravel some of the inner connections between the blessings of the River King and the mysterious letter in the Commissioner's desk.

"YOU AMERICANS are certainly the most adaptable creatures in the world," said a cheerful young patient in room No. 6 of the Shanghai Hospital to a nurse who brought him the good news of his early release. "Why, Miss McPherson, there doesn't seem to be any role that you can't play and play most successfully. Now who would have thought of your disguising yourself as a nurse?"

"Disguise?" she said with a smile, as she started to rearrange the flowers that some mysterious friend had placed on the table by his side. "Why, this isn't a disguise; this is simply putting on my old uniform again."

"Your 'old uniform'—why you don't mean to say you've ever done it before?"

"Done it before! Oh! so I look and act like an amateur, do I, then?" with a quizzical point that suggested some little hurt feelings.

"No, no, not at all—you don't understand—I mean—that is—"

"That is, you haven't seen my little gold badge. That cross and shield is the proof of my two years' training in old St. Luke's in Philadelphia."

"Why, how did you come to do that?"

"Oh, I just had a feeling that I would like to be practically helpful to someone in this world sometime—you know you never can tell when you may be needed, and I thought I should like to be ready—"

"And you certainly were needed here. I don't believe I should have been out of here for another two weeks if that rosy-cheeked creature from Guy's had continued dropping her 'h's' all over my floor. She means well, poor soul, but it made me nervous trying to pick them up after her. But it really was awfully good in you to come and help a fellow out this way. I don't know how I am to thank you—I—"

"Don't try to thank me, just accept my little penance, and"— she leaned over him and took his right hand in hers and held it for a moment—"you know all good people have to do penance sometimes. Just tell me that I am forgiven."

"Penance? Forgiveness?"—he held the hand and wouldn't let it go now—"why, Miss Florence, what do you mean?"

"Why, it was all my fault, that runaway, wasn't it? If I hadn't been with you that pony would never have bolted, would he?"

"Well, perhaps not, but then, you see, if he hadn't bolted, why you and I would not be here now, would we?"

"No, I suppose not; we might just be drinking tea at one of your awfully stiff English afternoons, and—"

"And then we shouldn't be alone, should we, Florence?" (Haughty boy he, to just drop the "Miss" before his nurse's name in this way without giving her any preliminary notice.)

"Alone?"

"Yes, and I shouldn't be able to tell you that I really am deeply religious—though I may not look it—and a profound believer in a lifelong penance?"

"But I don't want to be a nurse and stay in this hospital all my life," she gently protested.

"No, no, not in this hospital, but just in this dear old land of China, as the guardian angel of a heart-sick patient, you see?"

"And in memory of the event which brought it about, they would certainly call it 'a runaway match,' wouldn't they?"

"Who cares if they do?" was his reply, as he drew her nearer to him.

And so it came to pass that when Mr. Anthony Lowder of the Imperial Maritime Customs left that institution a few days later, the nurse who assisted him into his jinrikisha wore on the third finger of her left hand a sparkling decoration that was not strictly a St. Luke's Hospital badge!

"YES," REMARKED WANG FOO, in his closing interview with the Commissioner before his return to Hong Kong, "the ties of family relationship are still very strong in China. Now who among the Europeans would have thought that your office-boy, and Old Wang, the receiver of stolen goods, and the assistant priest of the River King were all brothers and all mixed up in the same family game?"

"Quite true," remarked Sir Arthur, "and who would have suspected that same sleepy old office-boy of mine of having energy enough—or even brains enough—to make a duplicate key to my desk?"

"Or, again, who would have suspected the guards on the pier of being foolish enough and careless enough to allow the River King's barge to tie-up right under the opium?"

"But how could a younger brother, under the strict rules of the Confusion ethics, ever bring an accusation against an elder one? Is not that a most serious violation of the teaching—in fact, a crime?"

"Ah, you see, that is just the point. That is where he 'saved his face' as we Chinese say; he didn't really accuse him, he merely suggested that we 'look through the goggles,' and so he freed himself and shifted the responsibility to our shoulders."

"And why did he call the old bridge 'The Compradore's Goggles?'"

"Why simply because that is a popular country name for it, and his brother, you see, had once been a compradore and had worn such goggles for years."

"What an ingenious play on words!"

"Yes, China is full of that sort of thing, and it means far more than the foreigners realize. He knew that if we stooped down and looked through the old arches we should see just that one old house—and that was the very place where the opium was concealed. And then, perhaps, he recalled that famous old saying of the Classics:

"Looking through the crystal spheres,
One can gaze upon the hidden treasures."

THE GOLDEN FILLET

"Yes," said Mrs. Addison Holloway, wife of the American consul at the great Chinese seaport, "we are looking forward with the keenest anticipation to Lady Cockrill's little party next Wednesday evening, because we are sure she is going to have some delightful new and startling surprise in store for us."

"She always does," chimed in the circle of ladies on the consular veranda, voicing their sentiment through the personality of Mrs. Bevington-Jones of the Indian Bank, whose long residence in the east gave her the privilege of being the first speaker on any local topic whatever. "I am wondering now what it is going to be this time. Let me see—we've had the Egyptian dancers and the Cingalese magicians and the Siamese fairies, and all that—"

"Perhaps she will have some European entertainers this time, Mrs. Jones," ventured to remark the young wife of one of the junior clerks in the bank.

"Mrs. Bevington-Jones, if you please," was the crushing rebuke administered by Shanghai's self-appointed society leader to this young upstart.

"Excuse me, I meant Mrs. Bevington-Jones," was the courteous reply. "I understand there are some wonderful Russian musicians visiting at their consulate just now, and she may give us an opportunity of hearing them."

"Pos-si-bly so, but I doubt it," drawled out the offended dignity.

"Well, ladies," put in Mrs. Holloway, evidently desiring to pour oil on the troubled social waters, "whatever it is; I am sure it will

438

"IT REVEALS HONGKONG'S COMPLETE PLANS OF DEFENSE: FORTIFICATIONS, GUNS, MINES, AMMUNITION, SUPPLIES, SOLDIERS, EVERYTHING."

be something well worth hearing and seeing, and I know we shall all be delighted." (The wife of the American consul was just beginning to get used to these little social frictions, so common in the far eastern ports.)

"We certainly shall," arose the chorus from the teacups and saucers.

Wednesday evening duly arriving at the British consulate, and with the appearance of the after-dinner guests came the announcement of the anticipated surprise. A dainty little program was handed around by the immaculate house boy and on it, after several musical offerings by resident professionals, was a notice to the effect that "Mme. Rodinsky, entertainer at the Russian court," would appear in her marvelous séance of mind-reading and clairvoyance.

EVERY ONE WAS ON THE TIP-TOE of expectation and there was just that little nervous feeling creeping around among the guests that always precedes any form of entertainment that proposes to give public utterance to one's private thoughts or future. Mrs. Bevington-Jones seemed to be more than usually sensitive on this point, and took occasion to remark to Mrs. Holloway, leaning over her waving ostrich fan: "Well, whatever she does, I don't propose to give her a chance to read my thoughts, my dear. No! not at any price. If I have any special thoughts—and goodness knows I haven't very many"—she giggled with her quaint little giggle as she said it—"I propose to keep them to myself, and not have them gabbled all over Shanghai."

Mrs. Holloway made no reply to this sentiment, but inwardly concluded—as probably every one else in the room would have done—that Shanghai wouldn't be much poorer by the loss.

Prof. Le Monte of the institute had played the piano, Mrs. Brevaine of the French concession had charmed the company with her operatic selections and the Misses Wilson of the American College were just finishing a duet, when Sir Rutherford Cockrill was seen reaching over to his wife and whispering something in her ear—

"Impossible! Why, what an awful disappointment," said the hostess. "You must explain to them at once, Rutherford."

"Ladies and gentlemen," remarked the consul, as he turned to address the company. "It is with feelings of extreme regret that I have to announce to you that Mme. Rodinsky is unable to appear before us this evening. The reason is given in her own words," unfolding a message in his hands. "Madame regrets that owing to the fact that the Golden Fillet, through which her manifestations are given, has mysteriously disappeared from her room in the hotel, she will be unable to comply with your request for a séance!"

"The Golden Fillet! The Golden Fillet!" was repeated from mouth to mouth.

"I wonder what that can be!"

"Perhaps, Sir Rutherford," asked Mr. Holloway, "you can throw some light on what this mysterious object is."

"Why," replied the consul, "as far as I can remember, from the entertainment that I saw her give in Government House at Hong Kong, it is a golden band which she has tightly bound about her head, after she goes into a trance, and which she claims has the magical power of catching the thoughts 'floating in the ether,' as she says, and conveying them to her brain. I really can't say whether there's anything in it or not, but she certainly does some wonderful things with it and she seems to be perfectly helpless without it."

"What you say only makes us all the more anxious to see her."

"Quite naturally. And I wish to say now, on behalf of Lady Cockrill and myself, that when the mysterious Fillet turns up—if it does while she is in the port—we shall expect you to do us the honor of being our guests on some other evening."

IT WASN'T THAT LIEUT. PIERSON of the *Charleston* was at all discourteous—indeed, what real American officer could ever be to a lady—but he certainly felt that the time had come when he would be obliged to tell Mrs. Puffington (the good soul who presided over the Methodist school for Chinese) that he didn't approve of her overstrict chaperonage. There could be no possible reason whatever, in his mind, why he shouldn't call upon any of the young lady teachers in the evenings, and yet Mrs. Puffington had distinctly told him, on this very afternoon, that she preferred to have him confine his calls upon Miss Atherton to the hours between 11 and 7. Perhaps he did not realise that the *Charleston* had been so long in the port—and the calls upon Miss Atherton had consequently become so numerous and so lengthy—that he was reported among the school authorities to have very serious designs upon the young lady's affections, and she, on her part, was accused of allowing that much-maligned little angel, Cupid, of seriously interfering with her legitimate school duties.

"I will tell the old girl just what I think of her," he remarked, as he put on his gold-laced cap and went down the steps of the school toward his jinrikisha.

"Oh, please don't do that, lieutenant," she begged of him, "it's better to see me in the afternoon than not to see me at all, isn't it? And the 'old girl,' as you call her, might make it so unpleasant for me that I would have to give up my work and then—then"—she took his hand to bid him good-night—"what would become of me, stranded out here alone in the far east?"

"Don't worry about that—"

"Why, who would take me home?"

"Take you home? Take you home?" he smiled, and before he thought of the full force of the words, he answered. "Why, I guess the United States Navy is good enough for that!"

"But the Navy ships don't carry lady passengers—"

"Miss Atherton, you'll catch your death o' cold out there!" screamed a female voice from within.

"Hang the old girl, there she is now!"

"Jump into the rickshaw before she sees you."

So ended the interview, and the coolie picked up the shafts and started up for the Nanking road.

"Yes! I committed myself before I realised it," he kept saying to himself as the little carriage rattled along. "I wonder if she'll take that as a definite proposal, I wonder!" But that was only wonder No. 1, for wonder No. 2 kept creeping into his mind all that night on board the ship, and that was the old, old wonder of the ages, namely, "What she would say if it was a proposal."

Now, Lieut. Pierson was not only a courteous man, but a brave man, and yet it took him three whole days to actually summon up courage enough to turn his footsteps again in the direction of the school. He could have responded instantly to a call to face a Chinese mob, but this—to face a poor and lonely woman—was a far more serious matter. He wandered down the Bund, half afraid to summon a jinrikisha, and stopped right in front of the hotel.

"Hello! Pierson, old chap; glad to see you. How is everything going?" said a friendly voice, which he recognised instantly as belonging to a brother officer of the British service.

"Fine! By the way, where are you coming from? Been to tea in the hotel?"

"Tea? No, indeed. I've been in to have an interview with that Russian clairvoyant, Mme. Rodinsky. I say, she's great. Most wonderful woman I ever met in my life! Told me all my future like a book. You ought to try her some time."

"Perhaps I will."

Now just what it was that induced him to seek an interview with madame, he never knew. It wasn't entirely his friend's advice: it wasn't his fondness for fortune-tellers, for he had never had much to do with them: it wasn't entirely his own unsettled state of mind— it must have been a combination of all these and something else, but in he went and it wasn't a very long time before the famous Russian seeress had read his mind, and read it as easily as most of them do with their love-sick clients.

"And what will the young lady's answer be?" he finally mustered up courage enough to ask as a definite question, after relieving himself of an exorbitant fee.

"Ah! That I cannot tell today. My fillet is gone, my precious fillet! I can read your thoughts by putting my hand upon your brow, but her thoughts—hers—hers—they are floating in the ether. I cannot draw them to my brain without the golden band. Come back! Come back to me again when I have found it, and I will tell you all." And so the lieutenant bade her adieu and passed out into the street, having at least eased his pocketbook if not his mind.

INSPECTOR JOSEPH MCARTHUR of the Shanghai police sat in his inner office in earnest consultation with Deputy O'Keefe. Turning to him, he said:

"Well, O'Keefe, what do you think of it? Clever piece of work, eh?"

"It sure was, chief," was the laconic reply.

"You don't suppose it was worth what she says, do you?"

"Not unless it was set with diamonds on the inside. Why, there couldn't have been five hundred dollars' worth of gold in the whole thing, and here she is claiming ten thousand—"

"Well, I suppose that's because she's putting her own estimate on it for what it's worth to her. You see, she's superstitious about it in some way; claims she tells fortunes and reads thoughts by it and all that sort of nonsense. I suppose she got it from some fakir in India or some place. That kind of person is always putting lots of faith in these things they steal from the temples."

"Yes, and their silly dupes believe all they tell them and then pay for it handsomely. Why, I'll warrant you she makes more in a month than you or I do in a year."

"Any report today from the native detectives on it?"

"Nothing since last night, but let us call in Ah Sam."

The office bell rang. "I want to speak to Ah Sam," said the inspector to the uniformed attendant.

"Can do," was the celestial's very brief reply.

"Now, Ah Sam," began his chief, as the skillful Shanghai detective entered the room, "we must get that golden fillet and get it quick, you savee?"

"My havee look see all piecee pawnshop, no got. Two more piecee man havee look see all placee Chow Chow Stleet (the Shanghai headquarters for stolen goods) him no got, too. My tinkee tiefee man hav' hidee—no hav', sell."

"Oh, you think they're hiding it somewhere, do you, until suspicion blows over?"

"My tinkee so fashion."

"Well, you and your men just keep on looking—and look till you find it. There's a big reward out for it, you savee? A thousand dollars—and half of it goes to you. Now go and get to work again as quick as you can. Try all the native games you can think of, but don't come back without it!"

The faithful Ah Ham's eyes glistened as he saw the thousand dollars floating in imagination before him, and five hundred of it dropping into the outstretched hands of himself and his friends, but he was too good and loyal an officer and had been too long in the service to seem to be moved by a bribe, so he merely bowed and said: "S'posee catcher tousand dollar—s'posee my no catchee one dollar, look see all samee, how fashion

"Nobly said, old boy," smiled the Inspector, "you're a credit to the department." Then turning to the deputy, "we may as well leave it in their hands, for they're the only ones that can get ahold of it."

But, as a matter of fact, they were not the only ones that could get ahold of it, nor indeed the ones that did get ahold of it, as the facts eventually showed, for the golden fillet was secure in the hands of a very different person!

IN THE UPPER ROOM of the basketmakers home, a visitor from Hong Kong was sitting quietly at a table and pondering some notes in a little leather book. Contrary to his usual custom, he had not yet called at police headquarters. In fact, his presence in Shanghai at this time was entirely unknown to the Inspector and his officers. He had special plans of his own which he wished to work out, and he thought it better to remain entirely incognito until he had done so. Now he was—to speak very candidly—just as much interested in Mme. Rodinsky's golden fillet as was the good lady herself, and this interest went very much deeper than that of the police, who were concerned only with the theft and the effort to apprehend the thief and secure the stolen property. And another still stranger fact in the case was that—contrary to all his usual procedure—he was not attempting at all to assist the department in their search for the culprit, but, quite the opposite, was exceedingly anxious that they should not lay hands on him at present!

The reason for this mysterious attitude on the part of the great detective appeared a few moments later. He rose quietly from his seat, securely barred the door of his little bedroom, carefully closed the shutters of the windows, and listened for a while at the thin partitions of the walls until he had thoroughly satisfied himself that the basketmaker and his family were sound asleep. "I think we are perfectly safe now," he repeated to himself, and proceeded to open the quaint old brass lock that secured his hog-skin trunk. He drew out several garments and, laying them on the chair, unfolded an embroidered vest of yellow silk. In the middle of the vest was a little package tied with a double red cord. He slowly undid the knots and out upon the table rolled the stolen fillet, right under the eyes of the self-confessed thief!

Was it possible that Wang Foo had actually stolen it? Oh, no, dear reader, not at all! He had not stolen it, he had simply appropriated it for a little while and for a very special purpose. He had simply "loong-ed" it, as the Chinese say, and every old resident in the far east has had, at some time or other in his career, to encounter that most felicitous term "loong." It is an ancient word, handed down from hoary antiquity, and is always used as a convenient term to explain a mysterious disappearance. For instance, you miss some day an article of jewelry or wearing apparel, or it may be some useful tool or implement, and when you interrogate the Buddha-like houseboy or coolie and ask them where it has gone the reply will generally be: "Tiefee man no makee stealee, my tinkee some piecee man hav' 'loong.' S'pose waitchee little time, can come back dis side." And there you are! There is nothing to do. There is no need of appealing to the police, for they are as helpless as you are. So you patiently bide-a-wee and in a few days you will almost certainly find the missing article in its usual place. Some one in your employ has lent it to a friend to examine or use it, or, what is more likely, he has rented it out for a small consideration, with the guarantee that it will eventually come back. It has simply been "loong-ed"—that is all! And so Wang Foo had "loong-ed" the golden fillet!

He took it up in his hands and carefully examined it. It was apparently a plain gold band, of pure and heavy metal, about an inch in width and long enough to be bound around a lady's head and fastened with two ingenious buckles at the ends. He ran his finger gently along the edge several times as if feeling for something rough. "Ah! I thought so!" he said, and, taking his magnifying glass from its little case in his sleeve, he discovered a delicate black line which appeared to be a joint in the metal. It was but the work of a moment to insert the blade of his penknife into the line and, with a little pressure, to cause a cover of gold about two inches long to fly open and reveal the interior of the fillet. Something white met his eye, and the glass showed it at once to be a folded strip of paper. Bending the silver cleaner from his tobacco pipe into a hook, he carefully drew it out without tearing and proceeded to unfold it. It proved to be a large sheet of fine white tissue, covered from top to bottom with the minutest writing and containing several mysterious diagrams. It took more than an hour to decipher it all, but when it was finished he leaned back in his chair and, drawing a very long breath, exclaimed with that feeling of intense satisfaction that comes to every great discoverer: "So, so! Madame Rodinsky, so these are the thoughts that you claim to 'catch floating in ether,' are they? How interesting! How v-e-r-y in-ter-est-ing; and what a wonderful thing clairvoyance is, after all!"

After breakfast with his host and the family the following morning Wang Foo remarked that he had some very important writing to do in his room and asked to be excused until noon. Taking from his hog-skin trunk his traveling ink case and pens he sat down at the table and never arose until he had completed two exact copies of the document, one in English and one in Chinese, which he carefully worked out from the Russian original by the aid of his little dictionary and phrase book. He then refolded the paper along the creases and, with the aid of the silver wire, pushed it back into the interior of the case and carefully closed the opening.

THE SECOND STAGE in the "loong-ing" process, to be sure, was a little more complicated and dangerous than the first stage of procuring the fillet from Mme. Rodinsky's apartment, but tactful native diplomacy—in which the hotel servants played their respective parts—

enabled the amah to say to the good lady a few mornings afterward: "O Missee, Missee, my hav' findee dat goldee libbon you
makes lose! Pleasee you come chop-chop look see!"

"You have found it! Where? Show me at once!" exclaimed the
astonished and delighted owner.

"All samee der inside hav' got. Hangee dat blackee hat down-
side. My can show you," and opening wide the door of the wardrobe she exhibited the famous golden fillet suspended quite innocently from an inner hook (where she herself had hung it that very
morning when she came in with the early tea-tray!).

The discovery proved a boon both to the inspector of police and
to the consul, for it enabled the former to announce in the *Daily
News* that "the supposed theft of some valuable jewelry from a
Russian lady at the hotel turns out, after careful searching on the
part of the department, to have been a mistake, for it has now been
found in a wardrobe where she mislaid it," and it enabled the latter and Lady Cockrill to announce to their friends that "the séance
of Mme. Rodinsky, which was unfortunately postponed, would take
place at the consulate on Thursday evening next, the day before
her sailing for Vladivostok."

When Lieut. Pierson read in the papers the notice of the recov-
ery of the golden fillet, he sympathetically opened his wallet and
drew forth a brand-new ten-dollar bill. "Ten dollars of good Shanghai
money," he repeated to himself, "ten dollars of good Shanghai money—
just five dollars of United States coin—well, it isn't very much, I
think I'll cancel that little dinner engagement at the French Hotel,
and risk one more chance on the old Russian girl's second-sight."

So, skeptic though he was in his saner moments, and poorer
financially, from his former visit, he did what many another love-
sick young man had done before him, and jumping into a jinrikisha
started for the clairvoyant's apartment. After some apparent re-
luctance, accompanied by exclamations that she was very busy
packing her baggage for departure, she finally consented to a "sitting" and, binding the mystic golden fillet around her head, proceeded to "catch the floating thoughts in the ether"—after having,
of course, relieved her victim of the aforesaid ten-dollar bill.

"Your fate will be sealed this very evening," she said, after mumbling over a lot of unintelligible nonsense (which he concluded to be a dialect of northern Russia and not the language of the spirit-world).

"This very evening? How and where?"

"At my séance at the consulate."

"But why not here and now? I've paid you for the young lady's answer, why can't I have it?"

"True, you have paid me, and the thoughts are floating in the air—I can feel them even at a distance—but they have not come near enough for me to communicate them to you now. At 9 o'clock tonight, yes, at precisely 9, you will listen very carefully and they will reach you."

"But I don't want my private affairs trotted out for the public," protested the officer.

"The public will know nothing," was the answer. "I will simply say 'he' and 'she' and the secret will be yours."

So ended the interview and the remainder of the afternoon was taken up with a regular naval attack upon old Mrs. Buffington at the school, to convince her that it was her most sacred duty to allow Miss Atherton to be present at the séance that evening. Though at first she put up a valiant resistance, she finally yielded on the condition of Mr. Holloway's constant chaperonage, and a solemn promise to be home "very early."

WHEN THE OFFICE BOY BROUGHT IN the tea at police headquarters on Thursday afternoon Wang Foo and the inspector were concluding a most important interview, which was destined to have a very decided effect upon Mme. Rodinsky's séance, though she never for a moment suspected it.

"And you feel quite sure that it would be better for us to wait until the evening, instead of making the arrests now?" asked the chief.

"Quite positive," answered the detective. "We cannot afford to take any risk of losing them. They are as 'slippery as eels' (as the Americans say), and we must not only catch them both together, but it will be much more effective if we catch them publicly in this way."

"Very well, Mr. Wang, you practically have the whole case in your hands, so we'll just let you manage it as you have planned."

"You will have Deputy O'Keefe there with several officers in civilian clothes, and see that every doorway and window is carefully guarded, so that there is no possible escape."

"He'll be there, sir, with his men, and you can rely on him to see it's thoroughly done."

"And now let us make our final call upon Sir Rutherford, and see that he clearly understands the arrangements."

The Inspector rang the bell and in a few moments more these two guardians of the secret of the golden fillet were speeding toward the British consulate. On arrival they were immediately ushered into the inner office.

When all had been explained by the officers, the consul said: "The program then, is this: After madame has told several fortunes among the guests, I am to request her to allow me to glance for a moment at the golden fillet. She will naturally not want to part with it, but as any hesitancy would be suspicious, she will unclasp it and hand it to me, and then I will hand it to Mr. Wang—and he will do the rest."

"Exactly so," replied the visitors, as they rose to take their departure.

Sir Rutherford and Lady Cockrill's guests arrived at the consulate precisely on time that evening, and looked forward with more than usual anticipation to the séance, because their curiosity had naturally been aroused by the story of the stolen fillet. All proceeded smoothly with the program, and after some introductory music, the consul escorted Mme. Rodinsky to a chair upon the platform and announced that her "marvelous exhibition of clairvoyance and thought-reading" would begin. Several persons in the audience accepted her invitation to come forward and have their fortunes told, and there was the usual mingling of astonishment and merriment at her visions of their future, to say nothing of the innocent smiles that were provoked by her amusing use of broken English.

One statement that she made seemed to mystify them more than anything else, and that was when, between two of her readings, she waved her arms over the heads of the company and cried: "Her answer is 'yes!'—Her answer is 'yes!'"

"Whose answer? Whose answer? Answer to what? Answer to what?" arose from different parts of the room.

"They will knew—they will know!" was the only satisfaction she would give them, leaving them all in that realm of indefiniteness which is the characteristic of her tribe—no, not all, all but two, and they were the very two in whom we most were interested. And that is the reason why, Lieut. Hereon, who had been sitting very close to Miss Atherton in the shade of the heavy parlor curtains, drew even a little closer yet and—relying on the friendly shade of the self-same curtains—seized her right hand in his, and, leaning over, whispered: "It's all right now!" And so, of course, it was, and consequently no one could blame her for calling her Chinese engagement ring "Ching Lien" or "Golden Fillet." in spite of all that happened later in the evening. And just what was it that happened? Why, simply this:

"Will madame kindly allow me to take the wondrous fillet in my hand for a moment?" asked Sir Rutherford of the seeress. She started for a moment, and then, as a strange pallor spread over her face, she instantly re-controlled herself and, unclasping the golden band from her head, handed it to her host with the words: "I am honored to have you hold it, sir, and I only regret that I cannot offer you its mystic power with it—but that, unfortunately, abides in me alone."

"Ah, then its secrets could not penetrate a Chinese brain—"

"It has never been tried, sir—I do not understand you—"

"Then why not try it now, its revelations may be more marvelous yet," and, suiting his action to the word, before she could even utter a protest, he handed the golden fillet to Wang Foo, and, placing him in a chair by the side of madame, bound the fillet around his head, and, turning to the audience, announced as follows: "Ladies and gentlemen, we are now to make the supreme test of the psychic world and ascertain whether the occidental 'ether waves of thought' can ever actually affect the oriental brain. My esteemed friend, Mr. Wang Foo of Hong Kong, has kindly consented to conduct the experiment."

"Gracious me! It makes me feel more uncanny than ever!" exclaimed the redoubtable Mrs. Bevington-Jones as she drew her shawl more closely about her and pushed her chair backward into the curtains, where she came within an ace of upsetting the prospective bride and groom.

"Mr. Wang, please state clearly to us what the golden fillet of mystery reveals!" said a stentorian voice from the middle of the room. All eyes instantly turned toward the speaker—he was none other than Joseph McArthur, chief inspector or police!

"It reveals Hong Kong's complete plans of defense—fortifications, guns, mines, ammunition, supplies, soldiers, everything—"

"Where?" cried the audience, in chorus.

"Here!" answered the detective, as he unfastened the fillet and opening the cover, revealed to their astonished gaze the incriminating paper concealed within. "Mr. O'Keefe, hold your man!" But the deputy had already made sure of the Russian trying to escape through the doorway. "Mr. and Mrs. Rodinsky will return with me to Hong Kong, where the government has long been waiting for them as a couple of the most dangerous spies in the colony."

"And what of the golden fillet?" asked the ladies.

"Oh, that we will present to Lady Cockrill as a memento of a most interesting evening," replied the ever courteous Wang Foo.

THE QUINNY HITE
MYSTERIES

CHINESE RED · HERE LIES THE BODY

RICHARD BURKE

ISBN 978-1-61646-247-5

COACHWHIP PUBLICATIONS

COACHWHIPBOOKS.COM

THE
DEATH
OF A
CELEBRITY

HULBERT
FOOTNER

AN AMOS LEE MAPPIN MYSTERY

ISBN 978-1-61646-263-5

COACHWHIP PUBLICATIONS

ALSO AVAILABLE

DONALD BAYNE HOBART
TWO MYSTERIES

THE CLUE OF THE LEATHER NOOSE • THE CELL MURDER MYSTERY

ISBN 978-1-61646-253-6

COACHWHIP PUBLICATIONS

COACHWHIPBOOKS.COM

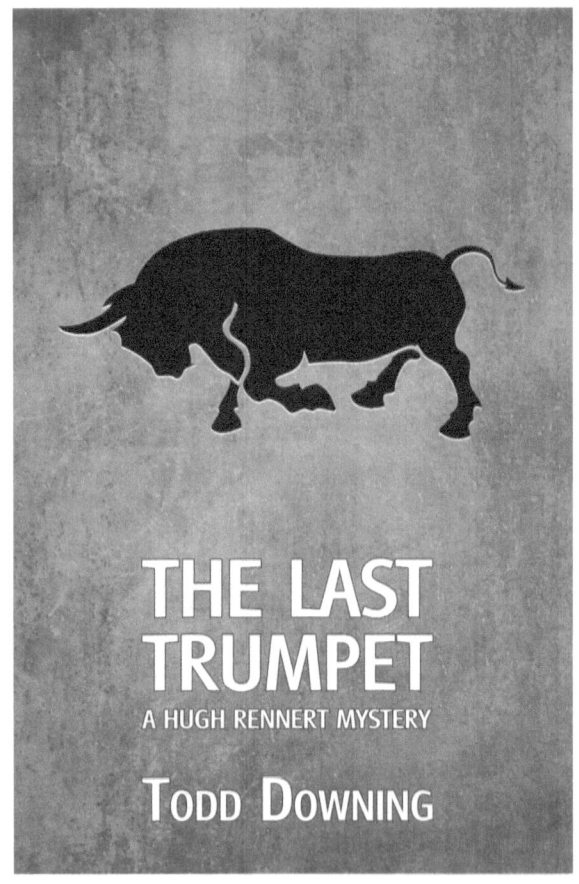

THE LAST
TRUMPET

A HUGH RENNERT MYSTERY

TODD DOWNING

ISBN 978-1-61646-152-2

COACHWHIP PUBLICATIONS

ALSO AVAILABLE

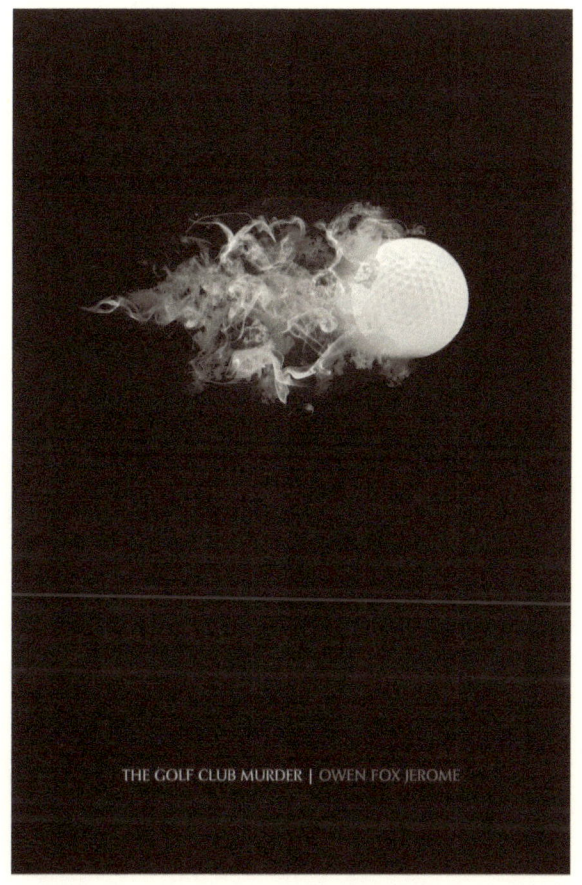

THE GOLF CLUB MURDER | OWEN FOX JEROME

ISBN 978-1-61646-279-6

COACHWHIP PUBLICATIONS

COACHWHIPBOOKS.COM

ISBN 978-1-61646-275-8

THE MUMMY
CASE MYSTERY

DERMOT
MORRAH

ISBN 978-1-61646-250-5

www.ingramcontent.com/pod-product-compliance
Lightning Source LLC
Chambersburg PA
CBHW021840010726
47493CB00005B/1487